"A memorable saga . . . Avery adroitly conveys the intricacies of the tea ceremony, 'the language of diplomacy,' and the subtle ways in which it was trans-
formed as Japan moved from a Shogun society to one ruled by the emperor.
At the same time, she illuminates vivid period details."

—*Booklist*

"In 1865, nine-year-old Aurelia Caillard is taken from New York to Japan by
her missionary uncle Charles while her ailing mother dies at home. Charles
soon vanishes in a fire (not the one of the title), leaving Aurelia orphaned and
alone in Kyoto. She is taken in by Yukako, the teenage daughter of the Shin
family, master teachers of temae, or tea ceremony. Aurelia, narrating as an
elderly woman, tells of living as Yukako's servant and younger sister, and how
what begins as grateful puppy love for Yukako matures over years into a
deeply painful unrequited obsession. Against a backdrop of a convulsively
Westernizing Japan, Avery brings the conflicts of modernization into the
teahouse, and into Aurelia and Yukako's beds, where jealousy over lovers
threatens to tear them apart. In one memorable instance, Yukako, struggling
to bring money in for the family, crosses class lines and gives temae lessons to
a geisha in exchange for lessons on the shamisen, a seductive (and potentially
profitable) string instrument. Eventually stuck in a painful marriage, Yukako
labors to adapt the ancient tea ceremony to the changing needs of the modern world, resulting in a breathtaking confrontation. Avery, making her
debut, has crafted a magisterial novel that is equal parts love story, imagina-
tive history, and bildungsroman, a story as alluring as it is powerful."

—*Publishers Weekly* (starred review)

"Avery writes with a self-assured lyricism . . . Quite arresting . . . confident
[and] original."

—*Kirkus Reviews*

"Readers who enjoy historical fiction will be dazzled by Avery's attention to
detail, savoring her descriptions. . . . Those who like plot twists will relish the
epic cast of characters. . . . An homage to Virginia Woolf's *Orlando* in both
style and theme, Avery's ambitious endeavor is the perfect companion for a
series of cold winter nights."

—*Library Journal*

The
Teahouse Fire

Riverhead Books

New York

The
Teahouse Fire

.

ELLIS AVERY

RIVERHEAD BOOKS
Published by the Penguin Group
Penguin Group (USA) Inc., 375 Hudson Street, New York, New York 10014, USA •
Penguin Group (Canada), 90 Eglinton Avenue East, Suite 700, Toronto, Ontario
M4P 2Y3, Canada (a division of Pearson Penguin Canada Inc.) • Penguin Books Ltd.,
80 Strand, London WC2R 0RL, England • Penguin Group Ireland, 25 St. Stephen's Green, Dublin 2,
Ireland (a division of Penguin Books Ltd.) • Penguin Group (Australia), 250 Camberwell Road,
Camberwell, Victoria 3124, Australia (a division of Pearson Australia Group Pty. Ltd.) •
Penguin Books India Pvt. Ltd., 11 Community Centre, Panchsheel Park, New Delhi–
110 017, India • Penguin Group (NZ), 67 Apollo Drive, Rosedale, North Shore 0632,
New Zealand (a division of Pearson New Zealand Ltd.)
• Penguin Books (South Africa) (Pty.) Ltd., 24 Sturdee Avenue,
Rosebank, Johannesburg 2196, South Africa

Penguin Books Ltd., Registered Offices: 80 Strand, London WC2R 0RL, England

The author gratefully acknowledges permission to quote from *The Diary of Lady
Murasaki*, by Murasaki Shikibu, translated by Richard Bowring (Penguin Books, 1996).
Translation copyright © 1996 Richard Bowring. Reproduced by permission of
Penguin Books Ltd. Material quoted from pp. 7 (text altered: Bowring's
translation reads, "You remind me of a fairy-tale princess!"), 20, 54, 56.

The author gratefully acknowledges permission to quote 74 words from
The Pillow Book of Sei Shonagon, edited and translated by Ivan Morris. © 1967
Columbia University Press and Oxford University Press. Reprinted with permission
of both Columbia University Press and Oxford University Press, Inc.

First Riverhead hardcover edition: December 2006
First Riverhead trade paperback edition: December 2007
Riverhead trade paperback ISBN: 978-1-59448-273-1

The Library of Congress has catalogued the Riverhead hardcover edition as follows:

Avery, Ellis.
The teahouse fire / Ellis Avery.
p.   cm.
ISBN-13: 978-1-59448-930-3
ISBN-10: 1-59448-930-0
1. Americans—Japan—Kyoto—Fiction.   2. Kyoto (Japan)—Social life and customs—
19th century—Fiction.   3. Japanese tea ceremony—Fiction.   I. Title.
PS3601.V466T43   2006   2006024042
813'.6—dc22

PRINTED IN THE UNITED STATES OF AMERICA

10   9   8   7   6   5   4   3

FOR

Sharon Marcus
Amanda Atwood
Elaine Solari Atwood

The
Teahouse Fire

1856–1866

W HEN I WAS NINE, in the city now called Kyoto, I changed my fate. I walked into the shrine through the red arch and struck the bell. I bowed twice. I clapped twice. I whispered to the foreign goddess and bowed again. And then I heard the shouts and the fire. What I asked for? *Any life but this one.*

I WAS NAMED AURELIA for my grandmother, Aurélie Caillard, who worked in Paris as a laundress. She had two children, my uncle Charles and my mother, Claire. My uncle was clever with books and won scholarships to Jesuit schools, where they puffed him up, my mother said, with dreams of power and glory in faraway lands. When he was twenty, a priest already, the Order transferred him to New York to shuttle between Irish and Italian immigrants downtown, using the office of school principal as a base from which to consolidate the Catholic vote. The post was less than he had hoped for; he petitioned regularly for transfer. My mother stayed in Paris, working as a maid in a convent. Uncle Charles said she took up with a wicked man, but—I admit my bias—I think someone at the church forced himself on her: she was fourteen. My grandmother offered passage money to New York and closed her door.

In 1856, when my mother arrived on Mott Street to wash her brother's floors, my uncle Charles pronounced her a young widow and gave her dead husband the surname Bernard. Early that May she gave birth to me. *Aurelia*, Uncle Charles insisted, not Aurélie. *An American name.*

We lived at Prince and Mott, my mother and I, across from the churchyard, in an attic apartment above Saint Patrick's School. My mother had black hair and black eyes like mine; her round face dimpled on one side in a private smile. Every morning, before even setting water to boil for Uncle Charles, she would lift me up to the sill of the garret window. I loved seeing the high sycamore leaves up close, and far below, the red brick wall around the churchyard, loved wrapping my arms and legs around her shoulders and waist. She was most my mother at the edges of the day; she was a radiant mantle folded around me. She would comb my hair back with her fingers and sing the jaunty song she loved: *Auprès de ma blonde, il fait beau, fait beau, fait beau.*

"But my hair is black! Can I still be your *blonde?*"

"You are my little blond crow," she would assure me.

"Your blond licorice?"

"My blondest black plum."

And then she would set me down and change her song: *Frère Charles, Frère Charles, Dormez-vous? Dormez-vous?* And with that she would pack up her dimpled smile, fold up her radiant mantle, and become, not my mother, but her brother's *bonne.*

Uncle Charles had his office—which doubled as his apartment—on the fourth floor, just downstairs from us. He had arranged our quarters this way because he disliked the smells of cooking. He also disliked climbing stairs, but living any lower than the fourth floor would have forced him into more frequent contact with pupils than he preferred.

Uncle Charles's features were small and his hands were large; his skull tapered like a fez at the back of his head and he flushed easily. He spoke only in French to my mother and—for my own good—only in English to me, his voice an oboe to my mother's cello. On Sunday afternoons when I was very small, after saying mass for the nuns and eating lunch with my mother and me, he would retreat with me from the spartan back half of his apartment (bedroom, dining room, untouched kitchen) to the nest of his office in front (hundreds of books, one enormous armchair). He would sit me on his lap in the burgundy velvet chair and teach me how to read the English Bible, just as he had taught my mother how to read the French one when they were children. He covered the bricks of tightly printed letters with blotting paper so that only the letter, only the word, only the line before me was visible: *Heaven and earth. Le ciel et la terre.*

Aside from those Sunday afternoons, three times a day we laid out Uncle Charles's meal on a tray, set it on a stand beside his armchair, and ate on our own upstairs. After breakfast, we would clear away the tray and do the shopping, me translating between rapid French and pushcart Italian-English, and then we would come home to make Uncle Charles's noon meal, the richest of the day. If Uncle Charles planned to be home in the evening, we would serve a soup made up from the lunch ingredients, together with bread, cheese, and wine. If he dined out, we would clean his apartment (quickly in back, slowly in front) and borrow his books. At night my mother would read to me, *le cigale et la fourmi;* and when I was old enough, I would read to her as she sewed, *If hairs be wires, black wires grow on her head.*

In the afternoons, once the dishes were washed and the soup assembled, my mother would rest until the schoolbell rang and the pupils clattered home, then go downstairs to mop the classroom floors. All I wanted was to follow her, so she made me a toy mop of my own from a broken broom handle and a tied-on rag, and together we danced with our obliging partners, noisy in the empty classrooms, quiet in the ones where the nuns lingered, bent over their students' papers.

My mother, though she hid it from them well, did not like nuns. I heard it in the lugubrious way she said the word *nun*, the way she sniffed at their wet wool habits drying on the roof next door. *Les nonnes.* I never learned what her life was like before I was born, when she cleaned for the convent in Paris. Though I was baptized, and sat in the back of the chapel on Sunday mornings when Uncle Charles said mass, and even took my First Communion with a holy shudder, my mother never joined me. She slept or sewed. The morning of my First Communion, when I asked her one last time to come, she said, "Aurelia Bernard. Who is this Bernard, tell me? The Church hates truth, and the nuns hate it most of all."

"Do you want me not to go?" I asked, confused.

"My dear, you need the Church as much as I do. At least until you're grown. You don't have to *bite the hand*"—she said the phrase in English—"but you don't have to lick it, either." *Lick* is *lécher* in French; the word pooled out of her mouth like honey, obscene.

I think she hated having no choice but to feel gratitude. We did need the Church; it fed us, it sheltered us. And in time, it educated me: my mother gave me a Saint Claire medal and my uncle gave me a tartan uniform; I put on both and joined the girls at Saint Patrick's, helping my mother in the afternoons. Once I started school, French became for me, not half my spoken life, but a secret language shared only with my mother as we glided across the floors.

All the girls in my class were Irish but me. Some of their fathers had been killed in the War between the States; some had killed policemen in the Draft Riots the summer I was seven. They were tough, those girls. I liked them: their games and the up-and-down way they talked, like horses and the sea, the way they laughed with each other in secret after the nuns beat them. *She took the ruler to me hand, the cow.*

But one day when I was nine, one of the nuns from another classroom came to show us a book of etchings of the Vatican. She asked my name. "Aurelia Bernard? Oh, I didn't recognize you without Claire," she said, holding an imaginary mop in both hands, gesturing. "Please give my regards to your mother."

I don't think she meant me harm, but at a desk nearby I saw one of the Irish girls take up the gesture and laugh. And after school a chorus of girls giggled behind me, their fists stacked one on the other in front of them, their arms circling as they cried, *Mopper! Mopper!* Our ballroom afternoons sounded grubby in their mouths. I walked stiffly upstairs, and a last girl called my name. I turned and saw piefaced Maggie Phelan laughing with her friends. "Please give my regards to your *mopper!*"

"Leave me alone!" I said.

"Leemie alone!" she mocked as I turned the corner, forcing myself not to run. I climbed upstairs and crawled into my mother's bed to hide. I pressed my face against her warm back: it was a comfort, her smell of soap and lemons, the purring stutter of her breath. My mother's afternoon naps were getting longer and longer, I noted, trying to be patient. I wanted so badly to tell her, to be reassured by her, defended. My mother stirred, coughed into a handkerchief, and petted me. "You look sick, *ma petite*, what's wrong?"

I opened my mouth to tell her, and couldn't. Instead, I heard myself saying, "I don't really help you so much, when we clean together downstairs. What if I did some of your morning work in the afternoon instead, like bringing in the water and the coal?"

"Hm, then maybe we'd have time to shop together in the morning before school," she mused. "I think Mrs. Baldini is cheating me." I wanted to protect my mother from all the Phelans and Baldinis in the world; I wanted the coarse, chewy English words to be easy for her the way they were, miraculously, for me. She looked reluctant for a moment, and then embraced me tightly. *"Ma petite,"* she said, "carrying such heavy things. It isn't right that a young girl should work so hard."

"I don't mind," I said. "I'll make lots of little trips." As she nodded slow assent, I felt as if I had gotten away with something: with not having to be embarrassed by her and not having to hurt her, either. My love and calculation formed a black wad in my throat. I held her close and said, "I'll start today."

EXCHANGING MY SCHOOL UNIFORM for a smock, I made my mother's bed after she went downstairs to the classrooms. I poured the stale water from the kettle into the dishpan and brought down the next day's fresh water from the barrels upstairs: it had rained recently, and the roof was closer than the tap outside. I took the scuttle to the cellar and brought up all the coal I could carry. I took the chamberpots downstairs and emptied them into the outhouse, washed them at the tap, and brought them back again, panting my way up to the fourth and fifth floors. When I returned Uncle Charles's pot, he looked up from his armchair. "Tell your mother I'd like you both to join me at dinner tonight," he said. His urine smelled worse than ours, I reflected on my way upstairs; I would have to ask my mother why. I explored our apartment when I was alone in it: brushing aside a handful of crumpled handkerchiefs, marked as if with rust, I dug out the basket my mother kept hidden under her bed. It held a pretty brown half-sewn dress, I discovered, just my size, with brown velvet ribbon at the waist and cuffs. Beneath it lay a rag doll wearing the same dress, made of white cotton with drawn-on features—brown eyes like mine—and a velvet kerchief in place of hair. Wriggling with delight, I returned the dress and doll to their hiding place, scattering the handkerchiefs again to cover my tracks.

Just as I crawled out from under the bed, I heard slow feet up the stairs and then my mother returned, flushed from the work below. "You did so much, my sweet," she said. "Shall we heat up your uncle's dinner?"

I told her of Uncle Charles's strange request, and she pursed her lips, amused and quizzical. "Has Sunday come early this week?" She glanced at the pot on the stove. "Well, soup for all, *quand même*," she decided. "He should have spoken up sooner if he wanted something else. Whatever does he expect us to wear?"

AT UNCLE CHARLES'S little-used table, me in my tartan and my mother in her good dress, we leaned forward, fidgeting through the long blessing. Then Uncle Charles began eating with a bachelor's silent, methodical speed, and my mother followed suit, leaving me to rock in my chair with frustrated curiosity. The two of them locked into what could have been called a contest if it weren't for my uncle's tonsured dignity and my mother's wry grace. When Uncle Charles had emptied his bowl, he set down his spoon with a rap, which my mother answered instantly, and the two of them surveyed each other with arms crossed over their bellies. "Well, that was fun, Charles; I don't see how you can bear to eat alone every night," said my mother.

My uncle offered a sniff of acknowledgment and began speaking in his preaching voice. "As you know, I have for some time sought permission to serve our Lord in a capacity commensurate with the gifts He has seen fit to bestow upon His creature."

"*For this I speak four languages?*" my mother mocked. "I haven't forgotten."

My uncle took a deep breath to continue in this vein, but then his joy burst forth in a shuddering exhale. "This morning I received a letter," he announced simply.

"You beat out Brother Michael, didn't you?" my mother needled.

"I have been chosen," Uncle Charles said, reddening, "to follow in the footsteps of the Blessed Saint Francis Xavier. To minister to a lost flock. To convert the heathen in a land that has finally opened her doors to the West." He leaned back in his chair and sighed. "It's not for me to say why Brother Michael's prayer went unheard while mine has been granted." As he looked heavenward, my mother flashed me a knowing smirk, which drained out of her face as she began to realize he was serious. "This afternoon I booked passage for all three of us," he said. "We leave for Japan in six weeks."

I DROPPED MY SPOON. Japan? My mother went white. What would she do, my mother, who could not serve a Sunday meal on a Thursday? Scream at him, curse him? Fling her glass of wine in his face? But instead she slowly pouted out her lip and rocked her head to the side, as if gauging her store of flour—as if to say, *We can stretch it.* And with uncharacteristic hesitation, she asked, "Do you think it's good? For the girl?"

"What could be better than to serve our Lord? Aurelia has the gift of languages, and you have"—he paused, groping—"the gift of the hearth." My mother, irritated, closed her eyes and pressed her lips together, and Uncle Charles chastised, "It is a blessing to be called to do God's work." His ruddy face shone, and then he looked down at me. "Now, the world is full of people who can speak French and English, but if Aurelia can learn Japanese as readily—"

"You could support yourself as a translator," my mother said. I saw relief for me in her face, and something gentler than envy.

"The Church has a place for all Her daughters, even the most unfortunate," said Uncle Charles, looking at her pointedly. My mother's nostrils flared. "Any order that Aurelia felt called to would be the richer for her learning."

"Or you could marry an ambassador," she daydreamed.

"In any case," said Uncle Charles, "the Order, at my request, has given us a second copy of the grammar with which they have provided me. Learn what you can," he said, passing me a black and gilt book stamped with the word *Nippongo.*

"Aurelia, thank your uncle and go upstairs," said my mother. "I'm going to talk with him for a while. Here, take a candle."

. . .

I PRESSED MY EAR to my uncle's closed door, almost falling in as someone opened it. "Go," said my mother, standing over me. "Now."

I LAY IN MY BED by candlelight with Mr. Nippongo's book. The blocks of text were sprinkled with drawings of parasols, pagodas, men in dresses called *kimono*, singular and plural, women in *kimono* and sashes called *obi*. The ladies were pretty as painted china plates: when I closed my eyes, I could see them in blue and white. In our pagoda, Uncle Charles would live on the ground floor and my mother and I would live upstairs, sleeping each night under our little tiered roof. Oh, to live up only one flight of stairs—and to never see Maggie Phelan again! I clutched the book to me, lighthearted and fierce.

I woke again halfway when my mother came in. She rustled in the room, kissed me, and blew out my candle. I heard her cough in her bed and spit into a handkerchief; it fell to the floor with a soft wet slap.

SIX WEEKS LATER I stood by her bedside. "Look, I wore my dress," I said.

"You look very pretty," my mother said drowsily. "Do you like the velvet?"

"It's soft." I nodded.

"Do you have a name for your doll?"

"Clara," I said, holding her up for my mother to see.

"Hello, Clara," she said in English.

I remember the attic, the wind in the sycamores, the vagrant bolts of light from the garret windows, the bright air buzzing with dust. A patchwork quilt from the nuns' box: red squares spreading in diagonal stripes on a field of soft white cotton. Under it: my mother. "I'll take

the next ship out," she promised. "I'll be there before you know it."
Her face was hot and flushed; her body seemed so flattened, so small
in the sea of Irish Chain.

"But I could go later, with you," I insisted.

She looked pained for a moment, then merry. "I think your uncle
needs you to come with him," she said. "He'll never say it, but I think
he'd be afraid to try learning Japanese without you." I laughed. "No,
it's true: you're younger; it'll be easier for you."

"If you'd come to New York when *you* were younger . . ." I said
tentatively.

"I wouldn't have had you, *ma blonde*." She reached with effort to finger my black hair. "You are the best thing that's ever happened to me,"
she said. "My *bel accident*." She was always tender with me, but never
solemn like this. I scratched my nose uncomfortably.

"Uncle Charles did the right thing by both of us," she said, out of
nowhere. "Did you know, he booked two cabins on board? The
cheaper thing would be to put us in the front of the ship, where all the
servants room together. That's how I came to New York. It can be trying, for a woman alone; I imagine your uncle didn't want any more *acci-
dents*." Because she laughed, I laughed, too, uncertainly. "So you'll get
the cabin we'd have shared. What do you think of that, having a room
to yourself?" she asked.

She closed her eyes and lay quietly, and I cuddled under the red-
and-white quilt. "I'd rather stay here with you," I said.

"My precious child," my mother began softly, and then she seemed
to gather force; her black eyes flew open and she broke off, hissing, "If
anything ever happened to me, you'd be at the mercy of the nuns. I
can't have that on my conscience."

"I don't understand," I said, burrowing my face into her neck.

"You will," she sighed. And then, very seriously, pushing me back
a little to look at me, she said, "Is there anything you ever wanted to
ask me?"

I looked her in the eye. I couldn't think of anything. And then I wriggled closer and whispered a question, and my mother laughed and hacked. "Oh, God, my Aurélie. Because he drinks coffee, darling," she said, brushing tears of laughter from her eyes and blood from the corner of her mouth.

When we had both caught our breath, she patted her shoulder for me to rest my head while she told her story. "When I came to this country," she said, "I got sick off the side of the boat so many times. All the adults did. You'd feel your stomach start to swoosh around inside you and—quick—you'd make a run for the railing. Meanwhile all the children raced around like it was Carnival. *Hurrah!*" she said, in a piping little voice. "*The boat's rocking like a pony, and our parents are too sick to keep us in line!*" We laughed again; she coughed and said, "It's better this way. If we were sailing together, I'd be so jealous—you prancing around, me throwing up—but this way I'll get to hear all about your adventures when I can enjoy them properly." We heard Uncle Charles's impatient tread up the stairs; she hauled her thin arms around me and clasped me so hard I gasped. "Now, *va-t'en*, shoo," she said, pushing me out of the bed. "I'm going to let your uncle say a prayer for me and I know you'll fidget." I shooed.

So many firsts all at once! My first trunk. My first ship, the *Lafayette*, just like the street in our neighborhood. My first telegram, before we even steamed away—Uncle Charles's, actually, but I had never seen a messenger boy up close, or his little leather satchel. My first view from the water of the pillared city where I was born. My first view, on all sides, of the sea.

My first room to myself, as my mother had promised: a tiny, windowless cell containing a stacked pair of bunks with high walls like the sides of a crib. I named the top my bedroom—my first ladder!—and the bottom one my parlor, like a fancy lady.

My first meals my mother hadn't cooked. I remember how exotic it was my first day of school, how sophisticated I felt, in my plaid uniform and Saint Claire medal, eating the apple and bread and cheese my mother had sent down with me. (She did not want me eating the nuns' food, she said. I was grateful; what I saw—and smelled—of the other students eating at the Saint Patrick's refectory was one long nightmare of soggy boiled greens.) Even so, how much more grown up I felt eating roast chicken on a tray by lamplight in my parlor bunk with Clara, while Uncle Charles ate with the other Jesuits in the dining room. *So this is how it is for him. The food appears, the dishes vanish. So easy. Auprès de ma blonde,* I sang to my kerchiefed doll. Later, my stomach hurt.

Maybe there was some truth to my mother's idea that children could learn languages faster. When the seven Brothers met each morning to study Japanese, I was always the first to raise my hand—*this, that, the other; here, there, over there; yesterday, today, tomorrow*—until Uncle Charles asked me to stop joining them for class. "The presence of a child distracts us from our labor," he explained, and so I studied on my own in the gloomy ship library, quizzing Clara—*I gave the book to the teacher; the teacher gave the book to me*—as Uncle Charles, daily, quizzed me.

After seven days, and seven letters to my mother on French Line stationery, we changed ships in Southampton, England, for the P&O Line. We took the *Poonah* bound for Alexandria—the very ship, the captain told us, on which the great acrobat Blondin had trained for his Niagara Falls feat by walking a tightrope strung between the main and mizzen masts. A framed engraving of the event hung in the ship's library: Blondin, blindfolded and barefoot midway, smoking a pipe. In place of the solemn volumes of French philosophy on the *Lafayette*, the British ship library had Shakespeare and fairy tales. I remember thinking, that first afternoon as we bobbed in the harbor, how lucky I was, sitting with my doll and all those books in that sunny window, savoring the promise of a letter from my mother when they passed out the Southampton mail the next morning.

At the end of the day, when I lay in my new compartment, this one even smaller than the last, Uncle Charles came in with a lamp to say good night. "There's only one bed this time," I said, rocking experimentally against the narrow sides of the new crib-bunk. "Where would *Maman* sleep?" I yawned.

Uncle Charles blinked in the darkness. Something in his face woke me up.

"What?" I asked, sitting up to see him in the light. Some unsaid anger—or panic?—scuttled across his features.

He composed himself. "The Sisters in New York sent a message," he said. "One of the Southampton Brothers told me."

My stomach twisted inside me. Of course I knew, but I wanted to make not knowing last longer. "She can't come on the next ship, either?" I squeaked. *Say nothing, Uncle Charles,* I thought.

"God took her just after we left."

I pulled the covers to my chin, and pressed my fists to my ears.

"The Sisters buried her in the churchyard at Saint Patrick's."

"No."

"God will purge His handmaiden of her sins," he said, "and draw her to His side in heaven."

"No," I said.

"I know you mourn, but you must rejoice for her immortal soul."

"Good night," I said, choking, and shut my eyes tight. I did not open them when he blessed me.

I KNOW I READ and ate and studied and slept on the *Poonah,* but I remember very little. I know we crossed the Mediterranean, took a nightlong train across the desert to Suez, and steamed off again on a new ship, but those numb winter months are lost to me. All I see is the engraving, the tightrope, the blindfold. We did not mention her, neither Uncle Charles nor I.

I began to thaw a little on the new ship, the *Singapore*, steaming the long warm weeks from one fragrant port to the next: Aden, Galle, Madras, Calcutta, Penang. There was one Japanese person on board: a skinny young cook, Mr. Ohara, who wore his ship's uniform stiffly ironed and sharpened his cleavers each day. It was easy enough to learn from him because he said the same things every morning when he brought food up from the larder: *It's dirty. It smells bad. It's not fresh.* He kept a cat, Maneki-*san*, a one-eyed mouser I was forbidden to feed. He gave me tiny cups of pale green tea and let me practice my new words in the early part of the day, then chased me away when he set to work on the noon meal in earnest. I read fairy tales then, or played School in my narrow chamber, teaching Clara *Nippongo* from my gilt leather grammar. There was no Mr. Nippongo. The word meant *Japanese*.

My name is Clara. I am a doll. I am a foreigner. I come from New York. I came by ship. My mother is French. My mother is in New York. My mother is sick. I don't speak Japanese. I don't understand. I don't know.

I remember the soft arms of the ship rocking me at night as I prayed for my mother: sometimes that God might hold her as the ship held me, sometimes that she would get well and come soon. That her passage might be safe. That she might be, secretly, an elfin princess, and come to me across the water on gauzy wings. And every day I woke still farther from her, to *umi, tori*: the vast blinding sea, flecked with gulls.

1866

WE REACHED YOKOHAMA that spring, after days of sailing north from Shanghai, the sea growing colder. I remember lurching on the dock, unsteady on my land legs, waving good-bye to Mr. Ohara, though he could not see me. Japanese people were forbidden to leave Japan, he had told me, trusting me with his secret, so he didn't want to go above deck until they reached Edo, where he could slip off the boat unseen. We had said our farewells in the kitchen; I remember calling him Ohara-*san* and bowing, him bowing back, pleased. While the other monks awaited their orders, a buttery French Brother, Joaquin, his pate above his tonsure beaming, met me and Uncle Charles amid a quiet crowd of pointy round hats and bare brown legs. "Welcome, welcome," he said. "You are now in Japan and it's February twenty-fourth."

"Why, it's the end of March," protested Uncle Charles.

"Of course it is. But the natives are still on a lunar calendar here," the monk chuckled. "The trick for us is keeping both dates in our heads at once. When in Rome, *n'est-ce pas?*" He laughed at his own wit as Uncle Charles fumbled with his valise. "Welcome to Japan," the monk repeated, his gaze falling on me, "though they told me to expect an adult servant, not a child, *mademoiselle*," he said merrily. He arranged to have most of our other things sent on to the next ship, and two Japanese men wearing straw hats and wooden sandals—and not much more—carried our smallest trunk together on poles behind us. Brother Joaquin led the way down a little gray street of little gray tiled roofs—he and Uncle Charles looked enormous—past gray doorways tucked behind billowing strips of indigo cloth painted with fluid white characters. We passed a bright red trellis twice the height of a man: two red tree trunks topped with two red beams. "That's a *torii*," he said. "The heathens think of it as a kind of spirit gate. You'll see it in front of all their shrines." The red *torii* commanded one side of the street, while a great wooden gate framed the other: beyond each of them I saw a garden, a tall building, a fat braided rope bellpull. "Buddhist temple," said Brother Joaquin, nodding toward the wooden gate. "Shinto shrine," he said, glancing at the *torii*. "Reincarnation and nature worship, respectively," he sighed. "It seems the natives follow both religions and believe in neither." I looked through the *torii* gate as we passed it and saw a wedge of bright colors, no, a dainty woman swathed in brocade, reaching for the bell-rope at a little gilded altar. Brother Joaquin continued, "One of them had the cheek to 'teach' me how to 'pray' at their shrines once: toss a coin, ring the bell, bow twice, clap twice, make a wish, bow again." As we walked up from the bay, the heavy, frail blocks of tile-and-wood gray houses became less tightly packed; new brick buildings, like the ones on Mott Street, appeared here and there, still under construction. "'And why is it you call this nonsense prayer?'" Brother Joaquin continued. "'Two-two-one system,' said the little fellow. He sounded so very pleased with himself." He chuckled.

"'Two-two-one system,'" Uncle Charles said with a shudder. "Tarting up idolatry in the finery of science."

A man in a black *kimono* strode past us with a look of bland distaste. He wore his hair in a horsetail queue slicked stiff with oil and pinned at the end to his crown, so that it looked as if he were wearing a tobacco pipe on the back of his head. He wore what looked like two sticks at his belt, one long, one short. "Those are swords," said Brother Joaquin. "He's a *samurai*. You'll see five castes here: warriors, or *samurai*, at the top, then farmers, craftsmen, merchants, and the unclean. They all have to follow the caste laws about every little thing: what kind of clothing you can wear, what kind of roof you can put on your house. Pay attention to the merchants; they're hungry for change. Officially they're low caste, which means they have pots of money and aren't allowed to spend it on anything. 'All men are brothers in Christ' appeals to them, because it puts them on equal footing with the *samurai*. Not a lot of *samurai* converts; they're the toughest nuts to crack."

As the streets began to look less foreign and more like New York, I kept glancing back at the proud *torii* gate. The higher crossbeam had ends that swept upward, like the prow of a Viking ship. I liked thinking of a spirit boat, sailing in the air through a red gate. "Is *torii* like *tori*, bird?" I asked.

"Seen and not heard, Aurelia," said Uncle Charles.

"The Church of the Sacred Heart," Brother Joaquin announced, stopping to nod toward three structures: a new brick church, a new brick house, and a blackened, roofless brick hall, half built or half in ruin. "Founded by our own Abbé Girard. To answer your question, young lady," he said, "every time I've asked a Japanese something like that—*torii*, gate, and *tori*, bird; *hana*, nose, and *hana*, flower—I get a queer little laugh and a bow, and the man says, 'Sorry, Father, different *kanji*.' Their words are all in those wretched Chinese characters, and two words can sound alike but look completely different on the page."

I had seen *kanji*, the difficult Chinese characters, in my grammar, and had learned only a few. I nodded.

"Well, here are your quarters for the night, right across from the main building. Japanese style, I'm afraid. The dormitory was almost ready last fall and then it went up in flames." He nodded toward the wreck across the street. "Fires all the time here; they build their blasted houses out of *shoji* paper. We're lucky more wasn't lost." He glanced back again at the ruined building, pained.

"Paper?" asked Uncle Charles. Following his gaze, it seemed to me that only the roofless brick building had burned—an especially remarkable fact, given the surrounding buildings: under the heavy tile roofs, I saw dainty wood lattices framing sliding paper doors and walls. I had been too young to understand what was happening during the Draft Riots in New York, but I knew they had been more than Uncle Charles was prepared for. "Is it safe here?"

"Oh, that bother with the British Embassy was a long time ago."

Brother Joaquin's reassurance had the opposite effect on Uncle Charles. "What bother?"

"Arson," said the monk dismissively. "Before anyone could move in. Nobody hurt, don't worry. Besides, that was four years ago, and times have changed. It was lightning, don't worry."

Uncle Charles did not look mollified. "Couldn't an evildoer have come under cover of storm?" he asked.

"You don't understand, Father. That was Edo, this is Yokohama. And we've hired our own watchman. You'll hear him at night: they beat wooden sticks together"—he clapped twice—"to scare off tres-passers, I suppose."

Uncle Charles looked wary as Brother Joaquin plowed ahead. "So, then. Have you ever been in a Japanese building before? Well," he laughed dryly, "welcome; behold. You'll need to take off your shoes whenever you step up into the house." He opened a sliding lattice gate and showed us the dark inside of a wooden house. The stone floor just in from the lattice was simply a continuation of the cobbled street. After the little stone foyer, the whole house stood on stilts a foot or two up from the ground, carpeted in a strange pale flooring. "This is what the Japanese call a *tatami* floor: thick mats made of woven rice straw. *Tatami* mats are all the same size, about six feet by three. That's how they measure their homes: *I live in a six-mat room,* and so forth. If you walk on *tatami* with your shoes, for them it's like you used the well for a privy."

I grimaced, imagining, and Uncle Charles glowered at me.

"So: you come inside and, if it's raining, leave your umbrella and your muddy things here—*arigato,*" he said, counting out change to the porters who set down our trunk. "And then you sit on this wooden step, take off your shoes, and put them in this cupboard, see? Dirty outdoor shoes on the bottom shelf, clean indoor slippers on the top. They all wear wooden sandals so they're not spending the day lacing and unlacing as we would." Brother Joaquin, I realized, wore wooden sandals too. "In the lavatory—indoors, but it's cleaned out daily—one must wear, mark me, *different slippers,* so that when you miss you'll not be tracking your mess into the house. On our mission, we'll each have a servant—a novice Brother, one of the natives—nonexistent, of course, under Japanese law. Anyhow, mine here raised all kinds of fuss when I wore the wrong shoes in the wrong place." Uncle Charles opened the door the monk indicated and looked at the privy, appalled. "Yes, well, you'll have to squat to answer the call of nature in Japan; it takes getting used to," Brother Joaquin said. "Tonight we'll have a boy take out your *futon* for you; it's their idea of a mattress—cotton wadding spread on the floor. You'll get to try their queer pillows too." He pointed to an empty corner of the lattice-and-paper wall.

"What is it, Brother?"

"Oh, sorry, it's a closet for your *futon.*" Magicianlike, he pulled the wall open—it was a sliding door—and revealed shelves laden with thick quilts. How strange the room looked, how empty: sliding paper walls surrounding straw *tatami* floors. Along one wall stood dark wooden cabinets I took to be dressers and cupboards, solemn with their sliding panels and metal fittings. Uncle Charles looked around as well, asking, "How is this place heated?"

Brother Joaquin pointed to a blackened metal cauldron beside the cabinets. "Charcoal braziers," he said. "Your boy will take them out tonight and get a fire set for you."

"I'm sure I could see to it myself," said Uncle Charles.

"Please don't," said Brother Joaquin. "They're fussy, the braziers." The church bell tolled five. "So. There's a loft at the top of the ladder, which is sure to break if I show you," said Brother Joaquin, rubbing his broad belly for emphasis. "And there's a garden in back, very quaint," he added. He and Uncle Charles blocked the garden door, so I looked around the back room: it had no furniture at all. One *tatami* mat against a side wall of the room was raised an inch or so higher than its neighbors; it was framed by raw wood posts and contained a statue of the Virgin. "What's that?" I asked when Brother Joaquin moved away from the sunny patch of moss and gravel behind the house.

"Aurelia, silence," said Uncle Charles.

"Our Lady, or her display alcove? The best room of every Japanese house, usually the one by the garden," Brother Joaquin explained, "has a niche like this for showing off one or two treasures at a time, usually calligraphy or ceramics. The statue came from Nantes, thanks to Abbé Girard. What else can I show you? We'll eat at the refectory, but there *is* a native kitchen, if you're curious. It's over here. Down a step, here we are, back on a stone floor again." He lowered himself with practiced grace into a pair of sandals waiting by the ledge. "You can come in through the kitchen, if you like—there's a side alley. Don't ask me what all these things are for; I don't know. Except here's a basin—I filled it for you this morning. There's a well down the alley; your boy will bring in more water for washing tonight. Unless you want to try one of the native bathhouses . . ." he laughed; Uncle Charles looked appalled. "It's kind of charming, really, in a squalid way: they all change out of their daytime dress and wear blue cotton *kimono* bathrobes down the street, as if they all lived under the same roof. I thought it was some kind of heathen rite when I first came here. And then inside—according to their

defenders—whole families bathe together like Adam and Eve in Eden."
Uncle Charles shook his head, overwhelmed. "So, the refectory at six,
then? You'll hear the bell."

Before dinner, I climbed the polished wooden ladder in my stocking
feet and looked up in the empty loft: *a three-mat room,* I counted. When
the bell called six, we wove our way through Brother Joaquin's promised
twilight procession: a streetful of clattering wooden sandals and blue
cotton robes. Two pairs of women walking toward each other bowed
and stopped to chat: I heard a hash of rapid syllables, the sound, *-mashita,*
-mashita, that meant they were using verbs in the past tense, and then one
of them glanced over at the sweet yawning baby on the other's back.
"Kawaii," she sighed. I understood! The baby was cute! I also noticed that
the women's mouths were strangely like the dark O of the baby's: they
had no teeth. No—one of them was standing under the mission lamp; I
saw—their teeth were black.

What's more, I noticed, the women had no eyebrows. Those walking, it seemed, *to* the bathhouse had eyebrow lines painted on their
foreheads; those walking *from* the bathhouse, moist and rosy, had none
at all. I held my doll closer and hurried to catch up with Uncle
Charles.

He looked at me in the doorway and seemed uneasy. "A child . . ."
he said darkly. And so I sat in my good dress in the kitchen, eating dinner on a tray. From time to time, I peered into the dining room to
watch the dozen-odd Yokohama Brothers entertain their guests, bragging about their boiled beets and tough chicken. I thought, not of my
mother, but of her steamed green beans, crisp and tender, potatoes
and garlic cooked in wine and cream, her meringues served with strawberries in June. I missed them terribly. The Brothers sat talking, talking, sucking at their chicken bones. A silver-bearded Father made
Uncle Charles stand with his head bowed as he pronounced upon "the
old capital of Japan, benighted Miyako, hard of access, the city most
steeped in pagan darkness, residence of the Emperor Komei, whom

they worship as a descendant of their sun goddess. Our son Charles, gifted with tongues, we have chosen, with our son Joaquin, to breach the city of Miyako. May they bring light into darkness." Uncle Charles flushed, bashful and radiant.

"But first things first," cautioned Brother Joaquin. "We aren't supposed to be in the Emperor's capital, not as Westerners, and certainly not as missionaries. But a group of Christians who have been practicing in secret since Saint Francis Xavier's time has asked us to come. We'll be guests of one of the feudal lords, who keeps a residence in Miyako. You'll meet Father Damian when we get there; we're to assist him. He'll install us in houses where we can minister clandestinely, at least until the laws change."

"And on that day," the Father boomed, "we will build a cathedral in Our Lord's name and gather up a new flock. We shall not use violence but exhort by word, by baptism, and by example, until they put their own temples to the torch, the better to make straight the road for Christ."

I remember resting my head against the wall for a moment as I listened to the Brothers, and then Uncle Charles set me down on a pillowy quilt. He propped something under my neck: a wooden box topped with a cloth pad. I blinked awake. "Are we in the Japanese house?" I asked in French.

"Yes, you're upstairs," he said in English. "Here's your nightgown."

So the thing under my head was a Japanese pillow, how uncomfortable. Pushing it away, I blinked and saw soft candlelight on the *tatami* floor. "*Tatami,*" I said, pointing. "*Futon. Shoji* paper. *Torii* gates. *Kanji* words. So many new things." I yawned. "How will *Maman* manage?"

"Aurelia," said Uncle Charles sharply.

I swallowed hard, my face flaming. My mouth tasted of sour beets and rank chicken. "Nothing, never mind," I said shortly. "Good night, sleep well."

"May the Lord watch over you," he said, as always.

I wouldn't need the Lord if my mother were here, I thought in the dark, beginning to cry, and no one punished me with lightning. I was that alone.

HIDDEN IN THE BELLY of a Japanese cargo ship, gnawing on the monks' bread and salted meat, we sailed for a week down the coast and upriver to great Osaka. On the seventh night, concealed in lacquered, cagelike boxes, we took a flat poled craft to Fushimi, the port for the Emperor's city. Come morning a group of Japanese men—servants of Father Damian's Christians, it seemed—transferred us, boxes and all, to a third boat, the narrowest yet, which brought us into Miyako itself. I sat with my doll in my lap on those voyages, not speaking, mostly sleeping. *My mother, my mother.* I felt nothing. Not the distracted, evasive, playing-house nothing of the past two months, where my prayers were really stories I told myself, but a square-on nothing, a blank mirror inside. The animal of my body wept and I felt nothing.

On the journey from Fushimi to Miyako, invisible in my lacquered cage, I peeped through the grillework at the world outside and at Uncle Charles's chair, lashed beside us, empty, bobbing, half-encased in rough cloth. The red plush bulk of it rose up from the loose wrappings, framed in dark worked wood: scallops and protruding cherubs, and at the top a hoop of wood carved into a ribbon arch. Through that arch I saw the sky, the distant wild mountains, the nearby slopes terraced into pools; I saw green shoots, like eyelashes, peeping through the sheets of water. I saw trees among stones, bare, a few trembling with white blossoms. I saw people on the banks of the canal: straw hats, wooden sandals, and so many *kimono.* They wore indigo, mostly, but also brown and gray and black, gray-pink, gray-green, grayed gold. I saw blue in every shade and stripes in every pattern; women wore great wide sashes tied at the back in every kind of knot. Children darted in and out of the frame of arched wood, back and forth like butterflies, the way my mother had once promised I would.

The sky framed by Uncle Charles's chair was white, a fog, a murky absence of color. And I was an empty sky as well, a bare tree. Other people talked, other people laughed, other people ate—even here, so far from home, with knitting needles, out of black lacquer lunchboxes, they ate. I wasn't hungry myself.

By the end of the day, our flat-bottomed wood skiff, a scant few feet across, had threaded its way up a shallow channel so narrow two such boats could barely pass each other. "Is this the Kamo River that runs through the city?" asked Uncle Charles, surprised at its smallness.

"We're alongside it," Brother Joaquin assured him. "The Kamo is rocky and quite shallow, except when it floods; you can't run boats on it. This is the Takase Canal. Dug more than two hundred years ago," he added.

"The natives are cunning," murmured Uncle Charles.

THOUGH A LIFETIME has since passed, I remember catching a glimpse of the river beyond the canal once the men hoisted up our palanquins: a shimmering ribbon flecked with bridges and sandspits, long streamers of new-dyed cloth rinsing in its waters. On the near side, I saw the flat wooden city; on the far side, three mountains: one green and low close by, built up with little houses, one at middle distance, a wedge of its flank stripped of trees. Carved into that bare hillside, I saw one of the few Chinese characters I'd mastered: *great,* pronounced *oh* or *dai.* Far away and north of me stood the tallest mountain, solemn as a sentinel, leading a fleet of smaller blue mountains behind it; they filled the sky like strips of stacked torn paper. A gust of gulls skimmed the river and I felt, in spite of my grief, a sense of lightness as we pulled away.

I remember Uncle Charles's chair, borne by two porters, heading off a procession of small strong men carrying us and our trunks. We looked like a file of pallbearers, a parade led by a chair. I remember watching it bob solemnly through the narrow gray streets like a holy relic, framed at one point by a red *torii* gate. Once we arrived in the new house and scrambled up out of our lacquered cages, the two men heaved the chair barefoot up a narrow flight of stairs. It muscled through the tight stair-passage as if newly born, a wooden cherub bursting through a paper wall en route, and at last stood at rest, monstrous in the sere little three-mat room. We looked at it, embarrassed. "Well, with a rug . . ." said Uncle Charles.

A pair of men appeared with a message and gifts of food, and Brother Joaquin talked with them, switching between Japanese and English to translate for Uncle Charles. "Stay here," said my uncle, his voice buzzing with excitement. I had never seen him so happy to meet someone. "Change into your good dress, in case Father Damian asks to speak with you as well. Be ready, in case you're sent for."

"Here, if you get hungry," said Brother Joaquin, passing me a small packet tied in string. "It's not bad; just don't eat the leaves."

Uncle Charles and Brother Joaquin folded themselves back into their palanquins and I was left alone. The townhouse was very like the one in Yokohama: entry and kitchen at street level, a few barren *tatami* rooms a step up, an extra room on the second floor—this one reached by stairs instead of a ladder. Uncle Charles had named them all: *ministry, bedroom, parlor, service,* and, upstairs, *study.* I was assigned a one-mat room under the stairs until I took over the novice brother's duties, Uncle Charles told me, at which time I would graduate to *service.*

Cold, I took Uncle Charles's coat upstairs and huddled with my doll in the wide red mouth of his chair. I had never been permitted to sit on it at home, except in his lap at reading lessons when I was very young. Uncle Charles read in this chair, ate in this chair, napped in it, surely. It smelled richly of pipe smoke and faintly of soured sweat. *"Claire,"* I said in his voice, beckoning to my doll. *"Un petit café."* I pulled his coat tight around my shoulders. "Tell your mother to put on some more coal," I grumbled, close to tears. Clutching the coat to my sides, I felt coins in the pockets. I found three nickels, a rosary, and an envelope marked *Telegraph Office, New York Harbor.* I opened it, and read.

HUNGER SUDDENLY TOOK hold of me. I felt hollow behind my eyes. I took up Brother Joaquin's box and untied the string. The little package seemed simple enough on first glance, but in the dimming light I saw a leaf of white paper peeping out from under the subtly textured brown wrapper. The two sheets of paper concealed a wooden box tied in green thread, partially covered by another sheet of paper—this one painted with a crude and vibrant tree in bloom. I broke the thread and peeled off the little painting, removed a cunning lid and discovered six little packages pressed snug together, each wrapped in a leaf. I had once touched a snake at a street fair: it was cool and dry, satiny and faintly ridged, like these boxed leaf packets. I pried one out and unwrapped it: a perfect cube, pink fish on white rice flecked with herbs. I nibbled at it tentatively: faintly sweet, faintly tart, faintly salty. I ate all six. When Uncle Charles came up the stairs with an oil lamp, flushed, I felt not at all hollow; the thing I had to say was a clear hard bell inside me.

"It's freezing in here," he grumbled, oddly jovial. "They keep promising, *Someone will take down your futon. Someone will light you a fire.* Have you seen this *someone*?"

"No," I said.

"I think I've gotten one of those braziers lit downstairs," he said. "I saw some wood around. Not that it helps up here," he noted, rubbing his hands together. "Father Damian's an astonishing man. An inspiration. He'll see you tomorrow, not tonight," he added. "No need to sit up waiting." His way of speaking was slack and lazy; he was not himself. He looked at me suddenly, as if only just seeing me. "In our chair with Dolly, are we? Wearing our coat?"

I held up the telegram envelope. Uncle Charles recoiled. I said, "We could have buried her."

"My child," he said, a little sobered, "if we had waited for the next ship, Father Damian would have taken on other staff. That snake Brother Michael would be here in my place. And then where would we be?"

"In New York," I said coldly. And then I tried to say it. "I could have seen her—" I began, starting to cry again.

"My Aurelia," said Uncle Charles. I expected a lecture, but he lowered himself onto the chair and gathered me in his lap. He smelled of liquor. "My child," he said, holding me as I cried, helpless and snuffling. I missed her so much, and all I had was Uncle Charles, who sat there offering me clumsy, bearlike pats on the shoulder. At first, knowing he meant to comfort me was of itself a comfort, my doll in my lap and me in his, the awkward arms limp around me; but then his grip tightened. "My child," he repeated, whispering, his breath harsh. His hands gripped my waist as he spoke. I looked at him uncertainly; his eyes narrowed, as if he were concentrating. He was lifting me up in his lap and setting me down, gently and rhythmically, but gravely. He would have this rhythm and no other. "My child, my child," he said, his big hands trembling and pulling me tighter into his lap, again, again; I was a rag, a doll. And then he lurched up and groaned and dropped me, and my own doll dropped to the floor.

I did not cry out when I fell because I did not want him to comfort me. I stood up and smoothed my dress and looked at him, flung back in his chair. His eyelids fluttered, his round peach face flushed ripe: veins jumped in his forehead.

The thought struck me: *I did not like my uncle Charles.* I took my doll by the arm and I walked downstairs. The last dregs of evening lit my uncle's big boots, splayed across the floor where he'd tossed them, and my small ones, too, tucked together in a corner. I sat on the step by the entrance and listened. Outside, far off, I heard a hoarse voice calling a

short phrase over and over—a peddler, maybe—and from all directions the slow clop of wooden sandals. Nearby I heard the pop of
wood burning in the brazier. Upstairs I heard nothing. Was he gathering himself to spring at me? I quietly put on one of my boots and
laced it. A loud sound scissored down from his room: I grabbed my
other boot. It was a snore. *I did not like him.* I laced my boot, took my
doll, and walked outside. It was so simple. I glanced back through the
lattice at Uncle Charles's sprawled boots and walked into the dusk,
one foot in front of the other.

I saw the curved tip of the red *torii* gate rising beyond a house
across the street; I walked toward it and saw the shrine glittering with
candles. Lights and flowers surrounded a golden statue of a woman
with a dot on her forehead. She was not God, but where was God?

I would pray to her, I decided. *Two-two-one.* I had no coin, but I
could leave my doll. I walked through the gate and tugged the bellpull.
I bowed, I clapped, I made my awful wish.

3

1866

I WASN'T SURE what to do next. I sat where I had stood, at the foot of the golden goddess, under the bell-rope, watching people, young and old, stroll by in their noisy clogs. Carrying towels, they wore coarse *kimono* in different shades of blue, and one walked with a lantern in the dimming evening: a pretty globe of paper with a candle inside, dangling at the end of a stick. People spoke, and from the staccato song-chains of their speech floated up, astonishingly, words from my grammar: *mother, father, pretty, excuse me.* I sat quietly, and as the night deepened, more lanterns appeared, passing calmly to and fro, *clop, clop, clop.* I was transfixed by the lights; I wanted to join, not any lamplit person in particular, but the whole street, the whole net of fairy lights bobbing in the dark.

Then suddenly the lamps stopped moving, and then they all surged in the same direction. The steady tap of wooden shoes became a hailstorm, and then the shouting started, and I smelled the fire.

Uncle Charles had left wood burning untended in a charcoal brazier in a paper house. Could the blaze have started somewhere else? Perhaps.

. . .

Two MEN in billowing priestly robes appeared from behind the shrine
and swept the calm goddess off into the river of frightened people;
she glinted gold and vanished. I crept forward in the opposite direction in time to see, by the light of the conflagration, our new gray
house, intact (I could see through the front gate, see Uncle Charles's
boots sprawled where he'd left them) but glowing like a paper lantern,
hollowed out by flame. As I backed away, the house trembled, and then
it roared, belching up a ball of fire as the tiled roof caved in and
brought the second floor heaving to the ground. Then fire fanned
down the block, and I began to run.

I do not know if Uncle Charles woke and wriggled through a window or staggered down the kitchen alley. Sixty-three years have passed
since that night. Much later I learned that the same spring I arrived in
Japan, Saint Patrick's Church on Mott Street caught fire. While the
churchyard where my mother was buried escaped untouched, the
church burned to the ground. No one could say how it started.

THE FIRE WAS a loud animal. It sucked the breath out of me. I groped
and staggered, forward, away, through the screams and the groaning
buildings. Men called for water to save their homes. *Mother! Mother!* cried
the thin voice of a child. A horse-drawn cart pushed past me, and I
thought, *I could have climbed up on that.* I was sure I had missed my chance,
but then one of the horses spooked, shrieking on its hind legs, and the
driver beat him about the head with wet rags to stop the falling sparks.
Now, I whispered: I touched my Saint Claire medal for courage and ran
toward the horses, shimmied into the cart, and flattened myself against
a load of silk. As we pulled away, I bit my lip: had that child found its
mother? When we had cleared the smoke and the press of terrified
people, I scrambled out again and ran, ran into the dark.

· · ·

I RAN, and then I walked, unseeing. My lungs felt charred. Occasional breaths of incense burst through my sobs, so perhaps I passed temples. I walked and walked until my breath sanded my throat. I was so thirsty. Beyond a dainty bamboo fence, I saw a patch of stone where the moon shone wetly. I climbed the fence: no water. I passed a rock tied with string—a boundary marker, I one day learned—and saw beyond it a rough stone pillar. Its smooth worn top formed a cup, holding water. Oh. I leaned into it and drank like an animal. When I wiped my mouth, mucus clung to my wrist from crying.

I was in a garden of moss and rock. I saw a tiny wooden house with a square hole in the side, like a door for a baby. A rough stone formed a step in front of the square entrance; I climbed up on it and looked inside. "Hello?" Nothing. I crawled in. I felt woven straw under my hands, a Japanese floor, so I untied my boots and kicked them behind me into the stone garden.

This is how, smelling of fire, snot drying on my face, I first came to the teahouse Baishian. I lay flat on the floor and slept.

WHEN I SAT UP in the dark, the fire felt as small and remote to me as a story. I was real. This house was real, all silvery wood and moonlight: the most beautiful place I had ever seen.

The room stood small and austere, two pale *tatami* rectangles with a wide dark polished floorboard between them. In the heart of the room, I saw a gap in the floorboard, a perfectly square hole like the door I had crawled through, but smaller. The moon crept in through scattered windows, turned the straw floor white, made the floorboard gleam, but left a perfect square of night untouched at the center. It frightened me; I looked away. In the corner beside me, a tiny step up from the *tatami* floor, I saw an alcove, three feet wide by some two feet deep. The brightest splash of moon fell on the alcove floor: a beautiful piece of wood, brown-black, with a thread of white running across it like vein of bright marble. The room was a mirror for the moon. It seemed to hold its breath.

All it lacked was its fairy-tale inhabitant, the spirit princess for whom the little hole I had crawled through was a wide gate, for whom seven feet by six was palace enough. Maybe she lived deep under the earth, and wafted in like smoke through the dark square in the floor. Would she be warm enough in here? I lay down, cold, and drew my knees to my chin.

Someone was walking outside. It was strange to hear a footstep here without the wooden clop of sandals, but I was not mistaken: *shff, shff, shff,* as if walking barefoot, a light, knowing step, quick. The walker paused, as if startled, outside the house where I lay. A female voice whispered a word in Japanese: *Older Brother?*

I heard a long pause, and then a head appeared in the square doorway. I shut my eyes, breathed deep sleeping breaths. *A little foreigner,* said the voice.

I looked again: the head was gone. A large object had appeared in its place. It was dark, a creature, a stiff dead dog, and then I made it out. It was a Japanese pillow, a wooden box topped with a cloth pad. A thin cloth followed the pillow, and then I heard someone pick up my shoes, all in one resolute motion, and set them on the cloth inside the room. Then a back, a grown woman's back, appeared in the doorway, shoulders moving; she was peeling off a pair of socks. I saw her arm reach in and set them on the cloth with my shoes. And then the woman herself crawled in through the little door, straightened, and loomed over me. Scared, I closed my eyes again.

Koneko, she said under her breath. A word I knew, less endearing than it sounds in English. Cats and kittens are dirty in Japanese, and by definition stray, only tolerated—like Mr. Ohara's mouser—if they earn their keep.

And yet she paused over me, then crouched. I felt her face near mine. A damp feather of her hair touched my arm. I tried desperately not to change my breathing. Why didn't she scream at me?

And what kind of person, clearly not poor, went barefoot? I heard a slow, distant *tok, tok:* a night watchman pacing with his wooden clapper. I figured it out. The woman was hiding too. *Older Brother,* she'd said: where was he?

I opened my eyes. A stark white face was looking straight at me, a monster with no eyebrows. I flinched. *Boo,* she said. A Japanese sound, *ba.* I cowered and froze up, gasping. Her ghost face eased into a faint smile, and I uncurled and simply stared back at her, my heart loud in my throat.

I saw a young woman, perhaps sixteen to my almost ten, with long alert eyes, a narrow nose. A long face washed clean, longer for the lack of eyebrows. She was like the moon, like the dark wood shot with white. Her long drying hair was a silk river. Her eyes were lights. I shivered, from the cold, and because she was so beautiful.

Her beautiful nostrils flared. Her beautiful face rippled with distaste. *Kusai,* she said. *You smell bad.* I hid my face in my hands, ashamed. She gave a tiny dry seed of a laugh and turned away from me. I opened my eyes and watched her. She wore two robes, a dark one over a light one. She stood, as if dispensing with an interruption, and took off her outer robe. She lay down on her side, facing away, on the pale *tatami* between me and the hole in the floor, settling her pillow under her neck. She sighed, and again I heard a hint of laughter. And then she spread her *kimono* so that it covered us both.

My eyes felt bald, I opened them so wide, with shock, with gratitude. *Foreigner. Little cat. You smell bad.* Even my mother chased stray cats off the roof with a broom. She didn't spread her clothing over them to keep them warm.

My mother was dead in New York. No. My mother was alive; she was safe and far from fever. A spirit princess, she had vanished down a square hole in the floor under her bed, and left a false body behind. I reached for my Saint Claire medal. I couldn't think.

The woman's hair had touched my arm. The woman's hand, the back of her hand, had flickered across my side when she shook her robe smooth over us. Who had touched me, since I left home? Only Uncle Charles. I couldn't think about that, either. The cotton of the woman's *kimono* lay across my cheek; it smelled of old incense, dark and sweet. I watched her breathe. Her narrow back was a tall ship lifting gently on the waves. She was a moon princess. She was a bright vein in dark wood. I slept.

IN THE GRAY DAWN, the woman sat beside me and pointed to her nose, the way Americans point to their hearts to talk about themselves. *"You,"* she said. Was she speaking English? I am you? You are you?

She picked up my hand and took my index finger, they call it the person-pointing finger, and pointed it at my nose. "Me," I said, not grasping the game. "You. Me. You. I don't understand. Aurelia?"

"U ra ya," she repeated.

"U ra ya," I agreed.

"Ura-ya," she said dubiously, as if I'd told her my name was Road Toll, or Wet Mop. Her face cleared, and she lifted my hand toward me again, gently. "Urako," she said softly, pleased with herself. *"Miss Urako."* So it was a name, then, Urako, a name stressed like Erica or Jericho. This morning it was mine.

I was the last thing she'd imagined finding here, her face told me, as she stared at my dress, my knitted socks, my necklace. What had she come here for last night, barefoot and in secret? *"Older Brother?"* I asked, remembering.

She looked at me for a moment, then realized that I'd tried to say a Japanese word, then understood what I'd said. Her eyes widened soberly.

She said something, and like her, I had to think about it for few seconds. *Dead.*

There was so much I hadn't learned, but I remembered a word from my grammar. "*Sad,*" I said.

"*Sad,*" she repeated. She looked down and away.

To cheer her up, I touched my nose for her again. "Urako," I said. Her face bloomed.

I WOKE TO GREEN: a square of bright sun and green green moss. I opened my eyes fully: not to a dark ship cell, not to Mott Street, but to the bare and lovely Japanese room, like a perfect shell tossed up by the sea. I was alone.

Though the day was cold, the room had a warm look lent by all the different shades of brown, from the pale straw of the *tatami* to the deep warm black of the alcove floor, with its bolt of white gold, like a stroke of lightning. The clay walls were fitted here and there with bamboo-latticed windows. When I looked at the low slanted ceiling, I felt as if I were in a cunningly made little basket: I saw woven slats of wood and ribs of bamboo.

At the center of the room, interrupting the foot-wide floorboard between the two *tatami* mats, gaped last night's strange hole, less sinister, but no less mysterious. The satiny floorboard, its wood grain blooming like oil on water, was really two pieces of wood, perfectly matched, on either side of the foot-square hole. The hole—I nervously crouched over it—was a perfect cube, a foot deep, and lined with metal on all sides. Was that all? I dared myself to touch the cool floor of the hole, and came up with the faintest film of black on my fingertips: soot?

I heard a soft quick patter outside and recognized the step from last night. It approached the little house where I cowered, paused with a light flap like a thin book dropped on a table, and receded just as quickly. And there, between me and the moss garden outside, just peeping into the small square of the doorframe, I saw two brown circles: the ankle-tops of a pair of leather boots. My shoes! Why had she taken them? And why had she brought them back?

On the rock doorstep between the garden and the house, my shoes stood together, facing out, as if to point me home. And home? Two boots lit by a burning house. A churchyard. A woman coughing blood on Mott Street. I gathered myself close.

Who would know to look for me? Had Brother Joaquin escaped the fire? Did he even imagine me alive? And with whom, if he found me, would I live? Nuns, I realized. I faced a life of boiled wool and boiled greens, soap and bone and waxy cold hands. Years without the reprieve of thinking, *I have the right to be here.* A lifetime mouthing my mother's sullen gratitude for bed and board. What other place was there for me?

Maybe here, I decided: this room, this house as bare as dawn. The woman had set my boots side by side outside the teahouse and I chose not to lace them on. *Not until I'm thrown out.*

I heard clogs approaching and then I saw a figure in a rosy striped *kimono* pause outside the doorframe. Wasn't it the woman from last night? This woman, however, gasped audibly, perhaps even operatically, gave a girlish shriek, and ran away in a din of wood on stone. A guess: I was not supposed to be there last night, but nor was she. In order to expose me, she had needed to conceal her traces: moving my shoes was a way to control when I was found first, and by whom. But if I could ever ask her, what would I say? *Me not here; you not here too?*

I did not think, hearing her clatter away, that I would be allowed to stay in that perfect little house. I sat in the doorway, my head just brushing the top of the wooden frame, my feet resting on the rock below, and looked reluctantly out at the stone pillar where I had drunk the night before. The path leading out—flat gray slates embedded in spongy green moss—looked like a series of distant lakes. A voyage. What was going to happen? I didn't want to run away, but nor did I want to face my fate shoeless.

As I laced my first boot, again I heard a clatter: *two* pairs of Japanese shoes. The young woman reappeared, almost running, leading a round-faced older lady in a dark blue *kimono*, who threw up her arms when she saw me. *"Ara!"* she cried—which is what Japanese women say when they are surprised—her thick face twisting in disgust and horror. She spoke; the younger woman spoke. Were they mother and daughter? They looked nothing alike, and the older woman wore cotton, while the younger woman wore silk; the older woman wore raw wooden shoes while the younger woman's sandals were covered with a skin of painted leather. The older woman pointed broadly at me; the younger woman, talking continuously, looked at me and pointed with restraint at her nose. As I slid on my other boot, the older woman approached me. As if seizing a chicken by the neck, she took hold of my arm and dangled me for a moment; all the mass of her flesh was muscle. As I hung, my unlaced boot half sliding off my foot, I saw very clearly the thin red stripes in her indigo *kimono*, her large arm, her puffy face and small eyes, her wooden combs bristling under a blue tented headscarf. The young woman looked down at me with a mixture of pity and amusement; I was embarrassed. My arm hurt in its socket. I whimpered, the young woman chirred, and the older woman let me down.

They each took one of my wrists and began to talk rapidly, arguing, as they marched me down the path. I panicked, stumbling on my shoelaces as their voices rose like tumbling gravel. *Three, three,* I understood, and *today,* and *doll,* and the two words—completely different— for *your father* and *my father.* I saw a blur of other gardens and more stone pathways, glimpsed the thatch and lattice of other little houses, tripped on cobbles underfoot. Today someone's *father* was going to chop me into *three* pieces and make my bones into *dolls.* It made sense: I was seeing exquisite dollhouses for child monsters; the square hole in the floor was a well for blood. They steered me toward a larger building and their voices got softer, if no less vehement. *Kekkon*, the older woman rasped, which I was to learn means *marry*. And I heard the younger woman whisper a word: *Baishian*.

They led me into a dark doorway and dropped me on a wooden step between a stone-floored room and a *tatami* one. One unlaced shoe fell off my foot and the older woman tugged at the other. "Stop it, you're hurting me," I protested in French. "This one's tied!" She dropped my foot, startled by my voice, and the two of them stood, watching—curiously, I realized—as I unlaced my other boot. Hoping to catch them at a moment when they seemed least likely to chop me into pieces, I made overdue use of the longest Japanese sentence I'd learned: *"Excuse me, please, where is the toilet?"*

The older woman gasped, then shrieked, setting off a gale of laughter from the younger woman. They tried to laugh quietly, the young woman covering her mouth, the older woman silently throwing back her head, cheeks jiggling. The young woman, eyes beginning to tear, took me by the hand and led me by my stocking feet to a closet where I could put on a pair of toilet sandals and crouch, relieved, over a hole in a polished board (had I just spent the night in a very elegant outhouse?), then sprinkle my hand with a dipperful of water from a clay jar. I was no longer terrified; I was humiliated, which was worse, hearing the nearby giggle of the young woman and the farther chortle of the older one outside the door. The squat wooden room was very clean, and I wanted to stay there until they stopped laughing at me, but a faint, needling odor pushed me out again—minus the toilet sandals—to the young woman, who led me back toward the stone-floored room, where I stepped down again into a different pair of sandals. The older woman looked at me and started laughing again. *Excuse me, please, where is the toilet?* she asked. Was it how I asked, or just the fact of me?

"Now," the older woman said in Japanese, crouching to fix me with her small eyes, *"your father?"*

"None," I said, as far as I knew.

The woman blanched a little, and persisted. *"Your mother?"*

Now I flinched. I didn't want to say it. *"None,"* I repeated. The two women glanced at each other. I felt queerly translucent. Saying the thing for the first time made it more real, but saying it in this language abstracted it from me, as if the moment were happening to someone else.

"Family?" asked the younger woman.

"None," I said, slowly blinking my eyes to push the fire away.

The women looked at each other again and, speaking, seemed to agree on one thing. They spoke to me in Japanese, quickly and slowly, the older woman's black teeth and the young woman's white ones clearly visible, but all I could understand was the word *arau*, wash. I watched them hopefully, but no sense emerged, and then the older woman started fingering my dress and the young woman brought wet cloths. I didn't understand what the older woman wanted with my clothing, but it became clear that my buttons were wholly foreign to her when she brought over a pair of Japanese scissors—butterfly handles and tiny blades—and I stopped her before she could cut the dress off me.

It was one thing to stand in my dress from New York while they stood in their *kimono*—my body squarely in my world, theirs in theirs—and it was another to unbutton my dress in the dim room and let the older woman sponge me clean. I felt so very naked.

"Kusai kusai kusai!" cried the older woman. It's true: I reeked. Something about the water mixing with the smoke in my skin made me smell even worse than before. She wet a small cloth bag filled, I later learned, with rice bran, kneaded it to make suds, and worked briskly and thoroughly, rubbing between my fingers, behind my ears, even into my hair. The cloth bag was rough and cold, and its attentions alternated with

buckets of cold water. The stone floor sloped toward the doorway and formed a gutter, draining water, suds, smoke, fire, Uncle Charles, ocean, and Mott Street away as I shivered, arms wrapped around my chest.

My teeth chattered as the older woman dried me off. We were in a kitchen: I saw a covered well, a wall of cookstoves, a row of jars. On a shelf in the corner stood the only photograph I had seen since my arrival, of a young Japanese man in a black *kimono* jacket, a severe expression on his baby face. I blinked, surprised by the Roman letters stamped on the bottom edge of the daguerreotype—PERKINS STUDIOS, YOKOHAMA— and looked up at the older woman curiously.

"My son," she said loudly and clearly. *"Little Nao."* His name sounded like the English word *now*.

The young woman reemerged with her arms full of bright silk: a child's *kimono!* She wrapped a white underdress around me, then tied the *kimono* with a wide *obi* sash and looked at me, pleased. Then she tugged white socks onto my feet: my big toe sank into a separate sleeve from the other four, which made sense when she slid my feet into little red wooden sandals: I could grip the thong between my toes.

Pretty, pretty, I understood them saying: so many beautiful colors, and so many shapes! Fans, flowers, ribbons, bridges, ocean waves, treasure boxes, fat babies—it made me a little dizzy. *"Pretty!"* I echoed, floundering in my uncomfortable new getup. They laughed again, occasionally hushing each other, and the older woman made me copy her walk, a pigeon-toed shuffle that kept her robe from flopping open and her shoes from falling off. Barely containing their laughter, the two women froze when a human shadow paused at a window, relaxing when it vanished. The older woman tucked a paper handkerchief into the neck of my *kimono*, slapped something from a pot into a bowl, poured green tea over it, and stirred. Then the women sat on either side of me, on the step between the stone kitchen and *tatami* house. I was so hungry. If they had poisoned the soupy bowl of rice, barley, pickles, and tea I drank, I hardly cared.

· · ·

ONCE AGAIN I CROUCHED at the low square door of the tiny house, only this time I was on the outside, looking in at the young woman as she had looked in at me. Her rose-pink *kimono* bound by a golden *obi*, she knelt quietly, sitting on her feet, her hands in her lap, her back very straight. Her painted eyebrows arched black and high. Her long face and swept-up hair made her look severe, like a face stamped on a coin. She glanced over at me and crossed her hands over her mouth: *Quiet!* The older woman stood beside me, a hand clamped on my arm.

The room looked the same—two *tatami* mats on either side of a floorboard and a square hole—but dramatically altered. The alcove, which was to the right of the young woman and thus straight ahead as I looked in on her profile, was no longer vacant. Instead, the woman sat framed by green leaves and faint colors on the wall. On a hook on the raw-wood post that framed the alcove hung a clay vase from which willow branches cascaded, shining in the chilly wafer of sun that fell in from one of the little windows: a stained-glass waterfall of green-gold leaves. I saw a branch of pink buds in the vase as well. On the wall inside the alcove hung a scroll, bordered in brocade, with a picture of a Japanese doll, smooth and armless in her layers of *kimono*. Surrounded by color and light, the young woman could have been a princess in a painting.

A sudden pop of wood: the young woman glanced over at us, alarmed, and the older woman pulled me away from the door. I pressed my face up to a bamboo-latticed window, and the older woman let me stay. I peered in at the empty mat opposite the fairy princess with her flowers and scroll. Directly to my left, I saw a modest paper door, which suddenly slid open a little. A hand knifed into the inch of empty space—the fingertips of a large blunt hand—and slid the door half open.

Behind the door, in a part of the little house I hadn't even noticed, sat a man like a mountain, like the great north sentinel mountain I saw when I looked across the Kamo River. Silver-haired but hardy, with a round solid head and thick eyebrows, he looked at the young woman with an expression of utter tranquility. If rain had been pouring in through the ceiling, I thought, he would have sat as still. If the young woman had been pointing a pistol at him, he would have looked at her as calmly. He slid the door the rest of the way open, stood, and walked into the room, then knelt before the young woman, setting a large basket before her. He bowed to her, and she placed her hands in front of her knees and bowed back.

Seated in the doorway, the man had looked like a priest or a king, and yet what he did was so humble. Was she a real princess, then, served by powerful men? A heathen priestess in a secret ritual? Was I a sacrifice? Steam rose from the hole in the floor; I clenched my fists, afraid, and the older woman clasped my shoulder all the harder.

The Mountain bowed in the doorway, a clay jar at his side, and walked in, setting the jar on the *tatami* mat opposite the one where the Princess sat. He entered twice more, each movement precise, controlled, setting down first a clay bowl and a shiny round box, then— pausing to slide the door closed—a metal bowl with a bamboo dipper laid across it. He and the young woman knelt silently, facing each other across the floorboard and the steaming gap. The man quickly drew a short round piece of bamboo from the metal bowl and set it before him, then rested the dipper on it with a deliberate clap of wood on wood. He adjusted the metal bowl by his side, tugged smooth his robe, and paused, as if gathering strength.

"*Father!*" The young woman's voice startled me. Really? I could see it in their cheeks, a little.

"*Yes?*" He asked, as if she hadn't interrupted. Was it her birthday, that he was showing her such deference?

The Princess placed her hands in front of her and bowed again, then spoke at length, first humbly, then bitterly, then seductively, never changing her position. The Mountain listened, impassive, his hands resting calmly on his knees. At one point he interrupted briefly, with a few short sentences that included a man's name—a Mr. Akio—and the older woman's grip on me tightened with surprise. The Princess gasped, then continued, unswayed. Both people were motionless, the woman's body taut, the man's relaxed. When she fell silent, he asked, *"Is that so?"* and her eyes flickered to the low door. The older woman took hold of both my shoulders. Me? My heart beat in terror as she pushed me into the little doorway, tugging off my sandals as I crawled in. I reached for my Saint Claire medal to steady me: it was gone.

I was too upset to stand. Father and daughter stared at me, and I bowed where I sat; it seemed like the safe thing to do. I heard the Princess say, *"No father, no mother,"* and then they spoke back and forth, bird and thunder, and finally the Mountain asked me in Japanese, very clearly and slowly, *"Where are you from?"*

I knew, in that moment, as I bowed in a silk *kimono* on a woven straw floor, that I was cheating the future I ought to have: that cold-fingered nun with her boiled dinners and her wooden ruler. I intended to cheat her as long as I could. If I said a word about New York, or my uncle, or the mission, or the fire, I was certain she would have me. I missed my Saint Claire medal, but I steeled myself. If I had lost it, then perhaps its very loss would protect me from the fate I feared. I had not been lying when the older woman asked about my family, but now I said, *"Koko,"* here. *I'm from here.*

"But before, from Yezo?" he asked, naming the northernmost island of Japan. I had heard of it from the British captain of the *Singapore:* he said Yezo was peopled by a hairy tribe called the Ainu, more Russian than Asian.

"From Miyako," I insisted. At my side, the young woman tensed, as if to correct me, as if to demand, *But what about your foreign dress? Why can't you speak Japanese?*

"And before?" the man said.

"I don't know."

He did not believe me, but he did not quite know what to believe, it seemed. *"What is your name?"* he asked.

"Urako," I said, and I felt the young woman relax with pleasure.

The Mountain looked at me, thinking quietly. *"Un,"* he said at length, a grunt that seemed to accept me. And then they spoke together again, back and forth, the young woman sounding, at last, forlorn: *Older Brother,* she said, and *Mother.* Her father relented, visibly, and said something with a sigh. The older woman still kneeling outside asked, *"Me?"* At the Mountain's nod, she crowded into the house with us, offering apology and thanks in the same breath, hands clasped uncomfortably before her. I sat between the two women on the mat with the alcove, while the man sat across from us, offering a shallow bow. *"I am Shin Sokan,"* he said, *"and this is Shin Yukako."* The young woman bowed in greeting. *"And this is Chio,"* he said, and the older woman bowed as well, never looking at the Mountain.

"And this is Shin Urako," said the young woman, Yukako, gesturing toward me.

The older woman's breath caught. Thinking quickly, I remembered the monks saying that the finer folk in Japan had family names, while their servants did not. The Mountain and the Princess, it seemed, had a family name, Shin, while Chio beside me did not. When Yukako asked if my name was Shin Urako, she was pushing her father to say what sort of person I was to be, and what my place was. In Chio's caught breath I heard questions: Was I above her or below her? Was I a Shin?

"Not Shin," the Mountain admonished. But he bowed back, and said, *"Miss Urako, welcome."* As Chio breathed again, I bowed deeply and thanked him, and thanked the young woman, and then thanked Chio. The other two laughed at me, as if it were silly to thank Chio, but the older woman gave me a benign nod, as if it were quite proper indeed. Yukako's father smoothed his already-smooth robe and picked up where he had left off.

I did not understand his slow movements, but I was drawn to the grace of them. He folded a silk scarf. He removed beautiful objects from his clay bowl. He reached into the steaming heart of the room and drew out—a flayed animal? A pumping heart? A metal pot-lid. Just as in my mother's kitchen, a billow of steam burst up in its wake. And then I understood, finally, what I was seeing: the hole in the floor was a little firepit; there was a cauldron of water boiling on a charcoal fire. He lowered the bamboo dipper into the cauldron and drew it out, a ball of steam at the end of a stick, like the paper lanterns from the night before.

I closed my eyes against the memory. Because I was safe, I began to sweat with fear as the red mouth of the fire opened over me: I remembered the stillness of Uncle Charles's tumbled boots in the hot light, and then the screaming rafters and the flames, the falling roof tiles, the terrified horses.

I opened my eyes and looked down at my particolored *kimono.* I was alive; I was lucky. I was so far from home. I felt the largeness of this world and the smallness of my life. I was a bubble in the ocean. I was a wisp of steam. I missed my mother so badly. Suspended in the Mountain's slow gestures, in the gathered concentration pouring from the women flanking me, I felt like a tiny fleck of light on the skin of an orange, this earth. The little house, so lovely empty, was a stage, I understood, for this quiet dance.

The Mountain and the Princess spoke, their voices drained of struggle. I looked at the rectangles of the *tatami* floor with its steaming sunken cauldron, the rectangles of the paper windows. The grids of window, walls, and floor framed the gentler shapes of natural things: the curved willow branches, the soft hills of our bodies. Yukako lifted the large basket before her and bowed. On a plate inside the basket stood a pyramid of pink, blossom-shaped cakes made, I was to learn, of dyed white beans and sugar: sweetness suspended in pure texture, rich and dense, the beans an even more self-effacing medium than cream. She drew a packet of paper from her *kimono* and laid it on the floor, then reached into the basket for a cake, which she set on her paper and ate. Then her father set the small bowl before her, and Yukako brought it to her lips.

After we each ate and drank in turn, the Mountain tucked away his silk cloth, solemnly gathered his tools, and bowed farewell, leaving the remaining three of us to make our exit through the tiny door. I did not know I was witnessing the ritual known in Japanese as *Chanoyu*, Hot Water for Tea; or *Chado*, The Way of Tea; or *Ocha*, simply, Tea. I did not know that the Shin family had been teaching tea ceremony to the most powerful men in Japan for three hundred years. I saw only the doll scroll and the willow branches. I tasted only the cool moist bean-cake and the hot green foaming tea, sweet mixing with bitter. I knew only that there was room in this small house for father and daughter, servant and foreigner alike.

4

1866

Two months after Yukako took me in, the Mountain had the Emperor's nephew to tea.

Yukako's father, I slowly learned, was the adopted patriarch of a merchant-caste family whose head had served for twelve generations as tea advisor to three of the Shogun's underlords. The post, like that of the keeper of a castle wine cellar, made the Shins both the servants of their liege lords and the masters of a body of art. The previous head of the family, Gensai, had had seven children, six boys and a girl. Waves of cholera took all six of Gensai's boys, then his wife, then Gensai himself. In his last days, Gensai adopted one of his apprentices, the Mountain, to marry his daughter Eiko, who died giving birth to Yukako, their second child. Their firstborn, Hiroshi, had died of cholera at sixteen.

Yukako and her father, the last of their line, lived with a dozen-odd servants and eight young men who flocked around the Mountain like bats in their black silk robes: four students and four apprentices. The students were lords' sons for whom a year or two of tea study was polish enough for them to make use of the teahouses and gardens they stood to inherit, while the apprentices were well-born and well-off boys who after long study hoped to hire themselves out to lords too busy to look after those same houses and gardens. As proud as the Mountain's lineage, and as highborn his disciples, none of them had ever met anyone as nobly ranked as the Emperor's nephew. A court favorite, the young man was known for his painting, poetry, and mastery of the Chinese classics, as well as for the esteem in which he was held by the Emperor and the fourteen-year-old Crown Prince.

The August Nephew's acceptance of the Mountain's invitation had thrown the whole household into a pother of anticipation. Every place the imperial guest's eye might fall was made new, every place his foot might touch. New *tatami* arrived, pale green and sharp-smelling, and the old mats were sent home with the sewing women as gifts: their fathers and husbands all gathered outside the kitchen one day to collect them, cloth sweatbands tied around their foreheads. The mats made up, somewhat, for the extra hours the women had to spend on the two dozen rolls of fabric that had arrived, each the precise amount of cloth allotted for one *kimono,* each in its own wooden box. Under the supervision of Chio's husband, Matsu, the gardeners, students, and apprentices replastered the outside walls, re-thatched the front gate and the teahouses, and replaced the *shoji* paper in all the walls and windows.

Two of the Mountain's apprentices were of merchant caste, a jovial, neckless fellow I called the Bear and an ill-starred creature I called the Stickboy: the first tea lesson I ever witnessed, a bowl broke of its own accord in the boy's long nervous hands. The Mountain's other two apprentices, like his one-year students, were *samurai* caste, young lords themselves, one of whom I could not help but call the Button, so pertly did his features seem dotted on his round brown face. The other was a compactly handsome young man named Akio. Though he was the best at lessons, with the blackest hair and quickest eyes, there was something about him I did not trust.

Akio was engaged to Yukako, and would have married her already if he had not fallen ill. My first morning at the Shins', the Mountain had informed Yukako of the match—when he said *Mr. Akio* and Chio clutched my shoulder in surprise—and that night I witnessed their Sighting, a formal meeting between marriage-minded parents and their eligible children. Chio let me spy with a serving tray in hand while Yukako sat before Akio and his father, Lord Ii of Hikone, a castle town north of Miyako, across broad Lake Biwa. Chio called him Lord Horse, because he was known for his stables, and from the way the old man sat at the Sighting—long-backed and crook-legged—I could picture him more comfortable in the saddle than the tearoom. Yukako knelt in a dark blue-green robe painted with white flowering branches, her eyes downcast throughout the meal she served. Once, however, as she poured rice wine, a lamplit drop fell to the *tatami* floor and her eyes met Akio's: I saw naked curiosity leap between them.

For two months after the Sighting, it was my task to bring Akio his meals in the Bent-Tree Annex, the tiny wing of the rambling Shin house that served as his sickroom. Each day when we heard a specific conjunction of iron clanks and lacquer taps from the kitchen, Yukako's face would come alive. The sound meant that Chio, her *kimono* sleeves tied back, the folds of her chin wobbling as she lifted the iron pots from their sockets on the charcoal stove, had made up the lunches, stubby hands delicate as she tweezed food into *bento* boxes, swiftly and precisely assembling each mosaic of vegetables, pickles, and rice. After Chio left the kitchen with her tray of soup bowls and her stacked tower of student lunches, Yukako would furtively doctor Akio's meal, imagining herself in his place as she held the black *bento* serving box. I once watched her gently remove the lid with a hollow lacquer *pock-pock*, set it aside, and look down at the spartan dishes: a scoop of rice, a little mound of spinach dressed in sesame sauce, a few cubes of sweet potato. Then I saw her smile slowly as she pictured him uncovering the cut of sparkling blue mackerel hidden under the heaped rice. And so those weeks I ferried petals of fatty tuna, whole peeled chestnuts, jeweled orange salmon eggs, and festive red beans to Akio's sickroom, each purchased by Yukako on our morning errands and tucked into his sober student *bento*. I had specific instructions to inspect each empty box before returning it to Chio: I felt as if my sleeves were burning with the tiny strips of paper handkerchief I slipped into them almost daily, each folded delicately and tied into a knot. I can attest he ate every bite.

YUKAKO TOOK MY NEED to learn Japanese as an opportunity to talk, repetitively and at length, about Akio, which in turn meant talking about her brother Hiroshi and Chio's son Nao, the boy from Perkins Studios Yokohama. He may have been a servant's child, but Nao was a year older than Hiroshi, thuggish and handsome where Yukako's brother was spindly and awkward. One of the first phrases she taught me was *that summer:* she meant the summer she was twelve and Hiroshi fifteen, when their father took in Akio. Yukako's brother had a kind of starstruck sweetness about him that made everyone he met want to shine, but until *that summer*, Nao had had no serious competition for Hiroshi's idolatry: the Mountain's students, all much older, had always come for a short year and left. Until then, Hiroshi had been the one to turn over his sweets and umbrella when no adults were present, and Nao had been the one to choose each game. *That summer*, however, Akio was just a year older than Nao, and there was talk of him staying longer as an apprentice.

The three boys quickly became a tight unit, bound tighter by the rivalry that flourished between Nao and Akio. Nao knew all the good places for swimming; Akio had money to take them to the theater. (Yukako would have to take me to a play before I could understand the word for *theater*.) Akio had finer clothes, but Nao was stronger. Nao taught Hiroshi how to smoke a pipe; Akio kept him flushed with *sake*,

a strong rice wine. Akio, a *samurai,* was allowed to carry swords, but
Nao had learned how to make Roman candles. That summer, *that summer,* they took rice balls to the river and lit *fire-flowers* all night long.
Hiroshi played his flute; Nao and Akio beat their legs for drums.
Yukako trailed after them one night and watched them swim naked,
piss in the river, light fireworks in their bare hands. Across the river
they saw a riotous parade of men with torches, stripped to the waist
and chanting. This was difficult to picture until I saw it myself: once a
year each neighborhood entertained its local god by giving him a ride
down the street on a golden palanquin. Drunk on *sake,* Nao and Akio
picked up Hiroshi and ran him down the riverbank, whooping in the
moonlight, their bodies bright as flares.

   Within a year, Akio had gone to Edo at his father's behest, to serve
the Shogun. Nao had run away from home, an act forbidden by law.
And Hiroshi had died. When Akio came back, his cocky abandon
ground into silence and quickness, he was one apprentice among four.
Yukako said the night she found me, she'd gone to sleep in the teahouse knowing the Mountain had planned a Sighting with one of his
apprentices' fathers, but not knowing whose: in the face of having
family chosen for her, that night she chose me for herself.

ONE DAY, INSTEAD OF FOOD, Yukako sent me to Akio with a cracked
flute made of speckled bamboo. It had been Hiroshi's: for Akio, she
had uncoiled the lonely weight of her brother's loss into a rope that
two could hold. I saw her the next morning with her father, grinding
ink into his inkstone without remembering to add water, gazing daftly
into the garden.

   A few nights later Yukako gasped when she unwrapped the contents of Akio's empty *bento.* I gave her the package as we lay on her
futon in the room we shared above the kitchen. The object was long
and slender, the size of a pen: Akio had rolled it in one of his paper

handkerchiefs and tied the package fast with red thread. Inside was a teascoop he had made from Hiroshi's flute: I recognized the flecked bamboo. A short flat wand with a curved end for spooning tea, it was a beautiful object, humble yet graceful, speckled, satiny, simple. *How did the carver shape the bamboo curve?* I wondered, asking Yukako, *"How?"* and crooking my finger.

"By fire," she said. She wrapped the teascoop tenderly in its paper again and tucked it into the hollow wooden base of her pillow where she kept Akio's little tied notes. She hunched in a ball on the *futon* in her night *kimono,* head hidden in her arms, pale knees exposed. I touched her bath-hot back, circling the soft blue cotton with my palm. *"Thank you,"* she said. She was crying. I began to cry, too, and she stopped. *"Your mother?"* she asked, and I nodded. *"I understand."* Folded close behind her, I listened to her heartbeat through her curled-up body, bent the way bamboo might bend in flame.

I had begun learning Yukako's family story in Baishian, the teahouse where she first found me. Though the Shins already had several rooms for tea ceremony, Yukako's grandfather Gensai had talked of building a little freestanding house called Baishian: Plum Thread Hut. Sixteen years before my arrival, when a retired imperial prince, now dead, had agreed to come to tea, the Mountain had built a new teahouse for his visit, calling it Baishian in his adoptive father's memory. When the death of Yukako's mother rendered the Shin house impure, the prince's tea was canceled, but the Mountain had never given up on his dream of expanding his network of allies by hosting a member of the Emperor's line. So he had kept Baishian empty, save for small family events, like his tea with Yukako the morning after she found me. As children, Yukako and her brother had claimed the teahouse for themselves as a secret place to play. They once found a hidden room in the teahouse, she claimed, a spy hole for a bodyguard. *"Show me?"* I asked.

"No," she said. Her brother had never shown anyone else, and had made her promise the same.

"Not even Akio or Nao?"

"Not even Akio," she assured me. "Not even Nao."

Though I pouted, I did not feel excluded. Just a few nights after I arrived, Yukako had led me silently to Baishian. She nested a sprig of tiny white blossoms called snow willow in a hole of her brother's flute and hung it in the wood-floored alcove. Above it she hung another treasure, a scroll mounted by her grandfather: her mother Eiko's first childhood attempt to write the family name, *Shin*, three splashes of ink undergirded by a single curved line. Yukako pointed to the crude fat brushstrokes—*Mother's*—and the smoke-wisp lines beside them: *Grandfather's. My brother*, she said. *My mother*, I replied, and nodded. (*Have you seen my Saint Claire medal?* I wanted to ask, but I could only touch my neck and say, *Where?*) We sat together sadly. When I embraced Yukako, she staggered, clearly startled, then woodenly patted my back. I pulled away, confused and embarrassed. I quickly realized that though she had folded around me in sleep, Yukako had never embraced me, just as I had seen parents carry their children affectionately, but never hug them. "*I'm sorry*," I said. Yukako gamely circled her arms around my shoulders and gave me an experimental squeeze. Then she had me formally drink *sake* with her from three red lacquer saucers: I felt blessed and dizzy. In the teahouse that night, over giddy solemn sips of rice wine, she asked me to call her Older Sister when we were alone.

To EVERYONE ELSE, however, I was to be her servant. During the day, while she ran errands and made calls, I trailed behind as porter and chaperone: without taking off my clunky wooden shoes, I waited on benches in chilly cloakrooms floored with the same stone or earth as the street outside while she stepped up out of her fine leather clogs into the warm soft *tatami* rooms within. At night I went out for my bath with Chio and the others, while the fine students soaked in a tub of their own and Yukako soaked in water only her father had used. When their water was a few days old, Chio boiled it down and used the fluid left to polish the wooden verandas and corridors: thus every inch of the Mountain's house was oiled with his skin.

The servants' public bathhouse made me anxious at first: there was a girl named Hazu who took an instant dislike to me when Chio made me give her candy I'd thought was mine. *"But you gave it to me,"* I whined.

"To carry," Chio snapped. She took me aside and scrubbed the scowl off my face. I handed over the sweets, but the damage was done: Hazu made faces and showed me the red of her eyelids. Even without bratty Hazu, it would not have been easy to sit naked in a room full of naked men and women who gaped, asking if I was one of the hairy Ainu of the far north. When Chio told them I was a foreigner, literally, an *outside person*, the others simply stared, until an old man in the tub, his jaw so long it almost jabbed into his throat—I was to recognize him eventually as the man who sold *tofu* door-to-door in the neighborhood—pronounced his verdict: *"That's no foreigner."* The rest agreed. (No one believed Yukako, either: after an embarrassing first attempt, she let them think as they liked.)

"After all, we had never seen a real one before," Chio told me some years later. "But we had seen pictures, and *everyone* knew foreigners were huge, piggy people with very long noses, very red hair, and very green eyes, so you obviously weren't one. Clearly someone was playing a trick on us with that clothing."

"Well, then, what was I?"

"We thought you might be from Yezo or perhaps you were the child of some girl in the water trade." She meant a prostitute or a singing-girl. "Maybe when she was pregnant with you, your mother tried to let you go, but she had you anyway, and that's why your face turned out like that. So sad. So when she couldn't hide you in the house anymore, she bought some foreign clothes at a curio shop, dressed you up, and abandoned you, hoping some kind person would find you, the way those fishermen dragged up the statue of Kannon from the waters."

"They thought my mother was a prostitute but they didn't think maybe my father was a foreigner?"

"Don't be ridiculous; even a whore wouldn't sink so low. And besides, we all knew what foreigners looked like. You just looked a little deformed. We all knew foreigners couldn't speak Japanese. You could; you just sounded like you'd been dropped on the head as a baby."

"Oh," I said, wishing I hadn't asked. "And did you believe them?"

"Yes and no. I mean, you couldn't even eat like a human being when we found you. But you're the one who said you were from Miyako," she sniffed.

I didn't understand what they said about me at the bathhouse. What I understood was the idea of "shade." When Japanese people say you should find an important person to protect you, they say, *Seek the shade of a big tree.* When you receive a compliment, you should, if it makes even a little sense, reply by saying, *Oh, it's only thanks to you:* literally, *It's thanks to your shade.* And what I felt at first, balled up naked on the edge of the wooden tub with my arms around my knees, was "shaded" from the staring men and women by the bulk of Chio's indulgence, her good humor, her occasional protective, if pitying, pats on the arm with a dripping warm hand, pruney from the bath. And if she felt at all afraid of their censure, she took shelter in the "shade" of the names she repeated: *Young Mistress Shin Yukako, Master Teacher Shin.* They had taken me in: who was she to turn me out?

WHAT I LIKED most about our bathhouse trips—until I got used to the scalding water, which I loved most of all—was the walk home single file with our lanterns, carrying inside our bodies the heat of the bath. I loved the bobbing round globe of the lamp I held before me as we snaked by files of other bathers. When we passed the neighborhood shrine gate, I thought with wonder of the night Yukako found me, how I'd watched the net of lanterns crossing before me in the dark street. Now I was a part of that net. I'd glance at the neighborhood *torii* gate as we walked past, as if there might be another girl beneath it, large-eyed and uncertain. All I ever saw, deep in the back of the shrine, was a candlelit glint of gold.

5

1866

U SUALLY THERE WERE twenty minutes or so between when I
came home from the servants' bathhouse and when Yukako
came upstairs from the family tub. One night, however, a week before
the August Nephew's visit, she came home much later.

In those days my Older Sister and I each made a kind of religion
out of our own attentiveness, mine to Yukako and hers—when it
wasn't fixed on Akio—to tea. I liked to pass the time before Yukako
came upstairs at night by playing with her tea ceremony tools, trying
to copy what I saw when we spied on the Mountain's lessons. Tea was
like church, boring and hypnotic, a tiny meal wreathed in solemnity.
This was what adults did. Already Yukako was teaching me how to be
a formal guest: how to enter, how to sit (painful!), how to use the
packet of paper carried in the breastbone fold of my *kimono*, how to
use the fan tucked into my sash. (Never use it to actually fan yourself, I
learned: it's a silent place-marker.) How to bow, how to receive sweets
and tea and offer thanks: *I humbly receive what you have made.* Yukako didn't
use the words *make tea* when she talked about the whole choreographed
ritual—the *ceremony* in what we call tea ceremony—she actually used a

word that sounded like *hand* and *before*—*te* and *mae, temae. I need to practice temae. His temae is a little stiff.* It meant *the next point,* as on a list, or maybe *procedure,* but without the bureaucratic coldness that clings to the word in English.

Just as there was a precise way to move through each stage of the *temae* as a host, there was a precise way to do each thing Yukako asked of me as a guest. I liked the way she reached her arms around mine to lift the sweet tray with me, *just enough.* I liked her sitting beside me, tea-papers in hand, folding a used sheet into eighths as I followed her in time. *Just so.* Everything I did mattered. I felt so seen. If the guest role was this hard to play, however, I feared that Yukako would never teach me how to play the host's role and make tea.

And so at night, when I had her room to myself, I would try to fold her red silk cleaning cloth into the tight pad she used for wiping the tea box, try to draw imaginary water from the jar with her same heron-like movements of the dipper. Recently, Yukako had been practicing a style of tea—a *temae*—that called for a little iron teapot instead of a dipper and a water jar; she carried in all her tools at once on a lacquer tray instead of making several trips in and out of the room. I liked this *temae:* the earnest little teapot, the way everything—even the tray—fit into a silk brocade bag, as if for an extravagant picnic. And it moved quickly, so I got my tea-candy sooner. The only thing I didn't like was that Yukako sometimes tied the bag closed with an ornate knot, since it was only when she'd neglected to do so that I could finger the smooth red lacquer tea box, the rough black bowl, Akio's speckled bamboo scoop.

The night Yukako came back late, when I looked for her brocade bag, it was gone. Had someone taken it? Should I tell Yukako in her bath? I had to use the toilet anyway. I walked downstairs. Most evenings a little light seeped from the family bathhouse lamp into the toilet-room window, but tonight the narrow room was dark, except for the moon. So where was she?

At the top of the kitchen stairs, I sat resting my elbows on my knees. I cast a line from inside me out to the darkness—*Yukako!*—and caught nothing. I could hear the mice in the ceiling, just like in New York, the *sluff-sluff* of the bamboo hedge outside, and the sound of water in the nearby Migawa stream. I listened. At a distance from the other buildings of the compound, the Migawa meandered past a two-storied white tower with fireproof plaster walls instead of paper: the Shins kept their treasures there. Passing the storeroom tower over a tiny burbling drop, the stream eased through the garden, then found the straight line of Migawa Street and flowed in a gutter past the Shin gate. As I listened to the stream, a regular soft rattle, almost imperceptible, came from Chio's hut off the kitchen: her husband Matsu snoring.

Chio and Matsu had a son, Nao, whom I knew from Yukako's stories and from the daguerreotype Chio kept in the kitchen, where she also kept a packet of his letters, one sent each New Year, always bearing the same good wishes. They also had a gloomy daughter named Kuga. She had recently been married to a man named Goto: when he took a pretty mistress, she sulked, and he divorced her for it. Kuga arrived at the Shin house not long after I did, bringing her little son Zoji, whom I petted and carried and trailed after as he learned to speak, repeating the Japanese words as he did. That very night, while waiting for Yukako's return, I had scrubbed one of Zoji's milky stains off my cotton *kimono*, kneeling by the water jar on the veranda.

Since Kuga's arrival, her family slept four to a bed in the hut by the kitchen. I saw them lined up one night when I lingered after our bathhouse walk: Matsu by the wall, already drifting off, then Chio, then Zoji, and, last, skinny Kuga, closest to the damp night air. I wondered if Matsu had always been so loud, or if he did it on purpose to punish Kuga for shaming them by coming home. He did seem to dote on the boy, though. As the head gardener, Matsu also served as charcoal-cutter, sawing each carbonized branch to the precise lengths required by the Mountain's art, washing each stick of charcoal and drying it in the sun to reduce sparking in the tearoom. I remembered Matsu teaching Zoji how to make pellets of household fuel from charcoal dust and stubs, spheres held together with wet seaweed. He looked as happy as a boy himself, building up an arsenal of black snowballs, while Zoji preferred to eat or wear the wet dark paste. Matsu was so careful and thorough afterward, washing his grandson's sooty little hands and face.

Suddenly, I snapped alert at a sound: a sniffle, too close to be the baby's. And then, because I knew to listen for it, I heard the soft tread of a shoeless woman.

I saw a figure moving through the kitchen, pausing at the step up into the *tatami* part of the house, saw her quick bunchy movements as she shucked off her split-toed socks, saw her *kimono*, whitish in the moon as she moved toward me, the rectangle of its front panel angling into a diamond shape as she gained each stair. It wasn't her bath *kimono*. "*Little Ura*," Yukako whispered.

"*Older Sister*," I said, rising to let her pass into her room.

"*Why are you awake?*"

"*Why are* you *awake?*"

Instead of answering me, Yukako thrust her brocade bag into my hands, threw herself facedown on the *futon*, and sobbed.

I had seen her cry once before, when she unwrapped Akio's teascoop, or rather *felt* her crying, her silent wet breath. But tonight she wept openly, rubbing her face into her quilt, smearing her eyebrow paint into the pale cotton as she gulped and sobbed. I had never seen her with her eyebrows on after a bath. It scared me: the alien moans, the contorted streaky face under her lacquer-perfect coiffure. "*What happened?*"

"*Nothing.*"

"*Did you go see Mr. Akio?*" At this she wailed afresh, pushing me away when I gingerly reached for her arm.

I wanted to help her somehow, or maybe I was afraid she wouldn't want me around. I brought a soft cloth to the water jar on her veranda and moistened it. *"Your eyebrows,"* I said, pointing.

"Thank you." She took a deep breath. She went silently to the mirror with the candle and cleaned off the paint in two slow, practiced strokes. Then, pulling down her stained quilt, she lay on the *futon* in her good *kimono*, fitted her wooden pillow under her neck, and began talking, her words punctuated with sighs.

Usually when Yukako told me things she paused first, isolated an essential word or two, and spoke in short clear bursts. Usually I understood her. That night her words spilled out like water, rapid, without pauses. These were her words as she thought them to herself, not the semaphore flags she flew for me. She was telling another story about Akio. I heard searching and hesitation in her sentences, repeated phrases, as if she were clarifying for herself what had happened. And toward the end, I understood more: the words *my wife, not, host.*

Yukako had gone to perform tea ceremony for Akio, I understood, putting the words together with the brocade bag—and he had rejected her. *You are not an entertainer,* he'd told her. It was another word I had to learn later. Women in the water trade did *temae,* I eventually discovered, a flashy and facile variant of the Mountain's art. But here at the Shins', I realized that night, there were no women students. And though Yukako was expected to watch tea lessons whenever she could, sitting behind a lattice in the classroom wall, I had never seen her take a lesson with her father.

Then why had Akio made her a teascoop? I tried to ask.

"My question too," she said, nodding. *"'For our son,'"* he'd said.

Yukako cried; I listened. I touched her shoulder and she let me. She wrapped the speckled teascoop back in the white paper handkerchief stamped with Akio's seal, tied the red thread he had used back around the package, and grimly set it on the shelf with her other tea things. Something else must have happened, too, that made her cry so bitterly, but I didn't understand. *"Go to sleep,"* she said. So I did. I drifted off to the sound of her on the balcony, scrubbing her *kimono* as I had scrubbed mine.

I wondered if that night would mark the end of my duties as courier. The next morning, however, we stopped all the same for a cut of pink salmon. I wanted to see what would happen when Akio discovered it in his *bento* that afternoon, but I saw a second pair of men's sandals by his door and heard him talking inside with one of the other students.

After we watched that day's lesson, after she practiced in her room and cleaned her utensils, pouring the tea powder out of its lacquer *temae* box and into an airtight one for storage, Yukako fixed me with a long look. *"Watch."*

She took the cylindrical lacquer box used in *temae*, set aside the lid, and showed me the inside, cloudy with a film of green powder. She wiped off the tea powder with a square of soft paper until the inside of the box shone as bright as its mirror-smooth outside. *"Can I put the teabox away now? Is it clean?"*

"Yes," I nodded.

"Truly?"

What was wrong? *"Yes?"* I asked, nervous. She set aside the box, took up the lid, and turned it over. *"Ara!"* She hadn't cleaned the inside of the lid yet; of course it was still dirty. Just as I had doubtless left it when I played with her tea things. I blushed.

"Ara," she said dryly. *"Next time don't forget."*

I hung my head. *"I'm sorry."*

"You want to learn temae, *don't you."* It wasn't a question. I nodded, guilty as charged. In the long silence that followed, I looked up to see Yukako smiling, proud and spiteful. It scared me. *"Good,"* she said, *"because I'm going to teach you."* And then she said something I understood later, when I reflected that her father had married into the family line, and Akio would too: *"I'm the real Shin."*

I hunched, uncertain, and her face softened toward me. *"I'm happy,"* she said. *"You're a good student."* That was when I realized her spite was for Akio. If he said no wife of his would do *temae*, she'd do *temae*—and teach it, too! I smiled.

"*Wipe the lid,*" she said. "*Now you will remember.*"

IN THE SHORT WEEK that followed, the household continued to prepare for the imperial visit and I continued to leave treats for Akio at his sickroom door, and to bring secret notes—in tighter, more controlled handwriting than before—to Yukako upstairs. Yukako came home each night promptly after her bath, added Akio's note to the stash in the hollow base of her pillow, and anxiously read through the whole cycle of his correspondence. I would often fall asleep before she could blow out the candle, but I'd just as often wake in the darkness to feel her turning restlessly beside me, sighing like some long-ago lady from the illustrated Heian classics she showed me: Lady Murasaki's *Tale of Genji*, or Lady Shonagon's *Pillow Book*. One night as I lay watching, Yukako opened her eyes and looked back at me. "*Feel my face,*" she said. "*It's so hot.*" It was as cool as wax.

THE DAY BEFORE the August Nephew's visit, Akio called to me from the bent-tree sickroom. "*Miss Ura!*"

"*Yes?*"

He talked and I bowed and smiled. There was a rumpled elegance to his sleeping *kimono*: the muted blue suited him, and I liked the daring checkerboard pattern of his narrow sash, gold and green. "*Did you understand?*" he said.

"*No. I'm sorry.*"

He repeated himself more loudly and I smiled weakly. "*Baka,*" he muttered. *Stupid.* After two months in a new language, I was used to it.

He tried again. "*Young Mistress lonely,*" he said, speaking bluntly of Yukako.

"*Young Mistress is lonely?*" I repeated nervously, not certain how much to say about her. He hadn't really spoken to me before; I was unprepared.

"*No,*" he said, exasperated. "*I am lonely.*"

"*Mr. Akio is lonely.*"

"*Yes.*" He started to say something about Yukako and broke off, collapsing into another cough. In Japanese you don't say, *I miss you,* you say, *I'm lonely for not seeing you,* but I didn't know that.

"*Tomorrow,*" he said, apparently changing the subject.

I didn't hear the rest of what he said, but it was a question. "*Tomorrow, important guest?*" I assumed.

He sighed impatiently. "*Tomorrow. Young Mistress. Doing what?*"

Oh. He was lonely; he wanted to imagine her day. Since the night Yukako had come home late, I had worried that he might not think of her as much as he ought. "*First, cousin's house,*" I explained, as well as I could. "*Then bring cousin here. Then hairdresser comes. Then help o-Chio. Then kimono. Then help important guest.*" Custom required, I was beginning to learn, that a wellborn guest in one's house be served, at least a token amount, by the host and his family, not by servants alone. While the Mountain planned to do *temae* for the August Nephew with his own hands in Baishian teahouse, the Imperial Guest would travel with a large retinue, who would receive a ritual meal separately in the Mountain's largest tearoom, a fourteen-mat hall, then be entertained by a troupe of hired singing-girls. While the students and apprentices had spent days preparing and rehearsing the *temae* for the imperial retainers' meal, it would still be seemly for Yukako to appear where her father could not, pouring a first cup of *sake.* There would be some dozen guests, so Yukako had enlisted the help of her cousin Matsudaira Sumie.

I had seen Sumie often: every few nights, when Yukako washed all the oil and wax out of her hair, I knew that the next day we'd go to Sumie's house, where a pair of hairdressers, husband and wife, came once a week to look after the men and women of the household respectively. Sumie, tender and breathless, was sixteen like Yukako. Her face was full and round, her feet small and vulnerable, her teeth tiny and white. She and her family had spent much of her girlhood in Edo, so she spoke more quickly than most people I met. Moreover, her language was elaborately feminine: when they chatted while the hairdressers plied their wax and combs, I could understand Sumie even less than I could Yukako.

"Cousin's house far?" Akio asked.

"Twenty-minute walk," I explained. It was nice to imagine him picturing Yukako's walk. *"Canal Street."* A grand but weathered compound, complete with a moon-viewing pond stocked with fat red carp, housed Sumie and her large *samurai* family: a severe and vigorous grandmother I dubbed the Pipe Lady for her hobby and weapon of choice, an ancient, papery grandfather, a long-suffering mother, and a brood of rowdy siblings, including a pair of little brothers who lived to torment me and tiny Miss Miki, the hairdressers' daughter. Though the Mountain had joined the Shin family through adoption and marriage, the Pipe Lady and her frail husband were his blood parents; his older brother, Sumie's father, was part of the Shogun's army, marching south this very month to punish a rebellious lord. Sumie was the second child of six; the oldest was a slouching prince who lolled about the house demanding cups of tea; I knew he wished he could go south and fight as well.

Distantly related to the Shogun, Sumie's grandparents thought well of neither the upstart merchant caste—including the tea family who had all but bought their younger son using Japan's unofficial currency, gold—nor of the *kuge,* the parasitic old aristocracy of the Emperor's court, whom the Shogun supported with bushels of Japan's official currency, rice. While the Mountain had for years seen signs of weakness in the Shogun that made him want to seek allies in the imperial family, his parents treated his efforts with indulgent derision.

When Yukako had asked for Sumie's help with the August Nephew's visit, the Pipe Lady had taken pains to point out a lavish gold screen she'd bought for a song from a penniless imperial courtier. *"Kuge,"* she sneered, before granting permission in her ailing husband's name.

IN THE SICKROOM, Akio's voice came clear and slow. *"Miss Ura and Young Mistress, walk together to cousin's house?"* he pressed.

"Yes," I said proudly. The character for sun in Japanese is a rectangle with a horizontal line in the center: when I followed her on errands, the rectangle of Yukako's flat *obi* knot was like the sun to me. All the other servant girls had to spend the day at home, washing *kimono* and wiping *tatami*. Since each time a *kimono* was soiled it required unsewing and resewing, the Mountain's household kept a small army of sewing-girls busy: I looked down on them.

"Young Mistress's room, upstairs, only Young Mistress and Miss Ura?"

I made Akio repeat himself before I understood. *"Yes,"* I preened. I alone did the work of attending Yukako. I dragged out the *futon* where we lay each night and folded it up each morning; I brought up each tray of the food we ate together, fine white rice for Yukako, rice mixed with coarse servant's barley for me. Every morning I slid wide her wooden shutters; every afternoon I refilled the brown ceramic washing jar on her veranda and wiped down her room and stairs; every evening I brought up a lamp and slid her heavy shutters closed. The tasks comforted me as much as my prayers once had. After I answered Akio, I thought of something. *"Tomorrow night, cousin too,"* I corrected, before wondering why he'd asked.

"Here," he said, producing a sheet of paper. On it was an outline of what looked like a fancy New York lady's bell-shaped dress with *kimono* sleeves—no, it was a drawing of a *kimono* spread flat. Across it, in care-ful black ink, spread the trunk and branches of a tree tipped with

white blossomy puffs. Yukako's *kimono!* I had seen her wear it only once, the night of the Sighting, when she served Akio and his father.

"*Young Mistress's,*" I gasped in recognition.

"*Yes,*" he said. "*I am very lonely.*"

I imagined Yukako walking toward him in her splendid *kimono,* blue-green with its flowering tree, the long ends of her silver sash left untied, a shimmering train down her back, her hair streaming loose like my mother's. The very sight of her would mend him. And then they could get married and Yukako would be happy and sleep well again. She could sleep between us; I wouldn't mind the drafty side of the *futon.* Akio might not like it, but, like Matsu, he would have to live with it. "*I will ask,*" I said.

"*Please don't ask,*" he said. "*Just bring it. Just to borrow.*"

"*I don't know,*" I said. I knew the shelf where she kept it folded; I knew its white silk lining, yellowed and spotted with age. Would she want his eyes on that? And why did he not want me to ask?

"*Just to see,*" he insisted.

I felt confused, and strangely ashamed. "*I don't know,*" I said.

"*Fine,*" he said, relenting. "*I'm a sick fool. It's too much, I understand.*" Was this the famed Japanese indirection? To treat *I don't know* as if it meant *Absolutely not?* On reflection, that's exactly what I did mean. "*But please don't tell,*" he added.

Unease pricked at the back of my neck. I looked up, away from Akio, and saw his pair of *samurai* swords hanging on the bent-treetrunk post that gave the room its name. "*Can I see—*" I wasn't sure what the word was, and pointed.

I clearly had him at a disadvantage; he took them down. "*Tachi,*" he said. The long bright steel slid from its lacquer scabbard without a sound. "*Wakizashi,*" he said, showing me the shorter sword.

They were more beautiful and frightening than I had imagined. "*Thank you,*" I said.

Usually people said *"No"* to say *"You're welcome,"* the way we say "It's nothing." But Akio bowed, put his swords away, and said it formally: *What have I done?*

That evening I wanted to tell Yukako, but I fretted as I hung her mosquito gauze, recently brought in from the storeroom tower. Would she be angry or happy? And if Akio found out, would he cut me with those sharp swords? *"Older Sister,"* I said when she came up from the bath.

"Yes?"

My mouth went dry. *"It's a warm night,"* I said.

THE MOUNTAIN HAD PLANNED the household's shift from winter to summer to coincide with the imperial visit: we put away our lined *kimono* and began wearing unlined ones; the season's new jars of tea arrived from the packers by oxcart. All the square sunken hearths—the feature by which I knew a tearoom for a tearoom—vanished, replaced by fresh green-gold *tatami*. The afternoon I talked with Akio, I lingered with little Zoji near Baishian until the students shooed me away: they were carrying a long board wrapped in cloth toward the small house, and carrying two smaller boards away. When I looked later, the square hole in the floor was gone; the satiny wooden floorboard stretched unbroken between the two mats. The sunken hearth was for winter use only, I learned; in the warm months tea people used a brazier in order to keep the heat away from the guests.

On the day of the imperial visit, even the great brown and red jars for water disappeared from the kitchen, the tea preparation rooms, and Yukako's veranda; when we came home from Sumie's house we were startled by the sight of a black-robed student tottering down Yukako's stairs with a heavy load. I looked up at Yukako, alarmed, when I recognized him: it was the younger of the Mountain's two merchant-caste apprentices, the Stickboy. While the *samurai* boys left the other merchant apprentice alone—the Bear was older, thick-bodied and jolly, and not above a little bullying of his own—they singled out the Stickboy for mockery and extra chores, especially after the lesson when the tea bowl fell apart in his hands. Fortunately, Yukako's water jar remained in one piece all the way down the stairs, though he flashed us an embarrassed glance. In its place, we discovered, he had left a new vessel, blue and white, cool colors for summer.

To MARK THIS DAY, every single one of us received a new *kimono*, unlined, each in a solid color, the men in black and gray and blue, the women in shades of red. My *kimono* was bright salmon orange, Sumie's a muted peony pink, Yukako's a dark wine. Each *kimono* was printed with the Shin crest—a crane—in five places, like five white coins: one on the back, one on each shoulder, and one on each sleeve.

Before we put on our new robes, however, we all had work to do. While Miss Miki and her mother sculpted Yukako's and Sumie's locks into the waxed and pinned conventions an imperial visit required, I helped the seamstresses wipe every surface clean, then we all followed Chio's direction in the kitchen, preparing the exquisite nine-course meals. Yukako helped her father as he bustled about with tea imple-ments, and she also walked Sumie through the formal gestures of serv-ing rice wine to imperial retainers. (Part of her task seemed to be calming Sumie's jitters: "*So many strangers watching,*" the girl would fret, chewing at the knuckle of her thumb.) I wiped and chopped and kept Chio's grandson out of trouble. The students and gardeners raked the gardens clean of debris, swept the gravel into subtle waves, and cut off every iris blossom in the garden. During the intermission between the Minister's ritual meal and the tea *temae* that followed, the Mountain planned to exchange the scroll in the Baishian alcove for a vase holding one perfect blue flower. I was sad to see the irises disappear, I told Yukako in the kitchen. She was counting out twelve red saucer-shaped cups for *sake*, inspecting each for scratches. *"They'll grow again,"* she assured me. *"Today, he'll see leaves, leaves, leaves, but no flowers. But then at last, inside Baishian: the flower."* It was a tease for the eyes.

No one seemed concerned about the overcast sky, the muggy weight of the air. *"Clouds,"* I worried, pointing outside.

"Gray sky, bright colors," she assured me.

"Rain?"

Yukako inhaled, to answer seriously, and then she smiled with anticipated pleasure as, very slowly, she made a pun for me. *"If it rains, our guest will remember these clouds forever."*

I repeated her, as I often repeated her longer sentences, and when I reached *clouds* I grinned with her, because the word was so close to Cloud House, the oldest of the Mountain's teahouses, built by Shinso, the founding ancestor of the Shin tradition of tea, great-grandson of Rikyu, the founder of tea ceremony itself. Because tiny Cloud House was the most important of the Shin teahouses, sometimes the name was used to mean the whole Shin compound, or the Mountain's tea school, or the Mountain himself. *"Cloud House,"* I whispered, savoring the word and Yukako's good humor, rare since the night she came back late.

When there was no wood left to polish, no radish left to grate, and we had changed into our new robes, the Mountain gathered us all into the fourteen-mat hall made ready for the imperial entourage. As Yukako promised, every colored thing—from our new robes to the moss in the garden behind us—seemed to vibrate against the gray-white sky. The Mountain spoke to all of us and showed us one of the earthenware jars that had arrived by oxcart. Shoulder-height on me, it was made of blackened clay splashed with green. The Mountain cut the seal, lifted the stopper, and beckoned us each forward. *"New tea,"* whispered Chio in her rust-colored robe. The Mountain would open a different jar for the imperial guest, and bid him take it home: this was the tea for Cloud House. Each person in the household approached the jar, scooping the air with one hand the way Yukako and Sumie did in their incense-guessing games. I smelled it myself: green and bright like new grass.

6

1866

I DIDN'T SEE the imperial procession, but I saw the palanquin outside. I didn't see the August Nephew, but I saw the bobbing top of his black lacquer cap as he rounded the bamboo hedge. I didn't see the tea ceremony in Baishian but I did hear a sound, sharp and near against the distant dull thunder, *couisse-eh, couisse-eh, couisse-eh:* the Mountain grinding tea leaves in a stone mortar. I didn't see the dozen members of the imperial retinue, but I formed part of a human chain passing dishes to the students and apprentices as they served each one. I didn't see them, but I heard the three singing-girls brought in to entertain the August Nephew's men, the slow drum and banjo-like *shamisen* they played, their caterwauling tunes. Yukako and Sumie poured each man a first round of *sake*, then went upstairs and let the singing-girls take over as I ran hot kettles to the doorway with Chio's daughter Kuga, vivid, for once, in rose. When I had a moment, I paused to run up and spread Yukako's *futon*. *"Thank you,"* she said, waving a hand to fan Sumie, who drooped against her. *"See? You didn't drop anything,"* she told her cousin.

"How long could they possibly stay, do you think?" Sumie murmured, dabbing at her forehead with a cloth.

"When they go, we'll come say good-bye," Yukako informed me, her speech a blunt foil to Sumie's.

When I went downstairs, baby Zoji—a jewel in his tiny aquamarine *kimono*—was fussing on his mother Kuga's back. It wasn't raining yet, but with every clap of thunder he reached up and tried to pull off the rosy cloth tented over Kuga's hair. Taking a *kasa*—a waxed paper umbrella that looked like a parasol—I carried him out for a walk to calm him, avoiding the teahouses, bouncing as I went. *"Auprès de ma blonde,"* I sang softly in the twilight. I thought I might start to cry, thinking of my mother, so I tried a Japanese song instead. Chio had sung it the month I arrived, when the cherry trees—the *sakura*—burst into bloom. *"Sakura, sakura . . ."*

I felt Zoji go limp against my back as I sang. When I reached the Bent-Tree Annex, I rested for a moment on the bench outside Akio's *shoji*-paper door. At my feet I saw a second pair of men's sandals next to Akio's: one of the other students was visiting him. It must have been hard for him, missing the whole affair; he probably would have been chosen for some prestigious task. Even the Stickboy had looked so pleased with himself, neatly arranging the retinue's bags and umbrellas in the entrance hall. It was kind of the other students to visit Akio; they all must have resented him for not doing any work and still getting to marry Yukako. I could hear the twanging *shamisen* from the imperial party deep within the house, the women's wailing songs, the men's laughter. No, that was Akio's laughter, so soft it sounded distant. And the singing voice belonged to his guest.

In my head, outside Akio's door, I formed a sentence, very proud of myself for coming up with such a long one. I found I could make long sentences when I was alone, mumbling to myself in Japanese; whenever I was around other people, my beautiful clauses evaporated in the panic of trying to understand what I heard. In any case, it seemed doubtful that I would get to use my new sentence very often: *The woman has men's sandals.*

My attention leaped to a sound beyond the gate, rumbling too near and for too long to be thunder. A large animal? I rarely saw horses in Japan, and the hooves seemed to thud instead of ring. Could it be an elephant? I didn't care if I never met the Emperor's nephew—I probably wouldn't be able to understand his Japanese anyway—but an elephant? My heart beat fast as I hauled Zoji to the gate. It was a horse.

I missed what the man with the lamp was saying as the animal moved from hoof to hoof, transfixed as I was by what those hooves were wearing: *straw baskets.* The horses that had carried me away from the fire had no doubt had straw shoes, too, but I'd had no time to notice. Why would you do that? I could understand eating seaweed and taking off my shoes in the house, but why would you tie baskets to a horse's feet? The little animal kicked one of them off entirely as the man swung from his queer high saddle and completed his rapid speech, giving me a slender wooden scroll-box. In the first falling drops of rain, I stared at him, trying to repeat what I'd heard. His face changed, as Akio's had when he called me into his room. *Oh, she's slow,* he registered. *"Master Teacher,"* he repeated.

"Yes!" I barked. *"Please wait."*

The man seemed as if he'd ridden a long way that night, but I didn't think I should interrupt the Mountain in the teahouse. Because of the imperial guest, I wasn't even sure I should bring the horseman into the kitchen, so I pointed to the shelter of the thatched gate and ran the box up to Yukako's room, Zoji still on my back. Sumie seemed to have recovered her spirits: the two of them whispered together over the notes in Yukako's pillow-box. Yukako glared up at me. *"Where is it?"* she asked, eyes hot with accusation.

Where was what? I stared at her openmouthed, then followed her gaze to the shelf where she kept her tea things, the whisk beside the bowl beside the teascoop. I gasped: there should have been a second teascoop just where she'd left it, wrapped in white paper and stamped with Akio's seal. It was missing.

The night before he had asked me to keep a secret, and now his teascoop was gone. I did not know what had happened, but it was probably my fault. Before Yukako could press me, however, she was stopped by the sight of my rain-freckled sleeves, the long box I carried. *"What's this?"* she asked, opening it.

"Rain. A man. An animal," I spluttered. *"Four legs. Like an ox, not an ox. Feet in baskets!"* They stared at me, smiling weakly. Sumie cooed at the baby on my back, then stopped; we watched alarm spread across Yukako's face as she read the brief contents of the scroll in the box. Panicked, she leapt up and swept downstairs, Sumie, Zoji, and me in confused pursuit. Sumie seized up umbrellas for Yukako and herself, and I paused in the kitchen for a bucket of water and a cup of tea for the horseman, who seemed affronted by the parade of women and children. Our solid-colored *kimono*, I realized, looked like servants' uniforms to him.

"I am Master Teacher's only child," Yukako began, speaking to the man proudly and carefully as rain darkened the stones around us.

Beside me, Sumie asked the messenger about a man who shared her family name, *Matsudaira*. Her father? My gaze drifting out to the street as the man gave his long reply, I could see the outline of a palanquin some thirty paces away, smaller than the Nephew's or the singing-girls', the tiny lights of its bearers' pipes sheltered by their paper umbrellas. Who were they waiting for? When I looked up again at the horseman, Sumie seemed to have been reassured by his response, Yukako made more upset. She asked him to stay in the thatched gateway, her face taut with anxiety as she turned to Sumie. What had the messenger told her? *"Should we tell Lord Ii's son?"* she asked. I had noticed it before, the way she avoided saying Akio's name in front of anyone but me.

"I wonder, is he awake?" asked Sumie.

"Yes," I said. *"There is a woman visitor."*

Yukako wheeled on me. *"What kind of woman?"* she asked sharply.

"A woman with men's shoes," I said, delighted with myself.

My pleasure at my burgeoning language skills was not shared. Yukako said nothing, but made straight for Akio's annex. *"Wait!"* said Sumie helplessly, holding out both their umbrellas. I took one and followed, panting, Zoji yowling on my back, while Sumie brought up the rear, the sound of her shuffling trot lost in the loud hash of rain.

We pressed in close to the house, sheltering under the eaves. I watched Yukako at Akio's door for a moment, her face lit by a lamp glowing through the *shoji* paper from inside. Through the rain, we heard a woman's singing voice waft toward us, followed by laughter. Yukako's eyes were wide, her mouth a thin line. We heard Akio chuckle, *"Little Koito."*

Yukako did not look back at us. She took a deep breath and called into the room, loud but shaky. *"Who is Little Koito?"*

I gasped as the voices fell silent. Sumie hid her face with her sleeve. We heard rustling from inside the room, then feet approaching the entrance, and then a female voice, low and firm. *"I am,"* a woman said, and slid open the door.

When he said her name, Akio had used a tag for babies and younger sisters, *bo.* I could not imagine calling this woman *Little* anyone. Perhaps nineteen to Yukako's sixteen, the woman looked down at her challenger with queenly self-assurance. All three of us stared at her white-painted face, coy and imperious, the feline moue of her brilliant red mouth. She was even more beautiful than Yukako.

I had never before thought of Yukako as anything but grown up, but at that moment, locking eyes with the smaller woman on the step above her, she seemed coltish, green. Where everything about Yukako seemed hard and bright and seeking, everything about this woman, Koito, seemed subtle and knowing. She shone, too, albeit with a steely shimmer, the black orchid of her hair fierce with pins. Where Yukako's sash looked crisp and formal, Koito's dark brocade *obi*, dotted with violet and tied with a silver cord, looked soft and lustrous, a flash of red silk peeping where the sash met the robe, blue-green in the rainy night. When I saw that color, I gasped, and looked again: she was wearing Yukako's *kimono*.

7

1866

THEN EVERYTHING HAPPENED very quickly: Yukako's hands on Koito's shoulders, Koito's coiffured head bouncing like a pincushion as Yukako shook her, livid, words repeated in the rain: *"Mine! Mine!"* Koito bending for her sandals, Yukako snatching them away. Koito a series of flashes lit by the *shoji*-paper wall of the house: black, red, blue-green, brown branch and white blossom, rain riddling her white face paint. Yukako's voice a knife. Koito's wet red split-toed socks as she turned away, defiantly not running. The white stripes of her ankles. One hand holding up her skirts, the other cupped over her eyes. Yukako staring at Akio, Koito's sandals falling from her hand; his face frozen as he took us all in, not in panic, but with disdain. At some point Sumie had taken Zoji, screaming, off my back: for a moment, as Koito rounded the house and Sumie bounced the baby, the only sound was the loud rain. Then Yukako turned her back on the lit room, composed her face, and pointed to my umbrella, then to Koito's wake. I stared at her, stunned, until I realized she wanted to protect the *kimono* Koito was wearing. *"That was my mother's,"* Yukako said. She had never spoken to me so coldly before. I ran.

Koito bowed when I caught up to her, a tiny bow, as if her sodden robe and shoeless feet, her melting face paint, were nothing to her. She took the umbrella nonetheless, serene as a dancer, and swept past the staring horseman at the gate. He looked to me for explanation, then remembered I was soft in the head and looked away. As I paused in the shelter of the gate for a break in the storm, I spotted the pipe-lights of the two men I'd seen before: their palanquin was for her.

I looked at the patient little horse, its fringed dark eyes reflecting the horseman's lamp. It was wearing new straw shoes, the old ones stacked neatly by the gate. The horseman gave a small cough and asked me slowly and clearly, *"Is he coming?"*

I didn't know, but then Akio approached, his swords at his sides, handsome wasted body all but twined around the stem of an umbrella as he approached the gate, shivering. He spoke with the horseman briefly and they mounted, one of Akio's arms wrapped around the messenger, the other holding his umbrella over both of them. Neither man glanced at me as they rode away.

I ran back to Akio's room: it was empty, the lamp still lit, the *futon* spread, the mosquito gauze stirring in the wet breeze. I sat quietly for a moment, rubbing the gooseflesh inside my soaked sleeves. I remembered the accusation in Yukako's face when I came up to her room: the teascoop he had carved was gone, and I was the obvious culprit. Of course she would think I took the *kimono*. Again I heard the ice in her voice, not simply shock, but rage: *It was my mother's.* If I did not act, what would become of me?

When I was older, I would wonder why Akio had dressed Koito in Yukako's *kimono*. Was he smitten with the woman—had he simply wanted to give her the loveliest thing to hand? Or did he chafe at his lot—did it give him a rush, to court the ruin of his soon-to-be marriage under his soon-to-be adoptive father's roof? Perhaps he was responding to his quarrel with Yukako: did he want the idea of her without the trouble of the real thing?

When I was older still, I learned that the very act of substitution generates its own erotic glamour. That night, however, scared of the fate I'd cheated thus far—of its nunlike fingers on the scruff of my neck—I was concerned, not with *why* he'd taken the *kimono*, but *how.* I'd been so stupid, so drunk on myself, telling Akio exactly what he needed to know. How easy it would be for him, while Yukako and I were at Sumie's house, to take back the scoop he'd made when he took the robe. However, I thought, if Akio had been able to walk about, he would have been pressed into service that morning like the rest of us, and he'd barely been able to stagger out to meet the horseman. He would have needed an ally, someone who would draw no comment entering Yukako's room, and I had turned him down.

I knew who did it. Perhaps Akio had simply asked for his teascoop when he asked for Yukako's robe, but there was a fair chance he hadn't. I would risk it, I decided, and blew out the light.

On the path to the thatched front gate, I saw Yukako standing with Sumie, waiting to bow her good-byes to the imperial party. Beneath her umbrella, her face was a cold mask. Stealing past her, I circled the house to the kitchen door. Gliding silently on the polished boards and *tatami* mats I wiped each day (looking, daily, for my Saint Claire medal), I passed through the kitchen to the nearby garden study where the Mountain slept and took his meals, down the hall to the Long Room, where the students slept, each on a wooden pillow painted with his name: I knew this because I sometimes helped Chio serve the morning meal. That night, my eyes adjusting to the bare expanse of dark *tatami* in the Long Room, I slid open the paper door that concealed the students' bedding. I guessed correctly: the pillow on the humblest shelf was the same one that stood in the draftiest spot in the cold months, the stuffiest during hot ones. It belonged to the Mountain's lowest-ranked student, the boy of the broken bowl. I could feel his painted name with my fingertips, its first syllable one of the few characters I could read, the same one I had seen carved on the hillside my first day in Miyako: *great*, pronounced *oh* or *dai*. What I was looking for in the drawer of the wooden pillow, I found by touch.

In Yukako's room again, I looked at Akio's teascoop, still wrapped in white paper stamped with his seal, the package still tied with red thread. Since the theft, however, a black line of calligraphy had appeared beside the stamped red seal: Akio's name, I later learned, and his *samurai* title. Yukako looked at me hard when she and Sumie came upstairs; the betrayed disgust in her face thawed when she saw what I held. She knew right away that the writing was not Akio's, nor could it have been mine; she nodded when I told her where I'd found it. *"Older Sister?"* I said. She stared at me as I told her about Akio asking me for the *kimono*, about promising not to tell. Stumbling, I tried to explain how the Stickboy must have smuggled it out of her room inside the water barrel (clever Akio!), how he must have taken Akio's teascoop then too. I could tell she was taking nothing in: not my distress, not my guilt, not my innocence. The despair she'd kept at bay by hating me flooded over her; she could not hear me.

"Ura-*bo*," she said numbly, and I took from the name what small comfort I could. Tucking the teascoop into her sleeve, she left to sit the night in Baishian alone.

As we lay in Yukako's room, listening to the rain on the rooftiles, Sumie answered my questions, flustered as she cropped her elegant soft language into the crude phrases I could understand. With Yukako's brother dead, the Mountain needed Yukako to marry a man he could adopt as an heir. (Once I understood the word *heir*, Sumie told me how Hiroshi had made her a kite the summer—*that summer*, I thought— before he died. How he had loved ginger. How his flute had sounded, achingly sweet.)

Akio's father was Lord Ii of Hikone, on the far side of Lake Biwa, whose kinsman had been murdered, I later learned, for signing a treaty with the foreign barbarians. Lord Ii had two sons, Sumie told me, Akio and his older brother, Tadao, the heir. The horseman at the gate had ridden for two days from a battle in the South to say Tadao was dead, and Akio had left with the messenger for the house his father kept in Miyako. Now that Akio, the only son, was his father's heir, he could no longer marry Yukako.

"And Koito?"

"It's good, maybe. It can't be helped."

As clear as she was on points of inheritance, Sumie was vague, though visibly fretful, on the subject of Yukako's distress. I prompted her, dredging my mind for the word I wanted: *jealousy*. "He has another *fiancée*," another *promised person*, I attempted. "She didn't know?"

You really *are* slow, Sumie's expression said. "Miss Koito is a geiko," she said patiently. A singing-girl, what my grammar had called a *geisha*. "Nobody marries a geiko."

But he loves her, I wanted to say, maybe more than Yukako. But the construction was hard for me, and—to my shock—I didn't know the word for *love*. "But he likes Miss Koito," I said.

"So?"

"So he should marry her."

"Liking and marriage are bad together."

"Really?"

I had thought someone who spoke so gently and vaguely would be wistful and romantic, but Sumie said, "All husbands like geiko. It is bad for a woman to like her husband. Liking is jealousy." There it was! I'd heard the word in stories she and Yukako read aloud to each other.

"Who is it good to like?" I tried to ask.

"Babies!" Sumie replied, as if it were the most obvious thing in the world. She brought the candle over to the ash-filled brazier where

Yukako practiced her *temae*. *Man*, she drew in the ashes with one tong: a crosshatched box over a character resembling the letter *h*. *Woman*: I could make out a big-bellied stick figure when Sumie showed me the head, trunk, and feet. *Baby*: a shape curved like the number 3, or, if I squinted, like little Zoji, with a long ribbon for me to tie him to my back. *"See?"* she said, drawing a new character composed of the previous two, "To like *is woman and baby, not woman and man.*" We lay down on the *futon* again. I would never be able to read Japanese.

"*Yukako likes Mr. Akio,*" I ventured.

"*That's a problem,*" said Sumie.

Jerking awake at first light, I remembered something I'd seen in Akio's room: the tiny round body and long slender neck of a singing-girl's three-stringed *shamisen*. When I hurried down to the sickroom, I found it on the floor. A large fan-shaped plectrum lay beside it, painted in a pattern of swirling water. I packed both into a box and bag I found in the corner, painted with the same watery swirls; maybe they'd help me get Yukako's *kimono* back.

Later that morning, after Sumie went home, a narrow-eyed servant girl came to our kitchen door to beg a word with my mistress, swirling water printed on her *kimono*, a letter in her hand.

I read Koito's letter many years later, the only other time I ever searched through someone's pillow-box without asking. I didn't find what I was looking for in Yukako's pillow, but I saw a life's worth of worried-at things. All her poems from Akio, folded into *origami* drums. A pressed spray of snow willow. A cut of yellowed white silk. And a note on flecked blue paper in a woman's hand, practiced and fluid, yet employed as if she were uncertain of her reader's degree of literacy. The words were clear and firm, almost block-printed, in the Japanese phonetic script, with none of the Chinese characters men used:

> She knew not she wore
> the wings of a crane. Can the
> mute thrush atone?

It was a less flat-footed poem in Japanese, the hard *k*'s and *a*'s of *to not know* and *mute* smarting with humility, *shirazu, kikenai;* the sinuous character for *tsu*—a single curved stroke—snaking humbly through the words for *crane, thrush,* and *to atone: tsuru, tsugumi, tsugunau.* In a city without street addresses, Koito put teeth into her apology by having me learn the way to her house: if I followed the maid, then Yukako could call on the mistress anytime, so long as I remembered the long walk to Pontocho, the *geisha* quarter near the Fourth Bridge.

When we arrived, I knew I'd been right: the package waiting for me in the cloakroom of the narrow house we entered was the size and shape of a *kimono*, but bulkier, as if the girl's employer had added some other tribute too. I felt very pleased with myself indeed. *"Would you like some tea?"* asked the girl.

She was my age, her eyes close-set and merry. I'd followed the knot of her yellow plaid *obi* from my house to hers, watching her posture straighten from hunched trepidation to buoyant confidence. When we first started walking, I couldn't make sense of the flat, loud voice offering me something—what? I began to understand her, however, by the time she led me through Pontocho, greeting people on the narrow street by name. *"Good morning, Aunt! How's the little girl? Do you have kittens yet? Think it'll rain again?"* Her bow was deeper than anyone else's in the singing-girls' quarter—where *shamisen* scales jangled from every window and hairdressers shuttled from house to house, their wooden workboxes almost taller than the servant girls who carried them—but her voice rang out as lustily as any street peddler's in New York. I missed most of what she said, especially to the old ladies, all called Aunt—from the sound of it, they were discussing ailments I wouldn't have even known in French—but I was pleased I understood so much. Clearest of all, I understood when they greeted her in return: *Miss Inko,* they sang back. Even though I hated this girl, Miss Inko, on principle—as the servant of Yukako's enemy—I envied the jaunty indifference with which she set the tray beside me on the cloakroom bench.

"*Did you like your sweet?*" said a voice. Looking down from the *tatami* interior of the house, her face unpainted, stood Koito. I tried to concentrate on the ghoulish vanity of her blackened teeth and missing eyebrows, but I had seen them so often on women at the bathhouse that I found myself dazzled instead by the silver in her gray gauze robe, by the red of her little bud mouth.

What had she said? I couldn't remember. "*Thank you very much,*" I tried to reply, more warmly than I'd meant to. When she heard my accent, she gave me a closer look. I saw in her face at that moment the same suppressed blend of curiosity, amusement, pity, and disgust I often provoked, usually before the looker concluded that I was an accident of nature, but I also saw something else, a flicker of recognition, or compassion. While Yukako forged her own kind of radiance, I had seen enough pictures in books to see that Koito was a living *bijin,* a Japanese ideal of beauty. What could she see in me to recognize?

"*You haven't tasted it yet,*" she teased, gesturing toward the tea and the lidded ceramic box Inko had set beside me.

Oh, right—she'd asked about a sweet! I lifted the lid to expose a fluffy globe of dyed bean paste, green on one side, violet on the other, topped with a dab of gold leaf. For me? I bowed low in thanks.

"*Ayame,*" she said, before she vanished: iris. Gold for the splash of yellow on each petal, I realized, delighted.

Koito's livelihood depended on charming others, even young girls who loved sweets as much as I. This didn't occur to me, though, as I carried home my heavy parcel, eager in spite of myself to see Yukako open

it. Above me, women had flopped their mattresses over their balcony rail-
ings to air; the Pontocho street was so narrow that the draped bedding
almost formed a *futon* arch. It would take a revolution and a civil war
before I saw this quarter again, before the changes that wracked Japan
nearly broke Yukako as well. That day the women came to their windows
often: I saw bamboo blinds moved aside, faces tipped up to the sun
among the thick clouds, hands extended, testing the heavy air.

AT THE TIME, I did not know why Koito had taken such pains with the
two *kimono* she sent home with me. That night, after her bath, Yukako
unfolded them, nodding cold approval as she spread the singing-girl's
gift in the lamplight. What looked at first glance like broad black and
white stripes, flecked here and there with gold, proved to be raw silk
gauze woven subtly in a pattern of fish in a stream, their backs golden
where they rose from the water. Yukako folded the robe calmly and then
turned to her own *kimono*, inspecting every spotless inch. Before, the
kimono, like most, had been lined in two fabrics. Any area that might be
visible—the sleeves, hem, and collar—was lined in soft red silk, a rich
and feminine contrast to the deep twilight color outside. Hidden areas
were lined in coarser fabric, often white, in this case yellowed and spotted with age. Koito, however, had relined the entire *kimono* in fine silk,
the color a precise match to the old fabric but the texture as lush and
supple as suede. She had included the former lining, a ghost *kimono*,
which Yukako spread in the air: her eyes widened when she saw that the
fabric was strained and ripped at the shoulders where she'd shaken the
geisha. When she cried in her bed, I curled around her: I could feel her
back expand as she gulped in air.

THAT MORNING Akio's father, old Lord Ii, had come to speak with the
Mountain while his servants emptied the sickroom. Lord Ii wore black

for his older son, and Yukako's vacant pallor matched his as she brought him rice wine. The Stickboy was missing from that day's lesson: I found him by the stream near the storeroom tower. Hidden from the house, he was hunching over something, scrawny and naked except for a loin-cloth. Padding closer, I saw he was scrubbing one of his *kimono* in the stream. The smell of human excrement drifted toward me and I under-stood the shape of Yukako's revenge. I was so glad she'd believed me: we had both seen him panting down the stairs with her big water jar, after all. I wondered why he had done it. I knew the Mountain's students, just as status-conscious as the Pipe Lady, kept up a kind of wall between the merchants' sons—the Stickboy and the Bear—and the *samurai* boys—Akio, the Button, and the others. Perhaps—I could imagine it—the Stickboy was flattered when Akio asked him for the help I'd refused to give. Perhaps he wanted to be someone like Akio. Enough to steal the teascoop? Maybe.

Yukako stopped crying. She lay on her side by the two *kimono*, motionless except for one foot rubbing an obsessive circle into her *futon*. "*I can't wear these,*" she whispered, staring into the darkness. She hadn't eaten all day. She gripped the old lining in her fists and called out quietly, and for the first time I will not write what she said in italics because the word went right in without pausing to tell me it was in Japanese. Forlorn, unadorned: "Mother—"

8

1866–1869

WHEN I FIRST LIVED in Miyako, now called Kyoto, brides were carried down the street in sumptuous palanquins, as they had been for centuries. The very rich rode this way all the time, in hammocklike sedan chairs borne by pairs of stout young men, or in elegant boxes like the one by which I was first smuggled into the city. How could any of us have known that in a few short years, only the dead would be carried this way, or that the streets would fill with noisy machines whose name no one had yet imagined?

AKIO AND SUMIE'S WEDDING was a quiet affair, I heard, a glint of color after the mourning black we all wore for Lord Ii's son Tadao, killed fighting southern rebels in the Battle of Mori.

Shaken by his firstborn's death, the old horse-breeding lord determined to marry off his younger son as quickly as possible, turning to the Mountain for advice to show that there was no ill will between them. I sat in the doorway the morning of his visit, ferrying courses for Yukako to serve the two men. I was there when the Mountain mentioned Sumie's name: I saw Yukako stop breathing for a moment. The flask on the tray she held wobbled; she sat very still. After Lord Ii left, she went to the storeroom tower, buried her head in a stack of winter quilts, and screamed. From the window where I spied, I could barely hear her: she was so muffled—so private—that I held back from going to comfort her. That was the day she took to her bed.

When Yukako missed their standing date with the hairdressers, Sumie came by with a gift of silk. "Make her go away," Yukako begged me in the upstairs room. I remember the way Sumie lowered her eyes when I passed on the message, the soft look on her face, both guilty and hurt.

Though the family no longer dressed in mourning, on the day of the wedding Yukako put on the same black *kimono* and *obi* she'd worn for a month. I felt disloyal for wanting to see Sumie's trip down the street in a palanquin, but I still asked, "Isn't today the wedding?"

"Oh, is it? Oh, well, I'm already dressed, aren't I? Please tell my father I can't go; I'm sick." She wasn't.

YUKAKO'S PROTEST LASTED not a handful of days before the Shogun died and all Japan wore black for *him*. An ailing boy of twenty, he'd gone to Osaka Castle to lead his thousands against the southern rebels, only to die inside the castle walls of beriberi, the city sickness, a disease no one knew came from living on fine white rice. For a year, thousands of *samurai*, Akio's brother and Sumie's father among them, had waited at Osaka Castle to strike the rebels, and each day Chio had chosen carrots and eggplants from her husband's little plot for a peddler who could buy them, pay passage to Osaka, and still turn a profit selling food to soldiers. During the weeks of mourning, we heard, Edo and Osaka rioted for rice.

The young former Shogun had been easily led by the Matsudaira, the most warlike among his relations. (Sumie's family was a minor branch of the vast Matsudaira clan.) By contrast, his replacement, a distant cousin, installed himself close to the Emperor in Miyako to ask His Highness to back an end to the former Shogun's doomed thrust south. For some two hundred fifty years, relations between the Shogun and the Emperor had been like those between the Pipe Lady and her bedridden husband: although she abased herself before him and acted only in his name, he was entirely dependent on her. With the arrival of the foreigners, however, the power of the Shoguns had begun to unravel, and they needed all the more to clothe themselves in the Emperors' authority. While the previous Shoguns had lived in Edo, two weeks' journey from Miyako by foot, the new one spent almost all of his short reign at Nijo Castle, some forty minutes' walk from the Shin house. For a year we had both the Emperor and the Shogun in Miyako, and Chio and Matsu's produce did very well indeed.

Just two days after the new Shogun's investiture, the old Emperor died in his bed, and all Japan mourned again. I remember my first winter in Miyako as a swirl of white snowflakes and black *kimono.* We cleaned house for days until the plum trees bloomed in the snow, and then New Year's burst in with temple bells and fireworks heralding the new Emperor: a fifteen-year-old boy.

I never learned the Emperor's name until I left Japan; it wasn't for the public to know. We called him the Emperor. But the following year he changed the name of the era from *Keio,* Great Joy, to *Meiji,* Enlightened Rule. Until Meiji, Japan had seen so much fire, famine, and cholera in such a short time that the court astrologers kept changing the era name every few years, in a vain attempt to dodge bad fortune. None of the past six eras had lasted more than six years. As part of his Enlightened Rule, the new Emperor silenced the court astrologers, announcing that henceforth the era name would change only with the Emperor. So today if you want to refer to him, you say *the Meiji Emperor:* the one who reigned from 1867, the year before Meiji One, until his death in Meiji Forty-five.

. . .

YUKAKO SPENT THE six months between the Battle of Mori and the Meiji coronation in the same black *kimono*. She lay in bed, reading the poems in her pillow-box and asking for something to drink. I brought so much tea up her steep slick staircase, I made a rope banister for myself after falling down twice.

I let her be. I learned Japanese with little Zoji. I brought her tea. I waited as long for her as I had traveled by ship, carrying my mother's death under my ribs, and then when the year turned I bullied her back to life again. "Tie my *obi* like butterfly wings! I want to go out and see everybody dressed up for New Year's! Sumie's pregnant? Who cares? Do you want six kids like Sumie's ma?"

She tied it. She took me. She said no. "I'll never marry," she decided. She put on a fresh *kimono*—white stars in a blue night, a flash of persimmon at the sleeves and hem—slid open her windows, and did *temae* for the first time in six months, hesitantly, but with resolve. She hadn't bought sweets since before Sumie's engagement was announced; she knelt beside me in the snowy wind with a tray of sum-mer fan-shaped wafers. I ate one; it had long ago surrendered its crunch to the moist months, but the tea washed it away in one green bolt. When I returned the tea bowl, she gave me a look, wan but firm, and a small nod, and I formally asked her, as much as I could remem-ber, to join me and drink a bowl herself. "No, bow this way," she said, correcting me.

"I forgot," I said. "Thank you."

"That's why I'm here," she said, just as her father would tell one of *his* students. Her own words seemed to surprise and please her. She poured water from the iron kettle, whisked the tea, then drank deeply, lifting the bowl to her mouth with both hands, her *kimono* sleeves stir-ring in the brisk air. A hard, clean shape against the sheets of falling snow, she finished her tea with a sharp intake of breath, the way she had taught me, but louder, as if sucking in this very day. And then, as teachers often do, she broke the rules, reaching over to sample the soggy August sweets. "Well, it was what I had," she said, disgusted. She cleared away the tea and straightened the butterfly bow of my *obi*. "Let's go out for a walk," she proposed. "Let's get ginger sweets."

IN THE MONTHS THAT FOLLOWED, the city filled with soldiers, both the Shogun's troops and the southern rebels, *samurai* from Satsuma and Choshu, who were allied with the new Emperor's maternal grandfather. Because of the uneasy times, the Mountain did not ask Yukako to consider marriage again that year. One night late in the Eleventh Month, after the first frost bleached the verandas, southern troops replaced all the Shogun's *samurai* outside the Imperial Palace and poured onto the grounds. Once the Emperor's Satsuma grandfather had gathered all the lords and nobles, the young Emperor appeared before them to read a scroll announcing that he was reclaiming the power and land his ancestors had entrusted to the Shogun's clan.

This was the Meiji Restoration: how the South used the Emperor to overthrow the Shogun. If the Shogun had been like a vigorous wife to a bedridden husband, I imagined the southern *samurai* rabble—pouring in with their cries of "Restore the Emperor! Expel the Barbarians!"—as the brazen young lass who supplanted her, to be just as quickly supplanted by the quiet and crafty older sister who had pushed her into his arms. The leaders of the ragtag *samurai* rebels gave way to an oligarchy of southern lords and merchants who thought Japan stood to gain, not by expelling the foreigners, but by learning from them. It was a brilliant move to stage a revolution and announce it as a restoration, but though the southern rebel *samurai* claimed power for the Emperor, they were not prepared for how he—counseled by their wealthier countrymen—would brush them aside to keep it.

· · ·

IN SOME PLACES the fighting lasted as long as a year and a half, but Edo was subdued by summer, and the Emperor went in person to see his newly claimed city. Our school lined the street with the rest of the city when he left with his train of nobles: we knelt with heads bowed to the dust as the imperial thousands passed in silence. I peeked. Bolt upon bolt of *kimono* brocade rode by; men sat mounted on slow horses simply so as not to let their robes trail on the ground. I had never seen anything so solemn, so kaleidoscopic, so magnificent. Yukako pushed my head back to the packed earth, but not before glancing up herself. On their return journey, just as splendid, we lined the streets again, and again peeped.

A year later, in Meiji Two, I turned thirteen. The Emperor went to Edo again, and for a third time we lay prostrate in the street. When I looked, I gasped. Yukako kicked me, and gasped herself.

In the year between these two processions, we had heard that Buddhism was illegal; all priests and nuns were to leave their temples and go back to lay life. All Buddhist images were ordered out of Shinto shrines; all Shinto images were ordered out of Buddhist temples. The priests and statues had scattered for a few months and reappeared, most of them as if nothing had changed. Similarly, two years later the *eta*, polluted descendants of butchers and leather workers, were declared full citizens. This meant nothing to me at the time: I neither understood the words nor saw new actions. On the rare occasions when the Mountain ordered pork for his guests, the same man came as always, and as always, Chio treated him charily, making her transactions outside the servants' gate, sprinkling the threshold with water after he left.

Just so, though I had heard the Emperor had modernized his court, I expected nothing new when hundreds of men processed down

the street, some on horseback, most on foot. In the distance a palanquin, like a shrine carried through town on a festival day, floated over
streets and crowds alike. There, however, the resemblance to last year's
progress ended: they were all wearing Western clothes. In the sweet
May air of the Third Month, this company of men with hair oiled
back in topknots marched in bright striped trousers and swallowtail
coats, their shoulders built up with absurd epaulets, their chests made
over into pincushions for sashes, medals, and braid. I had not seen
trousers in three years and they seemed to me like stalks, like stems:
travesties. Yukako and I could not speak of what we'd seen because we
should not have looked up to see it.

Between these two processions, the Emperor fought a last battle
with his greatest enemies, the Matsudaira clan, from whom the
Shogun's ancestors—and the Mountain's family of birth—had first
sprung. The Mountain had been right to seek allies in the imperial
house, but he had the tact not to say so to his parents. His brother and
nephew—Sumie's father and brother—as minor Matsudairas, were
summoned to the clan fortress north of Miyako to fight the imperial
troops that poured in. Not among those killed, they were marched to
Edo for internment; whenever we visited in those dark weeks, we heard
the Pipe Lady worriedly extolling the courage of the Matsudaira *samurai* who had committed suicide rather than be taken alive. Her addled
ancient husband slipped away between one battle report and the next
so quickly I later wondered if he had died by his own hand, convinced
he was doing his part.

AMID ALL THE UNREST of those years when I was ten, eleven, twelve,
and thirteen, the meaning of comfort became for me Yukako's blended
scents as we slept on her floor: the beeswax in her hair, the minerals
from her bath, the cedar-and-geranium smell of the herbs she used to
ward moths away from silk, and fainter smells, too, incense and pow-

dered tea. *Yu-ka-ko* meant Evening Fragrance Child: her compounded smell was sweet and sharp, like fresh earth.

BY THE TIME I was thirteen, in the second year of Meiji, I had a grasp of spoken Japanese that mirrored, I think, the way Yukako read and wrote: multiple strands of information spun toward us and we knotted together a meaning using what we knew and what we expected to hear. I understood what was said to me because it was said *to me*, and in due course I had heard many times over the few hundred things anyone— Yukako and little Zoji excepted—ever said to me. I could only understand what people said to each other if I listened very carefully; I could say much less than I could understand. Just so, Yukako read richly illustrated books written in both Japanese alphabets: the ideographic Chinese characters, or *kanji*, that men used, and the simpler phonetic *kana* used by women. Taking in pictures, *kana*, and *kanji*, Yukako came away with a story because she expected a story. She could read a sentence aloud and explain it in detail, but if I pointed to a *kanji*, she became flustered and irritable; she couldn't tell me what it meant on its own, even though she had just used it in context to explain the sentence. She understood far more *kanji* than she could write.

Perhaps because there were so many words in Japanese with the same sounds, and because words were written withoutspacebetweenthem, *kanji* traveled alongside *kana* as a sort of silent archeology, the way our spelling gives clues to a word's origin. An ordinary speaker of English knows what a *conversation* is, a literate person can spell the word, an educated person will know it comes from Latin through French, and a specialist will know that *con* means *with* and *verse* means *turn.* A poet will hear *conversation* as a *turning together.* All the layers are there in English too. The Japanese had a few proverbs that broke down *kanji*—Sumie's demonstration of the *woman* and *child* in the word for *to like;* men in the bathhouse grumbling about their mates by noting the threefold

repetition of the *kanji* for *woman* in the *kanji* for *clamorous, kashi-mashi*—
but mostly I had to learn to see the clues in the *kanji* myself, my efforts
by turns annoying and amusing Yukako. She never gave the matter
much thought, except when new words came along, like *jinrikisha*.

What was the new sound on the packed-earth streets in the summer of Meiji Two? *Jinrikisha, jinrikisha.* Two enormous wheels making
such noise as even a crowd in wooden sandals could never achieve; two
poles for a runner to pull, hollering in his straw bowl hat and loin-
cloth; one black lacquered or brightly painted wooden shell to hold a
passenger or two; an awning in case of rain: this new form of trans-
portation swept Miyako with the same effervescence with which the
bicycle would later conquer *fin-de-siècle* Paris. It quickly became the
most ordinary thing in the world: even the old pointy-chinned *tofu*
man threw off his yoke and tubs for a wheeled cart. But though we
took it for granted within a few years, and though it leapt the sea to
become the dusty Old World *rickshaw* of every traveler's Indian diary,
the *jinrikisha* came as a shock to us. It hailed from Edo, as did all things
stylish.

One autumn day we stood at the temple before solemn Kannon, the
goddess of compassion, paying our morning call. Though Kannon was
the Buddhist face of the Shinto goddess to whom I had prayed my first
night in Miyako, I found the first stop on our daily pilgrimage—before
Benten-*sama*, the golden goddess of the lute—more jolly. Yukako
brought her hopes to the many-armed goddess; over time I heard her
name her father, a tune she was practicing on the *shamisen*, a particular
sequence in her *temae*. In emulation, I would pray to learn things better
too: how to use three verbs in a sentence correctly, how to hold the tea
bowl so it didn't slip, how to deflect the taunts of Miss Hazu at the
bathhouse.

To the other goddess, Kannon-*sama*, my older sister brought her
heavy heart. At first, after Akio's wedding, Yukako's jaw would tighten

when she lit incense at the temple, but in the three years that followed, she began to offer a short prayer for the health of Sumie's first, then second, then all three children. With time the bitterness of her disappointment, it seemed, reacted with the fascinated horror I heard in her voice—at living so far across Lake Biwa in Hikone, at having so many babies so quickly—so that it wasn't long before her prayers took on a certain vindictive cheer. In the first year of Meiji, Akio was wounded in battle against the Emperor's army and Sumie suffered a very difficult birth; by that fall morning in Meiji Two, Yukako's prayers had settled into a wary sincerity. For me, the gray lady, Kannon, looked like Mary Dolorosa in her mantle. While Yukako prayed, I would try to call forth my mother's face, experiencing a twinge of grief when I could see her wafting in the incense smoke, a twinge of guilt when I couldn't.

As Yukako's incense burned that morning, we heard the exotic clatter and the runner's cry: we turned and saw, through the heavy tiled temple gate, a Buddhist nun alighting in a *jinrikisha*. We gasped at each other; she looked so dashing, like a charioteer. Just outside the temple, we noticed as we left, there was a new bench with a painted sign: a wheel and three *kanji*. "Look!" said Yukako. *"Jinrikisha."*

Yukako showed me each character and explained how it added up to *jin-riki-sha, man-powered cart*. Two-stroke *jin* meant *person*. *Riki* looked like the letter *h*, like the bottom half of the character for *man*. "Strong," said Yukako, miming a *sumo* wrestler. Then she told me that *sha*—a box cut into quarters with a cross above it and below it—was *carriage*.

"Carriage?"

"Remember Lady Murasaki's book?" she prompted. "The jealous Rokujo Lady in the carriage?" Suddenly I remembered a storybook picture of a lady flirting by letting a long sleeve drape out her carriage window.

I looked at the Chinese character a long time, and then I saw a clue in those crosses above and below the box. "I see a carriage!" I said, excited. "A box"—I pointed—"and two wheels!"

Yukako looked at me, delighted, as if a pet dog had taught itself a new trick. *"Little Foreigner,"* she cooed. It was part of our secret language, the way I called her Older Sister in private and Young Mistress in public.

Suddenly, a second *jinrikisha* flooded the street with noise. Yukako looked from the flashing wheels to me and a smile crept across her face. Until the nun, we had never seen a woman in a *jinrikisha*. But if *she* could—as the runner stopped beside our bench, Yukako's eyes snapped with light—then why couldn't we? "I have money, why not?" she whispered, and took my hand. The young runner who bowed to us wore a cotton scarf rolled thin as a shoelace tied around his head. "Take us to the Palace gates," Yukako said.

I had traveled to the wharf by carriage with my Uncle Charles. I had traveled three oceans by ship. I had taken a night train, the enormous animal of it hurtling down the route that would become the Suez Canal. As the *jinrikisha* man broke into a jouncing run, approaching with great urgency the speed of a gently trotting horse, Yukako squeezed my hand so hard that I asked, "Have you ever gone so fast?"

"No!" she screamed, laughing, her loud voice masked by the runner's cries: *Abunai! Watch out! Abunai! Danger!* Then the force of the man stopping threw us deep into our seat. Before us the northern wall of the Palace enclosure stretched in both directions. A brace of helmeted *samurai* stood by the gate. Yukako looked disappointed. Did we really live so close to the Palace after all? "Now Nijo Castle!" she cried.

The *jinrikisha* man ran the length of the imperial preserve, then jogged west. During the mile from the north edge of the Palace grounds to the gates of Nijo Castle, Yukako kept my hand in hers, her eyes flung wide, trilling now and then in pleasure and terror.

With the Shogun gone, the vast fortress was occupied by only a few dozen imperial guards. Nonetheless, it loomed impressively as we approached the wall made of massive stones, the louring tiled gate, the murky green moat. When the runner lurched to a stop again, Yukako sat breathless, her cheeks red as if with wine. Now what? The runner looked at her. I looked at her. She looked down, uncertain, and up again at the sheer stone walls. In the wooden cup of the *jinrikisha*, with its painted pattern of red leaves, she seemed to shrink a little. We didn't belong there. "Well, I guess we'll walk home now," she said, counting out the fare. My eyes widened when I saw him run off with so much of our money, painted leaves flashing down the street. "Don't fret," said Yukako. "We'll have *sanma*. This is the one good time of year for them, actually. Can you carry it?" She'd save money twice this way: once on the humble fish, and once again on delivery. Was it worth a few minutes of Yukako's pleasure, this long clop back to the market street, then the blocks home walking behind her, a fish bucket heavy in my arms with its brick of ice?

"*Mochiron*," I said. *Of course.*

We passed the low Imperial Palace wall again, tended by a flock of old women digging out the luxuriant moss—prized, until recently—from between the stones. After we passed them, I asked, "The Shogun's never coming back, is he?"

Yukako grunted: it was a silly question.

"And the Emperor?"

Behind the Palace wall rose red trees and bare trees, dusty-looking bamboo. The Emperor was still in Edo, newly named *Eastern Capital*, or *Tokyo*, just as Miyako had been newly renamed *Kyoto*, or *Capital City*. "I don't know," Yukako murmured.

"Remember those clothes?" I used another newly coined word, like *Tokyo*, or *Kyoto*, or *jinrikisha: yofuku*, Western clothing.

"You saw nothing!" Yukako said sternly, then held back a smirk.

"I saw nothing," I repeated solemnly. Yukako walked as if in a dream and I could see that procession floating before her eyes too:

those long, exposed chicken legs in their striped trousers, all that garish gilt and braid. I stood on tiptoe and made my voice ghoulish. *"I saw nothing,"* I whispered in her ear.

"Stop it!" she insisted, giggling.

As I COPIED OUT the character for *jinrikisha* under Yukako's watchful eye when we returned, the smell of grilling fish climbed toward us. Then Chio climbed the stairs herself: "Your father wants you to eat with him in Baishian," she told Yukako.

We looked at each other, surprised. "And I?" I asked.

"You can bring the lunches."

"PLEASE MAY SHE STAY IN HERE?" asked Yukako as I set the stacked *bento* boxes before the Mountain. Father and daughter faced each other across the polished floorboard of the little teahouse.

"She can wait in the *mizuya* in case we need anything," he said, no small concession considering how rarely an *in case* comes up in tea ceremony. I retreated to the *mizuya*, the little one-mat preparation area backstage from the tearoom. All the tea implements stood ready by the sliding door, while at the far end of the mat, shelves of utensils sat above a wet area: a barrel of water for cleaning tea things, a bamboo grille set over a drain. As I knelt on the polished wooden floor between the *tatami* and the drain, I heard a hollow metallic pop beneath me: in a teahouse, extra charcoal was stored in a metal-lined bin under the wooden *mizuya* floor. A tightly latticed window by the drain offered a look into the tearoom; I could see Yukako's face and the back of the Mountain's head. When she glanced at the doorway as if waiting for me, the Mountain, more sad than angry, chided, "You are not a little girl on Dolls' Day."

"Hai," Yukako assented. She bowed, visibly stung. As she and her father ate silently, I gnawed on the rice ball Chio had tucked into my

sleeve. The season for the sunken hearth had not yet come; instead, a cauldron of water sang over a brazier on the Mountain's mat: the charcoal glowed red in a carefully finished bed of scooped ash. The room was brightest by the crawl-through entrance, the square door left open to the warmish day. When they had finished, the Mountain cleared away the lacquer food boxes and began to carry in the tea implements, his face registering neither annoyance nor thanks when I moved the *bento* boxes out of his way.

Today he set before Yukako a single sugared rice cracker shaped like a leaf; I noted its meagerness with admiration: I had been with the Shins long enough to know the tearoom was no place to pile on sweets. In the sweltering summer, the Mountain had used a squat dark vessel filled with water drawn so deep from the cold well that the jar sweat dew. Now, in mid-autumn, the water jar he carried out was tall and narrow, brightly painted with gourds. Yukako had not yet let me learn the *temae* her father performed, but I followed as best I could his practiced, modest gestures.

My eyes were accustomed to the lurching, start-and-stop lessons of the new students, the almost angry vigor of the apprentices as they suppressed the desire to show the one-year students, *There, once and for all,* this *is how it's done!* And of course I was used to Yukako's crisp waterbird motions, the way her long body took all the space it needed on the host's mat. But I saw the Mountain make tea only when the whole household gathered for holidays, his *temae* quiet as spilt water spreading on a wood floor, natural as Chio cooking rice. Not effortless like sleeping, but effortless like walking, both awkwardness and fanfare long forgotten. How beautiful, to see something done simply and well.

Yukako drank deep and formally invited her father to join her. He bowed assent, cleaned the bowl, and spooned in powdered tea. Before adding the dipper of boiling water, he turned his kneeling body to face her. Her eyes widened at this break in form. "The teahouse and the world are separate," he began. "But . . ." I could not understand what he told her next. I leaned in closer, hoping he would repeat himself, wondering what could light her face with such grim comprehension.

"You still have your students," she assured him.

"I suppose," he said. I heard him say the word *marry*. "I am sorry you will have to wait."

Yukako bowed, expressionless. "You're a young man, Father." He was not a young man.

"I will write a letter," he said, and told her what he hoped a letter would yield. Yukako nodded. I didn't understand.

"It was good you bought that fish," he said. She flinched. I never heard a Japanese parent say, *I am proud of you*, but Yukako's father added, "Your mother was good with money too."

Yukako bowed deeply to cover her face. A yellow ginkgo leaf blew in through the open door. The Mountain made his bowl of tea and drank, less mournful, more hopeful. "This really is the one good time of year for *sanma*," he said.

After the last or only guest drinks, the host rinses the bowl with clean water, then pours that water out into a waste bowl. In that moment of pouring, if the honored guest is silent, it's a sign to the host to make another bowl of tea. Otherwise the guest says, as Yukako said now, quietly, "Please finish."

"No second cup?" the Mountain asked.

"WHAT DID YOUR FATHER SAY?" I asked that night.

Yukako sighed. She opened her mouth to tell me, then closed it. "You'll see soon enough, won't you?" she said at last.

"Did he hear about the *jinrikisha* ride? Was he upset?"

"No," she said, ashamed.

9

1870

Y UKAKO'S FATHER had told her what the Meiji Restoration would mean for the Shins. It explained why we had *sanma* more than once that winter, as Meiji Two became Meiji Three, even when it wasn't the best time of year for them. It explained why, instead of *kimono* fabric, all we servants received for New Year's were imperially mandated last names: I became Migawa Urako. And it explained why, when the cherry blossoms fell, no new students joined us, and those who remained were shepherded home by their fathers, newly destitute since the revolution.

With the students of the Long Room left the women of the sewing house, and even Chio's daughter Kuga took little Zoji away to go work for what was left of the Pipe Lady's family. Only women and children remained in the sprawling Canal Street house with the moon-viewing pond: Sumie was in Hikone; her father and older brother were interned in Edo.

When Kuga moved into the Pipe Lady's house, her husband Goto claimed their son. His new wife had a boy of her own, so he hired Zoji out for cash to pay off a gambling debt. Zoji's new master, Lord Ii of

Hikone, Akio's father, was a man known for his fine bay horses: small as Zoji was, he could still fetch water and curry what steeds His Lordship hadn't yet sold. I missed the boy terribly; Kuga must have missed him more.

Without students, gardeners, or sewing-girls, without Kuga and Zoji, the five of us—Yukako, the Mountain, Chio, Matsu, and myself—sealed all the unused furniture away into the storage tower, the quicker to clean the floors of the deserted house. Under Chio's instruction, Yukako and I struggled to sew up our own *kimono*, which required taking apart with each washing. We packed our showy robes in herbs and cedar and wore only dull, practical garb, while all around us merchants' daughters wore brighter colors than we'd ever seen, thanks both to the end of the Shogun's sumptuary laws and the influx of new British dyes.

I never knew when May second fell for sure, but I always knew my birthday came sometime in the Third or Fourth Month, when the peonies bloomed, both in the gardens and on the lavish gilt screen the Pipe Lady had bought from an impoverished courtier, a man of the *kuge* nobility she scorned. In the display alcove on Canal Street that year, however, I saw only a peony in a vase and a scroll with a pen-and-ink butterfly, standard fare for early summer. "Where's the screen?" I asked.

"You might as well give a gold coin to a cat," Yukako's grandmother snapped. "This is an antique." She gave me a hard rap on the side of the head with the metal bowl of her tobacco pipe, and Yukako repeatedly apologized for my rudeness. The Pipe Lady muttered a number of angry words, among them *kuge*.

"But—" I whispered.

"But what?" the Pipe Lady wheeled on me.

"Nothing, I'm sorry. I'm sorry. The butterfly is very beautiful."

I was spared more of her attention by the arrival of an older woman attended by a young girl carrying a *shamisen* case. The new guest was homely, her face constellated with moles, but she had a kind of threadbare elegance. She chatted stiffly with the Pipe Lady, and Yukako and I slipped away.

Later, at home in the abandoned sewing room, Yukako probed my temple with a fingertip. "Better?"

I nodded.

"I'm sorry she did that, Ura-*bo*. This has been hard for all of us."

I nodded again.

"You see, they hadn't finished paying off the screen. They had to sell it."

"Oh," I said, my voice very small.

"And the only buyer they could find was from the Emperor's court."

"The *kuge*?"

"Exactly." Until just recently, the *kuge*, nobility from the age before the Shoguns came to power, had subsisted on slender handouts from the Shogun, while *samurai* families like the Pipe Lady's took home ample stipends of rice.

When I nodded again my eyes were big with tears. I couldn't say why I missed that gilt screen so much. *I'm too old for this nonsense*, I thought, but again I whispered, "But—"

"But what?" said Yukako, more kindly than her grandmother had.

"But it's my birthday—" I tried to explain.

"Ura-*bo*," she soothed, pushing back a wisp of my hair. "How old are you?"

"Fourteen," I said.

"So grown up! We should find a husband for you soon."

"No!" I said. Did she want me to marry and leave her? "I'm too young."

"Well, then," she said fondly, "we'll tell the hairdresser to leave you alone another year." At the bathhouse, one or two girls my age had already shown up with their hair slicked hard with wax and combs, and even Miss Hazu had begun wearing ladies' leather shoes, changing her stylish clog-thongs every two weeks. I still wore my hair in a soft bun like a young girl and clomped around in wooden sandals. "Hm?" said Yukako, when I did not reply.

"Thank you," I said, and my heart flopped with relief.

The air was cool and misty, so we kept a pot of ordinary green tea on a brazier and drank it to keep warm; it was more pleasant to sit with the *shoji*-paper doors slid open to the day than to huddle inside with our lamps. Except for our bathhouse *kimono* and the robes we had on—and the lovely silks we'd packed away—all our clothes (and the Mountain's, and Chio's, and Matsu's) lay around us in various states of unreadiness: strips of picked-apart *kimono* and their linings, like fabric bundled with like. Tubs stood filled for washing, whether ready with clean water or already soaking out the worst dirt. Boards leaned against the wall with *kimono* fabric stretched over them for flat drying. All *kimono* fabric was woven to a width one-third the short side of a *tatami* mat—about a foot across—so the drying boards were long and narrow. We would peel the dried panels off the boards, then sew our long dull seams, fretting over how to set the neck strip right, how to make the curved corners match on both sleeves. Our necks hurt. Our eyes hurt. We kept strips of cotton ready to wrap our fingers, so as not to bleed on our handiwork.

All day I'd felt forlorn and achy. I was always a little melancholy this season, having to remind Yukako it was my birthday again. Though she indulged me if I pestered her, a birthday just wasn't something people fussed over: every year, no matter what month we were born, we all ate toasted soybeans on New Year's Eve, a number equal to our age plus one—and suddenly we were all a year older. I knew vaguely that little Zoji had been born in the winter, but there was no way I could have missed Boys' Day, with its irises and carp-shaped streamers, considering the little god Chio and Kuga would make of him each year in early summer. And both Yukako and I were cosseted and plied with emperor and empress dolls on Girls' Day, fed sweets in our very best silks. It was a fair enough trade, I supposed, but what I wouldn't give that day for dinner at a table, a new ribbon tied in my hair, my mother, yes, even my uncle singing to me, what I wouldn't give for potatoes and garlic baked in wine and cream. For a cake, a candle, a wish. I touched my throat, longing again for my Saint Claire medal.

Perhaps that's what the gold screen had meant to me, some birthday ritual: my stomach hurt with missing it, with my May melancholy, with indignation at being struck on the head, with the panic I'd felt when Yukako talked of marrying me off. Or maybe it was just something I ate. I set my sewing aside and rubbed my belly gently. I felt oozy inside. Did I need to go use the toilet? When I stood, I heard a soft tap and Yukako gasped. "Ura-*bo*," she said sharply, and swiftly slid the *shoji* door closed.

"What? What?"

"Very carefully, take off your sash," she said. I took a step back from a second soft tap on the floor and saw two round spots of blood on the *tatami* matting.

Yukako helped me unknot the cord and two scarves holding my *obi* in place. I turned slowly and she gathered the ten-foot sash into her arms. She peeled the *kimono* off me and held it in the air. "See?"

My *kimono* was mouse-blue striped with pale gray, a murky, forgiving color combination that approximated City Dust plus House Dust. It forgave nothing, however, of the blood that spread across the seat and tapped once again on the floor. "Do you have any others upstairs?"

"Just my bathhouse one, and——" I pointed at the half-sewn robe I'd been working on. "They're all here."

Yukako sighed. She put my stained robe in a tub to soak, then tugged my cotton underrobe so that I was bleeding snugly into it instead of onto the floor. "Stay where you are," she said, and wiped down the *tatami* with a rag.

"Am I dying?" I asked.

Yukako had broken down the crisis into tasks and was performing them as efficiently as possible. Her face softened at my question. "No," she said, careful not to laugh at me. I believed her. "I'll be right back."

WHAT HAD HAPPENED to change everything for the Shins—and what Yukako's father had told her on the day of the *jinrikisha* ride—was this: at the end of the second year of Meiji, the Emperor decreed an end to the feudal aristocracy. On the night of his restoration, he had announced that he was taking back all the land he had entrusted to the Shogun and his lords, and all the rice money that the land yielded. In place of a hereditary warrior caste, each man loyal to his liege, the Emperor now announced that in a few years' time he would establish an army conscripted from boys of all origins, loyal to himself alone. To do this, and to fund the new government, he cut loose all the lords and *samurai* who had benefited from the Shogun's largesse for two hundred fifty years. For the Mountain, this meant no more tuition from the students, whose fathers had paid him from their rice stipends, and no more income from the three lords he served as tea master, who until now had paid him enough rice to feed three thousand men a year. Worse still, the Emperor announced a program of *Bunmei Kaika*, Civilization and Enlightenment, dismissing tea, like falconry or incense-guessing games, as an archaic "pastime," better abandoned than subsidized. That spring the *samurai* fathers, with no money for tea, had taken their sons home from the Shins', while the merchants, amid the tumult, had cautiously followed suit. It had been very quiet at our house since the students left.

While news came that the Emperor was having all his lords and soldiers cut off their topknots, the Mountain waited fruitlessly for a response to the appeal he'd made for help. Every day he made extra offerings to the ancestors, setting a bowl of tea before the statue of his adopted forefather, Rikyu, then making one for himself in Cloud House.

Rikyu, the founding ancestor of tea ceremony and tea teacher to Hideyoshi, the most important warlord of his day, was forced to commit suicide once he'd ceased to please his master. The tearoom Cloud House was built in the style favored by Rikyu's grandson, Sotan, a man so beggared by his grandfather's disgrace that his favorite tea-scoop was the one worn on the side from years of use. When his luck changed for the better, Sotan had a one-and-a-half-mat hut built to keep himself honest, to honor the years he'd spent in his own company. A generation later, his oldest son Shinso built a copy of the tiny house on his own property, to memorialize his family's hardship: this was our Cloud House, where the Mountain drank his dwindling store of tea.

"Every rich man talks about escaping the world and living a monk's life," I remembered Matsu saying one night on the way to the bathhouse. "But it's so forlorn, his look when he sits alone in that little room. There used to be so many of us," he sighed.

"He'll be fine," Chio said almost harshly.

YUKAKO RETURNED with my bathhouse *kimono* and some packets of soft paper, which she taught me how to use and where to burn. She also brought a second iron kettle for the brazier. "O-Chio made this for you," she said, giving me a bitter-smelling cup when I rubbed my belly again. "It'll help." Then she set my underrobe to soak as well. "You can wash at the bathhouse tonight, but don't soak in the tub with the others when the blood's heavy."

"When will it stop?"

"In about five days," she assured me. That seemed manageable, if unpleasant. "And then you'll bleed every month until your first grand-daughter does." I laughed. "No, I mean it." Sumie had borne her first child at sixteen, but that still seemed like an awfully long time. I remembered then that sometimes Chio or Kuga didn't soak at the bathhouse; I hadn't thought about it before. I wrapped both arms around myself and groaned a little when the cramp came again. Like little Zoji, like a spoiled baby girl, I pillowed my head on Yukako's leg and kept sewing my dim seam where I lay.

"You miss your mother," she said. I nodded. She nodded. "I remember the feeling." I felt her awareness drift away—perhaps toward her own first monthlies, perhaps toward the little she knew of her own mother—and then felt her flinch as she cut her finger on the sharp seam-ripping blade, catching blood in her lap. "*Ara!*" she cried.

I pulled away. "This is your last clean one, too, isn't it?"

"Not anymore," Yukako said, putting her finger in her mouth and lifting her skirt-panel so the little spot wouldn't touch anything else.

Gingerly, so as not to dislodge my new paper diaper, I went to bring her clean water. If I had learned how to move around in a *kimono*, I could learn how to negotiate this too. "The water in the basin's red," I said. "I have to go out to the well."

"No, look at you," she said. She stood up.

"It's just a dot," I consoled her. "You can't even see it."

"Yes you can," she snapped. She sat down in a ball and hid her face in her bare arms. She sighed. No, she was crying. "I can't do this," she whispered. "Go to the well and fill two buckets and bring them back and fill a tub and take off my *kimono* and soak it and sew myself another one before dinner—" She broke off. Since the students and the sewing-women's departure, she had tied back her *kimono* sleeves like a servant and followed Chio's instructions to the letter, laughing at her own crooked work. Now she sobbed. "I didn't grow up like this. I'm not ready. I can't."

When she wept for Akio at sixteen, Yukako had seemed voluptuous, monstrous, womanly. Now, at twenty, she seemed thin and ashy, all girlish knees and elbows. I touched her tentatively, stroking her back. "Yes you can," I said gently. "You can get used to anything."

She looked up; she wore the same face that had frightened me the night she came late from Akio's. Her forehead was smeared, her eyebrow paint printed on her wrists, a black butterfly. "Maybe *you* can," she said.

My mouth fell open as the hard points of her words sank into me. My adaptability endeared me to her, but she did not respect it. This was the side of her that desperation revealed: a person who refused to *get used to anything.* "I'm not going to do this," she said calmly. "It's not my job."

Hurt, I watched as she untied her work-strings and her long sleeves spilled down. She reached into the brazier and lifted out the round iron kettle, holding it up as if to show me. In the *shoji*-filtered light, I could make out a pattern of sinuous dragonlike horses, iron on iron. Then a hint of smoke curled up my nostrils and I realized that Yukako was holding her sleeve over the brazier on purpose. "What are you doing?" I demanded.

Though a practical brown cotton, Yukako's *kimono* was cut in the showy style of an unmarried girl, her sleeves so long that as she stood there, the tip of a sleeve moved among the coals in the brazier, brushing white ash off their red faces. Her expression as she watched was devoid of anything but curiosity. The long banner of her sleeve smoked and charred, then flamed. It looked like a wing. The smell of burning fabric hit me square-on and lifted me into the air in a rage. I tackled her, using my body and my robe to smother her. "Stupid *baka fille!*" I screamed in three languages.

Her body under mine was hard and narrow. Soon I would be stronger. I was aware of this, and that as much as I wanted to shake or strike her, I didn't want to give the fire any air. So I held her, like a stack of drying boards. "Don't *ever* do that again," I panted. The air was quiet except for our frightened breathing. When I thought it was safe, I eased away. My own robe was blackened in places and the room stank.

Yukako blinked, stunned. *"Hai,"* she said. With deliberation, she drizzled Chio's tea over the remains of her sleeve to make sure any sparks were out, then attended to me and the floor. A charred fleck of cloth made a smear on the *tatami,* so she took the whole *kimono* off, inspecting her *obi* and sashes for damage as carefully as she had mine. When everything was tidily in place, she tied back her sleeves, knelt formally in her *kimono* undergown, and addressed me. "I'm sorry."

For hurting my feelings or nearly killing us both? "Thank you," I said sullenly.

"It was a stupid thing to do. I suppose we should start work again, no?"

We sewed all afternoon in the waning light, and with lamps into the evening. I sat very quietly with my needle. I didn't want to cozy up to Yukako: I wanted to watch what she did next. She sat quietly, too, perhaps as afraid of herself as I was.

After night fell, Yukako cleared her throat. "Before the Shin family adopted my father, he was a *samurai,*" she said, tilting her chin in the direction of Sumie's house. "You know, when they were boys, their father was rich, but they had to go without food for days. They had to go without sleep for nights. The monks would beat them if their heads drooped. They had to stand under a river." Yukako paused to explain the word for *waterfall.* I tried to imagine the Mountain and Sumie's father as boys, side by side in the drilling cold gallons. "Everything to get strong. But look what happened anyway."

I looked at her, still shaken. What was she driving at? "It's easy to be a warrior if there's no war," she said softly.

I didn't understand her. I didn't want to draw her out. She had scared me, and it was hard to forgive her. She tied a knot at the end of her seam and snipped off the thread. "Women get paid to do this," she said, as if this thought followed logically on the last.

"Not much," I said, curious in spite of my anger.

"Not much," she agreed. "We had a sewing-girl for every student."

We looked bleakly at the pile of sewing before us. "And as hair-dressers," Yukako said.

"What?"

"And o-Chio sells vegetables from Mr. Matsu's garden."

Oh. I followed her again. "Those old ladies digging moss out of the Palace wall last year, they probably got paid."

Yukako gave me a withering smile. "Yes, and whores and *geiko* make money too."

"Wait! Who was that lady at your grandmother's house when we left? The lady with the raindrop pattern?" I dotted moles on my face with my finger, groping for the word.

Yukako touched her face quizzically. "Oh, *hokuro!* Yes, that poor *kuge* woman; it's just the same as before the war; she's still going from house to house teaching music . . ."

Sumie's baby sister, like Yukako, like any *samurai* girl, studied flower-arranging and *shamisen*. Even now? From what I heard, Akio's father was that foolish, selling most of his fine horses to pay keep for a few, but the Pipe Lady's family too? "You mean they sold the screen and they're still paying for music lessons?"

Yukako looked at me hard. "Why, yes, they are," she said. She unwrapped her bound finger and looked at her hands in the lamplight.

On the walk home that night, dressed in one of Yukako's bathhouse robes, I saw Chio give me an appraising look. "It'll be hard to find a husband for you," she finally said as we walked some distance behind Matsu, "considering"—she gestured toward the Shin house to avoid speaking of their misfortune—"and considering"—she gestured toward my queer, big-nosed, droop-eyed face, to avoid speaking of its lack of appeal. With a flash of anger, I thought of Yukako setting her sleeve on fire. I could *so* find a husband; I could leave; let Yukako pay for her stupidity without me. But then I thought of Matsu snoring, the hair in his ears and nostrils. "I can wait; it's all right," I said. Chio nodded grateful approval.

When I came home, Yukako was kneeling in her room with all her silk robes laid around her. She looked up at me and nodded a tiny greeting bow. "Do you remember the way to Koito's house?"

10

1870

Even more than their beauty, *geisha* were known for their style. The morning after Yukako burned her sleeve, I shied from her touch. Still shaken, I dressed myself alone for the first time, struggling with my robes and ties. Yukako watched me coolly in her mirror as she painted on her eyebrows. "Not bad," she said. I could tell she was unhappy with the results, but I didn't want her help. I yanked and pushed, sweating into my gauze undershirt, and at length she rose. "May I?" she said, in a voice that brooked no refusal. She retied my *obi* knot and gave it a final pat. "I need you to look good today."

Koito's neighborhood, Pontocho, stood across the river from Gion, another *geisha* quarter. During the heady time when both the Emperor and the Shogun lived in Miyako, and the years of intrigue that preceded it, the southern rebels—among them, the man who would become the prime minister—drank and plotted in Gion, on the soft slopes of Maruyama, while the Shogun's loyalists held their parties— and their secret meetings—by the river in Pontocho. Now, since the war, most Gion *geisha*, including the woman who would become the prime minister's wife, had followed their patrons to Tokyo, while most

Pontocho *geisha* had stayed behind to mourn men dead or in exile. Only a few lucky ones still had patrons in newly named Kyoto, selling off their treasures one by one.

I walked the single slender street of the unlucky quarter, my wooden sandals clopping on the packed earth. The few other sounds seemed especially loud: a dog trotting up the street behind me, its toes clicking; an old woman splashing water across her stone threshold with a ladle. We both looked up at the sound of a single musician in an upstairs room, rending the street with a wail. A grim look flickered across the old woman's face as she gave the stones a final splash. And then someone stepped out of a fan shop: I almost shouted. "Miss Inko!"

Koito's servant wore the same yellow plaid *obi* as she had four years before. She recognized me. "Are you still with Miss Koito?" I asked. "May I follow you to her house? My Young Mistress wanted to see her—"

"Wait, slow down," said Inko. Her eyes widened as I explained myself. Yes, she still served Miss Koito. "But we moved in with her mother. You're lucky you saw me. I'm only here because she sent me out for this—" She pointed at her fan-shop package. "Do you have time to follow me? It's a long walk."

I *was* lucky. There was a family altar by the fan maker's house: I left a little coin in the box and went with Inko north again. "After you?" she said.

She was offering, I realized, to walk behind me, attentive to the difference in our mistresses' rank. It seemed silly: I didn't know where I was going. "Let's walk side by side," I said. She gave me a surprised smile. We walked almost three miles north and west to the weavers' quarter: I heard the sound of beating looms. When a great leafy shrine grove came into view, we turned onto a street of pretty townhouses bursting with screeches and twangs. The discord of women practicing many different tunes on many different instruments was welcome after the sour damp silence of Pontocho. "Here we are," said Inko. "Kamishichiken."

"*Kami* Seven Quarter? *Kami*, like gods? Hair?"

"*Kami* like north, silly," Inko chuckled. "A long time ago the shrine hall burned down in a fire," she explained, pointing to the nearby grove. "When they rebuilt it, they used the wood left over to build seven *geiko* houses."

Oh: the Northern Seven-House Quarter. "It looks different here." The buildings were unusual—tall, like temples, but close together like city homes: for a moment I could have been in New York. As we approached one of the long-faced houses, I heard a woman singing with a hand drum upstairs. "Young Mistress's mother," Inko whispered. "The best dancer of her generation." I understood the word only later, when I asked Yukako: what I had heard was that Koito's mother was the best dancer of her *height*, and I had tried to picture a very tall or very short *geisha*.

"I'll do what I can," said Inko. She brought in the little parcel Yukako had sent with me for Koito, had me wait on the cloakroom bench with a cup of tea, and ten minutes later reappeared. "Can Young Mistress Shin come tomorrow?"

WHEN THEY FACED each other for the first time since that rainy night years before, Koito again stood a step higher, looking down from inside the *tatami*-floored house while Yukako looked up from the packed-earth cloakroom. For a moment they simply looked at each other, the beauty and the colt. Yukako, holding in her tight jaw and sucked-in breath all the nights she'd spent awake hating this woman, had grown thinner and harder in four years, while Koito seemed as fresh and smooth as before. "Come in, come in," she said, after kneeling to bow her greetings. "You'll settle a quarrel between me and my mother. She insists that these sweets are from Toraya and I'm convinced that they're from

Tawaraya. We need an expert." I'm guessing this is what she said; she used the baroque speech of the singing-girls. What I heard clearly were the names of the two confectionery shops most relied upon by the Shin family. I think it was a ploy to make Yukako relax her guard: sweets had worked on me four years before; they worked on Yukako now.

I think Yukako imagined icily transacting her business with Koito in the cloakroom in a matter of minutes, to minimize her humiliation; she gave me a backward glance as Koito solicitously whisked her inside. What were they saying? I wished I'd gotten a second look at Koito's ensemble, instead of just a flash of pink and gold. I'd been too absorbed in looking at her face in that first moment as she registered Yukako's unease: though pleasant, it made me think of a *Noh* theater mask, white and impassive even without the thick layer of paint she'd worn for Akio. I was sitting with Yukako's two *kimono*, primed to get an eyeful the next chance I had, when Inko appeared and asked me to bring in my package.

I followed her to the room of honor by the garden, its *shoji* doors thrown open to the blooming paulownia tree outside. In a vase in the display alcove, a slender vine wound about a long white feather, while behind it hung a portrait scroll of a calm, graceful-looking old man with funny frog lips. He had long earlobes like Yukako's—like the statue in the Shin family shrine! And wait—wasn't the Shin family symbol a great white bird—a crane? The whole room was a letter to Yukako.

The two women faced each other over a low ebony table, where two steamed bean cakes had dainty crescents slivered out of them. "You can stay," Yukako said when I set the large heavy package down beside her. Flustered, I knelt, eyes fixed on the brocade edges of the *tatami* matting as Koito refused politely twice, as was customary, and then refused a third time. I had never actually heard someone decline a gift a third time, though I knew to do so meant a real refusal. I felt Yukako startle. I looked up.

Koito was layered inside the most brilliant, yet subtlest, plumage the new aniline dyes had to offer. While Yukako bloused up her long *kimono* at the waist like any practical *samurai* daughter, Koito's skirts trailed behind her on the *tatami* like a fine lady's; in deference to the season, she wore a robe of peonies—gold-green leaves and creamy pink petals—on a slate field. It was part of a set of five robes; I could see the nested vees of color where the collars of her underrobes were exposed: pale green, deep green, fuchsia, saffron. She wore a gold-on-gold *obi* in a pattern of feathers, with a deep-pink accent cord and dappled undersash. Clearly she didn't need Yukako's *kimono*. Her complexion was pearly and fine, her expression, as she threw Yukako's offering back in her face, was not cruel but serious. "I have another idea," she said.

Yukako listened as Koito wove her proposal in flowery, sidelong phrases. I had no idea what she was saying—conditional verbs, the words *art* and *treasure*—but Yukako understood, and knifed a brusque word through the web. "Absolutely not."

A direct no? I recoiled from the insult, but Koito calmly sipped her tea, *Noh*-faced, half smiling. My heart beat as fast as it had two days before, when Yukako burned her sleeve. *You stupid stupid!* How could you so affront someone whose help you've come to seek? And at the same time, I wondered, what had Koito proposed that would so offend Yukako? Did she offer to auction off Yukako's purity? (At fourteen, I knew from bathhouse gossip that a girl's *junketsu* was her treasure, and that whores sold theirs—this last repeated with disgust and fascination—but I was a little hazy on the details.) Was my sensible older sister being tempted into a glittering life of sin? Could I go with her?

Koito set down her cup and fired her dart. "Your grandmother taught *temae* after all, you know."

Yukako's spluttering cough dispersed my lurid fancy. The air in the room changed. Yukako gathered herself, stunned. "Indeed."

"Yes, she taught your mother."

Koito spoke again, like quick plucked strings. I heard *secret*, and
kohki—a word for *aristocratic* or for *opportunity*. Yukako had her eyes lowered to the table; she absentmindedly thrust at her sweet with its spicewood pick and ate it in large bites. Koito changed the subject. "In any
case, I'll draw you a map," she offered. "Shall I send Miss Inko along
with you?"

A map? To what? And how would Inko help? I didn't know; I just
heard that Koito was offering one favor piled up on another, and I
watched Yukako as she weighed her trepidation about a new place
against her distaste for being indebted to this woman. *I'm not afraid*, her
face said. "I can manage," she decided.

Koito's eyes lit, briefly, with respect. "As you wish."

I FOLLOWED YUKAKO down the long way to Pontocho the next day. She
gave me her sunshade to hold and squeezed my hand a little by the
pawnshop door, as if I were the one who was nervous. I heard an old
man's voice within, and the *tick-tick* of abacus beads. Upon leaving,
Yukako glided quickly through the quarter, her face hidden by her
parasol. She took the river route home. I know it was a pawnshop
because I had to carry the bundled *kimono* on the way downtown, but
carried nothing on the way home. "Did he give you a lot of money?"
I asked.

"Some."

"Will you spend it on music-teacher lessons from Miss Koito?"

"They're not for sale," she said. "I'm going to see if we can't hire
Chio's daughter back, for a spell."

"Are we going back to Miss Koito's house?"

"I'm not sure."

"Was that a picture of your ancestor she had in the alcove?"

"Yes," Yukako said impatiently, her voice flat and cold. She halted,
spread her empty carrying-scarf on the stone embankment, and sat

down. I knelt on the cloth beside her, looking down at the Kamo River, and across it at Daimonji, the green hill with the *kanji* for *great* carved in its side: *dai*. Large quick waterbirds blinked in and out of sight, snatching fish out of the river. Yukako threw them a toasted *sembei* now and then. At first the bits of rice cracker flew up, then arced down, but once the birds took note, they snapped up each cracker before it even reached the top of its tossed arc. We watched the river and the birds, their fluid white flickering bodies. They were wind made flesh. Then Yukako tossed a stone, and a bird snatched it from the air, unharmed. Her face hardened. *"Yes!"* she hissed, fierce and bright. "I'll do it."

"Do what?" I squeaked. I knew she wouldn't answer.

Over the next few mornings, always after the Mountain made his daily offering to the ancestors, always before he began to eat the meal Yukako set before him, I witnessed a series of strained, sidelong conversations between father and daughter. As I knelt in the doorway of the garden study, I heard the words *dream* and *Kitano Shrine*. I heard Kuga's name. Did she say that Kuga would work for food alone? I could not understand the whole of what Yukako said, but I knew she was lying.

WHATEVER WORDS HAD PASSED between Yukako and her father, a week later Chio's whey-faced daughter returned to wash and sew, sometimes with Yukako's and my help, sometimes alone. It was painful to see Kuga without little Zoji, to know her son was working off a term of indenture to pay his father's gambling debts. What had Lord Ii sold to pay for years of a boy's life? A horse? Half a horse? Kuga was an anomaly, a grown-up girl cast off by her husband, now childless. She was ashamed of imposing on her parents when the Shins had so little, so she'd worked like a young unmarried girl at Sumie's house until Yukako hired her back. Once again I trailed behind her back and forth to the bathhouse at night, and once again ate a silent evening meal with her and Chio and Matsu, feeling the sour weight of their disappointment.

The day after Kuga's return, I followed Yukako, bulky boxes in my arms, to the narrow streets and high walls of the northern *geisha* quarter. When the dense greenery of the sacred grove came into sight, Yukako pointed. "Kitano Shrine. I told him I'm coming here every day to pray."

"He believes you?"

"*Mukashi mukashi*," she began, which is how Japanese fairy tales begin: *Long, long ago . . .* "I know you remember the picture in Koito's alcove," she prompted me.

"Your ancestor."

"Rikyu. He favored a humble tea," she said, using a word that also meant *forlorn*. "Tea in a straw hut. Nothing showy, not even flowers in the spring. Just a shoot of green through the snow was spring enough for him." I was so happy; she was talking poetry and I could finally understand. "He was the tea master for the warlord Hideyoshi. They were very close for a time, and together they held the largest tea gathering the world has ever known, right here in these woods by Kitano Shrine. Then they drifted apart: Rikyu wanted a two-mat hut, Hideyoshi wanted a great tearoom made of gold. In the end, Hideyoshi required Rikyu to commit *seppuku*." Ritual suicide? I knew about it from the games of the noisy little brothers at Sumie's house. They were sober-faced young men now, but as children, between bouts of chasing their sisters and Miss Miki, the hairdressers' daughter, they had gigglingly ordered one another to commit *seppuku*. "I die for honor!" the older one cried. "I die for honor *and* forbidden passion!" shouted the younger one, giving pretty Miki's sleeve a tug. They'd mime slitting their bellies, then compose grim poems and die manfully on the veranda again and again, pushing their imaginary intestines back into their stomachs. I couldn't imagine it really happening—and certainly not to anyone in Yukako's family.

"And so I *do* pray here," Yukako continued. "That Rikyu's good fortune will befall us, and that his bad fortune will pass us by. Imagine this whole grove filled with tea people. It happened once," she said. She gave me a coin to toss in the shrine box, and I set down my packages, pulled the bell-rope, bowed, clapped, and bowed behind her. Then I followed her into the *geisha* quarter.

You might as well give gold to a cat, it took so long for Japanese music to grow on me. I had grown up on Latin hymns and New York street music—the accordion, the fife and drum, the Irish fiddle—and my mother's craggy French alto, her love songs and lullabies. These had not prepared me for the meowl, the twang, the start-and-stop of Japanese music. I sat in the packed-earth cloakroom at Koito's as I did when Yukako practiced at home, alternately bored and grated upon, happiest when Inko appeared with tea and treats, a glint in her eye. "Your Young Mistress is good, huh?"

Japanese is fraught with little crises of etiquette: say yes and risk the rudeness of bragging about your own household, or say no and risk the rudeness of disloyalty? "She's trying," I offered.

"No, she's quite good," Inko insisted brashly. "I live here, I should know." She vanished back into the house. Why had I been so careful? Wasn't this the girl who called her own employer's mother "the best dancer of her generation"? I liked her, I realized, her ready smile and funny close-set eyes. As the music screeched on, I wished I could hear what she heard.

When the *shamisen* lesson ended, I was summoned with my packages into the back depths of the house. Yukako opened the boxes and unwrapped tea utensils: a whisk, a tea bowl, a linen cloth, a bamboo scoop, a bronze bowl for catching waste water, a lacquer tea box and large round tray. Was she trading tea utensils for music lessons? I looked down at my lap, upset. She was lying to her father and stealing his things, and for what? Why not just sell the tea utensils outright? I took tiny comfort from the fact that these were her own tools, and not even her nice ones: it was the set she'd had me practice with until she could trust me with her good things. I looked over at Koito. Surely she could see that these weren't treasures. Was Yukako underestimating her? Insulting her on purpose? The worry that had begun to creep up on me the night Yukako burned her *kimono* bared its teeth. "Miss Urako," Yukako said.

"*Hai!*" I jumped. Me? She'd called me Little Ura all these years: what had I done?

"Do you remember your *temae?*"

Of course I did.

"Here is the brazier, here is the kettle, here is the host's door. Here are your sweets," she said, pointing to a half-eaten tray of *sembei* crackers. "Take these into the kitchen and set them up."

"*Hai.*" Was she going to do tea ceremony for Koito? I couldn't imagine a more grudging way to go about it, I thought, eating a broken *sembei* cracker—crunchy, salty, encrusted with black sesame—and arranging the rest on the tray. I couldn't understand what Yukako was doing. You were supposed to *invite* the guest to your home, ply the guest with your own sweets, set up the tea utensils with your own hands. I left the tray of *sembei* and the wastewater bowl outside the garden room door, then retreated to the kitchen with the rest of the utensils. The black lacquer tea box was round with a flatly domed top, mirror-smooth. I spooned in the powdered tea as Yukako had taught me, in the shape of a soft hill, with no lumps, no green dust on the shining walls of the box. Then I washed the tea bowl and sprinkled the tea whisk with water. The spokes of the whisk were fretted with black thread; I shaped the wet loose ends of the thread to a point like a man's queue. I wet the linen cloth, folded it into a stylized swab, and set it inside the bowl, resting the tea whisk on the cloth and the tea-scoop across the rim. I placed the bowl and the tea box one behind the other on the tray and set the tray by the door as well. "Young Mistress, it's ready," I announced, bowing. Then I looked up. The *shamisen* cushions and little tea table had been tidied away into a corner so that the brazier and steaming kettle took pride of place. Koito sat opposite me, calm and expectant. She seemed unmoved with Yukako's break with custom. Had she never seen a real Shin tea ceremony? Perhaps this was Yukako's way of satisfying Koito's curiosity while keeping the upper hand. After bowing, I half-rose to go back to the cloakroom and let Yukako take over, but then she spoke. "Use these," Yukako said, passing a fan to each of us. She was sitting on the mat off to the side of Koito, just beside the brazier. I gasped: She was in exactly the spot her father used when giving lessons.

Was I to do *temae*? The hair rose on the back of my neck as I set my fan before me and recited the phrase I'd heard the Mountain's students use with him, the phrase she'd taught me to use before our play lessons in her room: "*Sensei*, please be kind to me." Yukako set a fan in front of herself and we bowed together. Then, as the Mountain's students did for one another, I turned my fan, then my body, toward Koito and bowed to her as well. "Honored guest, please be kind to me."

"No, bow back *this* way," Yukako directed Koito. "Don't sit like an entertainer." My skin prickled. That was the word Akio had used when he told Yukako not to do *temae*. "If we're going to do this, you need to forget all the *temae* you ever learned in Pontocho. This is real Shin *temae*. Your fan goes *here*. Say *this*."

Koito bowed. "Thank you, *Sensei*."

Yukako passed me a silk tea-cloth, the emblem of the host. "Now, Urako, tuck this into your sash and make tea for your *kohai*." Her voice was a bright blade.

I backed my fan and my kneeling body out the door and flushed, finally understanding. Koito had asked Yukako to teach her Shin *temae*. Yukako wasn't stealing her father's tea things, she was stealing his art, his role, the very thing he and Akio had denied her. Her back was long and alert as she knelt on the teacher's mat; I saw in its firm line all her

years behind the lattice during lessons, permitted to observe, but not
to practice, the tossing nights after Akio said no wife of his would do
temae, all the lonely secret lessons in her room with me, like a girl with
her doll, her shock in Koito's parlor and her hissed *yes* by the river. This
was the bright blade in her voice: she *would* practice tea, she *would* teach
it, she *would* be her father's son and not wait to marry him, and if this
life offered only her old rival to stamp her will on, then stamp she
would. I heard the pleasure she took in calling Koito my *kohai,* my junior, my lesser-in-rank. Though an entertainer, Koito was the oldest,
most beautiful among us, and she had what Yukako wanted: the means
to support herself. But in this room Yukako had blown a small bubble-
world where the woman she hated was the meanest among us. Now I
saw: my dazzling older sister knew exactly what she was doing. My
hands shook as I folded the silk cloth into my waistband.

I brought in the sweets, then the utensils on their tray, then the
wastewater bowl. I wiped the tea box and scoop with the silk scarf,
poured water in the tea bowl, swished the whisk in the water, and
poured the used water away, wiping the bowl with the linen cloth. I
added powdered tea, offered Koito her *sembei,* and whisked hot water
and green tea together into a foamy brew. After the *geisha* ate and
drank, I formally restored the utensils to order and carried them
away.

I had done this *temae* so many times that Yukako did not correct me
but focused on her other charge instead. "No, like this, like *this.*" When
she'd spoken to Koito before, she'd used polite though not obsequious
language, but as soon as Koito bowed to her as *sensei,* she began using
the short, imperious verbs she used with me and Chio. *Chaimasu,* a
polite way of saying *It's different*—though I rarely heard Yukako disagree outright even politely with anyone but me—became *Chau: You're
wrong.* "Raise the sweet tray in thanks and set it down, *then* set your
paper pad before you—*wrong!*—fold-side *toward* you—touch the tray

with your left hand—*wrong!*—palm *up*—and take your *sembei* with the right hand and set it on the paper—*wrong!*—first *move* the tray to the right—*wrong!*—with *both* hands—"

Koito took Yukako's critiques with good humor, and even eagerness. I understood. Though she'd spoken with more affection, Yukako had been just as stern with me, just as precise, and I had loved how carefully she'd watched me. *Temae*, though mysteriously affecting, was not mysterious: each gesture took clear shape in the light of her attention. That day in Koito's garden room, *not* being critiqued, for the first time I felt while performing *temae* something of the solemnity and grace that I felt watching it. I felt the austere precision of the choreography, and my voluptuous surrender to it. I felt the desire to give something precious, this bowl of tea. I felt this one moment in all the world, three women in a room, doors thrown back to the bright day, the drunk bees in the purple flowers. I felt the alchemy of food made flesh. We were candles that burned on rice and salt. These ground green leaves came from earth, water, light, and air, and so did my guest's drinking body. And I myself was a leaf adrift, my own body borne down a river of *temae*. I felt my mind both river and leaf at once.

After I cleared everything away, I was allowed to stay and watch while Yukako walked Koito through the very first thing she'd taught me: how to fold the host's silk cloth from a large square napkin into the tight pad used for wiping the tea box. Of course there was only one way to do it. Patient and severe, Yukako broke the fluid motion down into twelve separate steps, demanding, as her father had demanded of his students and she had demanded of me, that Koito pay strict attention to the position of her back, head, limbs, and fingers. "Here. *Here*. Like *so. Wrong!*" she said, striking Koito's fingers with the flat rib of her folded fan. I was the daughter of a charwoman, trained by a missionary; Koito was the daughter of a dancer, trained by musicians: she learned so much more quickly than I had. She had already studied *temae* before, I consoled myself; she knew the style they learned in the *geisha* quarter. Still, as Yukako hectored and pushed, I felt envy as I watched Koito's body *remember* what it learned. When Koito could fold the silk cloth perfectly three times, Yukako grunted approval, just like the Mountain. "*Un.* That's enough for today."

"Tomorrow, then?"

"Very well."

Koito and I bowed the ritual end to the lesson, and then Yukako switched back to using polite longer verbs. "May I leave my *shamisen* here?"

"You don't plan to practice at home?" Koito chastised, a student no longer.

"I have another," Yukako said curtly.

"Oh, how could I forget? You don't want your father to see," said Koito, baiting her.

"Well, would you?" Yukako sniped. "Or do you even know who your father is?"

Smiling, Koito replied, "I would advise you not to presume." Or something in that vein. As she became more nastily indirect, I understood less. Four years before, I remembered, she had used the very long verbs of a flatterer or servant, but now, I realized, she spoke only just as politely as Yukako did. When had she shifted? Oh: when Yukako asked for help.

"Perhaps we should keep conversation to the lesson at hand," said Yukako.

"We stand to gain so much from one another," Koito agreed. "Of course you can leave it here," she added. "It's not bad. It has a nice sound, considering the quality."

Yukako's hand clenched around her fan. Too bad her hour as a teacher had come and gone: I knew she wanted to give those pretty little fingers another smack. She held herself in check, and bowed. "Thank you, *Sensei.*"

I'd felt so close to them not long before, and now I just wanted to leave. I was surprised that Inko even came to the door to bow us out, let alone smiled at me.

IN THE YEAR THAT FOLLOWED, as Western canes and bowler hats began to appear in the market crowds, the Mountain's fortunes slowly improved. He acquired a merchant patron, the portly new head of the Okura household, heir to a shipping fortune. The Emperor had seen no need to outlaw tea, assuming that without his support the traditional "pastimes" would die a natural death. He had not anticipated the way that those who had been denied the trappings of aristocracy during the Shogun's time would claim them now that they could: for a merchant like Okura Chugo to buy the services of a feudal lord's tea master was to declare himself that lord's equal at last. Following Okura's lead, other merchants began to seek out the Mountain, and in the spring of Meiji Four we had students in the Long Room again: three merchants' sons, including the Stickboy and the Bear. By then Koito had long since surpassed me as a student of tea, and Yukako, a quick learner herself, had been accompanying Koito on her music lessons for months. To conceal Yukako's identity as the tea master's daughter—and to conceal Koito's identity as a *geisha*—they posed as teacher and student from Tokyo, with Yukako as teacher and Koito as student. When the young pupils were ready, Koito told the mothers of the fine houses we called on, they would begin work with "Migawa Yuko" herself.

My only moment of alarm when Yukako worked as Migawa-*sensei* was one day when I spotted Miss Miki, the hairdressers' daughter, walking out of a comb shop in the *geisha* district. Yukako and Koito had already turned the corner, but Inko noticed me gasp. "You know Miss Miki?" she asked as Miki crossed the street in front of us, unseeing.

"Why? Is her mother your hairdresser too?"

"Oh, no," Inko said, as my heart thudded with relief. "They just shop there all the time."

KOITO PROPOSED WORKING incognito soon after she and Yukako began exchanging lessons. Yukako's need for discretion was evident, but when Koito mentioned her own, Yukako gave her a superior glance. "Beg pardon?" she said snidely, just to hear Koito repeat herself.

"If it were to circulate that a woman of a certain profession with a reputation for making money made in fact so little money that she had to find a second source of income . . ." Koito trailed off. I didn't quite understand her, but it was something like this, only more so.

"What a shame," said Yukako, almost sincerely.

"Listen," sighed Koito. Though *geisha* were dancers and musicians, not prostitutes, they were enough in that world that Yukako had just offered an insult that bordered on obscenity. "My mother is sick and in debt. When she dies this house won't be mine; Madam Suisho next door will take it over as payment. I have no tree to shade me, *Sensei.* I'm sorry I hurt you, with the young lord. But don't you see? It could have been any of us. I was a bought thing, I was a toy. And then I lost my heart a little. I waited for him to say 'I'll marry you,' and he never did. Do you understand?"

Usually Koito seemed all of a piece, as if the exquisite cascade of silk she wore simply clung to her like water, but for a moment she looked like what she was, a worried young woman who happened to be wrapped in brocade. Yukako couldn't meet her eyes. "I'll stop, *Sensei,*" she said. "I'm sorry." When Koito performed *temae,* Yukako was as finicky as ever with her corrections, but her *"Wrong!"* fell without venom. When she lit incense before the sober-faced goddess of compassion at the temple that afternoon, I heard Koito's name in her prayers.

. . .

THE FIRST TIME THEY GAVE a music lesson, at the enormous house of one Lord Mitsuba, Koito and Yukako split the few coins half and half. When I followed Yukako home, the tassels of her *obi* cord bounced with pleasure as she walked. After that day, she would spend the money on Kuga's wages or better food for the household, or simply tucked it away—*For Father,* she'd say—but that first time, she bought herself *dango,* rice flour balls skewered on a stick, grilled and slathered with sticky sweet sauce and toasted soy powder. She ate a whole skewer and bought another for me.

"It would take dozens of lessons to make what I got for one *kimono,*" she mused, after we stopped to greet the Pipe Lady. We sat on a bench by the moon-viewing pond, watching the sun ruffle the water. I saw fewer carp than usual: could the Pipe Lady's family have been eating them? And yet they'd just recently paid to march in one of the summer festivals. Just so, the Mitsubas—their house, though grander than Sumie's, in a far greater state of disrepair—had paid for music lessons. Yukako looked at the coins in her hand and tucked them back into her sleeve. "This is less money than I go out with to the market every day. But still . . ." she said.

"It's different?" I thought of her burning sleeve in the sewing house.

"*Un,*" she grunted agreement.

"You sound just like your father when you do that."

11

1871

T HE SUMMER OF MEIJI FOUR, after Yukako and Koito had been
exchanging lessons for a year, I turned fifteen and the weather
turned brutal. The early-summer rains came and went in a brief hot
shimmer. In the weeks that oozed toward Obon, the late-summer festival of the dead, the Kamo River slowed to a crawl, and the Migawa
and the Canal Street canal—never deep, except in the rainy season—
shriveled to dusty trickles in their banks. Even the moon-viewing
pond at Sumie's house shrank by half. In the Northern Seven-House
Quarter, Koito's mother was among those whose health flagged in the
sultry heat.

When she wasn't running to the doctor for the ailing dancer, Inko
would come with us to lessons, trotting along behind me with Koito's
shamisen. Except at the Mitsubas', the grandest house we visited, Inko
could always grease her way out of the cloakroom and into the
kitchen, where the other servants would give us cold barley tea and
press her for stories about Edo, which she would fabricate mar-
velously. Inko's most devoted listener was a wide-eyed old gardener at

the house of the Tsutamons, a fine *samurai* family whose son the Mountain had once taught. (Yukako fretted that she would be recognized each time we called, but the young man never appeared.) Bozu, the Tsutamons' gardener, was named for his hair cropped short like a monk's or a Westerner's; his wife and daughter-in-law had died of cholera, and he bounced his tiny grandson on his back as if perpetually surprised by the boy's existence. "Is it true, in Edo a monk burned his own temple?" he said.

"I know for a fact," Inko said, though she didn't, "that he did it after he saw a phoenix in a dream."

"No, what I heard was he did it when the Emperor passed by with his hair cut short like a foreign devil," said the cook, giving Bozu's shorn head a playful cuff.

"And is it true he committed suicide after?" asked the gardener.

"Who wouldn't, huh?" said Inko.

I liked it when we went to the Mitsubas' and waited quietly, as we'd been instructed, on the bench in the dim stone-floored cloakroom. We sat fanning ourselves with stiff paper paddles, making faces at each other when the Mitsuba girl played her lessons wrong, chatting in low voices. She loved it that I was as gullible as Bozu, and I played it up to entertain her. "How come everybody gets a new name except me?" I asked one day. "My mistress, your mistress, even you, Miss Namiko."

"But Namiko's my real name," she laughed.

"Liar."

"No, it is," she insisted.

"Then who's Inko?"

"You don't really think anyone's parents would name them Inko, do you?" And there I was, giving her that baffled look she loved to mock. "You *do!*" Sheltered girls were called "daughters kept in boxes," but in Inko's opinion, I lent new meaning to the phrase. "Born in a box," she sighed. "Have you ever seen an *inko*? It's a kind of noisy bird."

"Oh, like you," I teased.

"You bet," she said, cawing like a parrot while I tried not to laugh too loud.

I had no hope of impressing her, but she liked me anyway. "Namiko's pretty," I said, looking away. "Inko too." I still wore my hair in a knot held up with a pin: a style for girls past childhood but too young to be worth spending money on a hairdresser. At that moment my bun gave itself up to gravity and the sticky heat that weighed on the city. I took down my hair and Inko reached for it. Lifting my hair with one hand, she fanned the back of my exposed neck as I sat limp-armed and grateful. *"Soft,"* she whispered.

As we passed from unlined garments into the gauze of highest summer, I knew Yukako wanted to start teaching music lessons herself, but pride prevented her from asking. Koito, for her part, seemed subdued and distracted, and when she pronounced Yukako ready to trade places, it was with an air of embarrassed surprise. In fact, two days before the Obon festival, when Koito announced to Mitsuba that her little girl was ready to work with the great "Migawa Yuko" herself, she seemed positively gray. Yukako shone that day, coaxing the little girl through her tune as if she'd been born to the task. Even one as indifferent to Japanese music as I (alone in the cloakroom, wishing Inko had come too) could hear that all Yukako's work was paying off.

After we left, Yukako kept looking back at Koito for some nod, some grunt, some sign of approval. When I congratulated her, as I often did, she looked over to see if Koito would, too, but the older woman remained stony-faced for so long that Yukako finally turned, asking plaintively, *"Sensei,* I did badly?" Koito's *shamisen* case dropped to the ground and her head and shoulders slumped forward.

I went to catch her: was she fainting in the heat? *"Sensei,* do you want some ice?" I asked. "Some cold barley tea?"

"That was so selfish of me," apologized Yukako, fanning Koito with her hands, "I had no idea."

"I'm sorry, I'm sorry," said Koito as we steered her to a bench under a red parasol. It belonged to a stall that sold nothing but shaved ice with syrup, so we got her a bowlful. "It's all right, I don't need this, I'm so sorry," she kept fluttering, but then sighed, rested a hand on her chin, and took a bite. "Oh, it's good."

Koito gazed at the sweat forming on the sides of her lacquer bowl. Yukako and I traded an anxious look. "We have the one lesson tomorrow with the Tsutamon family and then none for a few days, because of the Obon festival," Koito said.

Yukako looked puzzled. "Yes?"

"I think Miss Ura should stay at my house tonight, if it's all right," Koito decided.

"What? Why?"

"If need be, she can come tell you to go to teach without me tomorrow," she said heavily. "My mother may not last the night."

"*Ara!*" gasped Yukako. She said all the pained helpless things one says, and then asked, "What are you doing here at all?"

"She asked me to do what I do every day. Otherwise . . ." Koito's voice wavered.

"I'm so sorry," said Yukako.

"So," said the *geisha* briskly, "unless Miss Ura comes to find you, tomorrow morning at my house?"

Yukako looked back twice with worry as she walked away.

I HAD SEEN KOITO's mother Akaito once, during the short rainy season that year, not long after a heavy storm leaked into a closet in Yukako's upstairs room. While clearing it out, Yukako found the brown dress my mother had once made me, trimmed in velvet and reeking of smoke. Through my closed eyes, I could see my mother, my uncle, my little brown-kerchiefed doll. Mott Street, the nuns, the ship, the fire. I stood still a long time with the dress held at arm's length.

"Put it on?" Yukako begged. I hadn't grown much in height since I was nine, but I had filled out dramatically in the last year: the fabric strained over my new breasts and hips. Who is this? I gasped, looking down at the young woman in my dress. I felt a wave of sadness that my mother had never known me in this body, that I had grown without her. Yukako clapped her hands with delight. "Show o-Chio!" she insisted.

I felt hot with embarrassment and old grief, but I hadn't seen her so giddy in years. Relenting, I started down the stairs to the kitchen, and suddenly found myself face-to-face with the Mountain. "What's this?" he exclaimed. Stitches popping, I scrambled back up the stairs. *I'll never wear this dress again,* I thought, peeling it off as carefully as possible. I folded it up and combed through the wet things dragged from the closet, fruitlessly searching for my Saint Claire medal. I had asked Yukako and Chio about it years before, once I had the words in Japanese: they had seen neither medal nor chain.

Whenever we went to Koito's house, Yukako exercised her privilege as *sensei* to choose the scroll for the display alcove, hanging a different treasure from the Shins' storeroom tower for each lesson. A few mornings after the storm, when Koito and I entered and bowed with our fans before the alcove to appreciate the flower and scroll, I gasped. Then Koito and Inko gasped as well.

Yukako had hung my dress in the alcove. Inko asked permission for something, and Koito nodded her away. We stared.

Sometimes, in place of a scroll, a painting appeared in the alcove, or a beautiful statue, an Ainu tribal mask, or even a piece of driftwood, magnificently rotted into lace. Was my dress such a precious find? With my fan before me and my hands and body bent precisely into an art-appreciation bow, kneeling by Yukako, all triumph, and Koito, all curiosity and frank appraisal, I looked at my mother's handiwork on the wall, hanging like a primitive artifact. I felt a great emptiness and, surrounding it, a crust of pride, of indignation, of grief, of shame.

"*You* wore this?" Koito asked. "Would you wear it for us now?"

"No," I said.

And then I was spared from saying more by the woman who swept in: the most beautiful old lady I've ever seen in my life. Not much younger than the Mountain, in a royal blue robe with a wadded russet train, with Yukako's height and Koito's bearing, stood the best dancer of her generation, Koito's mother Akaito. In seconds she observed the way we were sitting, knelt on the floor with her arms bent precisely like ours (but with more grace), took in an eyeful of my mother's dress, bowed, and sailed out, leaving Yukako, stunned and meek, to call after her, "Please, won't you stay for some tea?"

AND SO I WORRIED about Madam Akaito, too, when Koito asked my Older Sister to let me stay overnight. The doctor—with his servant and his pharmacy chest of little drawers—agreed to sit up with the patient until Koito came home from work, or all night if the fever didn't break. Koito's cook and Inko agreed to stagger their trips to the bathhouse so that someone could run up to the sickroom at any time. Before Koito had even finished painting on her lead-white face, the doctor declared the night a safe one for the elderly dancer but agreed to stay regardless: though we kept to our watches, we did so with lighter hearts than expected.

After the doctor's pronouncement, the curiosity I'd kept tamped down with anxiety flared free, and I made myself as helpful as possible in order to find out what a *geisha* house was really like.

It was just like any other house I'd seen in Kyoto, wood and straw and ribs of bamboo, the kitchen in a packed earth alley that ran the length of the building. Koito's mother slept upstairs in a room overlooking the garden, while Koito kept her things just behind the parlor where we held lessons: the milky doors slid open to reveal an inner room I had never seen, a little bower of bright fabric and makeup brushes. Beside a lavish mirror, in its own bed of ash, burned a black pellet of *neriko* incense, fragrant resin suspended in a ball of honey and powdered shell. An exquisitely pretty little girl named Mizushi came over from the *geisha* house next door to help Koito as she painted her entire face and shoulders white, leaving a snake-tongue of breathing warm flesh exposed at the nape. Then she painted in a pair of dainty eyebrows and a cherry-bud mouth, a hint of rouge at the cheeks.

After Koito painted Mizushi as well, dabbing red on only the young girl's bottom lip, a balding old silk-voiced dresser from next door—the only man permitted in a *geisha*'s house, Inko told me—helped Koito into an extravagantly beautiful costume: a set of five nested robes, the outermost a regal sweep of mountains and waterfalls, heavy with silver thread. At one point Koito pointed to a bundle wrapped in cloth: "Tomorrow's *kimono*. Could you help Miss Mizu bring it over?" Between us we could barely carry it, and I understood why Koito needed someone to help her into her night's ensemble: the *kimono* weighed a third as much as she did. While Mizushi washed Koito's brushes and laid them out carefully to dry, a chalk ghost flickering in and out of the room, the dresser arranged the next day's magnificent robes on a rack to air. "Tomorrow's *kimono*, I hope," Koito corrected herself anxiously.

Once Koito was ready, the dresser fit Mizushi into her *kimono* as carefully as if he were laying a yoke with balanced pails of water across her shoulders. While Koito looked majestic, like a human painting, Mizushi conveyed a kind of stylized antique cuteness, the long ribbons of her *obi* hanging untied down her back as if in homage to some long-ago little minx who'd run off before her mother could finish dressing her.

Koito ticked off a series of events and gatherings where they'd been invited to make an appearance, and two parties where they were scheduled to perform, one that called for a *shamisen* player, and one much later that required a minor dancer. "Little Mizu, take my place," Koito decided, casting a glance upstairs. "I don't want to be out so late."

"Older Sister, truly?" Were they really sisters?

"She won't fuss if I'm home a little early. You've practiced the Hotaru and Miyagino-no dances, haven't you?"

Mizushi's deep bow half-hid her excitement—as well as her embarrassment that she owed her pleasure to Koito's misfortune. "Older Sister, I humbly thank you," she said.

"Everyone likes a fresh face," sighed Koito.

"No, THEY'RE NOT SISTERS," Inko told me as we walked side by side to the bathhouse. We were the same age, but I felt so much younger. "Little Mizu's her *maiko*—her apprentice," she explained. "She came from Madam Suisho's house next door. They have so many *maiko* and we have none, so." Even though people often didn't finish their sentences— as a way of showing respect to both listener and subject matter—Inko's voice was so frank and emphatic that it always surprised me when she broke off like that.

"I've never seen her before," I noted.

"You've never been here at night," Inko said, almost reproachfully.

I didn't know what to say. "So it's you, the cook, Miss Mizushi, Miss Koito, and her mother, all living together?"

"Mizu sleeps next door with the other *maiko*. And the women who do the sewing are next door too."

I nodded. "So why is your Young Mistress going so many places tonight?"

"She makes a little money every place she's invited to stop in, more at the parties where she dances or plays. It's embarrassing, though. For a long time there was so little work, but now"—she tilted her chin back toward the house, looking up toward the sickroom—"people feel sorry for Young Mistress, so the *geiko* office is booking her at every party in the quarter. But where were they before?"

"That's hard."

"Can't be helped."

I was walking in an extra bathhouse *kimono* of Inko's; when I brought my hand to my face I smelled Koito's *neriko* incense on the sleeve, complex and intoxicating. "If Miss Mizushi isn't her real sister, is Mother"—Inko called the lady of the house Mother, although it was clear they were not related—"her real mother?"

"Sure. But Young Mistress grew up in the biggest *geiko* house in Pontocho. You saw what happened there when things went bad."

"But why didn't she grow up with her own mother?"

Inko was so unlike Koito I was surprised she'd worked for her all this time. Her speech was so straightforward as she explained things. "Well, fifteen years ago, Pontocho was the highest-ranking *geiko* district and this one was just a sleepy backwater. Still is. Silk merchants, ho hum," she sniffed. "Well, at least someone's making money these days. Young Mistress's mother wanted her girl to have chances she wouldn't have here, so she adopted Young Mistress out to the best house in Pontocho. She gave her daughter a name she could keep if she wrote it a different way."

"I don't understand."

"She explained it to me once. Mother's name is Akaito, *Aka-ito*," she said, sounding out the two separate *kanji*. The name meant, literally, Red Thread.

"So Miss Koito's *kanji* is *Ko-ito*? *Ko* like *small*?"

"Exactly." The name meant Little Thread. "But you can also read it *Ko-i-to*."

"What is that?"

Inko said *ito* a different way, so that it meant Famous Beginning. "Her Pontocho mother's name was Izakura," Famous Cherry. "And there was a Famous Crane, a Famous Maple, and a Little Famous Snow."

I remembered the day Yukako hung my mother's dress in the alcove. When we left, Koito stroked my cheek with her thumb. "It's hard to grow up without your mother," she'd said. I remembered the queer glance of recognition she gave me when we first met. I said, "But before you came here from Pontocho, Miss Koito's mother was all alone. Why would she send her little girl away?"

Inko shrugged. "Oh, she had other blood daughters, other *geiko* daughters, other *maiko*. Why, Mizushi used to live here. But remember when they kept changing the era name every year? Mother Akaito had one misfortune after the next. And then two of her girls died in the sickness, one right after her debut as a *maiko*. Mother had to borrow so much money from Madam Suisho next door. Then doctors' bills and hard times, so."

"Ah."

"Well, one by one, she had to sell off all her girls' contracts. Now Young Mistress will get everything, the house, the debts, and all."

"Once I heard her say she had no tree to shade her."

"Well, she can keep the house and take out a long contract with Suisho, make up the debt that way, I guess. Or she can sell the house to Suisho and find some *geiko* house to live in as a free agent. Suisho would take her, I think, but . . ."

"Poor Miss Koito," I said.

"Poor everybody," she agreed. The way she said it, I wanted to ask her more, but we'd arrived at the baths.

I was used to the bathhouse at home, and the people there were used to my bulbous body and misshapen face. Though Miss Hazu and her friends, now growing breasts of their own, sniggered at me, the adults respected Chio too much to say anything and the children didn't know any better. At the *geisha* bathhouse, however, everyone took in the new face with a nod, or often, on closer look, a sneer. "She's my cousin," Inko announced, when people stared. "She's visiting." Still feeling their eyes, I hurried through disrobing and scrubbing, then sat like a lump, hunching over my ugly new breasts while Inko chatted with everyone who walked by. "What are you waiting for?" she asked.

I looked over toward the hot bath. "I didn't want to get in there alone."

Inko ladled a last rinse across her back and stood. She wore an unmarried woman's hairstyle under a tented white cloth. Slim and sinewy, she had no hips at all and breasts that barely swelled beneath their brown tips. "You're fat," she mused, looking down at me. "They must give you better food over there." The way she said it, *fat* didn't sound so bad. She held out a hand for me to take and hauled me up off my stool. She stood with her arms akimbo, giving me a careful look with her close-set eyes. "It's funny, though, your middle goes in as much as mine," she said, poking a spot on the undifferentiated rectangle of her torso. "It's like your *shape* is fat."

"I want to get in the bath," I said.

"Sorry."

I was profoundly embarrassed, but I actually liked the way she said it, that my *shape* was fat. I sat in the bath with my eyes closed, partly out of shyness at being seen by strangers, partly to tease out what she'd said in private. I remembered ladies' magazines I'd seen in the ship library when I was a little girl, the advertisements for corsets with their baroque fastenings. It was hard, now, to remember words in English, but I dredged it up: I had an *hourglass* figure.

The one time my heavy breasts gave me pleasure was when I sat in the hot bath. I would choose the darkest corner of the tub and feel the rare weightlessness as they floated up of their own accord. As I sat in the unfamiliar bathhouse with my eyes closed I felt my breasts lick the surface of the water. I touched my little waist and the *fat shape* of my hips swelling out from it. The thought was absolutely novel to me: *I have a body that a corset would flatter.* The word I heard in my mind for *corset* was *korusetto.*

The only women I saw with breasts or behinds like mine were stout old grandmothers with bellies to match. Like me—once I correctly padded my waist and middle and the small of my back—they looked blocky in *kimono*. I envied those taut cylindrical girls at the bathhouse who wore their robes so effortlessly, envied Inko her loud, flat ease in the world: she wasn't pretty—neither was a crow—but she was as buoyant and raucous, as matter-of-factly unaware of her body. I envied Mizushi the beauty that gilded her ambition with charm. I didn't envy Koito, though all the teeth felt loose in my head when I looked at her: how can you envy an ideal? I didn't envy Yukako, exactly, when I watched her dress or followed as she walked, light-boned as a scull: I felt something less petty and more frightening. At night when I waited for her to come up from the bath, I thought sometimes about the long single brushstroke of her body and longed to fit mine to it, to press my moony cow breasts flush against her narrow back and weld them flat at last. But imagine, I thought in that *geisha* bathhouse, there was a word for my body other than *ugly*, a barely remembered, barely pronounceable word. *A-wa-gu-ra-su*. I savored it.

Inko's deadpan voice, always on the brink of laughter, snapped me out of my reverie. "Once, when we lived in Pontocho, Young Mistress went with some customers on a boat to see the water lilies. This time of year, if you go at night and wait until sunrise, they say you can *hear* them pop open."

"Really?"

"Well, *I* didn't. I just carried the picnic. And no way *they* did. They got so drunk, staying up all night singing and composing poems. Young Mistress danced in the boat and one of the men almost pushed her in."

"No!"

"Yes! But then she told him how much her *kimono* would cost to replace and *that* sobered him up. For a little while. Then he started talking all colorful to her."

"Colorful?"

Inko giggled, her voice dropping. "You don't have to *shout* it!"

"I'm sorry," I said, mortified.

Inko covered my ear with her hand and whispered, "He told her how he wanted to do it to her."

My eyes went huge and round, but I followed her lead and laughed.

BETWEEN THE DOCTOR and the cook, we weren't even allowed near Koito's mother, so we set up Koito's mosquito netting, spread her *futon*, and waited up to feed her and help her out of her *kimono*. We lay drowsing on Koito's *futon* with the lamp lit for her, burning a pellet of the rolled incense she used to blow away the smell of her lead paint. Lying next to Inko, I whispered my question. "Did your Young Mistress really have to do it with the man in the boat?"

"No!" Inko giggled. "*Geiko* don't *have* to do it with anybody. But when they *do* actually take a patron, why, there's so much money involved, it's a major event! Everybody in the neighborhood talks about it."

"*Ara!*"

"Most men, they pay *geiko* to sing and dance and talk and pour *sake* so that they can think about it, but then they pay prostitutes so they can *do* it, since they do like to finish what they start. Really, I think just being around a woman they can't afford gets them excited."

"Did she do it with Mr. Akio?"

"What do you think?" Inko rolled her eyes, but I could tell she liked being a know-it-all. "But he was her sweetheart so she did it for free. Madam Izakura was so mad when she found out!"

"Were they really going to get married?"

"I don't know why she believed him. Those are the oldest lies in the water trade. She says 'I love you' so he'll pay. He says 'I'll marry you' so she'll do it for free."

Though I knew we were alone—the cook and the doctor were upstairs with Koito's mother—now I cupped *my* hand over Inko's ear. I was so embarrassed to ask, but I kind of liked being embarrassed in front of her, and I knew if anyone would tell me, she would. "What do they do when they do it?" I whispered.

"You really *were* born in a box," Inko said, laughing.

I covered my face with my hand, humiliated. I could feel her gesturing so I made a chink with my fingers and looked. "*Ara!*" I said, putting it together with the floppy roots I'd seen on the bathhouse men, with what I knew of my own body. Sometimes, when I lay up waiting for Yukako, or when she curved around me spoon-fashion at night, I thought my monthlies were early, but they came clear instead. Giggling in bed next to Inko, flushed, I thought they might be early now. "Have you ever done it?" I asked.

"You're so *bad!*" Inko swatted my shoulder, grinning. "Well, there was a boy in Pontocho I liked and we did it once or twice, but then he liked somebody else."

"I'm sorry."

"It was fun too," she pouted. "I think my parents have somebody for me to marry when my contract's over, so I guess I'll do it a lot then, huh?" She laughed broadly.

"Have you met him?" I asked.

"No, but my contract isn't up for another year and a half anyway, so who knows what could happen."

"True." I marveled at Inko. When Yukako and her father faced their greatest hardship, no one had talked of hiring me out. Could I live like Inko, or like Kuga's son Zoji, bound for years yet to Akio's father? Could I be so cheerfully indifferent to my future? I liked the absentminded way she thumbed my wrist as she talked to me.

She flicked me a look I couldn't read, and said, "There was this girl Fumi, she worked in the Izakura house too. When we left and came here, Fumi's Young Mistress left too; they went to Edo. I miss her. We used to do it all the time."

"Excuse me?" My heart froze in my ribs when she said this, the same brash way she said everything else. I pulled my hand away from her.

She looked me in the eye, tough and wounded, and she shrugged. "It's karma from another life, you know? Can't help it. I bet she's married now. She probably has a baby."

I blinked, still stunned. I knew if I lay quietly, soon we'd talk about babies, or fall asleep. Was that what I wanted? I inhaled. *No.* I reached over, pushing through air suddenly dense with fear, my own. It was labor; it took forever. I took Inko's hand. And then, the way I copied Yukako's every gesture in our lessons, I stroked Inko's wrist with my thumb, gently and persistently, just as she had mine. I felt her sigh. "What did you do?" I asked softly, as if coaxing a bird from the air.

"Me and Fumi?" I had never seen Inko embarrassed. She looked away, then at me, then away. "Everything," she said, defensive. But it was a dare too.

I held on to her wrist and I lay there, watching the mosquito netting stir in the rare breeze from the garden. It was difficult to breathe. I remembered myself as a little girl, the way I stood watching the cart in the fire, and then the way I leaped inside. *"Misete ne?"* I whispered, leaping. *Show me.*

She smiled a nervy, slack-jawed smile, and then she showed me.

She touched me gently, moved down my body, and fit her head between my legs. At first I lay still, rigid with a terror that felt even larger than that enormous moment, and then I eased into her mouth and the fingers she slid into my body. By the end I felt like there were horses inside me, like I was the horse rearing up in the fire. And then, good tea student that I was, I copied her every gesture, at first afraid of the way she shuddered and sweated, then thrilled. When she rested, I took her in my arms and kissed her. "Why are you doing that with your mouth?" she said, so I stopped. I'd once kissed Yukako good night, and she'd said the same thing.

She didn't pull away, though. "I like it here," I whispered, my head pillowed on Inko's chest, my arm around her waist.

"I think we were foreigners in a past life," said Inko, lost in thought.

"Why?"

"Well, me because my voice is loud and my father makes foreign food," she said.

"He does?"

"He has a little *tempura* place in Pontocho."

"Oh," I said, confused. The dish had come to Japan from Portugal so long ago, I didn't know it was foreign.

"And I think *you* were one, too, because of that Western wrap your mother dressed you in. You look different too," she said. "And you walked next to me. Sometimes you don't remember words for things, and I know that's from the fire, but maybe it's because last time around you were a foreigner."

I laughed nervously.

"And that thing with your mouth," she said, kissing the air. "Young Mistress told me in the West husbands and wives lick each other's lips; can you imagine?"

It was difficult enough to imagine what we'd just done to each other, but I laughed with her nonetheless.

FROM OUTSIDE CAME the jingle and clop of hair ornaments and wooden sandals. We tied our splayed robes closed and hurried to the entrance as the slatted gate slid open. When Koito and Mizushi came in, Koito went straight upstairs without changing as we laid out the little meal the cook had left for the two of them: pressed rice, salted mackerel and seaweed, cold barley tea. We helped them undress and spread their robes on racks to air, and then the pair left again in their bathhouse *kimono*, still ghostly white. "When do they take off their makeup?" I wondered as we spread a *futon* for ourselves, one step up from the earth-floored cloakroom.

"At the bathhouse."

"Inko, Namiko," I said, whispering her real name. Beautiful Plant Child, clad in gold flowers and tender new grass. She felt so known to me, and so new. I folded my arm around her and she held my wrist. "Who did you lose in the sickness?" I asked, remembering something she'd said.

"A little sister and my baby brother. There were eight of us, you know?"

"I'm sorry."

"My mother stopped having children after that. She made the hairdresser give her a widow's *obako* hairstyle and wouldn't let my father near her anymore."

"Really?"

"I think she just didn't want to see any more babies go," she sighed. I stroked her back. "My brother was just born but my sister could talk by then. She'd wave her little arms and say *Onetan! Onetan!*" Oh, instead of *Onesan, Older Sister.* It was as heartbreaking as if she'd said *Thithter! Thithter!*

"I'm so sorry."

"It can't be helped," she said softly, and I held her.

We lay together quietly for a minute. "I'm sorry your mother dressed you up like that and left you," Inko said. "And then the fire? How awful."

"She had the sickness too," I said. "So."

"She was doing her best."

"Sometimes I forget her face a little," I confessed. "Every time we go to the temple, I pray to remember her better." My voice began to falter.

Inko touched my face and chided me with the gentlest possible words. "I always pray for the same thing."

"What?" I asked.

"To be happy."

KOITO CAME HOME from the bathhouse; I heard her and Mizushi bid each other good night, and then she stepped over me as Inko barred the door.

Once Koito padded upstairs, Inko twined around me. I felt her awareness slacken, now that she'd done the night's last task. When had the thought crossed her mind, I wondered, that I was someone she would want to touch?

"Inko?" I asked, though I felt her start to drift. "Why did you tell me about the man on the boat, you know, and the water lilies?"

"Because that's what you were like, floating," she whispered, cupping my breast by way of explanation. Her palm was so soft, holding me the way the water held me. She murmured something to me, half-asleep: "I would have had the best poem."

I SLEPT LIGHTLY, confused by the different night noises and by my own astonished body. The day starts later in *geisha* quarters than in other neighborhoods; what woke me the next morning was the absence of Matsu hauling charcoal, the absence of the pointy-chinned *tofu* man's hoarse call. I opened my eyes to Inko beside me and, bedded down next to her, the quilted sleeping bulk of Koito's cook. I lay awake by Inko, nervous and thrilled, and a little lonely for the sound of Chio yanking pots out of their sockets in the stove, for Yukako's loamy scent.

I helped Inko with all her tasks that morning, marveling daftly at the shape of her neck and hands. When she looked at me and smiled, I felt her fingers inside.

Koito said there was no need for me to go, and Yukako arrived before the cool of the night had wholly burned off, arms laden with the grasses used to decorate homes for Obon. "Did you sleep last night? How is she? Should we still have our lesson?"

"Miss Inko, take these for now," said Koito. "*Sensei,* may I ask you something?" She looked, though lovely, drawn and gray. She'd never used the *futon* we laid out for her. "Would you come upstairs with me for a moment? It would mean so much to me. Miss Ura, I'm sorry, would you bring up the tray in the kitchen?"

I knelt in the doorway a minute later, surprised at the tray in my hands. In the earthen-floored kitchen I'd been exquisitely aware of Inko unwrapping the Obon grasses, drawing a foot out of her sandal to scratch her calf with a toe, but I hadn't noticed that the tray I'd taken held *sake* and cups. Had I brought up the wrong one? The upstairs room was full, between the doctor and his boy, Koito, Yukako, and the woman on the *futon,* Akaito. A Buddhist rosary in her limp hand, she lay regal and devastated, with a shipwrecked face and pitted skin. The lead in the white paint, I heard later, takes its toll. She looked at Yukako. "You're here," she said.

Koito poured for her mother and her guest. Yukako, as puzzled by *sake* at a time like this as I, poured for Koito. The three women drank, and Yukako's eyes blinked open with surprise, then understanding. Curious, I dabbed at a bead of *sake* on the tray and tasted: water. I'd heard it in stories but never believed that people did this, drank water out of a *sake* cup to say a last farewell. Perhaps Madam Akaito had grown fond of Yukako's harsh correcting voice downstairs, the way even the mournful barking of the *tofu* man meant home to me now.

No one said a word. Madam Akaito's gaze rested on Yukako. Koito sometimes glanced from one face to the other. Looking past the patient's ravaged face, I realized that she was not so old as I had assumed. She was much younger than the Pipe Lady, in fact, perhaps in her fifties. I knew Yukako's mother had borne children late: she and

Koito's mother would have been around the same age. Yukako did not have many women her mother's age in her life, and certainly no one she looked up to: Sumie's harried mother was much younger, as was Chio, and I knew neither woman filled her with as much awe as the older *geisha*. As the three women drank in silence, I remained in place, sometimes listening for Inko in the kitchen below, sometimes wondering what Yukako was thinking. "Thank you," Madam Akaito said.

I WOBBLED PASSABLY through my tea lesson that morning, my whole body blushing at unexpected moments, and then played guest to Koito's *temae*, constantly looking past her to the open doorway to see if Inko would appear. Only two kinds of tea were ever made in tea ceremony: "thin" tea, the foamy broth I had tasted my first morning in Baishian, and "thick" tea, a runny paste of moistened tea powder, kneaded instead of beaten, that made my heart knock loud. Already compromised, I was glad Koito was making only thin tea that day. After I drank, I forgot to ask her to finish, and Yukako didn't prompt me. When I realized my mistake, I saw Koito was making a second bowl. Grief, weariness, and grace radiated calmly from her as she followed Yukako's maxims: "Make heavy things look light; make light things look heavy." The dipper of water was a heavy door she slid shut, the bamboo whisk was a great stone bell. And though she looked at no one, only deep into the tea bowl, I felt her attention focused on Yukako in just the way the Mountain told his students to focus on their guests: *for you. All this is for you.* She set the steaming tea bowl on the mat beside her, and Yukako watched her without a single harsh word. In fact—I looked closer, surprised—her face held the same compassion, the same hesitant tenderness, she'd brought to Madam Akaito upstairs.

Yukako ritually thanked Koito and drank. She'd brought this tea bowl especially for summer lessons; it was shallow, so the tea cooled quickly, and its thick green glaze formed bumpy translucent ridges, as if it were dripping with cold water. When she finished, Yukako set the bowl in front of herself to offer formal appreciation, but Koito spoke. "*Mukashi mukashi*, there was a woman of the floating world who loved a man of tea."

I felt Yukako cloud over, thinking this was a story about Akio. Koito's phrase *floating world*, like Inko's more matter-of-fact phrase *water trade*, described the nighttime world of men's pleasures—gambling, singing-girls, prostitutes—but it was a pun on the Buddhist idea of the world of human grief. This world of suffering is a transitory illusion, teaches Buddhism, so we should detach from it. This world of sin is an evanescent dream, the pleasure seekers counsel—replacing the *kanji* for *suffering* with one of its homonyms, the *kanji* for *floating*—so we should enjoy it to the hilt. *Water trade, floating world.* The silk merchants' money floated Koito and her neighborhood along: without it they'd be left high and dry like Pontocho. But at the same time, I thought, Koito and her neighborhood were the ones doing the work of water, while their customers were the ones being floated through the dreamy night.

Who had floated whom last night? I wondered, thinking of Inko until Koito continued, "The man of tea was married to a girl who bore him six sons and a daughter. He had so many sons, he taught his wife *temae* so she could teach them too. Then every single one of their boys died young."

"Is that so," Yukako murmured. *Six sons and a daughter.* I had heard the phrase before. I remembered: Gensai, the Mountain's adoptive father, had lost six sons before taking in a *samurai* boy to marry his daughter Eiko, Yukako's mother.

Koito continued. "The woman of the floating world who loved the man of tea, she bore him a daughter too. Though his wife's girl filled him with nothing but despair over her dead brothers, his lover's girl gave him delight. For the Seven-Five-Three festival"—she named the holiday for blessing young children—"when the girl received her first grown-up *kimono*, he did *temae* in her honor here in this house. She had never seen a dance so graceful, and she loved dancing best of all. *Teach me!* the little girl begged. *Let me do it too!* He refused and she begged; she begged and he refused. *You taught your wife tea,* the little girl's mother said. It was the only word of reproach she ever gave him, in all her years of loneliness and longing. *My wife, yes,* he said, looking at them both, *but not you.* The woman told him to go and never come back, and the little girl never saw him again." Koito's voice was brisk and restrained, but her story was so sad. Perhaps she had said *floating world* instead of *water trade* because the woman in the story had forgotten her watery work: instead of floating her patron on a dream of love, she'd succumbed to the dream herself.

"What is it you want to tell me?" Yukako asked, wary of the story and yet compelled, as I was, by the calm way Koito told it, *making heavy things light.*

"That I did not understand my mother's disappointment, or my grandmother's rage, until the young lord refused to teach me Shin *temae,*" Koito said. I noticed the way she, like Yukako, avoided using Akio's name in public. "Just as your grandfather refused to teach my mother."

"Your mother," Yukako murmured. And then she seemed to absent herself. Her hands had remained in front of her throughout Koito's story, in the bow held before formally inspecting the tea bowl. She straightened her back now, and lifted her hands, turning each one over slowly, looking carefully at each of her palms.

"She wanted so much to see you today," Koito said, and bowed in deep gratitude. "She—" Koito's voice caught. "She said she wouldn't mind if I stayed home with her now. Would you mind teaching without me today?"

YUKAKO PAUSED on the path out of the *geisha* quarter, gazing at the shrine grove. "So, is Miss Koito your cousin?" I asked.

Yukako raised an arm as if to slap me, and then stopped, looked at her hand again, baffled. "I don't know," she said.

JUST BEFORE WE LEFT, Inko and I had exchanged a grin, and she'd slipped a small white packet into my sleeve. Finally alone in the cloakroom while Yukako gave her music lesson, I took it out. Inside a sheet of paper tied like a letter, I found a few black pearls of *neriko* incense rolled in a scrap of mosquito gauze. I inhaled deeply, my body pulsing inside. Yukako would have kept the incense in her pillow-box, but having no coiffure to lift off the ground with a wooden stand, I slept on a bag of buckwheat hulls. Where could I hide Inko's gift? When would I ever have the privacy to burn a ball of incense undisturbed? It would be as impossible as trying to make love again, when I slept beside Yukako each night and Inko slept beside the cook. Inko couldn't read or write, I mused, and yet her gift captured both the *floating world* of our night together and the difficulty of repeating it. And it offered a solution: though incense smells more faintly when it isn't burned, it can keep for years, fragrant and intact. I rolled the incense back into its scrap of fabric, tied it back into its knot of paper, and tucked it back into my *kimono. I would have had the best poem,* she'd said.

Yukako was shaken all afternoon as I followed her to the fish market, the grocery stands, and home. She sat behind the lattice while her father worked with his new students, facing into the classroom without watching the lesson. That evening on my way back from the bathhouse—the ordinary gloom of embarrassment there lit with a ray of pleasure at my own floating breasts, how Inko had touched them— I saw a figure with a lantern crossing the little stream toward the storeroom tower. Yukako came to bed late that night, but she let me fold tight around her when she slept.

Were Yukako and Koito really cousins? Had Yukako's grandfather Gensai really had an affair with Akaito's mother? Over the next few days,

Yukako helped her father at a series of tea offerings for the Obon festival, first to her own ancestors, then at the household shrines of the merchant Okura Chugo and his friends. When she wasn't working, I couldn't find her—but sometimes she appeared, dusty and distracted, for a midday meal. She was in the dim plaster fireproof tower, it seemed, looking through the family treasures.

During the Obon festival, we would dance in circles with the ancestors each night, then light fires to send them home to rest, from the neighborhood temple bonfires at the beginning of the week to the great mountain fires at the end. On the faces of the mountains that cupped the city—including Daimonji, the hill I saw my first day in Miyako, its flank carved with the character *dai*—ten enormous *kanji* were shaped out of wood and straw and lit on the last night of Obon, so that the city was ringed with a poem calligraphed in fire. The morning of the smallest bonfires, Yukako seemed resolute again, changed. She sighed often, as if beating back a wave of disbelief. That evening, she had me carry a box behind her on the way to our neighborhood temple, where she danced a brief circle, and then I followed her when she slipped out of the crowd, walking the long dark way to the *geisha* quarter.

When we passed through a temple near Kitano Shrine, we paused: the circle of Obon dancers looked like a fairyland. I saw Mizushi there, lifting one hand at a time as if the world were watching, and Inko, too, her narrow eyes drained of merriment. I wished she could see me. And then we saw Koito, her movements stark and lovely as a tree in winter, tears rolling freely off her face. What had happened was clear: the three of them wore black.

On the walk home, I remembered dabbing at the water as the women drank from *sake* cups. I had drunk farewell with Koito's mother, too, even if she didn't know it. I remembered the way she sailed in to look at my mother's dress, her beautiful body bent in curiosity, her flowing russet train. And then I remembered—my heart caught in my throat a little—a sleeping woman in bright sunlight, a red-and-white quilt of Irish Chain. *Did you get to say good-bye to her—to Fumi?* I'd asked Inko.

No, she'd said. *I think it's better that way.*

I waited for Yukako to tell me what she'd sought and what she'd found. I asked her baldly that night why we'd gone to the *geisha* quarter. She turned her back to me and traced characters on the *tatami* with her finger; I couldn't read them. The next few days she was restive as she helped her father, itchy as we gathered on one of the Kamo bridges with her family, watching the Daimonji fires. Sumie's father and brother were still being held in Edo, I thought, looking up from the rice ball Chio had packed for me to the Pipe Lady bent over her lacquered picnic box. Her silk robes were threadbare, but she still had fine rice for her *sushi.* Carp, I noted. From her own pond?

At night I spread out Yukako's *futon* and waited up for her. *Tell me, tell me.* My desire to know mixed up with my desire for Inko—my desire to feel my own body alive again—and I remembered another impatient evening not long after I first came to the Shins, when I waited for Yukako on the stairs and she came up at last, weeping that Akio had rejected her *temae.* She and Akio had made love, I realized.

In the corner of Yukako's room I found the box I'd carried for her to the *geisha* quarter and back. Raw wood brushed with a black coiled river of *kanji,* it was wrapped in silk and tied with violet cords. I didn't want to be a sneak, I just wanted to know; inside the box lay two scrolls. Hanging each on a mosquito netting post, I lit another lamp and waited for Yukako.

I could barely read or write words that were block-printed or brushed very clearly, and Japanese calligraphy favors expression over clarity. In the bronze light of the lanterns, lying inside the luminous cube of mosquito gauze and drinking cold barley tea, I stared at the white panels within their silk borders, their brushed lines like the tracks of birds. The left-hand scroll I recognized: it was the child's character for *Shin* that Yukako had hung in Baishian the night she declared me her sister. The right-hand scroll was similar: a large childish center mark, surrounded by elderly wisps of *kanji*. The central character, however, was not *Shin*. A cross here, a sword there, two marks for motion, like a little pair of flippers at the base of the *kanji*—I had no idea. I traced it on my hand, to no avail. As for the smaller characters surrounding the crude center marks, I didn't venture a guess. They made me think of *miso* constellations, swirling in soup, or—on a hot night, I tried to think of cool things—smoke rising through snow.

"Miss Urako."

I all but jumped out of my skin. "I didn't hear you!"

"I suppose not." Yukako was sitting behind me, hands folded as if she'd been there for quite some time. "Are these yours?" she said coldly.

"Older Sister, I'm sorry."

Yukako entered the gauze enclosure. "I just—" I told her the truth. "I worried for you." Yukako looked at me and sighed, weary and fond. "What are they?" I asked.

"Proof," she said, taking down a scroll.

I didn't understand. "It's by your mother, right?" I persisted. "Shin Eiko."

"*Un*," Yukako said, nodding. "I wanted to show both to Koito, but this one is enough," she said, indicating the other scroll.

"What does it say?"

Yukako smiled grimly. "At the center there's the *kanji* for *aka: red*."

"*Ara!*" Didn't Koito's mother's name, Akaito, mean *red thread*?

Yukako paused. "At the sides, there's a poem by Lady Murasaki," she said slowly. Then she gave me a long look, and decided to tell me. "Two poems," she said. "Copied by two different people."

Leaning in, I saw she was right: the characters on one side of the page matched the spidery writing on the other scroll, while the characters on the other were firmer and clearer, as if writer did not take it for granted that he or she would be understood. "Gensai, Akaito,

Akaito's mother?" I asked, pointing at the calligraphy in three different hands.

Yukako made a harsh noncommittal sound. Then she rolled the *Red* scroll, fitted it into the box, and tied the violet cords tight. I meekly helped her roll up the other one. She said nothing as she knelt before our shelves, putting away the clean folded *kimono* she'd brought up from the sewing room. I saw her pause at my shelf. "Don't touch my things anymore," she said, tossing something my way. I caught it: my tied paper packet from Inko.

I LAY BESIDE YUKAKO, listening to her breathe. I tried to imagine Koito's mother as a little girl learning her calligraphy, proudly brushing her name. Why wasn't it *Shin*? I remembered the Mountain when we first met, speaking without defensiveness or anger, simply declaring me *not Shin*. With his voice in my mind, matter-of-fact, I could see a man looking at his lover and his daughter, hear his dispassionate choice: *not you*. I winced in the dark. Bernard was just as makeshift a last name as Migawa. If there was some living man in Paris with my face, I knew he'd never claim me. Inko wrote no note with her gift: even if the wrong person unwrapped it, there'd be nothing to betray her. "What were the Murasaki poems on the scroll?" I asked.

Yukako recited something in the dark. "The prince learns he has a daughter by a woman who is not his wife," she explained, "in faraway Akashi. In the first poem he promises to protect the baby. And in the second, the baby's mother sends her thanks. Do you understand?"

"Ah," I said. *Aka-shi. Aka-ito. Shi, ito:* the Chinese character for *thread* was pronounced using either sound. "Is the *ito* in Akaito the same as the *shi* in Baishian?"

"It is," Yukako said curtly.

"Didn't your grandfather want to build a teahouse called Baishian? Wasn't that where your father got the idea?"

"Could you please stop talking?" Yukako said, her voice thick with feeling. I knew how much she loved the teahouse—how much, though she knew her father had built it to make a name for himself in the Emperor's court, she thought of it as hers.

"I'm sorry," I said. I laid my hand on my chest, soft and newly dear. I breathed Inko's incense through my sleeve.

WITH THE OBON HOLIDAY behind us, we walked the next day to the Northern Seven-House Quarter, to collect Yukako's *shamisen* for her lesson with the Mitsuba girl and to offer condolences. "I don't imagine Koito will come with us to teach," Yukako said, "but I want to give her this." She gestured toward the box in my arms. She lingered at Kitano Shrine that day, praying until her candle guttered.

Passing out of the shrine gate, I thought of how in just minutes I'd wait in the cloakroom while Koito and Yukako talked, how Inko would appear, dressed in black, bringing me a cup of cold barley tea. I felt breathless. I imagined her sitting on the bench beside me, lifting her foot out of her sandal again, this time touching *my* calf. I wanted to trace her soft mouth with my finger. When we left the shrine grove, I almost didn't see Mizushi on the path.

"Shin Yukako-*sama?*" said the little girl. She was dressed for work in her whiteface and trailing sash, her absurdly high clogs.

"Yes?"

"My Older Sister asked me to wait here for you. You see, she left for Edo at dawn."

"Miss Koito?"

"Everybody was surprised. But after the funeral, she turned the house over to Madam Suisho and she packed up her *kimono* to go. Another *geiko* from her Pontocho days moved to Edo recently, you see."

"Did the cook leave too?" I asked. I couldn't say Inko's name out loud; I cared too much.

"Just Older Sister and Miss Inko and all those *kimono*. They had to take four carts!"

"Is that so?" said Yukako, dumbfounded.

"She left your *shamisen* in the cloakroom."

"Is that so."

"She wanted me to tell you that she left, and thank you, and good-bye," Mizushi recited.

Yukako shook her head in disbelief. "Thank you."

"I'm glad you got here because I've kept somebody waiting," the *maiko* said, smiling, then blurted out her news. "A famous artist wants to paint me!"

"Congratulations," Yukako said, the standard phrase hollow in the air.

"Miss Inko asked me to say good-bye to you especially," Mizushi added as an afterthought, giving me a tiny bow. She turned to go and, remembering something, bowed to Yukako again. "I'm sorry, that man who was going to meet you? I told him"—and when she said this she looked youngest of all—"there were no men allowed in the house, so he said he'd wait for you outside."

"Thank you," murmured Yukako, still dazed.

Mizushi bowed a last deep farewell and clopped down the path, the ends of her stiff gauze *obi* flapping like flags. Yukako and I looked at each other, stunned. "She went to Edo," she repeated.

"She's on a boat right now."

"Or on the mountain road." Yukako shook her head again.

"With her four carts?"

Yukako gave a humorless bark of laughter. "Oh, she'll go by boat, I'm sure." I was still holding the scroll box, tied in its silk wrapper. Yukako looked at it as if it were a bowl of blackened rice. "I can't believe I was going to give her anything."

Inko left! I could not parse it. I'd been about to see her and now I wasn't. How could that happen? "Who were you going to meet?" I attempted.

"I have no idea. Nobody."

How could she go? I could still feel the hard stem of her wrist where I'd been about to touch it. "Is it Mr. Mitsuba, about his girl's lesson?" I tried again.

"I wonder," she mused. "There must be many men who want to tell her good-bye." I heard a little of the old acid back in her voice. "But to see me?" She paused suddenly. "Akio?"

Could Akio know that Koito was leaving and have come, too late, from Hikone, to see both women who'd loved him? This seemed highly unlikely, if highly romantic, to me, but Yukako bore down the path as if a hard wind drove her. I trotted after, and all but smashed my face on her *obi* when she stopped in horror.

"Did you have a good prayer at Kitano Shrine?" the Mountain asked.

Yukako gasped. I gasped. He was sitting in the shade on the bench outside Koito's house. "Father—" she began.

He stood. "I admired your piety. I admired your forbearance. I admired your frugality," he said.

"Father."

"Those are the very virtues on which I based my plea to the Emperor to help the Way of Tea survive."

"Father, I—"

"But did you know there's a *geiko* in vogue these days who does Shin *temae*? Okura said she claims to be a descendent of Rikyu himself. He said one night, when she'd drunk too much, she bragged that underneath all the Western This and *bunmei kaika* That, the city was full of men who would pay dearly for the illusion that they were still the center of the civilized world."

"*Ara!*"

"Well, that's what *geiko* sell, my dear: illusion. And when that pretty young thing goes to the Eastern Capital and makes her gold at being The *Geisha* Who Does Shin *Temae*," he said, sneering as he used the flashy Tokyo word instead of the soft Kyoto one, *geiko*, "she'll do very well indeed. What a charming *pastime*."

His voice broke a little then, and I saw Yukako start toward him.

"How do you think the Meiji officials will consider my plea when they hear of this? They've set aside a fortune to build a foreigners' dance hall, but they've dismissed tea as a *pastime*. That was what they called it. When I wrote my formal letter of protest, I entreated them to support it as a *discipline*."

He cut off Yukako's words of encouragement with a bitter sigh. "If a few merchants like Okura want to play at being *samurai* and pass the time with tea, I'll thank them for their patronage. They're nostalgic for what they never had. But surely tea is more than illusion and nostalgia, Daughter?"

"Yes, Father," Yukako said, her head bowed low. Hearing *illusion* and *nostalgia* made me think of the phrase *the floating world*. I suddenly understood the Mountain's fury: for him, tea was not the *floating world*, it *was* the world.

"Surely tea deserves the Emperor's support?" he pressed on.

"Yes, Father," Yukako whispered.

"How much did you bargain away his support for, Daughter?" he said.

Yukako breathed deeply, unable to speak.

"Do you understand what you sold when you sold our *temae*?"

I saw Yukako's back tremble.

"I thought you were husbanding our money and you were burning up our last hope on a laundress and a bowl of white rice."

He struck Yukako across the face. I took hold of his arm. "Get out of the way, Urako," she said.

He struck her again and again until she sobbed, and then he stopped, watching her.

"I wanted—" Yukako gasped, her face red and puffy. She drew her packet of tea-papers out from the breast of her *kimono* and pressed them to her bleeding mouth. "I wanted to be like you."

I saw the Mountain echo Yukako's gesture of futility and disbelief. He held up his hands and stared at them, surprised at his own passion. "When Okura told me, I thought of that," he said slowly. "And so I have determined to award you permission to teach tea to the wives and daughters of my students. Okura wants his mother to look after his collection of tea things. You'll teach her *temae,* and you'll meet with me once a week for your own lesson."

Yukako looked up at him, surprised.

"When I wrote the Emperor, I said tea instilled filial piety, didn't I? I will decide who and where you'll teach, but you'll teach," he said.

"I humbly understand," Yukako said, using a servant's phrase. "I humbly thank you."

"Or your husband will decide."

"You said I might not marry for a long time."

"I hoped when the Meiji court replied, it would turn the tide in our favor. Now they may not reply at all. After I learned the depth of our misfortune, I received a request for a Sighting. I've discussed the matter with my mother, who was as appalled at the low birth of the suitor's family as she was impressed by its wealth." That, and the way the Mountain had looked at his hands, gave me pause: of all his family, birth and adopted, the only person he had left to consult was the Pipe Lady.

Many years ago Yukako had said she would never marry, and I had believed her. Now she carefully folded her bloodied paper into eighths and tucked it into her sleeve. "Yes, Father," she said.

"She berated me soundly and said this latest blow was due directly to my own neglect, letting you stray all over town with only a half-wit for chaperone."

I blanched, and Yukako flashed him a look in my defense.

"My mother has agreed to accompany you should you leave our home, until pregnancy precludes any further adventures in the floating world. Miss Urako, you'll work in the sewing house."

Pained, I stared at Yukako as she tried to keep her face composed.

"This is not my first choice," her father said. "But we are very fortunate that, having discovered what you've done, Okura offers us a choice at all."

"Mr. Okura?" Yukako breathed. Was she going to marry Okura Chugo, that fat, soft merchant, that giant mollusk?

"Are you half-witted too? He's the head of a household with a wife and son." But I'd seen the man; surely he was in his twenties. Was she to marry his infant son? "Tonight we'll hold a Sighting for you and Okura's brother."

I UNDERSTOOD ONLY PATCHES of what the Mountain said, and I have braided them in with what Yukako explained to me later as she dressed in the *kimono* he chose for her Sighting. But I understood Yukako's shame and contrition as she walked home behind her father, hobbling her long steps to keep pace behind his short ones. And I understood when she sent me out to collect her *shamisen* and tell the Mitsubas, the Tsutamons, and all her other students that *Sensei* had gone back to Edo for Obon and stayed, due to a family emergency. So sorry, but she might not return for a very long time.

At Yukako's first Sighting, when she wore the dark blue-green robe with the flowering painted tree, she had dressed older than her sixteen years, contrasting those sober colors with the dewy youth of her skin. The effect she achieved was the reticence of a flower in bud, a seductive modesty. Yukako grimaced when Chio brought the Mountain's choice upstairs. At twenty-one, Yukako was old for an unmarried woman, and very old indeed for a confection as girlish as this. The entire gauze *kimono* was a sunset seascape: turquoise water, puffy pink ribs of cloud. A troupe of fat babies tumbled across the golden sand, dressed in a rainbow of candy tints. "Can't you tell him it's the wrong season?" I groaned. During Obon she'd begun wearing a gauze robe patterned with *hagi*, one of the seven grasses of autumn.

"No, this is good until Jizo-bon," she said, naming the festival honoring the god of children, some ten days hence. "See?" She pointed glumly at the dumpling babies.

"Oh, no," I said, embarrassed on her behalf.

"The sleeves are as long as the ones on that *maiko*," Yukako complained. The sleeves she wore since burning her *kimono* were not so short as a married woman's, but shorter than these: to advertise her fading youth would reek of desperation. Assuming a cheer edged with hysteria, Yukako imitated Mizushi, coyly raising a hand to her mouth. "Will you marry me?" she simpered at the mirror.

"Tell him you won't do it!" I said. "Tell him you want to be a Buddhist nun!"

"Ura-*bo*, I've hurt him so much already." Yukako looked suddenly as serious as she had when she'd made her choice by the river, that day we watched the darting birds. And matter-of-fact as Inko, she said, "Besides, how else will he get an heir?"

"So you're going to marry just anyone?"

"He's not just *anyone*. My father *chose* him." Yukako said it firmly, with a tiny wobble at the end. Her father had chosen Akio first, after all.

The *obi* that the Mountain had set out for her was just as loud as the *kimono*: a vivid swirl of white and bright green, with a salmon undersash and a flashy red cord. "If you go to a Sighting, does the girl *have* to marry the boy?" I tried again.

"Well, either person can say no. But look at what a mess I've made of things on my own," Yukako said, shrugging.

"So you're just going to walk down that staircase and marry whoever's at the bottom of it?"

I was standing behind Yukako at the mirror. She fingered the red cord around her waist and spoke to my reflection. "Do you know what *Akaito* means?"

How couldn't I? "Miss Koito's mother. *Red thread.*"

"But what it *means*," she insisted. "There's a red thread that ties you to the person you're going to marry. I thought Akio was at the other end of mine, but he wasn't. It's not up to me. Do you understand? So it doesn't matter." There were tears on her face. She took my cotton sleeve and blotted her eyes without rubbing them.

And so I sat with a tray in the doorway again, five years after my first day at the Shins', when Yukako saw the face of her intended. I was supposed to clear the dish away and bring another while Yukako brought *sake* for the Okura brothers, but I sat unseen, transfixed, as Yukako poured for the gelatinous young man, and then for the boy in the shadows. He wasn't enormous—that was a mercy—but he was hard to see until he bowed his thanks into the lamplight. I saw his eager, hopeful face and I saw Yukako, a resolute woman in a girlish robe. I saw a bolt of lightning strike the blank night of her face, an appalled flash of recognition. It was the Stickboy.

IN BED AS I WAITED for my older sister, I wondered fiercely, how could *he* be at the other end of Yukako's red thread? That nobody, that knobby-kneed fumbler? How could I not have known he was Okura's brother? How could Yukako not have known? He was just always *there*, in his clumsy way: we'd never bothered to know. And once Yukako had taken revenge on him for stealing her *kimono*, he'd become invisible to her, to both of us: present on the grounds of our awareness, the way a privy is, but beneath notice.

I HELD INKO'S GIFT of incense to my face. I wondered if she was on a ship bound for Edo at that very moment. She must be happy, I thought, feeling, even amidst my greedy longing, a flash of hope on her behalf. If Koito was going to find the other *geisha* who moved to Edo to try her luck, wouldn't Inko find Fumi? Was Fumi at the other end of Inko's red thread?

But Fumi would likely be married, and Inko would likely come back to Kyoto in a year and a half and marry the boy her father chose. It all seemed so unfair. I knew Yukako had been sure Akio was at the other end of her red thread. How humiliating to be wrong, to follow the red line and find oneself tied to Okura Jiro, of all people. *It's karma from another life,* Inko had said. I'd once asked Yukako what *karma* meant, and she'd explained valiantly before giving up. But I understood now why Inko said it, why seducers said it in stories, why people said it all the time. It was a way to make the truth of the red thread less cruel. If Akio wasn't at the end of Yukako's thread this time, maybe he had been in another life.

Inhaling the rolled black knots of incense Inko gave me, I thought of her and my body quaked a little. I missed her, but I did not feel jealous of Fumi. I heard the splashing of Yukako's ablutions stop below, heard her climb up into the hot bath to soak. I felt a sparkle of contentment, knowing she'd be upstairs soon, and a splinter of despair: she could marry anytime, and then these would be lost to me, my nights in this room, inhaling beeswax and powdered tea, her curved back my horizon. At that moment it was Yukako I longed for most of all, my brisk and stormy older sister, my teacher, my brushstroke, my prow, my heart. I wished she were at the end of my red thread.

YUKAKO WAS IN NO MOOD for talk when she lay down. "I'm going to sleep now," she said. I felt her wide awake beside me, and I held her, my body rapt. I took her wrist and touched it gently with my thumb. "Stop that," she said. I pressed my ear to her back and felt her breath quiver, like slowly ripping paper.

"Are you crying?" I asked softly.

"No," she lied.

12

1871

Dᴜʀɪɴɢ Yᴜᴋᴀᴋᴏ's ʙʀɪᴇғ ᴇɴɢᴀɢᴇᴍᴇɴᴛ to the Stickboy, the Pipe Lady came to announce the imperial court's latest outrage. "They're rounding us up and marching us to Edo," she told the Mountain over tea.

"Tokyo, Mother," he corrected blandly. "Surely that can't be." Only the stillness of his face conveyed alarm.

"Bad enough that they took your brother," she lamented. "Now they want us, the Tsutamons, the Mitsubas, all of us." She went on to name other feudal lords throughout Japan who had fought on the Shogun's side, including Akio's father, Lord Ii. "I'm eighty years old," she said, sucking on her pipe in disgust.

Mɪss Mɪᴋɪ ᴀɴᴅ ʜᴇʀ ᴍᴏᴛʜᴇʀ were working on Yukako's hair upstairs when I came in with the news. I had expected Yukako to shake off her depressive torpor long enough to ask about Akio, but it was Miki, passing a comb to her mother, who showed most interest. "The whole family?" she asked, her little mouth falling open.

Miki's uncle, also a barber, had moved to Tokyo, where he learned to meet the new demand for Western hairstyles: the *random crop*, the *chestnut burr*. On a visit home, he taught Miki's father the new cuts, and now her family was starting to see wealth they'd never known before. Lovely, fourteen, and solvent, with no brother to head the household, I like to think Miki whispered to her mother that she'd never forgotten the boy who'd once tugged her sleeve, Sumie's youngest brother. Perhaps a match would keep his family from having to leave Canal Street.

A week later, after a go-between brought forward an extremely deferential and tentative request for a meeting between the two children, I overheard the Pipe Lady tell her son that Miki's father—*that climber!*—was a poisonous schemer who thought he could buy his way into a *samurai* family. "We don't need them," she scoffed. "Besides, we're not the only ones who plan to stay." Akio's father, she heard from her granddaughter Sumie, had left Hikone and gone to Tokyo alone to beg the court not to uproot his family. He had seen enough politics for one lifetime: just as Yukako's father had pleaded for Imperial support for tea, Lord Ii claimed that he could best serve the nation through breeding horses on the mild shores of Lake Biwa.

After receiving this news from her granddaughter, the Pipe Lady made inquiries, and within days Sumie's two youngest brothers—almost fourteen and fifteen by Japanese reckoning—were engaged to a pair of *samurai* sisters from Hikone, distant relatives of Akio, just as poor as the boys themselves.

With two new mouths to feed, the Pipe Lady pressed one of her maids on us, Chio's doughy niece Ryu, whom we took on as another laundress. Kuga was glad for the company and worried aloud to her cousin about little Zoji. "Lord Horse has no more money, either. He's sold my boy's contract to some man called Noda." By Sumie's report, the Hikone rice merchant Noda was an uncouth upstart. "Noda, hm? His family name's no older than ours," Kuga grumped.

"He could still be a good man," counseled Ryu. She was the sort of person who had nothing but compassion for people she didn't know, and nothing but mockery for those she did. When the Tsutamon family left Kyoto on the Emperor's orders, they left the Mountain with a pair of their servants as acknowledgment of tuition unpaid: a grandfather in his forties and a grandson under two, the boy's parents lost to cholera. Although he recognized neither Yukako nor myself, I remembered the crop-headed man right away: it was Bozu, whom Inko had regaled with tales of an Edo she'd never seen. He called his little grandson Toru. "After the queen of England!" marveled Ryu. "What a fool!" Chio and Matsu's tiny cottage could not sleep six now, she insisted, and Kuga was grateful to be bullied into decamping with her cousin to the three-mat room by the kitchen door.

THE NEXT TIME MISS MIKI came to do Yukako's hair, both young women were engaged. Kuga's estranged husband, Goto, never one to leave money untouched, took advantage of Miki's embarrassed rejection and quickly got her promised to his son Zoji; they would marry when the boy finished out his contract with Noda. "Congratulations," Yukako said, her voice consoling.

"Some girls have to leave their parents," Miki said, resisting her own disappointment. "We're the lucky ones."

A BRIDE'S FAMILY would have sent silk and lacquer, all the *kimono* and furnishings a woman would need in her married life. Okura Jiro, the Stickboy, was to marry into his wife's family instead of the other way around, so his brother sent cash alone. On Yukako's wedding day I saw, ceremonially laid out in brocade wrappings in the display alcove of her father's study, my first *koban*, gold coins of the old style, more like small saucers than coins.

Yukako and I sat together in front of the *koban*. Looking at the money made my skin crawl. "The worst thing is, a year from now this gold will still be worth something, and all the money I saved for Father won't matter a bit."

She was right: not only had the Meiji authorities taken back the lords' rice fields, they had announced a new currency, controlled from Tokyo. In place of the familiar disks of thin blackened silver, each pierced with a square hole, heavier coins of grosser metal had just begun to appear, their Japanese and Roman letters circling a central imperial chrysanthemum. Within months the old coins' worth would vanish, sure as the power of the lords who had circulated them. Suddenly bereft of even their patrons' unwisely spent savings, we heard, the downtown *geisha* had announced that for the first time ever they would hold public dances each year.

"It's like we never spent that year at Koito's," I sighed, missing Inko.

"All that work," Yukako agreed. "Father said he doesn't want the money, so I have to spend it on something while I can. O-Chio's been grousing about sharing quarters with Bozu and Toru. I'll get the old shed by the storeroom tower fixed up for them."

"That's generous," I said.

"The money was for the Cloud House, not for me. I might as well help someone with it." She was looking at the display alcove as she spoke. She held her breath. I saw her close her wet eyes and shut out Okura's gold.

I FOLLOWED YUKAKO upstairs to her room and sat with her, surrounded on three sides by clothing stands hung with the robes she'd wear that night: first an all-white *kimono* with long girlish sleeves, the robe, she said, without a breath of morbidity, she'd be cremated in someday. "I'll wear it for the first part of the wedding, when we drink three cups of *sake* three times."

"Oh," I breathed, remembering the night we drank *sake* together in

Baishian. Many years later I learned that in the *geisha* world, older and younger sisters bound themselves to one another with *sake* as well, but at that moment I was too stunned and hurt to ask.

"After that, I'll wear this one," Yukako said, pointing to the last long-sleeved *kimono* she'd ever wear: a crane-flooded riot of colors even louder than the tumbling beach-baby robe she'd worn for the Sighting. "And this one last." After the wedding feast, she would change once more, into her married life's first short-sleeved robe: a formal five-crested *kimono*, black with a morning-glory pattern climbing almost to her shoulders. The pattern on the formal robes sank lower with a woman's age, such that on formal occasions the Pipe Lady wore a black robe with a pattern of forest mushrooms that climbed barely past her ankles.

Surrounded by those robes, Yukako had Miss Miki and her mother wax, comb, sculpt, and pin her first married woman's coiffure. And then, for the first time, she blackened her teeth with a solution of iron filings and oak gall while the hairdressers applied themselves to me. First they shaved off my mother's sleek black brows with a thin blade and painted on new ones. Then, with hot wax and scalp-cutting combs, they tortured my hair into its first unmarried girl's *shimada*. Miss Miki gave me a wrapped package to open later, and then they went downstairs to work on Chio, Ryu, and Kuga. My head burned. My scalp burned. My face felt peeled and raw. Okura Jiro, of all people, I kept thinking. The Stickboy. "You could still say no," I told Yukako as she put on her white robe.

Since the day the Mountain struck her, a certain vacant, steely expression had made its way into Yukako's repertoire. Favoring me with it, she said, "Now you look like a grown-up young lady."

THAT NIGHT I SPREAD out bedding for Yukako and Jiro upstairs, and then went downstairs to sleep by the kitchen entrance with Kuga and

Ryu. I spent the night listening against my better judgment for sounds from the upstairs room, revolted on Yukako's behalf, bereaved on my own. The one thing that saved me from despair was the packet Miss Miki had given me, sent from her cousin in Tokyo.

Kyoto transplants in Tokyo, it seemed, were quick to find each other. Besides Koito, only one person in Tokyo knew me, a girl who, like me, had once recognized Miss Miki when she stepped out of a comb shop in the *geisha* quarter. When I could bear the night no longer, I opened Inko's gift. Unspooling a puff of white tissue, I found a water-lily–shaped wafer of pressed sugar. I had not been forgotten; my eyes stung from gratitude. The sweetness dissolved on my tongue, and I smiled in spite of my exile, cupping my full breasts in the dark. *Yes. You would have had the best poem.*

Inko's sweet had been tucked into the hollow of another wrapped object. I peeled back the paper: it was a *sake* cup, white as bone. I dipped it in one of the kitchen barrels and drank. *Did you get to tell Fumi good-bye?*

No. I think it's better that way. "Good-bye," I whispered aloud.

FOR THE NEXT FEW MONTHS I saw Yukako alone only when I joined her in Baishian, playing host or guest to her one student, the Stickboy's mother. At first, I lurched around after the wedding in a sleep-deprived fog, the lullaby of Yukako's breath beside me replaced by the effort of trying to keep my head from rolling off my new wooden pillow as I slept, so as not to crush my grown-up-girl's coiffure. After those filmy, wretched days had passed, I realized that a change had come over Yukako, one I'd been too selfish to witness. Her steely bleakness seemed to have dissipated. I cannot say she seemed to like her husband more, but she seemed to have set her dislike of him aside, as if she had better things on her mind. A month or so after Jiro came to the Shin house, when Yukako and I had a moment alone in Baishian, I summoned up

Inko's gumption and asked her, "So, what did he say to you on your wedding night?"

She gave me an arch smile, and I realized that she took fierce satisfaction from the fact that Akio, not Jiro, had been her first man. And that she was pregnant, and glad of it. "'*Well, we have to do this now,*'" she said.

13

1872

THE DOOR WAS OPEN when I brought Young Master's tea, so I didn't close it.

A raw wood box, an ink brush, a young man kneeling at a low desk. At the end of the First Month in Meiji Five, Jiro, the man I'd once called the Stickboy, seemed happy. "You enjoy calligraphy," I said with a nod to his brush when I set down the tray.

He thanked me with a curt dip of the chin. "Now I do," he said. To warm his fingers and preserve his fine wet writing-point, he tucked the brush in his mouth and took the cup with both hands. Poised for a moment like a bird with a twig, he looked past me through the doorway to the snow silvering the thatched roof of his favorite teahouse: the dim humble four-and-a-half-mat hut called Houseless House, Muin.

He was lucky indeed. Spared a ledger boy's life bent over the inkbrush, he was free to indulge in its pleasures. After a childhood spent catering to his tyrannical father and brother—the very name Jiro meant Second Son—and a youth spent year upon year as the lowest-ranked apprentice, he was suddenly the Young Master, the heir to the house, second only to his father-in-law, Master Teacher. He had also—like Yukako's grandfather Gensai and her father, sometimes called Yosai—received an art name, Insai, that announced his new status to the world. All the teahouses would be his when the Mountain was gone, and already he had been named special protector of Rikyu's own One Pine teahouse at Sesshu-ji, the Shin family temple south of the city. Young Master's conjugal duties dispensed with for the moment, he was free to spend as many nights as he pleased at Sesshu-ji, as he claimed, or trawling the floating world, as seemed more likely.

Jiro had wanted a study of his own in the Shin house and received it: the Bent-Tree Annex, where Akio had lain sick years before. He had summoned the queer-faced servant girl for tea, and she had come. He had just asked his adoptive father for permission to orchestrate, single-handed, an informal tea ceremony gathering of his own every new moon, and permission had been granted. That night he would host the Master Teacher alone, and from then on once a month the Mountain would be, not a teacher, choosing the scroll for each lesson, interrupting with corrections at any time, but one ordinary guest among a handful, offering private counsel after the event. It was for this first tea gathering—this first *chakai*—that Jiro now prepared, brushing letters on the lid of a wooden box.

He plucked the brush from his mouth, sipped his tea, and set to work again. "What are you writing?" I said. Jiro didn't abuse me when I spoke to him, or dismiss me outright. I wouldn't have dared to ask the Mountain questions, but sometimes Jiro even answered mine, showing me how pine-based black ink had a blue cast to it, while the undertone of bamboo-based black ink was brown. The things Jiro taught me didn't make up for how much I missed my place at Yukako's side, but they made me hate him less than I wanted to.

The pale raw pine was the brightest thing in Jiro's room: a box for a tea bowl, it stood some eight inches square, with slots cut in the base for a woven strap. The lid couldn't have been simpler: a flat square panel with two wood strips tacked in back for a snug fit. In his old black student robe, Jiro, brush in hand, seemed somehow apart from his scarecrow body, his dark-browed, long-nosed, cheese-wedge face. All his awareness was gathered in his soft eyes, in the ink-soaked tip of the brush, rising and arcing, touching down with a wet flicker and rising again, like a bird on a current of air. He brushed two large characters on the box and sat back from his work, content.

His head, from the side, looked like an upside-down flatiron: high temples, cheeks that tapered to the chin, his pinned-up queue a handle. "Did you say something?" he blinked.

"What did you write?"

"*Inazuma,*" he said.

I'd asked Yukako once why the word for *lightning* sounded like the word for *rice plant* and the word for *wife.* For once, she didn't say *Different kanji:* "When the lightning hits the paddies it makes the rice grow big," holding her arms out in a hoop as if swollen, as she was now, with child.

"Then why isn't it the rice's *husband*?"

"Why why why?" she'd teased. "Ura-*bo,* I don't know."

"Can I see it?" I asked Jiro, gesturing toward the form in the box, something tied in red silk.

The Mountain would have struck me. Yukako would have shot me a glance I called The Look. Jiro looked up in genuine puzzlement and explained, "Father needs to see it first."

"It was rude of me," I apologized. "Should I close the door when I go?"

"No. But bring in another brazier, won't you?" he said. Holding the brush in his mouth again he crossed his arms against the cold, looking dreamily outside. "Tonight I'll make tea from a kettle of snow."

. . .

THAT NIGHT, after the Mountain watched Jiro lay charcoal and brush the lacquer hearth-frame with its bundle of feathers, Yukako set the first tray from the kitchen in the corridor outside the Muin teahouse. Pausing, she looked over the utensils laid ready to enter the tearoom, including Jiro's calligraphed box, set out in the place where a tea bowl would go. "*He* named it?" she whispered, her mouth a black zone in the lamplight. During the intermission that followed the Mountain's ritual meal, Yukako helped Jiro replace the scroll in the display alcove with flowers, then settled backstage as Jiro began to do *temae* in earnest. *Come on*, she mouthed, waving as I lingered by the closed host door.

Didn't she want to see the new tea bowl? I made a gesture of licking a finger and dotting it on the *shoji* door to make a peephole. *No*, she whispered. This from the girl who'd spied on every lesson? But she got tired so easily these days. With an embarrassed smile, Yukako leaned against a post and closed her eyes, her panting short breaths relaxing into long ones in a matter of seconds. I moved the lamp to keep my peephole from shining like a star in the wall and leaned in.

Muin, a thatched hut nine feet square, was the most restrained of the Shin tearooms. Lacking the broad expanses of the classroom or the fourteen-mat hall, lacking the clever floorboards of Baishian or Cloud House—tricks to make a tiny room seem bigger—it stood a simple four and a half mats, with the four rectangular mats arranged like petals around the center square half-mat: a square within a square. The winter hearth was cut into the half-mat, and I saw steam in candlelight. I saw the pale-gold *tatami*, the ceiling like a dark plaited basket, the two darkened windows. A candle lit a shimmer of sand in the clay-plastered wall, lit a camellia blossom and the white tips of a budding plum branch in the alcove. A second candle lit Jiro and his red-lacquered tea box, a spot of color counterbalanced by a dab of green on the sweet tray. The flecks of green and red emphasized the quiet black-white-adobe palette of the tearoom, as did the occasional spark rising from the charcoal fire.

The Mountain bowed appreciatively over his sweet, its swelling green center visible through a white outer layer, and asked Jiro its name.

Shitamoe, he said, *shoots under snow.* It was a nod to the hope of spring returning, to the ancestor Rikyu's simple tea, and to the new life, unbelievably, slumbering inside my older sister. I felt a deep sense of *alignment* radiating from the two men, of serenity, of rapport with each other, with the beauty in the room, with the snowy night outside. The only sounds in the room were like breath: the soughing of the boiling water, the whisper of the tea whisk in the bowl. Then Jiro set the tea bowl on the *tatami* beside him, and the Mountain moved forward to retrieve it.

I saw a flash of black and gold. Yukako didn't stir when I gasped. I looked again. I saw a rough black vessel that shone like a hot thing newly formed, flung up from the earth: I recognized it. It was the lesson bowl from years before that had fallen apart, as if of its own accord, in Jiro's hands; I remembered the wet loose sound it made, the faintest sandy grinding, like unglazed dishes rubbed together, the way he froze, eyes and mouth wide at the chunk of fired clay still cupped in his left hand, the two black petals of the bowl trembling on the *tatami* floor. It was the same bowl, humbly saved and mended with soldered gold. I looked at Jiro with new respect. The gold vein was like the white thread of moon in the wood at Baishian.

The Mountain remembered the tea bowl too. I heard a grunt of recognition: *"Un."* Jiro all but beamed as the Mountain drank deep, then held up the bowl for a closer look. I had seen a chipped tea bowl or two mended with gold, a vase from Rikyu's time. And once, to celebrate the fifteen-day moon of the Ninth Month, the Mountain had chosen an ancient iron kettle, a perfect sphere that had once broken and been mended with silver, the bright lines like striations on the full moon. But I had never seen a tea bowl broken so badly and mended like this, the gold arc like the seam of an orange. Where had he gotten so much gold? A new bride's *kimono* and lacquer were her own; perhaps Young Master's wedding *koban* had been his own to melt and use.

I could picture Jiro, a shy, humiliated boy, hiding the shards of the black bowl. I remembered how he always took the last seat in the room, how the *samurai* students would tease him by hanging a wooden sword up with his clothes, since, as a merchant, he was forbidden to bear arms. "Did you forget something?" they'd say when he ignored it. I remembered a young lord striking at him in the air, daring him to fight back, when to raise a hand against a *samurai* was punishable by death. The Stickboy had crossed his arms and turned his back. How beautiful he must have found tea, how brutal its disciples. I remembered again his stealing Yukako's robe for Akio, his calligraphy next to Akio's stamped seal.

I wondered how, after the Shin fortunes fell and his father died, he had persuaded his brother that it was worth making a life in tea, even without the support of a great lord. What had he said, so that Okura was now our staunchest patron? And how could I not have known he was Okura's brother? My eyes must have glazed over, like Yukako's, with disdain. But here it was, the fruit of his forbearance, the gold vein in the dark matrix, like an underground stream.

Turning the bowl in his hands, the Mountain gave a softer grunt, a breath of approval: *"Un."*

Basking, Jiro announced, "I named it Inazuma."

The Mountain gave a third grunt, like a cloud crossing the sun. He composed himself and returned the tea bowl, asking the next question of ritual importance. *What happened?* I wondered. Now the old man seemed just as content as before.

Yukako blinked awake, and I joined her, tucking myself out of Jiro's sight as he carried out utensils no longer needed: the ladle and the lid rest, the bronze bowl for wastewater. I heard the Mountain move to inspect the tea box and scoop while Jiro cleared away the water jar and tea bowl. When Jiro reentered the tearoom, Yukako picked up the bowl and gave it a close look, fingering the line of gold. She gave a nod and a wan smile.

We heard Jiro, in answer to the Mountain's questions, identify the lacquerwork of the tea box and then the origin of the teascoop: carved by one of Rikyu's great-grandsons, it had the poetic name of Nestled Rice Fields.

Father and adopted son offered ritual thanks to each other, and then I heard them settle out of *seiza*, the formal kneeling contortion required during *temae*.

"How pleasing," the Mountain said, "to see the white hill of snow melt and then boil. Nestled Fields and Shoots under Snow conveyed similar feelings, but were different enough so as not to cloy. Your restrained use of color shows maturity. The tea bowl was a daring choice, and I compliment you on it. My adoptive father told me never to use it, as it was cracked. But he also said it was made for Rikyu himself by the potter Chojiro, so I kept it for lessons. It seemed a crime to never use it. A quandary, no? You've solved it well."

The Mountain paused. "However. Though the bowl's name has been lost, it is not yet your place to give poetic names. If you've inscribed a box for it, you'll have to burn it and make a new one when you become Master Teacher."

The floor gave a soft pop as Jiro rose again to sit formally and bow. "I humbly apologize," he said.

The Mountain remained in place. "That aside, a good first *chakai* event. The first of many."

"I humbly thank you," Jiro said, as if choking.

"And I have saved this auspicious night for more good news. I have, at last, had word from Court." Yukako's sleepy eyes went wide. The Mountain named the August Nephew we'd once hosted, now the

August Cousin. "Thanks to him we have both the Emperor's countenance and his support." Yukako grabbed my wrist and shook it, trying to contain herself.

The Mountain named an annual figure worth roughly a hundredth of what he'd once received, enough to keep thirty men in rice for a year instead of three thousand. Yukako nodded, sobered but still hopeful. Even that much put the Mountain's house in far more comfort than many, including the Pipe Lady's family. And if the Emperor no longer condemned tea as a backward "pastime," that was cause for hope too: more students, more tea events. Yukako exhaled quiet relief. A look of vindication briefly crossed her face: she hadn't dashed her father's hopes by teaching Koito after all. And then betrayal took its place, and she dropped my hand. She looked stricken. She mouthed a few words: "He didn't tell *me*."

I had been straining for the Mountain's words as he announced his news, but I was also aware of a certain damp unease coming from Jiro ever since he'd been reprimanded. "This is great good news," Young Master finally said, his voice queerly breaking. "We owe all our good fortune to you."

A last emotion took its place on Yukako's face as I realized, and doubtless she did, that Okura hadn't been their last hope after all. In the next room, Jiro said nothing, and then a sound cut the air: a sniffle.

"I too am overcome with joy," said the Mountain. But it was shame, not joy, in Jiro's silence, shame at being chastised, shame and disappointment and no small anger. I watched Yukako as he sniffled again. I could see her contempt.

14

1872

"IT'S QUIET TODAY. Is my son here?" Jiro's mother asked, after bowing thanks to Yukako for her lesson. She was a gray-faced gloomy creature whom young Okura Chugo had pressed into service to assist with tea gatherings and keep his utensil collection clean. I liked her, I'm ashamed to say, because she was so awkward that she made me feel less hopeless about my *temae*.

"He didn't go with the others," Yukako said, shifting her awkward bulk out of *seiza*. "He said he wasn't feeling well."

As I led the older woman to her son's bent-treetrunk room, she fretted over her *temae*. "As soon as I stand up, I forget everything," she sighed. "My feet go numb and my memory does too!"

"You remembered both ways to exit this time," I consoled her. "*Sensei* didn't even have to remind you." She gave me a shy smile as I went to help Yukako clean up after the lesson.

It was the end of cherry-blossom season; on all sides, the petals shimmered down through the still air. The Mountain had welcomed five students this year, up from three the year before: four new faces and the Young Master. He was taking them all on a visit to the Raku

Master Teacher, the direct descendant of Chojiro, the potter most favored by Rikyu.

"Young Master didn't seem sick this morning," I mused, tactfully maneuvering Yukako away from lifting the heavy kettle herself. That morning, because the men's excursion would have left Yukako alone with only servants in the house, the Mountain had asked the Pipe Lady to come. (The idea of Yukako, swollen-ankled and runny-eyed as she was at this point, waddling off to go cavort with *geisha*, strained credulity.) The older woman hadn't even descended from her *jinrikisha* before Jiro waved her off with some formal words and a cut of silk; he wasn't well enough to leave today, so there was no need for her to trouble herself. Truth be told, he seemed vigorous enough stopping that *jinrikisha*.

"He's not sick. But Father's choosing tea wares, and you know how the man is after studio visits."

I did: ever since his first *chakai* event with the Mountain, Jiro would come home from studio visits glitter-eyed and sullen, shutting himself away in the treetrunk room. He'd paint tea bowls and Chinese characters on cloudlike paper, sending me off for candles and cups of *miso* broth. *He must be naming them*, Yukako said when I asked her about the paintings.

"It's so strange," I said. "He loves pottery." We were sitting backstage in the Baishian *mizuya*, a one-mat-plus-wooden-sink annex to the two-mat hut.

"He loves it too much," Yukako shrugged, coaxing the powdered tea back into an airtight vessel for storage.

I finished scrubbing the green dust out of the linen cloth and wiped down the boards of the *mizuya*, checking the level of the water in the ceramic barrel a last time. I could see the silhouette of my face in the water, the peaks and mounds of my coiffure. When I scratched my forehead I felt stubble where my eyebrows used to be: *I should get them shaved again soon*, I thought.

Yukako put out the fire in the floorboard pit, and I sat with her quietly. *When she found me in this room, she was the age I am now,* I marveled. The host's door to the *mizuya* was open, as was the outside door beyond—the push-up skylight, too, the small windows and the little crawl-through door—so that the bleached-bone gold of the house was lit on all sides by green air and pink petals. The very house seemed to be breathing light. Above the lovely dark board with its whitegrained streak, a calligraphed scroll hung in the alcove, edged in sky-blue silk. Beneath it, in place of flowers, lay a small pair of flower-cutting scissors, their butterfly handles gleaming. "Why?" I asked, pointing.

"Why?" Yukako teased. "What flower is most beautiful of all?"

It was a matter of catechism, not opinion. *"Sakura,"* I answered.

"Sakura only bloom a few days a year," she said. "And now they're everywhere. To cut a branch of cherry blossoms and bring it into the teahouse is too much, don't you think?" She nodded toward the alcove. "This is just enough, the shears alone." Walking back through the moss-and-slate garden, the fresh spring air blowing petals my way, I felt joy, joy, at how I saw the outside world more intensely for having seen the world Yukako made inside. No wonder Jiro resented not getting to choose and name the tea bowls himself; every aspect of speaking through tea gave pleasure.

As a young man, the Mountain had asked the Emperor for permission to present tea at court, and he had done so every year until Meiji. Now that the new court had approved the Mountain's declaration that tea ceremony was a laudable discipline of body and mind, they had also granted permission for him to resume his twice-yearly tea offerings. The first date he was permitted to appear fell during Yukako's confinement, and so Chio's watch was shared by the two women who had adopted out their sons to the Shin household: Jiro's mother and the

Pipe Lady. On a moonless night not long after my own birthday, they sent me running for the midwife in the dark.

I sat up all that night with Yukako, and after Chio, the midwife, and the two older ladies had fallen asleep near us in the upper room, I reached over to touch the tiny boy on Yukako's chest as if he were my own. *"My treasure,"* Yukako whispered, her face slack at last. "I'd like a bath," she said, and fell asleep. The little creature's hair spiraled out from the crown of his head in a dark whorl. His ears were the softest things I'd ever touched.

Jiro and the Mountain came home on the wave of eggs that arrived, sometimes thirty in a box, as gifts for the newborn. The entrance looked like a series of white staircases, each box wrapped in white paper and tied in red-and-white string. Jiro seemed a little dumbstruck by the boy: when I brought up Yukako's morning tray, I saw him beside her on the *futon* I'd laid out, quietly tracing the dark swirl on his son's scalp with a finger. "His hair's as thick as scales on a *tai*," he bragged to the Mountain when I served their breakfast. Images of the *tai* fish, or sea bream, usually showed it under the arm of one of the gods of good fortune, robust and cheerful as the new baby. Giddy with pride, the Mountain gave Young Master a tea box named Omede-tai, a pun on *sea bream* and *happy occasion*. It was a family treasure that had belonged to his adoptive father Gensai: the glistening red curve of muscle and scale fit perfectly on the round lid of the box. On the baby's seventh-day festival, when we dyed rice red with lucky beans, Yukako, Jiro, and the Mountain went to enter the boy's baby name at the local registry: Tai.

15

1872

THE MOUNTAIN SEEMED invigorated by his experience in Tokyo—buoyant, enthusiastic with his students and the round of tea events, often using a word I hadn't yet encountered: *eppo, eppo.* I first became aware of the Kyoto Exposition of 1872 not long after Tai's seventh-day festival, pouring breakfast tea for the Mountain as he talked with Jiro of this *Eppo,* and of something that required a *tei-bu-ru.* A table? I wasn't sure, but I could see that Jiro, though he smiled and bowed, was gripping both chopsticks in one hard-knuckled hand. When I cleared the meal away, the lacquered edges of the chopsticks were dull where he'd ground them against each other. I followed him to the bent-treetrunk room to gather up any dirty dishes, and asked, as he ground ink in water with unusual vehemence, what was an *eppo.*

Jiro glowered at me and burst out, "He's creating a new *temae!*"

"Really?" Why did he seem so angry?

"No one has created new *temae* in generations, and now these, what, these *swine* float in with their boats and guns, reeking of butter, so we'll have a pig *temae* in a pigpen? You might as well give a cat a *koban,* but the mood of today is *Oh, let's!* Let's make a tea whisk that fits on a trotter!

It's too hard for a pig to lift a tea bowl: let's change the *temae* so they can push their big snouts into a bowl on the floor! Indeed, why use a tea bowl? Let's have Rikyu's family design a special *trough!*"

I had never heard him speak like this. "Ah, I'll just take these," I said, nervously stacking up his dishes.

"Look here," he ordered, brushing ink across the page.

I took a tentative step forward.

"The barbarians have an enormous kettle with wheels," he said. A kettle? "It slides on a metal bar like a door slides in its groove."

I stared. Had the trip addled him?

"And they're bringing it to Edo! Pardon me, *Tokyo.*" Jiro sneered. "The Emperor has more than granted permission; he's paying his *hai kara* crony Sono to have these metal bars laid," he said, using an English phrase—*high collar*—coined to describe those who aped foreign fashions.

I took a step closer and saw a spare brushed rendering of a curved train track. *"Ara!"* I remembered something the monks on the ship had told me: when Admiral Perry's black ships came to scare Japan into trading with the West, they brought a miniature steam train—with cars just big enough for a man to straddle and ride—and set it up on the shore to astonish the natives.

Jiro pointed to the train track: "It looks like a long scar in the ground," he said. "They call this kettle a servant, but I can see it's one of their gods, *look.*"

He showed me a woodblock print of a *bijin*—a beautiful woman in a fashionable *kimono*—except there was something wrong with her face. What was it? "Why, she's smiling!" I cried. I had never seen a print like that.

"Look at her eyebrows! Look at her teeth!"

"Eh! Is it a little girl in a grown-up *kimono?*"

"No, this is how barbarian women go about," he said, shaking his head in horror. "And this is no woodblock artist's fancy. The very *Empress* has started tricking herself out like this, and so now all Edo is full of these faces." He groaned. "It's a city of aging girls. And don't they see?" He dotted his finger along the woodblock beauty's smiling mouth, then along each white tooth of negative space formed by the curved train tracks and straight railroad ties. "Every time I looked at a court lady? *Torakku, torakku.*" As he said the English word *track,* he bared his teeth and clicked them together in a mockery of a smile.

Could the woodblock beauty have been Koito? Or did all *bijin* look alike? "When you were in Tokyo—" I broke off. Should I say *Edo* to please him? "—did you hear about a *geiko* who does Shin *temae*?"

Jiro's eyes widened at my poor taste for mentioning Yukako's unsavory past. "What would *you* know of the floating world?" he asked, with a certain lazy menace. I shifted from foot to foot, flustered. He relented. "If there was one, they kept the news away from Father. *Tea is the language of diplomacy,*" he said, imitating the Mountain's grunted pronouncements.

He sighed. "Bad enough to see what's become of Edo. Bad enough that the foreigners have been granted a new settlement so close to us." He was talking of Kobe, a not-too-distant fishing village where a new port had been built for Westerners en route to Osaka. "But now Miyako? Obon has been forbidden this summer, but we'll have a barbarian festival to make up for it in the fall!" He snorted. "Maybe Master Teacher will build a *torakku* for the *Eppo.* He can *slide* the tea bowl to the foreigners."

Before the Meiji coup, I had heard protesters crying *Sonno! Joi! Revere the Emperor! Expel the Barbarians!* I shrank back, wondering if Jiro had been one of them. Surely when those protesters fought, they had not imagined their revered Emperor's ban on Obon festivities: for ten summers, we would see neither dancing nor bonfires.

"They belong over there, we belong over here," Jiro continued. "We need to learn how to build their cannons to *protect* our beautiful things. We don't need to learn how to make our beautiful things ugly like theirs. Father says Shin *temae* looks frivolous when women do it, but I say a *bijin* would grace a tearoom better than some diplomat pig in a *furokku koto.*" A what? Oh, a frock coat.

"On your trip, did you say any of this to Master Teacher?"

Jiro gave me an appalled look in reply. "He's my *father,*" he said.

I NOTED, then, Jiro's peculiar silence the next day at breakfast, when the Mountain said to me, as offhandedly as if calling for his pipe, "For the little one's thirtieth-day festival, tell my daughter to start now. She shouldn't blacken her teeth anymore, or"—he pointed at his eyebrows and made a gesture. "It's not how Her Majesty does things." Before I could stop myself, I looked up at Jiro and saw his downcast eyes, the way his jaw worked behind his closed mouth. When his own mother came to see the baby, her eyebrows and teeth left untouched according to the new style, I saw the way Jiro shrank from even her.

And so I understood a few days later, when Yukako's teeth emerged (gray, then yellow, then white) and the stumps of her eyebrows began to sprout, Jiro's retreat to the bent-tree annex at night. "Should I serve your morning tea in your office tomorrow?" I asked when he hadn't slept upstairs in days. I tried not to sound too hopeful.

"Thank you, yes." Jiro rolled his eyes and imitated his son crying. Tai *had* begun to fuss at night a bit, but Jiro hadn't seemed to mind at first. *"Anything that cries out at night delights me—except babies,"* he said, in an affected, world-weary tone.

"Is that from a book?"

"How did you know?"

"Just the way you said it."

We were sitting just after breakfast in the room by the garden where the Mountain slept and took meals with Young Master; it also served as his library. I noted the authority with which Jiro walked his fingertips through his new father's small book collection: he found a thin volume and pulled it down for me. Light for its bulk, it was bound in a pattern of exposed violet thread, illustrated with dozens of black-and-white woodblock prints. It was written all in women's *kana*, run together, like all Japanese writing, without spaces between the words. Even worse, this book had almost no *kanji* characters to show where words began and ended. But I saw a page numbered like a list: *one, one, one, one.* And I picked out nouns here and there: *snow, moon, egg.* Before she married, Yukako had read to me aloud from a book of lists by a Heian court lady named Sei Shonagon; was this it?

"Who taught you how to read?" Jiro asked.

"*Okusama,* a little, four or five years ago," I said, meaning Yukako. Her title had changed since her marriage, from Young Mistress to Madam.

"Is that so?" he said, unbelieving.

"Why don't you borrow it?" said a voice from the doorway: the Mountain. Startled and embarrassed, I all but dropped the book.

"I'm sorry, Father," Jiro said.

"No, I mean it," the Mountain said to me. "Wash your hands first." I bowed deeply, alarmed. He had never paid me so much attention before. Though I had neither time nor ability to read, refusing seemed even more impudent than looking at the book had in the first place, so I bowed again, and thanked him. I could feel them both looking at me as I carried out the tray.

WHEN I FIRST TOLD Yukako her father's orders regarding her teeth and brows, she'd simply shrugged and moved Tai to the other breast. "Does he think I've had time to fuss over my face up here?" She craned her neck and grimaced at the mirror. "I haven't left the house in days. It's just as well," she said. She rubbed one of her stubbly eyebrows and laughed a little. "Ask him if I grow these out so long they cover my eyes, will they double our stipend?" I giggled. "What if I paint my teeth bright white?"

TODAY, as she prepared for Tai's thirtieth-day festival, she gave the mirror a longer look. When it seemed like Jiro wouldn't be coming back upstairs, I had quietly but decisively taken my place in her bed again, and so I sat with her as she dressed. For the festival she wore a married woman's black formal *kimono*, but she looked just as she had all the years before her marriage, younger even, with her girlish expressive brows. "I thought everything would be different when I was older." Yukako glanced from the mirror to me. "But here we are. There's only one thing different," she said fondly, taking Tai out of my arms and inhaling his baby smell. "Tai-*bo*! My Tai-*bo*!" she crowed. We tucked three gorgeous little *kimono* one inside the other, laid them on the floor on top of a sash, and placed the baby faceup on the *kimono*-wrappers. Yukako lifted each arm into a set of nested sleeves, then belted the baby into his clothing with a single knot. For a moment as she stood with the baby in her arms, I saw a flash of the old Yukako, my indomitable sister, armed to stride off in the sun to the temple, to dedicate her boy to her own special protector, Benten-*sama*, the goddess of water and the arts. Then I saw a look of shock and despair cross her face. Did she still pine for Akio? She thrust the baby at me, aimed her face at her breakfast tray, and heaved. "Oh, not again," she groaned.

For another week, the cloakroom looked like a world of staircases, as we orchestrated dozens of black lacquer boxes to send out as thank-you gifts, each on its own fine tray, each wrapped in brocade. We filled them with *mochi* cakes and lucky rice, and they all came back, as custom decreed, unwashed. The Mountain went overnight to Kobe to talk about returning the next year for a temple tea presentation: when he left, the entrance hall was full of laden boxes; when he returned it was crowded with empty ones. When we had cleared out the cloakroom—washed every box, stacked every tray, and folded every strip of brocade—there was a curious box left in the corner, easily missed by anyone passing through the cloakroom, anyone whose task wasn't, like mine, to clean it.

The box was full of books. Not Japanese books, either, with their exquisite thread bindings and cunning boxes. Western books, cloth and leather bound, some stamped with gold. They smelled, oh God, like *books*, like long voyages by sea—like ink and rags and glue—like a ship's library, like, to a certain stomach-twisting degree, my Uncle Charles. I laid them out one rainy day and sorted them on the stone floor. There were two in unfamiliar alphabets, one blocky, one curving—Russian and Greek, maybe. Two or three were in Roman letters, with queer large *b*'s in the center of words and a forbidding font, like bat's wings and diamond-paned glass. German, I think, or maybe Dutch. A few looked like Italian, but could have been Spanish or Portuguese, all those lovely staccato *t*'s and Latin vowels. One book with very clear type was freckled with umlauts, barred with diagonal lines through its *o*'s. And three books were in languages I recognized: a British guide for visitors to Paris, a slim illustrated French bird book, and an old friend—I almost cried—*Tales from Shakespeare* by Charles and Mary Lamb. The book had been difficult when I was nine, having read English with help for four years. At sixteen, when I opened the volume, all the fusty moths of its scent dancing toward me, I was baffled. I recognized the cover and the language, but when I looked at a particular phrase—*Tarry a little*—it entered my mind as sound and nothing more. When I looked at the pictures of birds I'd never seen, I saw arrangements of letters that looked familiar—*French*—at first glance, but on closer inspection yielded nothing I could grasp. All the same, I kept the three books. I stacked the others into their wooden crate and set it in its overlooked corner, padded upstairs as Yukako bathed the baby, and set my new treasures with the Japanese book the Mountain had lent me, under my best *kimono*. I felt rich. In the time between coming home from my bath and Yukako coming up from hers, I could learn how to read again. Not only had he (thanks to the Mountain) given me a book; by leaving Yukako's bed Jiro had given me the time and privacy in which to read it. *Anything that cries out at night delights me:* he'd sounded so surprised when I asked if it was from a book. Even if I couldn't read Sei Shonagon, I loved her for making Jiro feel glib and clever about giving me what I most wanted. I came alight thinking of Yukako coming up to me, the milky baby falling asleep between us. And as I waited, I paged through the bird book, pausing when I saw a familiar picture: a *karasu*, its dark body glossy as the bird that flew through my mind when my mother once called me by its name, fingering my black hair. I sounded it out, my voice thin and halting as I struggled with the old sounds. *My blondest crow,* I murmured, the way she'd say it after singing her favorite song. *Ma plus blonde corneille.*

A FEW DAYS LATER, when I mopped down the cloakroom, I noticed that the box of books had vanished, and the next day, when I laid breakfast out for the master and his heir, the Mountain stopped me. "Miss Urako."

"*Hai?*"

"In three months Kyoto will host a great festival. People will come from all over Japan, and from foreign countries as well. Even now, carpenters have started building foreign-style halls for this *Eppo.* It's a chance to show the world that we are just as civilized and enlightened as foreign countries, if not more so. For this *Eppo*, I have developed a *temae* that can be performed in a foreigners' room."

"I humbly understand," I said, not looking at Jiro.

"And you will speak to our foreign guests about it."

"Me?"

"In English and French. Don't tell me you can't."

I hung my head. Of course! He'd gone overnight to Kobe, the port town full of foreigners! Why hadn't I thought before taking those foreign books?

"I saw you in that foreign dress on the stairs last summer," the Mountain said. "I saw the way you looked at that book, as if you'd grown up with them, and yet I know you can barely read. So I brought the books from Kobe, to see what you'd do."

I felt a violent panic in my stomach. I breathed a shallow breath and then pressed my forehead to the ground in supplication. "Master Teacher, I have no home in this world but yours. Please let me stay," I panted.

"Who said anything about you going?" said the Mountain dryly, amused. "I'm your employer. This is your work." I kept my forehead down. "You'll wear this," he said, and I looked up to see my mother's dress in his hand.

"I—yes, sir—I—" I really did feel faint. "It's too small," I gasped.

"I'll arrange fabric for you," he said. "Make another."

A WEEK LATER I sat in the sewing room with a bolt of silk dug up from the storeroom, a tight pattern of red and gold leaves for the fall event. It was the same width as all Japanese fabric—just over a foot across—so my first task was to join three panels of silk together in order to have fabric wide enough to cut for a Western dress.

So much less had changed than I imagined since the Mountain gave me his orders. Yukako was the same toward me. The Mountain told me that when the carpenters had finished building what he needed for the new *temae*, he would teach his students, and I should observe those classes behind the lattice. That—and the silk he found for me—aside, he favored me with the same benign indifference as always. When I returned his copy of Shonagon after Tai tried to chew on it, he made no comment. Chio and the sewing-girls, meanwhile, treated me with mild curiosity, their coolness toward me for having moved back up to Yukako's room tempered with pity that I'd been chosen to be exposed to so many butter-smelly barbarians in such a monstrous garment. "Glad it's not me," Kuga said as we walked to the bathhouse. It was the week the wall went up between the men's and women's sides of the great soaking tub, in compliance with a new imperial edict. Where I once saw the old pointy-chinned *tofu* man straight across from me, I now saw a wall of cedar panels. *That's no foreigner,* I remembered him saying. "Can you really read those barbarian languages?" Kuga asked.

"Or did you just take the books for the pictures?" said Ryu.

"No, I can, a little. I don't know why," I said, cagey. "I don't remember much before the fire."

"You were a foreigner in a past life," Chio said philosophically. I remembered Inko once coming to that very conclusion, and I blushed in the twilit street.

I floated among the students as before, unseen except when they sent me back to the kitchen for more tea. Only Jiro treated me differently: suddenly the *miso* I brought was too hot or too cold; I laid his *futon* out askew, or too early, or too late. He was quick to dismiss me when before he'd let me linger with questions, and his speech, which had used to trail off vaporously as I awaited instructions, now fell curt and clipped. I was, I suppose, the enemy.

How WAS I GOING to make Western clothing? I fingered my mother's dress in my lap. A more visually skilled person—Chio, no doubt, or even Jiro—could have copied a child's dress for an adult just by looking at it, but not I. I turned the dress inside out. My mother's stitches were small and persistent but not precise. I could see her impatience as they loped wide sometimes, or danced crooked on the fabric. I could see her renewed heart—or candle—as they shrank, for a spell, into demure tidy lines. She'd loved me so much. I had never seen her make either of us a dress from whole cloth: she usually mended or altered whatever came in the church box at Christmas. But she'd bought new fabric to make this for me, found new velvet ribbon to match. *She knew she was dying*, I realized. I closed my eyes and breathed deeply. I opened them.

The most precise thing to do would be to cut out each of my mother's stitches, press the pieces of fabric flat onto paper, and trace them with a compass to my grown-up size. I couldn't do it. I demanded paper, scissors, a brush, and ink, and then, in the sewing room, I laid out my work. When I took apart *kimono* to wash them, beyond the long straight seams, I'd see the woven selvage, compact and self-contained. Beyond each of my mother's seams, however, was a half-inch of raw fabric where she'd cut the triangle pieces of the dress from a length of new cloth. The raw linsey-woolsey was a soft fringe. Tenderly, I brushed ink on the ragged hidden edges, then pressed the piece flat on the white page. A rough inked outline of the dress emerged one piece at a time.

There was a goddess to whom the sewing-girls offered a prayer when they made the first cut into a new bolt of fabric. Once a year when they held a funeral for their old needles, the girls sank the dulled and broken spines into a cake of *tofu* and left it at her shrine. As I rolled the inked cylinder of a sleeve slowly on the page, I said a small prayer: *Please let this work.*

Straightaway the goddess replied to me in French: *Don't cut the silk yet.* I laughed for a moment, at such a swift no-nonsense answer from heaven, and I cried too. It was my mother. As I traced my pattern larger by the inches I had grown, I resolved to ask Yukako for a bolt of rough cotton to practice on.

ALL THAT WEEK, as the trees in the garden blazed red, I had wondered how I would explain myself if I met a foreigner at the *Eppo*. Where was

I from? How did I get to Japan? How had I learned Japanese? *Don't flatter yourself*, I chastened. *They won't ask, they won't care, and if they do, you can just say you don't remember anything from before the fire.* After all, there hadn't been a year without a fire *somewhere* in Kyoto since I'd arrived. In the last few days before the *Eppo*, I had less time to worry: between wrapping and loading the Mountain's lacquer table and stools, looking after out-of-town guests, and running messages back and forth to the confectioners', I didn't even have time to see the hairdresser when she came.

Each guest at the Expo was to receive a sweet cake stamped with a chrysanthemum and wrapped in festive paper, presented in a silk pouch printed with the Shins' crane. The day before the Expo, as Ryu, Kuga, and I threaded violet cord into dozens of bags, I closed my eyes for a moment in the sewing room. I went to get a cup of tea to wake myself and saw a man at the gate with a cane.

He wore Western dress, his arms and legs sharply outlined by his clothes, which made him look like an animal on its hind legs. His trousers and *shatsu* were two different colors of black, which sat awkwardly together, unmitigated by a single breath of color or contrasting lining. How jarring! The only place for an eye to rest was a spot of white at the throat, which hardly counted, and in fact drew undue attention to his unlucky face: he had a large ugly nose and waxy pale skin. I blinked: he had blue eyes, like a dog, or an infant. What was wrong with him? Was he not a he, but an *it*—a fox spirit?

"Excuse me, I'm very rude," the spirit said, as if its mouth were full of stones. I hid my face with my sleeve, but stood firm before the open gate. I didn't want his evil touching Yukako or the baby. "*Mukashi mukashi,*" the spirit said, except awkwardly, as if it were speaking some other language: "Moo cashy moo cashy."

I blinked again. It was my Uncle Charles.

The man had aged before his time, his tonsured hair a silver wreath around his wrecked but still-young face, the scarred and twisted lip, together with the cane, suggesting that he hadn't left the fire unscathed. He spoke, the same voice reedy and nasal, but hoarse, as if he were still inhaling smoke. His speech was a string of poorly pronounced nouns, a few verbs in their rudest forms: *"Jesus Christ. Church. Seven years. Fire. Girl. Aurelia Bernard. Now I search. Now I go. Paris."*

As he spoke, I lowered my sleeve. He saw a dark-eyed servant girl in *kimono* and *obi*, her black hair oiled and pinned in a neat *shimada*, who spoke to him in Japanese. No recognition lit his eyes. "There's no one here by that name," I said stiffly.

"Pardon?"

He was looking at me and he didn't see me. I was speaking to him and he didn't understand me. I felt a jolt of rage, and of cruelty. With impunity, I said the stock phrase kept in reserve for guests who have overstayed their welcome, a phrase that implies that they've eaten you out of house and home: "Would you like some tea poured over rice?"

"O-cha-zu-ke?" he repeated, as if his tongue were made of wood.

"I see seven years haven't done much for your Japanese," I said.

He heard the word *Nippongo* and he thanked me, with an air of one used to being complimented.

I affected the elaborate speech of the singing-girls. "So sorry, but as your query poses insurmountable difficulty, perhaps you would be so kind as to . . ." I said, the word *depart* left to the imagination.

He blinked at me, dull and hopeless.

"Go Paris!" I said, making shooing motions. *"No girl here!"*

He bowed in comprehension. *"I understand,"* he said, using the crude verb of a lord or a nursling. He looked me straight in the eye without seeing me. Hadn't anyone ever told him it was rude to stare?

I looked at him, this lightning-struck tree. I looked the same rude way he did, like an animal, straight into his face, and I saw a glint of the man who'd held me on his lap with his French-English Bible, teaching me one word at a time. And then I remembered his hands around my waist, his breath hot with drink, and I said the one thing I'd wanted to tell him that night, matching his imperious form. *"Amari suki arahen,"* I said. *I don't much like you.*

I closed my eyes and opened them: I was in the sewing room. "Don't make us do your work, Sleepy," said Ryu, half smiling.

16

1872

M Y DREAM of Uncle Charles proved prophetic. No one asked me to account for my Japanese. In the Exposition Hall the next day, an enormous blue-eyed Englishman with hairy nostrils and ears like oyster shells looked down at the little maid in her Japanese coiffure and maple leaves, groping for substitutes for dozens of tea words: *temae, chado, chashaku, chasen.* As I choked out yet another article-less, pronoun-less sentence with the verb at the end, he asked me, "How did you learn such good English?"

With a giggle that hid my outrage, I raised an arm to curtain my face, but my narrow tube sleeve offered no shelter. "From the church," I piped.

WE HAD WITNESSED an opening ceremony—in which a very large man received a very large imperial medal—and served tea for two seatings of guests before any foreigners came to our enclosure. It was already clear, however, that Jiro was not enjoying the Exposition. He fidgeted through the speeches granting the large man, Mr. Kato—*a Satsuma nobody*, he muttered later—the post of Special Advisor to the Court for Kyoto in thanks for his work planning the Emperor's new conscript army, based on the Prussian model. Jiro also seemed overwhelmed by the displays of steel and ceramics and power looms, and while he was glad to see friends—among them his elder brother Chugo and his old classmate Shige, the Bear—there were far more people present whom he found distasteful. He liked neither hangers-on nor those on whom they hung, and the Exposition was rife with both. Okura Chugo, I saw Jiro note, had made a gift of his own tobacco kit to elegant Mr. Sono, the Satsuma art collector whom the Emperor had tapped to run the railroad that outraged Young Master so. And neither man had seemed able to tear himself away from an exhibit by a pair of Dutch hydraulics engineers, displaying plans for a fifty-mile canal north of Tokyo.

"If someone like you were leading the project, Mr. Sono, I'm sure it could be done," said a man Kuga told me was Noda, little Zoji's current employer. Though the frog-lipped Hikone rice merchant had made it down from the shores of Lake Biwa for the Exposition, we saw neither Zoji nor Akio that week.

"Thirty-five mountain tunnels? That's quite a few men digging," reflected Sono.

"You're a wise man, an exceptional man," oozed Noda, caressing the ivory *netsuke* fob that hung from his sash on a Western metal watch-chain. "But Satsuma's crawly-bug full of men who can't move with the times like you. Send them to prison and your problem's solved and your tunnels dug," he declared.

"Troublesome as my countrymen are, as a Christian, I can't condone what you're saying," burred Advisor Kato, the big Satsuma man from the opening ceremony, still wearing his palm-sized medal. The essence of *hai kara*—*high collar*—Western fashion in his swallowtail coat and trousers, he was flanked by two white American ladies, one tall and rough-hewn, one short and dumpling-shaped, astonishing in their crinolines and flounces. "Such a canal could do a great deal for Japan, but the Bible, like the Buddha, says *Do not kill.* A prisoner's life breaking rock would be a short one."

"But surely you killed your share when you fought the Shogun, Advisor Kato?" asked Noda.

"The Emperor's cause is holy," Kato explained good-naturedly. "The canal's cause remains to be seen."

As greasy Noda croaked with laughter, Advisor Kato moved closer to our booth, arms braced akimbo. "I never had the leisure to learn tea," he said as Jiro bowed before him with a slice of sweet bean cake.

"I imagine not," said Young Master dryly. I looked over at Advisor Kato to see if he'd acknowledged the insult, and then looked back to see Jiro's knees lock in alarm: one of the students in the *mizuya* backstage had neglected to lay out a spicewood pick with the Advisor's sweet.

Over the appreciative murmurs of the two American ladies, I could almost hear the hiss of students blaming one another behind the screen. In the narrow strip of backstage *tatami* visible from where I perched to welcome guests, I saw a plate appear with a single sweet-pick. Jiro turned to fetch it as graciously as possible while Advisor Kato, unaware of any problem, nodded in thanks for the sweet *yokan* and looked over our displayed utensils. His gaze fell on the One Meeting teascoop, a pale wisp of bamboo carved two hundred years before by Rikyu's great-grandson, the Mountain's founding ancestor Shinso. As Jiro stood with the missing sweetpick, Advisor Kato called after him, "Don't worry! What's this here?" Reaching into the display alcove set up in our booth, he took One Meeting and dug into his sweet. "I'm a problem solver," he chuckled at himself. "This is delicious."

The Mountain looked up in the long silence that followed and watched pained horror cross Jiro's face. "Excuse me——" Young Master spluttered, his right wrist clamped in his left hand.

"Advisor Kato, congratulations and welcome," the Mountain interrupted jovially. "Is this how the Westerners do it?" he joked, and before the Advisor could snap One Meeting in two and use it to pick his teeth, he detained both Kato's hands by shaking them. As they laughed and spoke, Jiro, mortified, cleared away the Advisor's half-eaten sweet—and One Meeting.

NOT SURPRISINGLY, Jiro was frayed and snappish by the time my oyster-eared Englishman sat down to tea and asked how I'd learned to speak his language. Thanks to my long, slow hours sounding out my Lamb Shakespeare tales, I could understand the man's English, though sometimes his accent bent familiar words queer. He was a dealer in rabbits, he told me. Never before seen in Japan, the exotic lop-eared pets were all the rage in Tokyo, the calico-spotted ones pulling in a thousand American dollars each. Having made himself a fortune in just days, my companion was intent on enjoying his stroke of good luck. "In Tokyo I could have spent all day in the archery booths. Each one had a pretty little girl just like you. You'd shoot, and then she'd clap her hands if you hit the target or laugh at you if you missed. And then the little huntress would pour you a thimble of spirits and she'd shoot. They'd always hit, but they shot like girls, wide. So you'd cozy up and steady her bow. They were like little almond-eyed dolls. They'd laugh some more and have at you with their fans if you got too fresh."

"These barbarians don't stop talking," said Jiro as the Mountain serenely wiped the tea bowl.

"He said he liked Tokyo very much," I explained.

"There's no better country for wasting time. Archery! Delightful! Hot baths! Delightful! And tea! Who would think it could take so long?"

Impervious, the Mountain sat on a stool drawing water from a kettle on a brazier set into a lacquered table, the wastewater bowl behind him on a stand of its own.

"Though if there were a pretty girl like you to watch," Oyster Ears continued, "I wouldn't mind at all. In Tokyo everyone was talking about a famous *geisha* who does the *ocha* ceremony, but the Jappers have got her all sewn up. There's no seeing her for the likes of me."

Jiro looked at the man abruptly when he heard those three words: *geisha, Tokyo, ocha*. The Mountain raised an eyebrow. "He said there's a famous *geiko* in Tokyo who does tea," I repeated, sliding down the bench away from the encroaching Englishman. In Yukako's defense, I said, "She's very popular. Everyone's interested in *ocha* now."

Another foreigner had paused to watch, slimmer and darker than Oyster Ears. "I've heard of her too," he said, in an American accent. "I can't imagine anything more charming than a Japanese girl making tea according to some ancient solemn rite, but when I visit my new friends at home, their wives and daughters never know how."

Apprehensively, I translated as best I could. Jiro's disgust was evident. The Mountain looked mildly perplexed. "Why would you want to pass the time with a man's wife and children?" he asked, and I conveyed his words.

"Especially when you could meet him at night in the company of women far more delightful?" Jiro added politely.

"Why would a Christian man go out at night?" the American rejoined.

Without a moment's hesitation, my leering benchmate chimed in, "What more does a man need than the haven of his family?"

I translated, and Jiro and the Mountain exchanged a barely perceptible glance of disbelief. Then they each extended an olive branch to the barbarians.

"Tell them that in Japan we think family is important too," said Jiro.

"Tell them the *temae* they're seeing is the true discipline as Rikyu taught it, *samurai* and warlord *temae*," the Mountain said. "If they want to watch pretty young girls make tea, they can go to the floating world," he added dismissively.

When Jiro flicked a glance at his interlocutors, his eyes held a tiny look that said, *I'd rather be there than here.*

"So it's men who have the tea parties in Japan?" mused the Englishman. "It rather goes well with wearing dresses, eh?" he nodded at the Mountain's *kimono.* I translated, when pressed, but I did not want to.

With his right hand, the Mountain turned the tea bowl twice on his left palm and passed it to his guest. The Englishman gazed at the bowl in his hands and gasped, bemused. "Why, it's so *green,*" he declared. "Rather like algae, wouldn't you say?"

"What is *algy*?" I asked.

The red-haired man laughed out loud, earning me a sharp look from Jiro. He turned to the American and made as if to pass the bowl on. "Cup of tea, good man?"

"Oh, after you, surely."

"'*Let the cup pass from my lips,*'" said the Englishman, like Jesus in Gethsemane. The American looked at him with disapproval.

"What's wrong? It's getting cold," said Jiro.

"It reminds them of their holy book," I said.

"Do you have any black tea?" the man asked, looking slightly stunned at the bubbles of the frothy tea, which had already begun to pop and dissipate. "Or coffee? Have you ever heard of a *cappuccino*? They get a good head of foam on top when they steam the milk. Looks just like this, but perhaps not quite so green."

"Powdered tea, or *matcha*, has been used in tea ceremony for some three hundred years," I admonished, I hoped graciously.

"Behold the Irish cappuccino," he announced, pleased with himself. "How about if I just have a taste and give it back? Do you think old Sourpuss will mind? Or I could take a little sip and you could finish it for me?"

"Sir, please enjoy the entire cup of tea," I said, reciting the instructions the Mountain had asked me to translate. "When you have finished, it is customary to show appreciation with a loud final sip. Then the guest is invited to inspect the teacup."

"You can't very well call it a cup, now, can you, if there's no handle and no saucer," the Englishman objected, stalling. "It's rather *bowl*-like, in a crude way, though, isn't it?" I'd chosen *cup* because I wanted to appeal to the English and their love of high tea. Perhaps, however, we wouldn't come off so poorly if I were to shock them a little with *bowl* next time, I thought.

"Come on, Pappy, drink your medicine," said the American.

"Cheers!" said the Englishman, knocking back the tea in one wincing gulp. "So now the guest inspects? Well. Lovely," he said. "But don't you think it's funny they couldn't come up with anything nicer?" he asked the American before turning back to me. "I mean, just two booths over, you can see some really good painted china; they'd probably lend it to you for the Expo, if you like."

"They *strive* for unevenness and accident," explained the American. "It makes them feel closer to their nature gods." He was more or less accurate, though he made the Shins sound more quaint and tribal than they were. The Mountain had used a large black Raku bowl freckled with white, in one place so densely that it seemed to blush a band of white cloud.

"The head of the Shin family named it Amanogawa," I recited, "whose meaning is River of Heaven, or Milky Way. In heaven there were once a shepherd boy and a weaver girl who married and fell in love. Their love o'ertopped all things to such degree"—as I spoke, they stared in such a way that I realized I'd been alone with Lamb's *Tales from Shakespeare* too long—"that the shepherd boy neglected his sheep and the weaver girl left her loom. So," I said, grimacing at my stilted, breaking voice, "God set a river between them, so to keep them at their travails. And now they are two stars, and once a year they can cross the river and spend the night in concert."

"How charming," said the Englishman.

"Wait," said the American. "They married and *then* they fell in love?"

"And so here are Japan and the West, treating across the ocean," I concluded, finishing the Mountain's story. It was months late for the season, but the tale had been too fitting to pass up. The other two tea bowls we used for the Exposition were named First Frost and Leaf Brocade, which balanced out the unorthodox first choice.

"Very poetic," said the Englishman.

"Japan has a winsome grace we'll never capture," sighed the American. "I would love to take an *ocha* tea set home to my mother. Could you box one up for me, with a little powdered tea?"

"I'm sorry, these are for demonstration only, not for sale."

"Now, don't be like that," he cajoled. "This teacup, for example, how much would you charge for it?" He named a figure twice the annual stipend awarded us by the Emperor, and the Englishman raised his eyebrows.

"What are they *saying?*" demanded Jiro. I explained. "Ocha *set?*" he sniped.

I translated the American's astonishing offer. Jiro and the Mountain exchanged a blank look of outrage. "They don't know," said the Mountain, regaining his composure. Unblinking, he named a figure fifty times what the American had offered, which I repeated, my heart racing.

The two men looked at each other, flabbergasted. "I apologize. I misjudged the situation. Perhaps this is some priceless family antique," murmured the American sheepishly.

"This tea *bowl,*" I said, experimenting with the word, "was made this spring by the direct descendent of the Shin family's first master potter, and was chosen by the Shin family head especially for the Kyoto Exposition," I recited.

"So it's not an antique?" The American looked at me, at the two men in *kimono*, and back at me again, his face fallen in confusion and anger. "For demonstration only," he repeated. "I see."

"He didn't know what it was, and he offered all that money?" Yukako repeated that evening. "That's crazy."

"I couldn't believe it," I said, bouncing Tai in his sling on my back.

"And even crazier, they had nothing to sell him," she said, cupping her hand over her belly. "What are you going to eat, Baby Two?" she asked. "My father's not a foolish man. But until two years ago, *samurai* went from birth to death without ever touching money." Yukako smiled with an exaggerated ratlike leer and stooped over, as if telling beads on an abacus. Then she flung back her shoulders like a *samurai* and grunted disdainfully, "*That stuff's for women and merchants.*" In her own voice, she sighed. "The foreigners aren't ashamed of money, and look at where they are now." She reached behind me and stroked her son's head. "My father gave up his sword when he became a Shin, but he's still a *samurai* about money."

"And this one's father?" I said, bouncing Tai. "He's a merchant by birth."

"One who'd rather marry out," Yukako said tartly.

17

1873–1876

K ENJI—NAMED VIGOROUS Second Son to make up for coming small and early—was born on January 24, 1873. I say this with authority because the Emperor moved Japan to the Western calendar that year, decreeing that the third day of the twelfth month in Meiji Five was now the first day of Meiji Six. Meiji Five, cheated of its last month, was shorter than any other year in Japanese history: Yukako's second son was born just before New Year's would have fallen in the old calendar.

We were all uneasy about the lost month. Were we to put out New Year's decorations twice? When the usual greetings from Chio's son Nao arrived at the same time as they had the year before, we wondered, were they on time or late? We had already eaten toasted beans on New Year's Eve to mark that we were a year older, but now that the plum blossoms had arrived a month later, should we eat them again? (We did.) Should we add *another* year to our ages? (We didn't.) And one afternoon just after Kenji's birth, Jiro decided to make another of his frequent trips to Sesshu-ji temple, this time in order to ring the bells for New Year's Eve.

"New Year's Eve has come and gone," admonished the Mountain.

We were sitting that morning in the study by the garden with my *Tales from Shakespeare.* The Mountain had just announced that the next day he would need Jiro's help teaching the younger students *temae* for tea in a Western-style room, and once again the next day turned out to be one that Jiro had long ago arranged to spend in contemplation and prayer. Wily enough to know he was being thwarted, and bent on leaving behind an heir able to meet the barbarians on some wisp of common ground, the Mountain had recently insisted I explain each of my *Tales from Shakespeare* to him and Jiro in Japanese. The week before, we had worked through *A Winter's Tale*, my favorite, in which the lost girl Perdita is found, her dead mother secretly alive. Now we were reading *King Lear.*

After the Mountain spoke, I could hear Jiro's resistance: his father hadn't explicitly *prohibited* him from going to the temple, after all. Maybe if he kept silent, the Mountain would forget to forbid him. "Why should your monks hold themselves above the law? Even Advisor Kato doesn't; he didn't start his Christian school until this year." It was true: now that the ban on Christianity had been lifted, effective Meiji Six, the Imperial Advisor had finally executed his plan to run a Christian school out of his home, employing the two American ladies from the Expo as teachers.

"So, how did Advisor Kato's lesson go?" asked Jiro, making an attempt to be polite. Solicited by Kyoto leaders eager for a word in the Emperor's ear, Kato was in turn eager to pursue the refinements that would identify him as worthy of their solicitude. Though Jiro snubbed Advisor Kato's friendly overtures, the Mountain had stepped in to save the relationship and, though his mother the Pipe Lady grumbled at how far he'd fallen, had begun teaching Kato *temae* once a week.

"It went very well," said the Mountain coolly. "And he was so touched by the gift you sent in return."

That was a jab. The Imperial Advisor had recently given Jiro a tea bowl which he had on good authority was of the age and style preferred by the Shoguns before even Rikyu's time: a glossy Chinese piece stippled like a fawn. While the correct thing to do would be to return the gift with a piece of equal value, Jiro had responded with a tasteful but undistinguished incense holder he'd picked up at the monthly shrine market.

"I wasn't convinced about the authenticity of Advisor Kato's gift," Jiro said, his words quiet and clipped.

"Maybe so. But you *can* be convinced that the Advisor believed the piece was genuine," said the Mountain. "If I had known you would not behave accordingly, I would have chosen the return gift myself."

"And so I should have given him, what? One of Rikyu's tea bowls? Are you sure that's the best way to dispose of the Shin treasures?"

"Elegant words," the Mountain grunted. "One of the Shin treasures is time. Yours. And I am the one who will dispose of it."

Jiro shrank back. "I only go to the temple to become a better tea person," he groveled. "As you say, '*Tea and Zen have the same taste.*'"

The Mountain nodded, indulged. "You may go to Sesshu-ji today if you can be back by dawn tomorrow to help me teach. And you will treat Advisor Kato as if he were taking food away from his own parents to give us our imperial stipend. Do you understand?"

"I humbly understand." Jiro bowed. When the Mountain left the room for a moment, Jiro glanced over at me and my Shakespeare *Tales*, the book left open to *King Lear*. "Maybe the king was in the way," he said.

I WAS ONLY too glad to leave Jiro and the Mountain and join the hairdressers, who had arrived during our play-reading session. I kept an eye on the babies while Miki and her mother worked their combs through Yukako's hair and shared news from their family in Tokyo, who were currently visiting.

"Remember that English Rabbit Man from the Expo you told me about?" Miki asked.

"How could I forget?"

"He went to jail."

"No!" cried Yukako. Though spent from giving birth just days before, she was still glad for a laugh.

"Yes! You know how the calico ones fetch the highest prices?"

"He killed all the others and sold the meat as beef?" I asked.

"No."

"One of the spotted bunnies attacked an imperial guard?" Yukako guessed.

"No! They caught him painting on spots with persimmon juice!"

"*Eh!*" we cried.

"Of course, he's British, so he's out of jail already." Thanks to Britain's unequal treaties with Japan, he would have been tried under British law instead of Japanese, which no doubt resulted in his swift release.

"And how's your cousin?" I asked, but I really meant *How's Inko?* Her contract of service with Koito was due to end anytime now, which meant soon she'd come back to Kyoto and get married. *And find me!* I hoped.

"She sounds well. She said last summer, there was a big announcement that everybody would be sent to school, boys and girls, but nothing's happened yet. And she told me a couple months ago she saw the first steam train leave for Yokohama. If I ever go to Tokyo, I want to see that," Miki said, the little cleft in her chin deepening as she grinned. "And she asked me to pass on another gift from your friend Miss Namiko."

"Oh?" I said, containing my delight. I knew Yukako didn't like being reminded of Koito; I saw her eyes narrow reflexively when Miki said this.

"I brought it," she assured me. "Miss Namiko's parents moved to Tokyo, too, like everybody. They found a boy for her, another Kyoto transplant. His family ran a sweetshop in Pontocho; they just opened a place in Tokyo last year."

"Oh." I had Tai strapped to my back as we talked, and was swooping from side to side to entertain him. When she said this, I stopped. Of course Inko would get married; I'd known this. But some part of me must have thought she'd always be fifteen, that she'd be coming back to Kyoto soon. "When is the wedding, do you know?" I asked, my voice strangely high.

"It was in the fall," Miki said, pulling a small box wrapped in paper out of her mother's comb chest. "So this is her new family's New Year's gift, flower-petal *mochi*."

My heart sank. It was an absolutely standard New Year's confection, an absolutely standard gift for a confectioner's family to send all its acquaintances and business associates, like a print shop sending out calendars. The Shins did the same thing, sending out folded pads of tea-paper each year. Being remembered like a cordial stranger was worse than not being remembered at all. "The outside's probably too tough to eat anymore," Miki said, "but my cousin said they were *so* soft when they were fresh."

"Thank you," I mumbled, my breath shallow and tight. "And please thank your cousin for her kindness."

AFTER MIKI and her mother left, while Yukako and the babies slept, I numbly unwrapped Inko's third gift to me, the box under its layers of paper and blue cloth. It was a toughened circle of rice dough enfolding a stem of candied burdock and a wad of *miso*-flavored pink bean paste. I gnawed at it morosely as I balled up the wrappings and the box, then realized what Inko had sent: the blue cloth wrapper smelled of *neriko* incense. It was a piece of fabric from the robe she'd worn our night together. I gasped. She was so clever, sending a gift only I would recognize. Since she would have needed help writing a letter, and I would have needed help reading it, she would no doubt have felt obliged to send New Year's greetings as bland as I'd feared her gift might be.

I was so lucky, I thought. And quickly, before Miki's cousin could go back to Tokyo empty-handed, I resolved to reply in kind. I found an unsent packet of New Year's tea-papers and dug through Chio's mending box for the brightest thread she had.

THOUGH MIKI'S COUSIN was to marry and leave Tokyo before I could learn if my gift had been received, for years I would take comfort in the fact that she had promised to give it to Inko as soon as she arrived. In a place you could spot only if you unwrapped the tea papers yourself, I embroidered Inko's namesake onto the fragrant strip of indigo cloth she'd sent: a noisy bird, unfurled and cawing, the color of new grass.

I WATCHED OVER Yukako as I sewed and brought food when she woke. "I'm always sleepy," she laughed at herself. "You've been so good to me, Miss Ura." She bowed wearily as I helped her gather up both babies to nurse.

"Of course you're tired," I said.

She exhaled deeply. "I didn't expect to get pregnant again so soon." She gave a sound that was half-sigh, half-laugh. "But I wouldn't wait around for Baby Three. Young Master didn't expect to have a barbarian wife," she said, pointing at her teeth and brows. She pressed her face to their fuzzy heads each in turn. She glanced around as if someone might hear her, and then whispered, "You are both so beautiful. More beautiful than peaches. More beautiful than *sakura*. More beautiful than either of your parents." I was in love with them too. Kenji suckled all the harder when I grasped his little foot, and Tai gurgled at me. I never heard Yukako praise her children to their faces once they were old enough to understand, but her eyes never lost that drunk look for them, either.

Those were the years I would have married, when the boys were tiny. I turned sixteen the year Tai was born, and by the time Kenji had outgrown the need for a nursery maid, I was twenty-two: by then, every girl at the bathhouse my age was married with children of her own. Like most Japanese girls, I did not relish the thought of leaving home and family to work for strangers and die in childbirth, but unlike most I had no parents who needed to dispose of me, no would-be parents-in-law eager for grandchildren with my features. If I had reminded Chio regularly, she might have said something charitable about me to the most desperate mothers of unmarried sons in the neighborhood, but I did not. I made sure to scowl at such women. I was not unfeeling: at night sometimes I would long so much for someone to touch me that I'd bite the heel of my hand. But I wanted no one to take me from my bed beside Yukako, no one to give me children in place of those who were already dear to me. My dream, with Inko lost to me, was to care for those boys and their mother until I was so old they took care of me.

"Two Shin boys is plenty," Yukako said proudly, that day that should have been New Year's Eve. And then, because she had lost so many, she closed her eyes in prayer. "Now grow," she whispered when she finished. "Live."

AT FIRST WE HAD THREE small children in the house: Tai, Kenji, and the gardener Bozu's grandson Toru, a little older, who was sadly proving as slow-witted as I was said to be. In Meiji Nine, three years after Tai was born, we gained a fourth. That New Year's, the note that came from Chio's son Nao—the boy in the Perkins Studios Yokohama daguerreotype—was unlike any we had ever received.

I hope someone will read this to you, Mother, read Yukako in the sewing room while Kenji napped on my back and I kept Tai quiet with a game of cat's cradle. In a painstakingly clear hand, Nao wrote—or someone wrote for him—*I am working on the Asaka Canal, north of Tokyo. It will take years. In places we can use explosives to tunnel through the mountains; in others the danger is too great. I lost a friend in a blast; he was like a brother. My sensei says I have learned enough to be put to more precise and demanding use. It is an honor, but I regret that I will risk less for Japan than my brother did.*

Yukako puffed out all her breath at once and bit her lip, the way she did when she thought about her own brother. *But none of this is your concern,* she continued. *Due to a misunderstanding, I was recently hurried into a marriage I did not want.* At this, Kuga and Chio exchanged a startled glance. *If you encounter a woman who claims to be pregnant with my child, please feel obliged neither to harbor nor reject her.*

"*Ehhhh!*" the three women each exclaimed in turn.

"Well, well, well," tutted Yukako. She opened her mouth to speak and closed it. "And he sends you best wishes for a happy and prosperous New Year."

So WE WERE NOT entirely unwarned that June night—soon after the rainy season ended and the little Migawa and the Canal Street canal were at their whooshing highest—when the little girl appeared. That day Yukako had received a letter from her cousin Sumie, which she had saved for the cool of the evening to read in her upstairs room. As she sat with the letter, she quietly pushed a fingertip into the ridge of her teacup until the nail went white: I had not seen her so upset in years.

"How is Sumie?" I asked.

Yukako did not answer me directly. "You know how some *samurai* are wearing Satsuma cloth these days?"

"Yes?" She was referring to a particular pattern of servants' cotton cloth, indigo sprigged with white. I *had* seen a number of well-to-do men in Satsuma cloth: their *kimono* differed from their porters' robes only in that the indigo, not yet washed out with years of use, looked as if it could come off on your hand.

"Do you know why it's so popular these days?"

I didn't.

"Do you know who Saigo Takamori is?"

"I've heard the name, but I don't know."

"He was a Satsuma *samurai* who fought on the Emperor's side against the Shogun. But he doesn't like the way the new *high-collar* government's been all sticky with the foreigners," she said, using a word that actually meant *sesame grinding* as she ground sticky imaginary seeds in her palm. "So he's gone back south and started training *samurai* in the hills, to fight the barbarians back to their boats. They blow up government offices to impress young men into joining them. They think if they bankrupt the rest of us by invading Korea, it will scare the foreigners away."

"And the Satsuma cloth?"

"A lot of people think he's right, even if they don't think he's wise."

I nodded. I remembered the men I'd heard murmuring about unrest in Satsuma years before, at the Expo. "And your cousin?"

Yukako paused. "Well, Akio's gone to Satsuma."

"I don't understand. To put down Saigo's rebellion?"

"No. To join it."

"Ara!"

"His father's still in Tokyo, begging for permission for them all to stay in Hikone. Sumie's up there alone with four children and her mother-in-law; who knows what they're living on? And now he's gone. How could you leave your parents like that?"

"But wait. Didn't his brother die fighting the Satsuma rebels?"

"He died as a *samurai*. And I suppose Akio wants to die that way too." It was hard to read Yukako's voice. "He left a letter for his father that if he had to choose between Satsuma and Meiji—'the upstart mer-

chants, the hayseed conscript army, the forced move to Tokyo, the crippling taxes raised to pay indemnities to foreigners—'" she said, reading Sumie's letter aloud, "he'd choose his fellow *samurai* in Satsuma."

"He just rode off one morning and left a note?"

"In the letter, he said he was fighting to get the family rice stipend back. And maybe he thinks that, but the truth is, he ran away. And he was always such a *good* son too," said Yukako bitterly.

True: he'd married as his father wished without a murmur of protest. "Will you start wearing Satsuma cloth too?" I asked, wary.

Yukako rolled her eyes. "Those *samurai* can cut off all the *high-collar* heads in Japan and they'll still have to fight the barbarians and their guns. And if they invade Korea, why, then the foreigners won't have to do it themselves." She crossed her arms, scoffing. "All those men on Saigo's side, can he give them rice?"

She looked away then, fingering one of her combs. "I don't think they've sold off their place in Kyoto yet. Akio could have stopped here on the way south if he'd wanted to."

"He didn't want to," I said.

Before she could respond, Tai rushed in, calling, "Mother! Mother! The stream's on fire!" We dashed outside to see the Roman candles whistling into the air, *one, two, three.* Set on a flat dry stone in the stream where they'd be least likely to cause any harm, the *fire-flowers* leapt and sparkled all on their own, glittering into the water like sequins. While the boys stared, rapt, we looked around to see who'd set them, and found no one.

"I only know one person who knows how to make *hanabi,*" Yukako murmured to Chio. I knew Akio was still on her mind, and seeing the fireworks must have taken her back to that summer, *that summer,* when Nao and Akio were at the Shins' and her brother was still alive.

"Look!" cried Kenji, pointing to the tiny bundle of blue cotton by the thatched gate. As we all gathered toward the baby, I looked back at the stream, where a puff of leftover smoke rose and spread into a lamp-lit haze. The stark, dirty face of a girl, suspended as if among the trees, looked back at me once and disappeared.

"Let's call her Maki," said Tai. She *did* look like a little *maki*, a *sushi* roll bundled tightly under the gate.

"Perdita," I said, under my breath.

"She looks just like my Nao-*bo*," Chio breathed, taking the baby in her arms. I tried to see the daguerreotype boy in the tiny face: maybe a little around the cheeks.

Kuga watched her mother holding the girl. I remembered how severe Chio had been when her daughter brought home little Zoji, under circumstances far less unorthodox than these. "Let's call her Naoko," she said, her voice flat.

Everyone looked to Yukako. As *Okusama*, the lady of the house, it was hers to say if the baby could stay. She took the bundle from Chio, and a bubble of spit formed between the girl's tiny lips, glistened in the dark, and popped. "We'll call her Aki," Yukako said.

The baby arrived with no written information and only a servant's shabby blue-and-white robe for a blanket. We all heard at the bath-house about the woman's body found that week, not far from us, in the rain-swollen Kamo River. At the bathhouse, bratty Miss Hazu, now grown up and stylish, whispered about it with her friends behind her paper fan. I shuddered at the news. I'd looked back a last time when we brought the baby in: I thought I saw a glassy flicker by the stream, like light on a pair of eyes.

18

1876

L ong after both boys were able to eat grown-up food and patter down to the privy on their own, Yukako cuddled and suckled
them in bed at night, and so I was surprised by the firmness with
which, when Tai was four—but five by Japanese reckoning—she exiled
him from the upstairs room to sleep with his grandfather.

On the fifteenth day of the Eleventh Month in Meiji Nine, the
same year Aki came to us, all the girls who had turned three and seven
that year by Japanese reckoning, and all the boys, like our Tai, who had
turned five, were dressed up in their best *kimono* and brought to the
neighborhood shrine for blessing. Poor Kenji, suddenly condemned to
babyhood: tied to my back, he struck his head gloomily against my
shoulder as Yukako dressed Tai in a smart new robe, again as she and
Jiro stood with Tai before the shrine priest with all the other parents
and little boys, and yet again as the Mountain filled Tai's sleeves with
lucky red-and-white candy. He cried when Yukako brought Tai down
to take the first bath with his father and grandfather, instead of the
second with his mother and brother. Tai had seemed perfectly happy
to lord his luck over Kenji all day, but that night I came home from my

own bath to the sound of his sobbing; when I came in through the kitchen, I found Yukako walking him down the stairs. "It's Seven-Five-Three day," she repeated, just as she had that morning. "None of the other little boys you saw at the temple are suckling like babies tonight." Tai gulped his tears and swallowed. "You're not going to cry in front of Grandfather, right? If you cry, you can't learn *temae.*"

Tai wiped his face with his sleeves.

"What did you have for dinner tonight?"

"Rice. And mackerel," the boy sniffled.

"Who bought the rice?"

"Mother."

"And who earned the money to buy the rice?"

"Father."

"No, Grandfather earned it. People give him money so they can learn *temae,* and he gives us money so we can have rice. This is what grown men do," she said. Her voice was tender and hypnotic.

Tai gave his mother a tentative look. "Me too?"

"You too," she crooned. "Once you learn from Grandfather, people will come from far and wide to learn *temae* from you. And they will give you money, and I will find the best price for mackerel so you can have it every night, and o-Chio will make rice balls just the way you like them. But first you have to spend as much time as you can with Grandfather," she said.

"*Hai,*" Tai whispered.

Her voice was firm and clear when they talked, but after leaving him, Yukako sat down on the stairs for a moment and gave me a sad smile. Pressing the corners of her eyes, she permitted herself a quick wet sigh before going back up to Kenji.

UNTIL THAT NIGHT, whenever Yukako walked into a room, the two boys held up their arms for her to carry them. The next morning, with

Kenji strapped to me as I helped Yukako bring in breakfast, I saw Tai sitting between the Mountain and the Young Master, the way his face lit up when he saw his mother, the way he leaned forward to go to her, then looked back and forth from his grandfather to his father and stayed in place. "Thank you, Mother," he said when she knelt before him with his tray.

"You're a man," said the Mountain. "You don't have to say that."

"Just bow," said Jiro. "No, not so deep."

"Starting today, you'll take classes with the other students," said the Mountain. Tai nodded, his eyes enormous, as Kenji twisted in his sling to get a better look. "And tomorrow you'll go with all of us to the Raku kiln."

It seemed that Young Master had failed to make plans to be away this time. Jiro's face tightened before Tai could even pipe up, with a child's unerring instinct for the uncomfortable question, "Papa too?"

Yukako broke the balky silence. "I know you've been sick this week. Would you like me to go in your stead?" She gave a brief, pointed glance at Tai. Even a careful small child—even one being treated, suddenly, like a grown man—might need looking after in a room full of breakable treasures.

"Please," said Jiro, his nodded bow a hair deeper than he'd instructed his son.

"We'll go tomorrow afternoon, then. In the morning you'll have a new student," the Mountain told Yukako.

"I will?" she asked, surprised. She had not been asked to teach any students since Okura Chugo's mother, who had studied for just a year: plenty of time, the big merchant felt, to learn to keep his collection of tea things in order.

"You'll teach Advisor Kato's wife," said the Mountain. "He just married the daughter of the man who bought land for the Angli-can church." That explained it. While most men went out at night,

Christians stayed home and relied on their wives and children for entertainment, a practice of which, given my experience, I did not approve.

I WAS NOT REQUIRED for Yukako's first lesson with Lady Kato, so I served green tea to the elderly Pipe Lady when she visited her son that morning. She asked about his autumn trip to Tokyo and the Mountain told her of the Emperor's Sword Decree: given the threat of Saigo Takamori's rebels in the south, the wearing of swords, beginning in the tenth year of Meiji, would be forbidden throughout Japan. The Pipe Lady was outraged. By law, only *samurai* had the right to wear swords, so this came as yet another blow to her family. "They will not rest until they have stripped us of everything," I heard her say, her voice like sand and splinters.

I kept her pipe and teacup filled, and humored Kenji as he fretted in Yukako's absence. Suddenly deprived of his brother, he'd begun pointing more and talking less, nursing for comfort, even rummaging hopefully in my *kimono* for milk. And so, in a morning spent ferrying teacups to the garden room, making twists of sucking cotton soaked in sweet soy milk, and distracting Kenji before he could take every pot, jar, and ladle off its shelf, I saw Lady Kato for only a moment, when she said farewell to Yukako. She was a pudgy child bride, younger than myself, with sweet bubble cheeks and a rosebud mouth. Her hair had not been oiled by a hairdresser, but instead stood piled up on her head in a swirling, pouffy bun, like a mountain of extruded chestnut paste. Just as strange, I'd never seen anyone wearing a *kimono* and a necklace before, and it had been years since I'd seen a little gold cross worn at the throat. I touched my neck reflexively, feeling for the thousandth time the absence of my Saint Claire medal. "I'd like to practice before next week," the girl said timidly.

"That's a good idea," Yukako agreed, her voice betraying some annoyance at the girl for suggesting the obvious.

"But I have no tools," Lady Kato said, looking down.

"Isn't your husband studying tea with my father?" asked Yukako.

I popped a candy into Kenji's mouth so I could lean in as the girl whispered, "He doesn't want me touching his things until I can do *temae*." Given his own experience with other peoples' tea utensils, I could see why Advisor Kato would say that; I smirked, remembering the One Meeting teascoop.

The Mountain had one set of practice tools for each of his eight students (now including Tai), so Yukako lent Lady Kato her girlhood practice tools, reclaimed from Koito when the *geisha* began buying fine utensils of her own. When Kenji seized his mother by the legs, Yukako lifted the boy absentmindedly, listening to the *jinrikisha* that wheeled Lady Kato away. Something was on her mind. "What if I have *two* students?" she mused.

We heard a voice. "Is my *jinrikisha* still out there?"

We turned to see the Pipe Lady, flanked by her son and grandson-in-law. "Have you ever seen anything so hideous?" she marveled.

"It was like a bird's nest," Jiro shuddered in agreement. He was perhaps overdoing the invalid's part, his silk robes covered in an out-of-season wool *kimono* jacket.

"I believe that's how the foreign women at the Expo wore their hair," said the Mountain, looking at me.

"I don't remember," I said, from habit, looking down.

"I've heard that Western women fix their own hair, which both protects them from the gossiping tongues of hairdressers and saves money for the household," said the Mountain. Then he almost laughed. "But I'm not sure what I think of the results."

Yukako rocked her son on her hip thoughtfully and gave me a sly look. "You do *so* remember," she said, so that only I could hear.

. . .

KENJI HAD THROWN himself at Yukako and even bitten her when he thought she'd leave without him, so I sat with him that afternoon in the entrance of the Raku showroom. I suppose I'd been imagining an atelier full of clay and potter's wheels, because I was disappointed to see an ordinary, if lovely, reception room with a scroll alcove and vase of autumn grasses, where a twinkling, thick-bodied gentleman unwrapped one bowl at a time for the gathered observers.

I wasn't expecting this. Twice a year we received shipments of tea utensils: whisks, ladles, and linen cloths, each fashioned by its own workshop. A messenger would deliver, say, a score of tea whisks, and offer a little gift of sweets or fruit to Chio, who would serve him tea and whatever she had on the fire for the sewing-girls. At his leisure, the Mountain would look over the delivery, and Yukako, before her father's dictum and her children's needs had confined her to the house, would walk to the workshop herself to handle payment. Now Yukako kept the books and counted out coins twice a year for Jiro to bring instead. I remembered, vaguely, the man Yukako used to deal with at the tea-whisk shop: kindly, sawdusty, and curt, proud of his family's craftsmanship, no doubt, but never one to sign his work or try to make it different from his fellow artisans', never one to boast of a tea whisk's antiquity or pedigree. The delicate, birdlike creations were made to be used, not to express the unique essence of their creator or materials. Like the ladles and linen cloths, they weren't even meant to last a year.

How different it was, then, to peek into this formal room knowing that the man before me was the eleventh-generation descendent of Rikyu's potter, Chojiro, and that his ancestors and the Mountain's had met twice a year in this very room for the past three hundred years. Any sense that we'd drop by to pick up a crate of tea bowls and head home was quickly dispelled as the courses of a small ritual meal, each served in exquisite ceramic dishes, were laid out before the assembled company.

The Mountain sat in the place of honor while the students, in order of seniority, lined up beside him, Tai last, with Yukako just behind the boy, not served and not eating, an occasional yawn betrayed by the stirring of her jawbones.

After the trays were cleared away, Chojiro's Heir laid out a series of plain pine boxes. One by one, he opened each box, unfolded a set of silk wrappings, and displayed the black, red, or smoke-colored bowl within. I felt the tension of the students as they watched the Mountain for his response. Often he sat quietly, and the potter would silently pack the piece away. Occasionally, however, he would nod, and the potter would pass the bowl to him. I could picture Jiro growing frustrated with the game of trying to guess when Master Teacher would nod. I wondered if the whole process was just a way to keep the students from presuming they could know the master's taste. I wondered, too, if the Mountain would actually choose any tea bowls at all, and if so, by what discreet, ceremonious means Chojiro's Heir would fix a price and receive payment.

For each bowl that earned a nod, the Mountain would inspect it as if he were in the tearoom, lifting and caressing the vessel briefly and expertly, then passing it to his students for their inspection too. Tai, though clearly bored and drowsy, watched his fellow students intently all the same, copying their precise movements: he bowed, braced his elbows on his thighs, turned the bowl in his tiny hands, and offered one last bow. He was very patient as the Mountain and the other students looked at some nine pieces, handled three, and chose, in the end, just one, but when the group made ready to go, he could no longer control himself, complaining, "I thought we'd get to see them make the tea bowls!"

Yukako hushed him and the Mountain glared his way, but Chojiro's Heir asked the Mountain graciously, "Would that be of interest?"

Able to keep an eye on his mother at all times, thanks to the cloak-room's proximity to the parlor, Kenji had long since relaxed into sleep. I lashed him to my back and carried him to a large handsome outbuilding, redolent with the scent of mud. The dapple-gray tea bowl the Mountain had chosen, though I'd only glimpsed it, seemed to embody, in its mod-est uneven form, this thatch-roofed, heavy-timbered building, this room of half-naked men building each bowl by hand. Awestruck, Tai reached up and took the potter's sleeve while the Mountain's gathered students clumped together, nervous for their *kimono*. Bringing up the rear, Yukako halted—surprised—and caught my eye. I looked: the shelves lining the studio walls were *filled*, brimful, with tea bowls by the dozen, more than I'd ever seen in my life, none too different, to my untrained eye, from the one her father had chosen.

"What are these?" Yukako asked.

"My apprentices made them," said Chojiro's Heir. "I'll critique them and then break them up." In response to Yukako's widened eyes, he explained, "Madam, our good name depends on releasing only our very best wares. I'm draining a marshy corner of the garden; I'll use the shards for tile." Yukako lowered her head in thanks for the explanation, giving the tea bowls a backward glance as we left the building.

PERHAPS JIRO WAS NOT showing enough gratitude for his miraculous recovery, because the next morning, as I helped Yukako serve breakfast, the Mountain was more severe with him than usual. "Your son was a welcome face yesterday."

I had not known that the appropriate reply was abject apology until Jiro said, "I hope he had a good time."

I had only seen the Mountain's anger unleashed once, outside Koito's house years before, but I caught a barb of it now. "I'm sure Raku was impressed I had fathered a son in my dotage."

Jiro ate a pickled plum, his face curdling. "So, will you unveil your new tea bowl at New Year's?" he asked.

"Perhaps you mean to flatter me into thinking I'm a young man. Perhaps you think that because my mother still has enough wits about her to scoff at foreign styles, it doesn't matter if you go to the kilns or not"—saying nothing, Jiro prised the plum pit out of his mouth with his chopsticks and reached to set it self-consciously back in his empty bowl—"but Raku has a son your age who was there," the Mountain said. His unspoken accusation filled the room: *You embarrassed our family.* If the heir sulked at home like a boy, waiting for the Mountain to die, the world would see no man in place to lead the Shins in the next generation. The faint tap of Jiro's plum stone was loud in the thick silence.

Yukako saw her moment and broke the tension. "Mr. Tai was very serious and responsible," she said. I could see Tai preen, and both the Mountain and Jiro melted a little with pride. "I'm so grateful we're able to patronize the Raku kiln again, even if in a limited way," Yukako added, nodding to her father. Their means had once allowed them, in the days when Akio was being groomed for Jiro's role, to bring home seven or nine tea bowls a season, which they had kept or circulated into the families of their patrons and highborn students.

The Mountain nodded curtly.

Jiro, a boy in those days, bowed his head. "It's a lost world," he sighed.

The moment of shared melancholy cleared the air. Then Yukako spoke. "I am so grateful to you, Father, for ensuring our future. I am so grateful to both of you for making the long journey to Tokyo to keep us from being a 'lost world' in the Emperor's eyes. But it's a new world too. We've lost our old patrons, but we don't have to lose our new ones."

"Why ever would we?" Jiro looked guilty and angry as he spoke, as if she were accusing him of planning not to go to Tokyo once he became the Master Teacher.

"I don't mean the Emperor," Yukako said. Her voice deepened, then, as if she had been waiting a long time to speak. "I mean the *high-collar* men, I mean barbarians, I mean women, I mean Christians, I even mean *geiko*."

The Mountain glowered. Yukako bent her head in apology, but pointed out, "We don't survive on the grace of a few rich families anymore. But look around, the Long Room is full. More people want to learn our *temae* than ever before. And they're prepared to pay for it. They may never be able to afford the best Chojiro's heir has to offer, but when that foreign man at the *Eppo* asked to buy a tea set for his mother, we should have had something to sell him. Not the best things, of course, but something he could afford. When Lady Kato told me her husband wouldn't let her use his tea things until she learned *temae*, I shouldn't have *lent* her my practice things, I should have *sold* her something. Raku's studio is filled with tea bowls his apprentices made that he plans to break into pieces and bury: it's gold he's burying!" she said, heated.

Jiro and the Mountain looked at each other, stunned. Yukako pressed her advantage. "Right now you choose one or two prize tea bowls every year and give them away, or you sell them for a fortune once they become antiques. Not everyone has a fortune. But everyone *does* have a little something to spend more than they ought to on a bowler hat or a French ribbon, or a new Satsuma *kimono*, if that's where your heart is."

She continued, speaking very quickly now. "What I propose is this: that you also approve an apprentice grade of tea bowl. It doesn't have to have its own box or calligraphy or a poetic name. Just a tea bowl that's the right shape that costs a little more than most beginners want to pay. They'll know they're not getting an antique. But they'll be getting the approval of the Shin Master Teacher, and look: the more of a beginner you are, the more that means to you. We can sell the Raku apprentice bowls—"

"Do *what?*" asked the Mountain.

"We can *say* they're made by Raku apprentices. And if they lack the master's touch, even better: it will whet people's appetites for the real thing."

"You're turning my stomach," Jiro said. He had clearly been wait-ing for the Mountain to say something, anything, to give him leave to speak. "A tea vessel is not a bowler hat or a French ribbon," he said with slow condescension. "People don't want to learn Tea in order to buy cheap ugly things. They want to be surrounded by what's finest in Japan before it's gone."

"There's a certain *wabi* charm to using an apprentice's tea bowl," the Mountain reflected, using Rikyu's word for *humble* or *forlorn.* "But the measure of a *wabi* tea person is his ability to make do with what he has, not his willingness to go out and buy what he's told. As for Lady Kato, she should use her husband's utensils; the man's being unrea-sonable."

"Father, if you bought a few hundred of these every year, you could give one to each person in the Emperor's court and start a fad for learning tea. You could post your students to teach at court, once they graduated, and have them send a portion of the fees back to Cloud House."

The Mountain looked at Yukako in reply, pointedly saying nothing.

The children had glazed over a little, confused, but some under-standing seemed to cross Tai's face in the silence that unfolded. "Toru wants to learn *temae* too," he announced. Jiro's lip curled to think of the gardener's blocky, dull-witted grandson in the tearoom. "Could I have a tea bowl to give to him?" the boy asked.

"Absolutely not," said his father.

"Can I have a tea bowl for Aki-*bo?*" asked Kenji on my back.

"No!" I whispered. "Hush!"

Spent, Yukako shivered. The two men seemed as of one mind as they had when Yukako first married, long before the Mountain had put Jiro in his sullen place. "I only wanted to help," she said softly.

"Yes, I seem to recall you saying that before," said the Mountain. Yukako winced. "Daughter, would you like to help your family?" he asked softly.

"*Hai*," she whispered.

"Do not speak to me of this nonsense again."

"I humbly understand," she said, bowing to her father, husband, and son. Her forehead touched the floor, but I could see from the back that her feet were clenched like fists.

19

1877

THE PIPE LADY died in the tenth year of Meiji, on a flower-viewing picnic with her large family. The two little boys who had once tormented me now had children of their own, both girls, and the dowager had just been telling their wives what to eat to ensure they had sons the next time around. She leaned back to look at the sunlight through the curtain of cherry petals, closed her eyes, and didn't open them again.

Her body was burned with all due office. Though Akio was still missing in Satsuma and Lord Ii was still waiting at court to see if his family would be permitted to stay in Hikone, the Pipe Lady's grand-daughter Sumie sent word that she planned to leave her four older children with her mother-in-law and attend the fifty-day memorial service. Not everyone could. Sumie's father and oldest brother were still interned in Tokyo, where the Pipe Lady's family had been ordered to move years before. Failing to do so meant that Sumie's younger brothers were not allowed to take the army jobs Advisor Kato offered to arrange for them. They stayed for the sake of their grandmother's dignity, and lived off it slimly: the Pipe Lady's trips to the antique dealers were all that kept them in rice.

I realized that the last time I'd seen the Pipe Lady alive, just a couple of weeks before, must have been her last trip to the pawnshop. As always, in preparation for the Buddha's birthday, the Mountain had sent Yukako to his mother's house with a flask of hydrangea tea for the family to wash the Buddha statue in their little chapel. As we approached the moon-viewing pond and the sprawling house, now more weathered than ever, the Pipe Lady greeted us from a *jinrikisha*.

"She was carrying a sword across her lap that day," I remembered the night of the funeral, when Yukako had come home.

Everyday life had hardly changed under the Sword Decree: it was a little easier to move through a crowded street, and the curio shops were suddenly glutted with swords. But I heard loss hang in the air when Tai asked the Mountain about the sword rack outside the Muin teahouse: "The only time a *samurai* lets go of his sword is in the tea-room," the Mountain said. He paused, a confused creaky old-man moment, and added, "In the old days." And I saw the stubborn set of the Pipe Lady's mouth, her hands tight around the long silk-wrapped scabbard.

Yukako remembered it, too, as she nursed Kenji. "That must have been her husband's sword. My grandfather."

"She can't have gotten a good price for it," I mused. "How could she let it go?"

"I think it's what he would have wanted," Yukako said, thinking aloud. "It would be disloyal to disagree with one's lord in secret. The honorable thing would be to state your grievance plainly and then kill yourself."

"Oh," I said, shrinking.

"Some *samurai* really need the money, but most are selling their swords as a kind of public suicide."

I almost understood. I shook my head in disbelief.

"It's what my father would have done, if he hadn't been adopted out," Yukako said.

"She looked like you, in the *jinrikisha*," I said shyly.

"Am I that old now?" teased Yukako. She was twenty-seven to my twenty-one.

"Strong," I insisted. "Like she'd seen everything in this world."

"You think?"

Jiro went alone to present tea to the Emperor that spring, as his doubly adopted status removed him from any impurity connected with the Pipe Lady's death. The Mountain fretted, though silently. He performed *ocha* for himself each day in Cloud House, as he had when the family's future seemed most uncertain, and shut himself away with Jiro for two days before allowing the young man to go on retreat.

In June, fifty days after the Pipe Lady's death, Yukako seemed nervous as I helped tie her thin summer *obi*. "I haven't seen her in eleven years," she said, as Kenji tried to engage her in a kind of three-card monte using teacups and a breakfast tray.

"We just saw her in the Fourth Month. In the *jinrikisha*, remember?"

"No, my cousin Sumie," Yukako said, choosing the wrong cup.

"Stop letting me win!" pouted Kenji.

"Does it still hurt?"

"We'll play again, and this time I'll really watch," Yukako promised. "Yes and no. She was just doing what she was told. He was just doing what he was told." She closed her eyes briefly and exhaled. "I would have liked to have been the thing he betrayed his parents for," she said simply. "But I wasn't. The middle cup, Ken-*bo*," she said, without opening her eyes. She was right.

· · ·

I was no better companion for Kenji at the service that day: I kept looking over at Sumie, baby on her back, surrounded on all sides by brothers and sisters. She had the same heartbreaking prettiness she'd had at sixteen, but she seemed more defined, now, less stylishly pliant. And yet she softened when Yukako threaded her way through the crowd and stood beside her. I saw them look at each other, briefly but steadily, and then look up again at the chanting priest, the incense rising among the narrow wooden memorial tablets.

And so it happened that they were together again, leaving the pickets of the graveyard, when the horseman came. Sumie looked up at the man wearing the crest of Lord Ii and called him by name, surprised.

"Ii Sumie-*sama*," called the horseman, and she looked at him quizzically. Why was he acting like a stranger? Even I remembered him, from the night of the August Nephew's tea, when we discovered Akio and Koito together.

Sumie went to his horse and looked up: I watched her as she listened, and I watched Yukako as she watched her. I saw shock cross Sumie's face, and then she closed her eyes and pressed her lips together. Yukako glanced backward and caught my eye. There was only one thing he could be telling her. I held Yukako's gaze and nodded, and then I saw her go to Sumie, my chest flooding with shock and with a kind of pleasure that of all the people gathered, Yukako had turned to me.

Akio was dead. The Meiji army had routed Saigo's men and only a few stragglers remained. He had died like his brother, just as Yukako predicted, except he was fighting *for* the southern rebels, not against them. Sumie stayed with us that night, and the two cousins sat up whispering long after Kenji fell asleep and I pretended to. Yukako's voice was gentle and steady, her own loss set aside, while Sumie's had an edge of rage I'd never heard before.

The next morning Sumie sat in Yukako's room, blinking and abstracted, oblivious even to Kenji's questions. Yukako fed Sumie with her own hands, and when Miss Miki and her mother came as scheduled, Yukako offered Sumie her place. Sumie sat numb, occasionally seized by fits of tears and anger. "I should have done this last year, when he left," she said as Miki trained her locks into a widow's *obako*.

After the hairdressers left, Sumie sat nursing her baby, a tiny girl named Beniko. "Grandfather," she said, meaning her children's grandfather, Akio's father Lord Ii, "is still in Tokyo, but he's paying money he doesn't have to get the body brought back to Hikone. I should leave today." She looked worried. "I wonder if he'll sell another horse for this." She held Beniko over her shoulder and patted the baby's back. "You know, a buyer from a *geisha* house offered to take this one when she's three." I heard the Pipe Lady's *samurai* pride in her calm voice, and her arms tightened around the girl.

"Oh, Sumi," Yukako sighed for her cousin, pained. She looked at her humbly, and bowed. "I never even said good-bye last time."

"I know," said Sumie, forgiving her.

WITH THE PIPE LADY gone, there was nothing holding her family back from heeding the Emperor's summons to Tokyo, and so Sumie's mother made the long journey to the capital with her four youngest children, hoping to find her husband and firstborn son. Advisor Kato bought their empty compound, moon-viewing pond and all, and offered his townhouse near the Palace to the two American ladies for their Christian school. Akio's father Lord Ii, meantime, was told at last that his request was not accepted and sadly moved his family to Tokyo too. Outside the temple one morning, gazing at Mount Hiei, the great northeastern sentinel that reminded me of the Mountain, Yukako sighed. "For a long time, I'd think, *Akio is just over that mountain, just across Lake Biwa.* And now he's gone, doubly gone, triply gone. Not even Sumie's left there."

She stood very still. I touched her shoulder. "When did you know you liked Mr. Akio?" I asked. "When exactly?"

Yukako watched her sons absorbed in drawing with sticks in the dust outside the temple. "Only you would ask that," she marveled, sitting on a shady bench. Her face softened and she ran her thumb along the top ridge of her *obi.*

"It was that summer before my brother died, when Akio was here. And Nao," she added, naming Chio and Matsu's son as if delicately tonguing out a stray tea leaf. "Sumie's family had just moved here after all those years in the Shogun's court." I watched her remember her cousin as a young girl. "My brother stole one of Sumie's *obi,* just to be troublesome; I think he was sweet on her. I was on my way to the storeroom tower to look for it one night, and I heard them in the woodshed by the stream, where Bozu's living now. They were just talking about this and that, smoking pipes, pretending to be grown men. My brother asked Akio about his home, how many days it took to get from Miyako to Hikone. 'You walk over the Eastern Mountains,' Akio said. 'That's a day, and then you sail across Lake Biwa: that's a second day.'

"'Why do you have to walk? Why can't you go upriver?'" my brother asked.

"'It's too shallow,'" Akio told him. 'The Shogun keeps it that way so he can mass troops where the river meets the lake.'

"'I heard the punishment is death if you dig the river deeper, but it's so shallow that every year, when the lake floods, the fields flood,' Nao said. 'The farmers dredge the river at night. They fill baskets with mud and say they're gathering shellfish if anyone asks.'

"And then I had the strangest picture in my mind," Yukako said. "It was so powerful and clear. Akio and I were farmers together in another life, filling baskets with mud in the dark, scooping out the riverbank.

And as if in answer to my thoughts, my brother said, 'Imagine that, a farmer with his yoke and baskets full of earth. In black on black lacquer, as a tea box for the rainy season.'

"Then I heard Akio's voice: 'If we need it shallow, we need it shallow. I wouldn't want to lose a horse in high water.'

"And then their talk turned to *sumo* wrestlers. I found Sumie's *obi* soon enough, but I could not shake that image. Me and Akio, together in some other lifetime, stealing wet earth in the dark." As Yukako told her story, her thumb never stopped tracing the top edge of her *obi*. She turned to me. "Only you would ask," she repeated gratefully. She shook her head to clear it. "Look at me now," she laughed. "Don't eat that, Ken-*bo*, it's dirty."

FOR TWO WEEKS after Sumie left, Yukako spent her nights at Baishian alone once Kenji fell asleep. For even longer, every morning, no matter what color she wore on the outside, I saw her belt on the black gauze robe worn under summer mourning. She roused herself to teach Lady Kato and the handful of other women the Mountain chose for her, but mostly she shut herself away in the upstairs room while I netted minnows and chased butterflies with my little charge. Sometimes we went to observe lessons in the practice room the way Yukako and I once had, and Kenji would spy longingly on his big brother while the Mountain watched Jiro teach the other students. After each student took his turn as host, the young men would file backstage into the *mizuya* to prepare for the next lesson while the Mountain berated Jiro for his mistakes. "If your students don't lay the ash and charcoal right, you need to teach them how. If they don't understand, don't keep repeating the same instructions louder, *baka!* Find another way to say it!" The Mountain had once embodied calm itself, but his mother's death had brought out a side in him I'd never seen. Perhaps, in an effort to bring her back, he had borrowed her spleen. Once he even made Tai watch as he castigated the boy's father. The Mountain's eyebrows had grown wild and long in the past year, and when he corrected his heir, both boys turned away as the black-and-white hairs jumped and fell and the spittle flew. The old man was all gentleness with Tai as he taught him the first steps of the tray *temae*, but that was not enough to keep Jiro from eating his breakfast in injured silence each morning, or from going on retreat on even the most obscure religious holidays.

THE MOUNTAIN DIED that summer, at the age of sixty-eight, after playing main guest at Tai's first formal *temae*. He wept openly as his grandson whisked the tea with his little hands and carefully set the bowl before him. The next morning Tai came running up the stairs, his eyes round and wide. "Grandfather won't wake up," he said. Shaking, Yukako went downstairs to lay her hands on her father's chest, to hold a silver mirror to his nose, but even as she pressed her sleeves to her eyes, she announced that the old man had surely choked on a fishbone, a lie spun to protect Tai from the inauspicious sign. Like her, I think the Mountain died of relief at witnessing his grandson's skill. I think he died of joy.

I wish I could remember the last thing he said to me. I think he held up his pipe and nodded at me to fill it. It was his mother's little pipe, which he had since started smoking: a long pale shaft made from a porcupine quill and those brass fittings the side of my head remembered well. Though toward the end I saw him beat Jiro's hands with his fan to exact the right posture from the young man, he never struck me, not even once. Good tool that I'd been, I was beneath notice.

20

1877–1885

JUST AS A GREAT STORM pulls all the other clouds down from the sky, the Mountain's death blew Akio out of the shrine of Yukako's preoccupations. While that summer she had belted on her secret mourning robe in a voluptuous trance of self-pity, that fall she dressed herself and the boys in black with a kind of solemn vigor. After the funeral, she installed Jiro in the family shrine to copy sutras for the Mountain's soul while she paid dozens of calls on her father's friends and former students to share the sad news, and on his tradesmen to ask for a month or two's grace on bills already long due. She drafted letters to a list of the Mountain's far-flung contacts and, having set Jiro to writing them, cleaned house. She moved her husband's possessions from the Bent-Tree Annex to her father's study by the garden and moved her father's things from the study to the storage tower. Jiro showed initiative by going through the fireproof tower himself, excavating the treasures of twelve generations of tea masters, trying to identify scrolls and tea wares worth enough to pay for the funeral but not so precious as to compromise the family honor by selling them. After all his work that season, he ordered brocade bags made for a few venerable pieces—including Inazuma, the Rikyu tea bowl he'd broken and had mended—but sold nothing.

At first, Tai slept in his same spot in the garden study, by the side of his father instead of his grandfather. But one night after the first week or so, he came creeping up the stairs and refused to go back down. "Miss Ura, would you go see what the matter is?" Yukako asked. For a woman who went downstairs to see her own dead father, there was a queer catch to her voice. As I groped in the dark from stairs to *tatami*, my feet acutely aware of the textures of looping wood grain and woven straw, I wondered why. As I'd suspected, the moonlit study was empty: Tai was afraid of sleeping alone. This *was* the room where his grandfather had died.

Jiro had spent most nights away from home for six years, I thought: why should Yukako sound surprised now? *For the boys,* I realized. *They don't know this.* From what Inko had once told me, it was fathers who introduced their sons to the floating world—but maybe not at ages four and five. "I think you should let him sleep up here tonight," I said firmly when I came back.

IN MOST MARRIAGES, I knew from bathhouse talk, the wife stayed awake all night until the husband came home from his roving, to help him change and to heat his bath—but in most marriages, I suspected the husband didn't avoid his wife's *futon* as emphatically as Jiro did Yukako's. At first Yukako neither acknowledged Jiro's nocturnal ramblings nor turned Tai away when he stole, nightly, upstairs. But that fall, after Kenji's Seven-Five-Three day at the temple, we had only a handful of nights as they should have been, with both small grown-up boys asleep downstairs. (I had a bad cold, I remember, so wretched I couldn't even enjoy having Yukako to myself after all those years.) After that, once we started having *two* little ones padding back upstairs at night, Yukako dropped the charade of sending the boys to bed with their father. Instead, while Jiro and the boys bathed first each evening, Yukako would lay out one of her husband's stylish *kimono*—heavy dark silk with an extravagantly painted lining—and leave a bathhouse *kimono* tied into a carrying-scarf for him as well. If he wanted a second bath before bed, he'd have to get it at the neighborhood bathhouse.

Yukako threw herself into raising her boys. She taught them all the writing she knew, and then, since Jiro was otherwise occupied, she hired a writing master to teach them the Chinese characters she'd never learned. I ground sticks of ink for the teacher, tracing each new *kanji* into the water, forcing the boys to help me read their texts out loud after each lesson. The year I outlived my mother, Yukako asked me to teach the boys how to talk with foreigners, and I was glad for the chance to hear my own voice speaking Claire Bernard's language. However, when Jiro heard his sons counting in French, marking out the numbers in a spiral like the *arrondissements* of Paris in one of their three textbooks, he put an end to it. He did encourage them, however, after their morning tea classes, to repeat each lesson with their mother. Yukako also hired a music master to teach the boys to play the long bamboo flute, and a martial arts tutor to teach them how to fight with staff and fists. The bamboo flute-staves were used by mendicant monks both to earn money and to defend themselves, she told us, but I think Yukako also took bittersweet pleasure, not unlike mine when I spoke French, in hearing her brother's music on her sons' lips.

But music masters cost money, and so do the pleasures of the floating world. The Emperor's stipend, when all was said and done, paid for the two long yearly trips to Tokyo to thank him for it, and while the students of the Long Room kept us in food, their fees weren't enough to pay off our mounting debts. Now that he finally had authority to name tea utensils, Jiro lacked the funds to commission them, though he was still welcome twice a year to the Raku studio, where the very act of his naming a favorite tea bowl—whether he bought it or not—raised its value. Jiro largely satisfied himself with calligraphing boxes for odd old pieces he'd dug up from the storeroom whose histories had been lost. There was no lack of treasures to choose from: even with his now weekly tea gatherings, even with his paid invitations to officiate tea events at shrines, temples, and the homes of newly rich merchants and imperial flunkies, he could still go through a year never using the same tea bowl twice.

The two elements of a *chakai*, or tea gathering, that Jiro could fashion himself were the scroll, a pleasure he only permitted himself yearly as they cost so much to mount, and the bamboo teascoop, which was inexpensive to make if one had grown up, like the Mountain's students, learning how. Moreover, they were stored in cheaply made bamboo tubes that invited lush calligraphy. Almost every *chakai* gathering included a moment where one ritually examined the teascoop and asked its name and maker, and this gave Jiro the chance to add his own fillip, his own shining word, to the poem of image and gesture that formed a tea event.

Jiro's life was arranged around duty—his dreaded trips to Tokyo, his morning lessons with young students, his evening lessons with grown students he'd inherited from the Mountain (minus, pointedly, Advisor Kato), his paid tea events—and pleasure: his *chakai* gatherings with friends, his longed-for retreats to One Pine at Sesshu-ji temple, his nightly visits to the floating world, his afternoons devoted to calligraphy and carving. He liked to wander through old temple gardens or poke around construction sites, such as at Advisor Kato's wood-and-paper townhouse near the Palace, which the two American ladies had knocked down to build their brick school. He'd return with a few choice sections of bamboo to work: some green, some gold, some blackened by hearthfire. His carving lacked the sturdy inevitability of Akio's but had a playful grace of its own: he was proudest of a piece made from a weathered cottage timber in which an insect had bored into the bamboo just below the node. The result was a slim blackened teascoop whose like I'd never seen, one tiny hole perfectly centered on its stem.

While Jiro wasn't earning much money, he was at least making an effort not to spend it on tea utensils. And he seemed to spend less and less of it on his nightly prowling as the years went by: the subtle perfume of *geisha* incense in the seams of the robes I laundered gave way to louder, cheaper scents, until his clothing began smelling harshly of grain alcohol and faintly of urine and bile. Jiro's mother had taken holy orders at the family temple near Third Bridge, and bathhouse rumor had it that she was the force behind his sudden lack of funds. People whispered that once his older brother Chugo stopped paying his bills, Jiro was barred from running a tab at one gay house after the next until he reached the tier of pleasures he could afford to pay for up front with the allowance Yukako doled out to him. He did not contest her right to the strongbox: although he was a merchant's son, Jiro regarded the Shin ledgers as if they were some kind of dense embroidery, intricate and squalid with the sweat of women's fingers. Meanwhile, having ground ink and taken notes for the Mountain all those years, Yukako merely had to pick up where her father had left off.

Yukako taught the students in the Long Room only when her husband was on retreat, and when she did she focused on the *temae* her father had created for use with tables and stools, as Jiro refused to teach it. Since Jiro would rather have seen a *geisha* than a barbarian in the tearoom any day, she did have her husband's permission to teach tea ceremony to singing-girls, but the fad for Shin *temae* had come and gone among them, so she earned money teaching a handful of Christian women and a few older ladies from the imperial family who had chosen to remain in Kyoto. When the boys were old enough to study with their father, I attended her on those lessons, some in the women's own homes, some at Baishian. It felt so strange to walk behind Yukako carrying her tea utensils, just as I'd once carried her *shamisen*, doing in earnest now what we'd done half in play with Koito years before.

ENTERPRISING HAIRDRESSERS like Miss Miki's father continued to see good times as more and more men wore their hair Western-style, such that by the time the boys were twelve and thirteen, Jiro's topknot put him in the almost eccentric minority. Listening for news of Miki's cousin—fruitlessly hoping she'd returned to Tokyo so I could hear from Inko—I learned instead that her father did so well for himself that he let Miki buy a camera, cumbersome and fragile, for her child-husband, our Zoji, who began teaching himself how to make portraits. He was popular, as the streets were full of people eager to show off: men in *kimono* and bowler hats, *kimono* and leather shoes, *kimono* and Western umbrellas—called "bat" umbrellas in Japanese for their blackness and their curved struts—*kimono* jackets and wooden sandals worn with Western trousers, here and there a man dressed head to toe in a Western suit, while the blocks sang with the squeaky-leather sound of progress: everyone, even the gardener Bozu, was doctoring their Western shoes to make them noisier.

Though shaved brows and blackened teeth were dramatically in the minority, women's clothing changed less than men's, noted Hazu and her bathhouse friends, among them Chio's niece Miss Ryu, who'd left us to marry a thread-winder's son. *High-collar* families aside—only two kinds of Japanese women wore full Western dress: "sheep," or mistresses of white men (who walked, the bathhouse girls whispered, *side by side* with their women! Opened their doors! Helped them into *jinrikisha*!), and teachers, of whom there were a visible few.

Most noticeable of all were the teachers employed by Advisor Kato's two American ladies, whose brick school for young women lay between us and the Palace wall. The ladies' names were Sutoku-*sensei*, Miss Starkweather, the big rawboned woman indeed shaped like a stalk of corn or a sunflower stem, and Pamari-*sensei*, Miss Parmalee, who unfortunately resembled the nervous Pomeranian she carried everywhere in a little lidded basket. In halting Japanese they exhorted anyone they stopped on the street to come to church, and a good few of the young men went, the better to look at the teachers.

Miss Starkweather and Miss Parmalee had hired a handful of English-speaking Japanese women as teachers, and had the young women wear their own mended castoffs until they could get dresses made to fit by a tailor from Kobe. How ungainly those Japanese girls seemed at first, with their unfamiliar silhouettes, their corseted waists and bustles and protruding bosoms, their tight sleeves and showy hats. And so many buttons! On the other side of the bathhouse wall, we heard a carpenter's son announce that the teachers wore fourteen buttons down the bodice alone.

Just a handful of students attended the Christian Ladies' School at first, though more came with time, and I would stare at the girls as they walked up the street in pairs and threes. In less than ten years, their numbers swelled to two hundred. Like the rest of hopeful young Kyoto, they wore what Western clothes they could: leather shoes here and there, often gold crosses. A girl might carry a frilly French parasol instead of the round oiled-paper one she'd grown up with, or a *kimono* sleeve might lift to expose the ruffle of a Western blouse-cuff underneath. You'd see a sprinkling of hats decked with fruit or flowers, and here or there an entire Western dress on a girl from a very well-connected family. However, with time they all began wearing their hair like the wife of their school's patron, who was none other than Yukako's first Christian student, Lady Kato. Her soft, unoiled Gibson Girlesque pompadour was called a *sokuhatsu*, a word evoking the eaves of a broad roof, for it sheltered the face with "eaves" of hair swelling from a central topknot.

One Western article of dress that enjoyed faddish pride of place in those years, worn by both men and women over *kimono* and suit alike, was a plaid wool shawl called an *ami*, or net, because the crosshatched pattern looked like the mesh of a fishing net. Advisor Kato, the man responsible for getting the new army into Western-style uniforms so soon after Meiji's revolution, left his touch on the Christian Ladies' School in a way even more visible than his money by requiring each student, no matter the welter of familiar and Western clothes worn underneath, to wear an *ami* shawl over her shoulders at school: gauze in summer, wool in winter. Though almost all the girls wore *kimono*, together they made an incontrovertibly modern picture, walking up the street to school, brisk and breezy in their plaids and wisping hair.

We knew none of these students well, probably because Jiro lobbied so hard among his own contacts to foil Advisor Kato, both because he disliked the man and because he was averse to Kato's latest pet project. Won over by the success of the Asaka Canal in Tokyo, Kato talked about canals with a convert's zeal, taking advantage of his position as Imperial Advisor to promote his brainchild. In spring, when he introduced the public dances of the *geisha*; in summer, when he opened the Gion Festival procession; in fall, addressing the crowds gathered to see the maples at their peak, he announced his dream: a canal from Lake Biwa into the city. We'd have cleaner drinking water, which would fight disease; our little canals and streams would flow high all year round, which would fight fire; we'd have a clear and taxable waterway all the way from Osaka to the cheap rice of Hikone, which would fight poverty. Kato had a Dutch waterworks team agree it was feasible. He had an award-winning young engineer from Tokyo with plans in hand. He had most of the money lined up from the Meiji government. All he needed, we heard ceaselessly, was the support of Kyoto's merchant community. Though Hikone types like Mr. Noda, the greasy rice merchant who wore his *netsuke* fob on a Western watch chain, were eager for the canal to be dug, Jiro's merchant friends, suspicious, gave Kato and his engineer Tanabe as wide a berth as possible in their tiny social world, promising to consider his

request and waiting to see what their fellows would do. Thus, the
Christian Ladies' School taught mostly daughters of Meiji officials,
like Advisor Kato himself; the merchants were more likely to hire
Starkweather and Parmalee's teachers as tutors than send their girls to
the Americans' school.

For example, the silk merchant Shige, whom I'd first thought of as
the Bear when he and Jiro were both the Mountain's students, had a
piano teacher from the Ladies' School come and teach his girls, but he
went out of his way to ask if Yukako could teach tea to his wife. Over
the years we observed a number of women teachers going in and out
of the Shige house, and Yukako's attention was drawn by their full
Western regalia: French and English teachers had worn Western dress
from the first, but now Japanese music and dance teachers were also
dressing in Western style. Chio, graying but strong as ever, was startled
to learn at the bathhouse just how much more the Japanese women in
Western clothes were paid than Yukako, and just how much more the
English and French teachers were paid than all the rest.

It was a spring morning in Meiji Eighteen when I passed this information on to Yukako, the month we brought Tai to the temple to pray
for wisdom in his thirteenth year, while Jiro was in Tokyo making his
tea offering to the Emperor. Yukako frowned over her accounts as she
listened, but I knew I had her full attention by the way she held the
loaded brush over the grinding stone to catch wet ink as she thought.
"How interesting," she said.

21

1885

A WEEK AFTER LEARNING Chio's news, when we went with the boys to the spring temple plays, Yukako slipped away home without us, complaining of stomach pain. That night she gave me a smug look and said, "When we teach at Shige's house tomorrow, wear the Western dress you made for the Expo."

The next morning, as I waited at the gate for Yukako, exposed and ungainly in my grown-up-child's dress, I saw a white lady with a parasol leave our house. A missionary, no less, from the clipped-gait S-curve look of it. I halted, afraid. No time had passed; I was a stray cat hiding from nuns.

The way she walked, was the lady ill? Drunk? She lowered her parasol: it was Yukako. "I think it fits well, don't you?"

"What happened?"

Yukako smiled triumphantly in her Western clothes and Japanese coiffure. "I bought it from that engineer Tanabe's sister. She teaches at the Ladies' School; she's just my size."

"When did this happen?" I asked, flabbergasted.

"Yesterday, when you and the boys were at the play."

I blinked. "You just walked up to her and *bought* it off her back?"

"Not the one she was wearing, her other one. Western fashion changes every season, can you imagine? Now Miss Tanabe can buy a new one. What do you think?"

"Well . . ."

"I *did* give her a lot of money. But I'll make it all up fast, if I play my students right."

"Come back inside with me; I think some of those hooks are on wrong," I said. In the cloakroom, I laced and tugged until she looked a little less queer, incredulous that she'd gone and had this adventure without me. She looked more than a little foolish, truth be told, a pencil-shaped woman in an hourglass dress. But more strikingly, she looked like *someone else.* "I would have helped you carry it home," I said, my tongue thick in my mouth as we went outside again.

"I wish you had," she admitted. "I felt so conspicuous, walking home by myself with that big box. I wore her plaid shawl so people would need to look twice to know it was me." Yukako, pigeon-toed in her leather shoes, kept looking back at her bustle with surprise and distrust. As best she could, she watched herself walk up and down the stone path. She looked like a man in a dress. "It's a bit tight, no?" she asked gaily, laughing at the picture she made. And then her laughter died mid-breath.

I turned to see what had caught her eye: a man at the gate. He looked at Yukako carefully, his controlled face betraying no shock at her clothing. She was afraid. I followed her gaze to the man's hand as he passed her a brocade-wrapped scroll case: he was missing the tip of his fourth finger, what we called his medicine finger, the one used for testing powders and spreading balms. His bow was deep, his *kimono* was clean, his tone was humble as he apologized for troubling our home. But Yukako shook a little as she accepted his message, staring at the blunt club of the man's fourth finger, at the gap between sleeve and wrist revealing a flash of red and green scrollwork down his forearm. A tattoo!

Yukako started to slip the scroll into her absent *kimono* sleeve, stopped, and steadied herself, bowing as the man departed. He was swept off in a cunning and flashy *jinrikisha* painted on every side with flowers and beauties, their layered robes rivaling the blooming cherries overhead. "Anyone can have an accident," mused Yukako, reaching for her own fourth finger.

"But only a few people have missing fingers *and* tattoos," I said, shuddering. I had never seen a mobster, but who hadn't heard of them?

"Don't say that word!" hissed Yukako.

"Tattoo?"

"Stop it!"

WE ONLY OPENED the man's message much later, long after Yukako had negotiated with the Bear's wife for more money and changed back into her familiar *kimono.* We sat with the mysterious scroll in the privacy of Baishian: it did not contain a letter, just three lines of text, written plain enough for a woman to read, with explanatory phonetic *kana* on the side. A date: the first of August, some four months hence. A place: the central *geisha* booking office of Pontocho. And a sum of money: a very large number, a figure against which the Shiges' raise was a trifling amount.

When Yukako opened the terse message, a little brocade bag fell to the floor: a talisman from a temple. Mothers bought these for their homes and children for every occasion: a safe voyage, a successful endeavor, a good wedding. I picked up the talisman; it was embroidered with characters that looked familiar, but even more striking was the scent. I recognized the subtle perfume that once suffused Jiro's robes after his nights out, in the days before his brother stopped paying his bills. When I passed the bag to Yukako, she inhaled, met my eye, and nodded sourly. Then she glanced at the strangely familiar *kanji* embroidered on the talisman and her eyes widened, her jaw went hard. Oh! I had just seen dozens of brocade bags adorned with these very characters on the day we presented Tai at the temple with his agemates. To send this talisman was to suggest that the boy might need its protection, that the tattooed man was prepared to do whatever it took to make Jiro pay his debts. Yukako dropped the little bag, chilled. *How dare they threaten my son?*

That night another bad omen befell our house. Chio's husband Matsu, now deep into his seventies, seized his chest and stopped breathing for two full minutes. He didn't die, but when he opened his eyes again the next day, he didn't recognize anyone. His hands reached involuntarily to cut lengths of charcoal, to mold charcoal stubs and seaweed together into spheres for fuel, but he could no longer speak, and his tools were foreign to him. Morning and night he sat by the fire, gazing at the opposite wall.

We went to the temple every day that week, and we prayed for Tai's safety. I had never noticed how Benten-*sama*, Yukako's patron goddess, carried not just musical instruments but swords and arrows in her many arms: on one statue, her plump, mild face leered in victory. Yukako took my spot by the drafty upstairs door at night, in order to place her body between her sons and danger. We prayed, too, for the return of Matsu's wits. Since the gardener Bozu had been working under Matsu for years, Yukako asked him to continue in the old man's place, and assured Chio that she had no intention of turning Matsu out on his own. Mostly, however, we prayed for money.

After five days, only leaving her prayers to give lessons in her Western dress, Yukako took action. First she laid out all her *kimono*, as she did when misfortune first came to the Shins. As she set aside the dazzling

brocade robes that she, then I, had worn as little girls, we heard Kuga
come stumping up the stairs to deliver a letter from two visitors who
had dropped by.

I watched Yukako anxiously untie the month's second unexpected
letter, this one addressed to Master Teacher, then saw her face relax as
she read. The city was holding another Exposition that summer, after
the flamboyant Gion Festival in July, and would the Shin family be willing to participate again?

With a quick, sure hand, Yukako wrote a response, "signing" it
with her husband's square jade seal. He would be delighted to participate in educating the barbarian world about the cultural triumphs of
Japan, and was prepared to offer his time—and a priceless thick-tea
container from Rikyu's day—for a small fee: here Yukako unhesitat-
ingly copied the enormous figure presented by the tattooed man.

Full of hope, Yukako continued her rounds of teaching in ladies'
homes. Jiro's trip to the capital was timed to fall after the old year's students graduated and before the new year's class began, but Yukako's
hands were full nonetheless as she coached her older son through the
duties usually performed by the head of the household this time of
year: washing the Buddha in the family shrine with hydrangea tea,
organizing flower-viewing events and memorial offerings to honor
great patrons of the past. With Jiro away, I was allowed to follow
behind Yukako and the boys on the annual Shin pilgrimage to Sesshu-ji
temple, where the family offered tea at One Pine House to mark its
construction three hundred years before. Because Jiro usually made the
offering, or her father before him, it was the first time Yukako had ever
seen the old temple or its garden, a long white wedge of raked stones.
Though cleaned by the monks daily, One Pine—a handsome four-and-
a-half-mat-house with a great round window—had long ago crossed
the line from *wabi* to shabby, its paper walls torn and poorly patched, its
tatami yellowed with age, its thatched roof balding. Tai made a handsome and assured picture, lifting his offering of tea to the ancestors as

Yukako, with as much decorum as possible, removed a large crawling thatch bug from her hair. I could tell she took grim satisfaction from the scruffiness of the place: at least her errant husband wasn't spending all their money *here*. I had been trusted with the tea utensils, while seven-year-old Aki carried the ceremonial charcoal made from the last of her grandfather Matsu's precise widths of oak, each cut to its ritually prescribed length. As the weak sunset light charged the path home, I heard Tai say to his brother, "Next year, you be the host, no?"

Long and weedy like their parents, the boys had shaved heads like the other tea students, and both wore white strips of cloth around their foreheads to mark them as pilgrims. Kenji had lassoed a fat dragonfly with a silk thread when we stopped at a hillside shrine to eat on a picnic veranda and drink at the spring; now, as his brother spoke, he let the insect go. "Don't talk that way," he said. He was so beautiful, everyone talked about it, even handsomer than the boys chosen to ride on the Gion Festival floats. Aki reached for the dragonfly as it lofted away; Yukako watched her sons, breath drawn taut.

"You'll be old enough then; why shouldn't you?" asked Tai.

Kenji looked away, laced his hands behind his back, stretched. "I'd only take your place if you were dead," he said simply.

Yukako flinched. Kenji continued explaining. "When you're the Master Teacher, I want to be the first of your students. And when you have a son, I want to teach him everything I know. That's all. I just want to be your younger brother," he said.

"You *are* my little brother, *baka*," said Tai, uncomfortable with Kenji's sincerity.

"*Baka* yourself," said Kenji peaceably. I wondered if most boys with fathers seemed as self-made as these two.

April was also the season for plays and pantomimes at Mibu Temple. Nights, the boys would imitate the *samurai* that the actors played onstage, making gargoyle faces at each other and swordfighting with their bamboo flutes. And just as Hiroshi and Nao had done before

them, Yukako told me, Tai and Kenji dug the Mountain's *hakama* out
from storage for their games: the wide pleated trouser-skirts that had
formerly been worn only by *samurai* were now only worn by actors playing *samurai*—and boys playing actors playing *samurai*.

The year before, they had been allowed to go to the plays by themselves and eat roasted sweet potatoes and grilled rice cakes, but this
year Yukako insisted that her sons only eat food from home, and—
under guise of giving the servants a treat—that they be attended by at
least two of us at all times, each armed with small sharp knives.

One day when the boys were away at the theater, I followed Yukako
home from her lesson at the Shiges'. Although it was rare and strange
to see Yukako in her bustle and buttons, taking possession of a new
way of moving in her body, for my part I felt like a clown in my Western shift, and always passed through our gate with relief. Today, however, a familiar figure blocked the path to the house.

"*My honored lord.*" It was Jiro, his voice dripping with sarcasm. "*I've
been waiting for you night and day. When I haven't been praying for your safe return,
I've been grinding rice with my own hands to make fine flour.*"

For a moment I was flung back to another meeting on another
path: I remembered Yukako's father striking her outside Koito's house.
I looked up at her, my heart thrashing. And then I saw all the fear and
anger, all the poison that had filled her since the tattooed man came to
visit, cross her face at once. Beside Yukako's, Jiro's rancor seemed fussy
and thin. She slowly peeled off her long white leather gloves and stood
very still, looking at her husband, his adze-shaped head, his bushy
brows, and said to him coldly, "Shall I draw you a bath, my lord?"

It was a task that usually fell to Bozu or Chio. "I'd like that, yes,"
he said.

And so she did. I unhooked and unlaced her; we changed quickly
into our *kimono* and I brought in fuel while Yukako fanned the bathhouse embers into a glowing bed of coals. We carried in bucket after
bucket of water while Jiro napped, then came out to watch us, pleased

with Yukako's penance. While the water heated, he scrubbed himself, working his bran bag into the crevices between his fingers, soaping up the back of his neck and behind his ears. He winced at Yukako's touch when she washed his back. After he had poured bucket after rinsing bucket of cold water over his body, Jiro settled into the hot bath and began questioning Yukako.

"I wouldn't have known it was you on the path if the servants didn't talk of nothing else." He glanced at me. "You and your *lady's maid*"—he spat the phrase in English: *reidizu meido.* "What shall I tell my guests when they ask me why my wife parades herself all over town dressed like a foreign whore?"

"Tell them to look around and see for themselves," Yukako said. "This is what women teachers wear. Surely you've seen them at the Ladies' School?"

"I've had better places to go," he replied.

"Yes, I suppose you have," said Yukako, her voice dripping with acid. "As for Miss Ura, isn't it obvious? It's humiliating to see those foreign ladies running around with Japanese servants and *jinrikisha* boys. I've dressed us both like this because I mean to earn as much as foreign teachers do."

Jiro crossed his arms over his bare chest and scowled in the steam. "Did you know, I've just spent two weeks at Edo hearing the same non-sense every day? The Prime Minister"—here he spoke of Ito, the man whose *geisha* mistress had followed him all the way from Gion—"has poured rivers of gold into a pavilion called The Belling Stag, where lords and ladies learn to dance and eat like barbarians, so that the barbarians will shift their treaties in our favor. They each cut their own plate of ani-mal meat like butchers, and they bray to each other about how good it tastes. They learn barbarian dances where men and women touch and leer. There aren't enough wives willing to dance, so they press whores into service to fool the foreign guests." At this, Yukako raised an eye-brow, while Jiro went on to condemn *gorufu, tenisu,* and the other Western games he'd been forced to witness or endure, his crazy words spilling over each other. He was lounging in the bath and she was standing in attendance, so he had to crane his neck up to see her.

"You'd best get all this nonsense about barbarians out of your system before the Second *Eppo* this summer," said Yukako. "You're presenting tea for them again."

"*What?*" spluttered Jiro, seizing Yukako's wrist so that she all but staggered against the tub.

"They accepted your terms this morning. They pay well," said Yukako. "And we have debts." I saw the unsaid words flash across her face: *You* have debts.

Jiro saw them, too, and dropped her wrist, dumbfounded.

"Would you like me to go in your stead?" Yukako offered gently. "The foreigners won't know any better, and then people here will know where you stand." Jiro gave a barely perceptible nod, and Yukako, emboldened, pressed on. "The city's full of men who would applaud you for taking the barbarians' gold and shaming them at the same time."

Jiro's head dipped again and I realized that he was nodding not in gratitude but in disgust. "Very well, then," he said.

IF JIRO HAD SHUNNED his wife's bed before that spring, he took his avoidance to new heights after, ostentatiously wiping the place where her hands had touched the tray at breakfast, insisting that the servants, me excluded, lay out his clothes at night. Of course, he didn't trust their taste enough to dress him, so the task fell doubly on Yukako both to select the robes and to walk the other women through handling them. On a graver note, he sabotaged Yukako's decision to use the Expo money to pay off debts: one day, a week after Jiro's twice-yearly visit to the Raku kilns, Yukako received a second bill for a staggering figure, this time from Chojiro's Heir.

"The man's full moon *chakai* is tonight," Yukako said, holding the bill at arm's length between two fingers, as if it could pollute her. "We may find some answers there."

"I'll try," I said, bowing.

THIRTEEN YEARS AFTER Jiro's first *chakai* in Muin, the stark foursquare Houseless House where the Mountain had first chastised him, where Yukako, heavy with their son, had first brought in food at his bidding, that very son Tai set bowls of young simmered sweetfish before his father's guests. In his early thirties, Jiro had lost the rawboned anxiety of his first *chakai* but retained a certain unsilvered look of eagerness, of wanting to be admired.

And I knew right then that he was succeeding, in the eyes of his main guest, the silk merchant Shige. Though I had seen his wife at lessons, I had not seen the Bear himself since the Expo crowd in Meiji Five. I knew Shige could see just how much Tai resembled his father, could "read" the pattern carefully chosen for Tai's narrow *obi*. Like the Edo-chic checkerboard weave popular a generation before, it was a series of alternating rectangles, navy and gray, of which all the navy blocks bore almost-imperceptible *fleurets* worked in gold thread. The ghostly gold medallions brought to mind, in as delicate and tasteful a way imaginable, the fact that if merchant sons like Jiro and Shige had worn such thread when they were Tai's age, they could have been punished with death. Though the moonlit branch of young cherry leaves in the hanging vase mourned the loss of blossoms, of *samurai*, of bygone days, the very fact of this young boy marked a triumph for Jiro and his guests, finding their fortunes in this untried world.

After thirteen years, half spent under his adoptive father's thumb, half spent in stinting on all but his basest pleasures, Jiro had set a new pine box by the tearoom door, calligraphed with a new name. I made out the *kanji* for *spring*, and another two below it. *Rain:* a stylized window, its bamboo blind rolled up to reveal a stylized storm, four quick diagonal flicks of rain. And *field:* a square box quartered by a cross. Spring Rain Field. It made sense, as blossoms gave way to greening trees, as Tai joined his father in the tearoom. I felt a dormant jolt of warmth for Jiro, even as I itched to open the box, to steal back whatever tea bowl he'd bankrupted us with.

I couldn't see the tea bowl at first as I leaned toward the room, listening to the main guest drain his *matcha* with gusto. "Spring Thunder," declared Jiro, when asked the tea bowl's name: Shunrai. He had chosen it, he said, out of all the bowls made this season by Chojiro's Heir.

"Perhaps a better name would be Kaminari," Shige said, nodding toward the cherry leaves. What did he mean? He spoke with a certain misty gruffness used by men when they were being poetic, but his words couldn't have been more ill-chosen. I had never forgotten Jiro's first *chakai*, when he named the mended Rikyu tea bowl. Would he sulk again this time? Argue with his guest? Coolly put the Bear in his place?

Jiro answered, however, with noncommittal cheer. "You think?" *Kaminari, Kaminari,* I groped mentally. Of course, it was another word for Thunder! I'd been reading *Rain* and *Field* separately when together they formed the *kanji* for *Thunder.*

Kaminari versus *Shunrai, Thunder* versus *Spring Thunder,* cherry leaves versus cherry blossoms. You couldn't find a fussier, more hairsplitting lot than tea people, I thought, crowding in toward the peephole I'd made thirteen years before.

I saw the delicate cherry leaves, the mica glitter of sand in the clay Muin walls. I saw a flash of moonlight on black glaze, like the shining eye of an animal: I nearly gasped. Had Chojiro's Heir known he was making, not a copy, but an uncannily similar cousin to the bowl Jiro had broken all those years before?

I heard Shige sigh deeply. "I was there, at that lesson," he murmured. He had seen the bowl break too. I saw, glowing in Shige's shrewd hands, the same dark asymmetrical solemnity that had arrested me all those years before, as if never broken, never mended, as if flung up from the volcanic earth intact.

After a long silence, the merchant set down the tea bowl. "When your brother hears about this piece, he'll be jealous," he said. It was a nod both to his brother Chugo's well-known taste as a collector and to his vast wealth.

"You think so?" repeated Jiro, pleased with himself. "Perhaps I can make tea for both of you in it sometime."

Breaking a rule more often honored in the breach, the Bear turned talk away from the tearoom. "Have you heard anything from him recently, about Advisor Kato's canal?" he asked.

Jiro chuckled. "Has that boor asked you to invest yet?"

"I plan to follow your brother's lead, whatever he decides," Shige said. The other guests nodded sagely. Advisor Kato had recently asked Okura Chugo for more money than all the other Kyoto merchants combined.

"I'm sure he'll laugh the man out of town," said Jiro.

"He was going on about those looms from France that run on water power. Can you imagine?"

"He doesn't know a thing about your trade and he's telling you to import equipment," Jiro scoffed.

"The man's full of nonsense, but he tells a good story," said Shige.

"*Un.* If my brother wants to spend his money on Kyoto," Jiro said, distastefully using the word in place of *Miyako*, which he still preferred, "I have a better idea."

"Yes?"

"Everywhere I turn they're knocking over lovely old homes and putting up brick boxes," Jiro sighed. "Kato's school, and so forth."

"True," Shige nodded.

"There used to be an exquisite four-and-a-half-mat room called New Moon Arbor behind that house. And now? The building, the garden, New Moon Arbor, gone. Girls are probably sewing American flags right on the spot where the teahouse stood." Jiro paused a moment, lost in thought. "I should have you over at One Pine House sometime," he said.

"One Pine . . ." murmured the Bear nostalgically.

"It's really gone tatty since our student days. What I'd like," Jiro said, "would be a fund to restore One Pine and buy up teahouses before they're demolished. I'd move them to Sesshu-ji and the City of Kyoto could sell tickets. It's counter to the purpose of a teahouse, of course, but it would draw men of taste and means like no *Eppo* ever will."

"A place for houses of retirement to retire. A hermitage for her-mitages. You're a true poet, my friend," Shige bowed. "You remind me what to treasure most." With that, he lifted the blocky dark tea bowl again and set it down, offering it a deep parting bow. Primal, ungainly, the bowl pulsed like black sand stuck by lightning. I bowed, too, before my peephole, a tiny gesture of awe.

THAT NIGHT, long after Shige and his friends left, I crept backstage into the *mizuya* where the tea bowl sat drying on the shelf. I packed Shunrai up into its new pine box and brought it to show Yukako. "This explains the Raku bill," I said, unwrapping my find. We looked at it together on the veranda while the boys slept inside.

"I can see why he had to buy it," she murmured, unexpectedly ten-der in the moonlight. When I told her of Jiro's dream, she nodded, wry and sweet. She turned the bowl in her lovely hands, offering its maker, as the rest of us had, an unconscious bow.

THE NEXT MORNING, after bringing in the breakfast dishes, Yukako laid another tray before her husband. I saw the pine box and an

unfolded letter: the bill from Chojiro's Heir. Without a word of accusation, Yukako asked humbly, "Shall I go to him and ask for a few
months' time?"

"If you insist," Jiro shrugged, though his words were crisp. His distaste for Yukako's unsolicited offer of help, for the Expo—for the foreigners whose money it would bring in *a few months' time*—crackled in
the air unstated. And then Jiro looked up at Yukako as she rose, nostrils subtly flaring with desperation, saw his sons shrinking into themselves against him. "Though you'll see there's no need to meddle," he
added, his voice a little shrill.

THE VOICE OF CHOJIRO'S HEIR was reassuring and generous. "A few
months is nothing in the shared history of our families." Nearly sev-
enty, he'd hardly aged since our long-ago visit, when Kenji slept in
my arms and Tai asked to see the studio: now, as then, he seemed as
roundly sturdy as a horse chestnut. Outside, the spring rain hissed
softly on the stones, while inside the roasted tea the Heir served gave
off a cozy smell of earth and iron.

Yukako had dressed carefully for this meeting. She was a wife in
straitened circumstances with two half-grown boys, but she was also a
beautiful woman in her thirties, nearing, though her nights with Akio
and Jiro were long past, her sexual prime. And so she dressed just a
little older than she needed to, chose a pattern of early summer grasses
that climbed a bit lower than necessary, tied her *obi* and *obi* cord just a
hair lower than convention required, in order to contrast the heaviness
of her burden with the relative freshness of her face. But those young
white grasses bent against a slate-green silk landscape, a coy cousin to
the blue-green that had flattered her as a girl, and she exposed just a
breath more nape—a white appeal against the brick-red collar of her
underrobe—than anything in her sober ensemble prepared one for.
Chojiro's Heir could not help but lean toward her. "I need to prevail

upon you for something more," her voice came hesitantly as the soft rain fell outside.

"What is it, *Okusama?*"

"My husband has an unusual request," she said. "I don't know how to broach this."

"It can't be so bad."

"You can't be surprised that he has fallen in love with your work. He has made a box for your tea bowl with his own hands and named it Shunrai." At this, Chojiro's Heir gave a pleased nod. Yukako continued, "In a tea gathering this past full moon, he even paired it with Rikyu's own Teardrop teascoop." Because, within a given tea event, all the utensils had to have a similar rank, this gesture showed the new tea bowl high regard indeed. I watched Chojiro's Heir suppress a smile.

"But you know how things are for him," she concluded. I could see her face in only quarter view, but her chin wobbled as if she were a little girl about to cry.

The prospect of taking back a tea bowl that had only increased in value, together with the project of consoling a beautiful woman, seemed to blunt the Heir's concern over seeing the money he was owed. "Sometimes one has to return a thing one can't pay for," he said.

"No," said Yukako soulfully. "Here it is. This summer our family will perform in the Second *Eppo.* They will pay well."

Chojiro's Heir nodded, Yukako's plea for time made clear.

"And we need gifts to give everyone involved. So . . . Well, my husband begs you to consider trading the Shunrai bowl for a hundred of the tea bowls made by your students as practice."

"Why, I would give them to you for the asking," laughed Chojiro's Heir.

"I couldn't have the world knowing that," Yukako explained. "Surely you understand. It would look better if they were traded for Shunrai." Of course: a gift that people heard was won dearly would be treasured more.

She continued. "But if the *Eppo* went better than expected, if it happened that we were able to buy Shunrai from you a second time, would you be willing to not raise the price?"

I watched as beauty, vulnerability, and the guarantee of easy money did their work on Chojiro's Heir. "Don't be silly, *Okusama*," he assented, and basked in the trust and gratitude streaming from Yukako's eyes. "When would you need them?"

"We can bring Shunrai here and pick up the student bowls the first night of the *Eppo*," Yukako said, her quiet voice a little too quick and firm.

Yukako's shift in demeanor jerked the Heir back to his wits a little. "I don't worry about foreigners at the *Eppo*," he said. "But I don't want these bowls making their way into the market here. We can't have shopmen passing them off as real Raku," he explained.

Yukako nodded, girlish again. "Maybe you could cut a notch in the foot of the bowl to show it was made for practice," she suggested meekly. "Or my husband said you could stamp the bowls with something like this," she said, passing him a small box from her sleeve: it held a carved stone seal used for stamping documents or clay.

Yukako kept her face studiedly blank as Chojiro's Heir carefully read the reversed *kanji* aloud: *"By students of Raku, for students of Shin Chanoyu."*

"Really?" asked Yukako, playing the illiterate.

Chojiro's Heir seemed put off by the stone seal, its deliberateness and its presumption. "I see he has anticipated my concern," he said stiffly.

"I'm ashamed," Yukako said humbly, her face luminous, her head drooping on its graceful stem. "Please take all the time you need to consider this importunate request." She used language so self-abasing I cannot reproduce it in English, but she gazed right at him as she spoke, her eyes bright, her lips delicately parted.

· · ·

"You planned the whole thing," I marveled, as we sheltered from the rain on a covered bridge. "You designed that stamp! You knew you'd ask for those student bowls when you offered to go in Master Teacher's place!"

Yukako smiled sadly. "Do you remember my wedding day, when we sat looking at Okura Chugo's gold?"

"Yes?" I remembered her crying through closed eyes.

"I felt so small," she said. "I'd worked so hard, remember? Even if I hadn't gotten caught, even if the new currency hadn't come along to make what I'd earned worthless, it was so little next to those *koban*." Setting her jaw, she explained, "I decided I never wanted to feel that helpless again. *Migawa Yuko* was never going to get as far as *Master Teacher's Wife*, right?"

I felt glum hearing her say that, but I nodded.

"That's why I offered to go as a favor instead of sneaking off on my own," she said. "Same with offering to present at the Expo in Master Teacher's place." A sly grin played across her face. "But . . . maybe I didn't tell him everything."

For the next month Yukako relieved me of all my duties attending her at lessons and serving meals. Through the long rains of June, she posted me on the veranda closest to the kitchen door to pick apart seams of soiled garments and sew up seams of laundered ones, so that I could observe every messenger that came. And so it happened that I was the one to offer tea and cakes to the boy from the Raku studio, to tuck away the answer he carried, to present it to Yukako late that night. It was a box containing one tea bowl, humble but handsome, with a pair of notches cut in the foot. The base bore a large square stamp: the very seal Yukako had had made.

. . .

AFTER THE BOWL ARRIVED, Yukako sold all her gorgeous girlhood *kimono*. I fingered the robe I'd once worn a last time. "I'll never have a daughter," Yukako said pensively on the way home, her sleeve full of coins. *But you had me*, I thought. I followed her to a series of shops where she placed a number of large orders, the most interesting of which involved another object of her own design.

AFTER THE MOUNTAIN'S DEATH, Jiro was no longer beset by frequent, mysterious illnesses. So one evening, a night he'd planned to dine with Shige, not long after Advisor Kato plied the silk merchant with the gift of a water-powered jacquard loom, we were surprised to discover that Jiro was ill.

Because the boys were still in the grip of their acting craze—making speeches in *hakama* and bashing away at each other with their bamboo staves—they asked me to read one of my Shakespeare plays for them to act out in the garden. Just as we were discovering how ill suited Lear was to their taste for blood—"Now you, call him a *waterish duke!* Now you, *beseech them to make good their professions!*"—we were surprised by Jiro, who jerked his study door wide with a noisy rattle. We turned to him with dropped jaws.

"You don't all have to look so shocked," he said. "I *do* live here. I have a fever; I'm staying in." As the boys bowed to apologize for bothering him, he waved them away like mosquitoes. "A foreign girl in a foreign dress, telling a foreign tale, that's what I like to see." I was still in the shift I wore to accompany Yukako to lessons. "It all goes together so well." His sarcasm held an edge of approval that surprised me. "You two, on the other hand, look ridiculous. Put those away," he said, gesturing at the boys' *hakama*. "Bring me something to eat."

Jiro's outburst jolted the boys out of their acting mood and into their other favorite game: *Jiyu Minken.* Throughout the countryside, we heard, taxes had gone so high that farmers of the *Jiyu Minken,* or People's Movement, had begun blowing up government offices, echoing the Satsuma rebels of years before. One boy would play a tyrannical tax man, and the other would tiptoe around his "house," whisper-singing the most popular ditty of the eighteenth year of Meiji: "Dynamite, Boom!" And then the "house" would explode and one boy would roll on the ground in agony while the other sang as loud as possible. Out of concern for their father's health, they mouthed the words instead: *For our more than forty million countrymen, we're not afraid of wearing convict red . . .*

Due to his sons' solicitude, no doubt, Jiro recovered with astonishing speed and was out the next evening until dawn.

22

1885

J IRO KEPT Lightning and Spring Thunder, his two prize tea bowls, side by side in a special cupboard in his study, on a wave-shaped shelf behind a sliding panel. Rikyu's gold-mended bowl sat a little higher than the one Chojiro's Heir had made, but the two together formed a kind of hypnotic unity, like a pair of dark eyes. Yukako easily located the two bowls and their calligraphed boxes, and that summer she visited the cupboard often to make sure the Shunrai bowl would be there when she needed it.

On the morning of the Expo, however, Shunrai's elegant box stood empty on the cupboard floor. The bowl itself was gone. I followed Yukako as she paced anxiously from Jiro's study to the classroom where he sat at lesson with his students, kneeling by the lattice window as if she could pry an explanation out of him just by looking. Halfway to the fireproof tower—had he locked the bowl away in storage?—she halted. "Isn't he holding another tea event tomorrow night?" she asked, embarrassed with herself. "Go look in the Muin *mizuya*."

"I don't think he uses the same tea bowl more than once a year with guests," I demurred. I was right: Muin's backstage preparation area, though its water barrel stood full and its plaited basket waited newly stocked with charcoal, yielded nothing.

"We don't have time for this," fretted Yukako. "Let's look in *all* the *mizuya.*"

We looked quickly, even checking the classroom *mizuya*, though it required some creeping around, but none stood in readiness like Muin's. "What about *inside* the tearoom?" I asked.

"Where would he put it?" she snorted. But sure enough, no calligraphy hung in the scroll alcove. In its place, like a pert little apple on a windowsill, sat a plump silk bag tied with bright cords. Opened, the bag sank flat into a perfectly round disk of brocade, on which Shunrai glowed like polished jet. "You were right," Yukako said contritely. Relieved, she took the tea bowl, and with a backward glance, replaced it with its gold-veined brother.

"Can you just *do* that?" I whispered, as we stole away.

"After that bill, he should be glad I didn't replace it with a cabbage."

In the old calendar, the festival of the dead had often coincided with the first whispering days of autumn coolness: early September with its clearest air, through which the dead could pass as easily as bonfire smoke. Now it fell in the dog days of August, the limbs of the circle dancers moving heavy in the blunt night heat. Just so, August, that worst of months, had once featured the Gion Festival, in which young men stripped to the waist hauled two-story floats crammed with pipers, drummers, and sacred boys, and girls in gauze robes panted by the river, limply lifting their moon-shaped fans. Every gesture at Gion Festival used to speak the words *Enough. After this, the heat breaks.* Now the festival fell mid-July, squarely in the hot eye of summer, with weeks to go before a breath of fall air.

Into this foundry, the city of Kyoto (all gauze and paper fans, bare feet and shaved ice on its night verandas) welcomed the foreigners: leather shoes and stuffy linen, bone corsets and smelling salts. "What an oasis we'll be," Yukako said, claiming the breeziest booth at the Expo for the Shins. She borrowed a few armchairs—the kind a foreign lady could wilt into—from the Expo offices to mix with the spartan stools of her father's design, and hired a shaved-ice man from one of Kyoto's most prestigious confectionery shops to work backstage in the *mizuya*. "I hear they like sweets, so I need to remind the Toraya man to use twice as much syrup," she noted. Although she seated her guests, she decided to forgo her father's tabletop *temae* and had *tatami* brought in for her own use. "It gives a cooler feeling," she determined. After a calculated look up and down the hall at the booths in progress—an uncertain array of technologies and products, from brocades to velocipedes to a headache's worth of maps for Advisor Kato's ambitious canal, drawn by his protégé Tanabe—Yukako nodded to herself. "I think the foreigners will like seeing us on the floor."

She gave me a writing set and a few leaves of paper and set me to work in our booth. "Make a label in the foreigners' language for the tea things," she told me, rushing off to deal with the shaved-ice man. I wrote rarely, and my hand around the brush was a stiff child's fist, but the coarse paper emboldened me. I experimented with English and French, ran roughshod with my spelling, wrote short and long descriptions, from the crudest—*Tea Things*—to the first sentence of what could have been an essay on the history and cultural importance of tea. Yukako reappeared and chose one of my labels by sight alone:

implements for
the Japanese
Rite of Tea

"Is this a dictionary?" she asked, pointing to another sheet I'd filled: a column of tea words and their English explanations—*Chawan*,

Chasen, Chashaku, Natsume, Kensui. "Let's take it home for the boys to learn someday." Then she sat on the *tatami* beside me, pulled aside her right sleeve with her left hand and stamped a red pigment square on the label using a stone seal similar to the one she'd given Chojiro's Heir. She took the brush and added two *kanji* characters to my taut little label: *Tea* and *Road, Cha Do,* the Way of Tea. "There," she said. "Now leave it to dry."

THE FIRST DAY of the Expo was reserved for only the most important foreigners. Though Yukako's sense of what the foreigners might want to see in her was acute—seated on the floor instead of at a table, dressed in a *kimono* just a touch more showy than appropriate for her age and station—it did not extend to me, and so I sat on a stool beside her in my overgrown girl's dress cut from *kimono* fabric, my hair oiled into a *shimada,* my voice pitched feminine-high, my English rusty with archaism and disuse. Facing the well-upholstered British ambassador, his bone-china wife, and the large-nosed entourage behind them, I was too embarrassed to know whether I was an embarrassment.

I began the speech Yukako had prepared for me, after hours of questioning me on foreign habits. "If you go to empty church and listen for Voice of God," I said, my articles slipping along with my confidence, "and then you go to a botanical garden and look at a thousand flowers, and then you go to a museum and look at a hundred paintings and sculptures, and then you go to a ballet—*the* ballet," I caught myself, "—and see twenty ballerinas, and then you go to a restaurant and eat a ten-course meal, and then you sit up talking with a roomful of friends, will you not be tired, Eminences?" I asked. My words felt false, baroque, and yet it seemed bald and crude not to add that tag, so humble in my mind, so pompous on my lips. "Especially when such-like heat should tax the limbs?" Just *speak,* I told myself, be natural! The gathered company looked indulgently at one another, suppressing

laughter, but a few women, plying their feathered fans, nodded in agreement. "Eminences, please imagine, if you will," I said, preparing to
invoke the pair of words most beloved by the Meiji regime, "A Civilized and Enlightened form of art experience." At this, I caught an outright rolling of eyes by two young women in back, gloved hands
holding lace parasols. Everywhere they turned in Official Japan, no
doubt, they heard the phrase *bunmei kaika*, Civilization and Enlightenment. In the silence that fell as I lost my nerve, I heard, off to the side, a
precise little man—the American missionary I recalled from the last
Expo—translating for his flush-faced companion into a harsh Ger-
manic language. "*Ah, bunmei kaika,*" he added, when he finished my last
sentence, and the two men shared a laugh at my expense.

The American's Japanese accent was wretched, I thought, and those
frilly parasols were redundant in the deep eaves of the Expo pavilion, a
waste of space. This jolt of superiority, however petty, gave me the
momentum to press on. "In *Chado*, the Japanese Rite of Tea, you are
invited to spend time with *one* flower, *one* painting. To touch and
taste from *one* piece of sculpture, to sample a *few* delicacies, to watch
the balletic movement of *one* trained artist. You are free to converse, or
you are free to contemplate in silence. Is this not a restful and salutary
activity?"

My syllables felt wrong, stiff, like pennies dropped in a tin pail, but
the travel-weary foreigners seemed to understand, and nodded among
themselves, self-congratulatory in their pleasure. Relieved, I concluded: "All the arts of Japan circle *Chado* the way"—here Yukako had
pushed for a little more *bunmei kaika*—"all the planets orbit the sun.

"Before we perform Tea Procedure for you," I said, fumbling with a
poor equivalent for *temae*, "Shin Yukako will display the utensils used
for *Chado*." I was finished! The worst of my humiliation was behind
me, my blush steamed into the humid air as the harsh translating voice
trailed away.

Years of training in tea had made it easy for Yukako to kneel quietly while I rattled on in my gasping stilted English and the foreigners stared at her gauze *kimono*, her waxed hair, her *almond eyes*—which looked nothing like almonds—her tea-with-milk skin. She bowed in welcome and held up a cloth bundle for their inspection. When I had told her about the foreigners at the first Expo, she had been intrigued by the notion of a Tea Set. "How can you show your skill at coordinating tea utensils if they come all together in a set?" she'd puzzled, with much more doubt than she'd expended on the notion that planets revolved around the sun. And while she never showed much interest in the foreigners' language, let alone bothered to remember that there were *languages,* plural, the word *set* charmed and distracted her. *"Setto, setto,"* she'd murmur, the word none too distant from *Seto,* a famed ceramics region. And now, smiling as I translated, she announced that her cloth-wrapped package was a *Chado no Setto.*

"It looks like a hatbox," one of the Parasol Girls whispered to her friend.

It did, if slightly smaller. Yukako's version of a tea *setto* was wrapped in humble cotton—navy striped with white—and tied with red cord. My label on its straw-flecked sheet seemed to glow against the dark cloth. "Japanese paper is so rustic, so charming," I heard the Eminent voices agree. Then I remembered Yukako inspecting my slim collection of foreign books, and realized she'd chosen the paper that would seem least familiar to her audience. *And cheaper besides,* I noted.

Tucked into the red cord, placed diagonally across the calligraphed label, the implement we called a *chashaku* gleamed like a pale twig. "A bamboo teaspoon," I announced solemnly. It sounded so silly in English, but I kept my face grave.

Ah, responded the crowd.

Yukako untied the wrappings and lifted the lid of the hatbox, laying it before her: it was a raw wooden version of the lacquered tray used in the simplest *temae.* Inside, like a series of nested dolls, sat a wooden wastewater vessel with a white linen wiping-cloth laid across it, and inside that, one of the Raku students' bowls, and inside *that*, wrapped in a tea host's silk napkin, resting on a packet of powdered green tea, sat a bamboo cylinder. Clever Yukako! The top and bottom of the cylinder fit together to form a humble but serviceable tea box, while a center tube housed the *chasen* whisk.

"Is that a badminton birdie?" I heard someone ask. "A shaving brush?"

"This is a whisk for tea. When you beat the clear part of an egg"—I had never learned the word in English, I realized—"you can make a *mousse* or *soufflé*. Insomuch, beaten tea is a likewise airy trifle." *I shouldn't improvise*, I groaned inside.

The gathered company, however, was prepared to be delighted. In this respite from sun and rickshaw and seaweed in soup, with no one asking them to agree what a Civilized and Enlightened nation they were visiting, they were receiving a special glimpse of Old Japan, never mind that it had been concocted for their benefit. Yukako's *setto* couldn't have been made from cheaper materials, and yet the foreigners murmured and gasped at each new implement as if she were firing off Roman candles. They sighed with pleasure when I mentioned the three-hundred-year-old relationship between the Shin and Raku families. They all but cheered when the whisk emerged from its bamboo tube.

I slowly became used to the strange translating echo from the American off to the side, and to his young friend who nodded constantly, wavy blond hair bouncing in a pageboy bob. I didn't mind the harsh sentences trailing after mine, but I minded the way the blond man looked from Yukako to me and back again, flat and appraising with his dog-blue eyes.

I looked away, uncomfortable, and saw a ghost of that same look in the face of a Japanese man from one of the other displays, drawn by the crowd. A young-old man with the fine high cheekbones of a lord and the heavy apron of a craftsman, he watched Yukako in a hands-on-hips stance I found distracting. He looked away, attention caught by something to the left: his master waving him back to his own booth. I saw him glance back at Yukako as she finished packing up her *setto*. She bowed to the British ambassador, extended the box to him, and bowed again. "Please accept this gift on behalf of the Shin family," I said.

The deep and gracious thanks of the ambassador and his wife unleashed a flurry of envious glances and whispers among the Eminences. "Would it be possible," began one of the parasol girls, her voice remarkably loud for its blue-blooded fragility, "to find other tea sets?"

Before I translated, I knew Yukako had heard the word *setto* clearly: though she controlled her face, her visibly filling lungs betrayed her glee. "We'll have them here for sale tomorrow," I said, my words practiced and clear.

"For how much?" asked a man, clearly indulging his wife.

I did not need to translate the question, but I did, knowing that the words would be more welcome from an oracular fairy queen than a wheezy buffoon. Echoing Yukako, I allowed a tiny pause and coolly named a figure large enough to deflate the men but small enough to make the women's eyes gleam brighter.

We made no further mention of money as Yukako knelt before the brazier to begin *temae* with her own utensils, brought from home. The foreigners leaned from side to side to note variations on the objects they'd just seen.

"It's that same silk square: look at how she's folding it."

"And there's the tea box again; this one's black."

"There's that shuttlecock."

"Have you ever seen anything like this in Holland?" I heard one of the Parasol Girls ask the blond man. He smiled at them with his big square teeth, his friend gamely translating. There had been Dutchmen among the foreigners at the last Expo—canal engineers, I remembered vaguely—but I had never seen one up close.

And then the company exclaimed over the gaily colored robes of the girls from Toraya wafting in with their sweet trays, and silence fell as the guests lifted the lids off their lacquer dishes and smelled citron syrup poured over shaved ice. All was well. Yukako whisked tea for the ambassador, a subtle incense burned in the scroll alcove, and the Eminences sighed over their sweet, sweet ices.

THAT NIGHT, Tai and Kenji, sworn to secrecy, arrived with the hundred Raku student tea bowls. They didn't know that Yukako had paid for the shipment with their father's Shunrai bowl, but that detail aside, they were enthusiastically aware of Yukako's plan as we sat together at the Expo site, assembling *setto* by the dozen. I copied out and stamped my label fifty times as the boys slid whisks into tubes and lined wastewater bowls with linen wiping-cloths. The heaped assembly of cloth-wrapped tea sets called to mind the days when the boys were newborns, the way the cloakroom filled with all those boxes of gift eggs. "They'll buy them all tomorrow," Tai predicted confidently.

"What will we do with the other fifty tea bowls?" Kenji asked.

"We'll keep them for new students," Yukako explained. "Do you remember when you were little boys, and you wanted Aki and Toru to have tea bowls too?"

The boys nodded, and I could see them looking eagerly at Yukako, wanting her to say more. I could also see Yukako making room for them to reach her conclusions on their own.

THE NEXT DAY, Yukako decided, I was not to accompany her. She didn't want the foreigners asking questions; she wanted them to pay their money and go. I don't know how Tai and Kenji convinced their father to let them go in my place without revealing Yukako's plan, but I know they were desperate to see the big-nosed blue-eyed monsters for themselves.

Jiro seemed none too pleased by this arrangement, but his most advanced students welcomed the privilege of being asked to assist at that evening's tea gathering in the boys' place.

JIRO WAS IN FOUL SPIRITS, his breakfast interrupted by a messenger from Shige, one of that evening's guests. He was so sorry, there was nothing he could do, but that hayseed Kato had begged to accompany him to the *chakai* and he was indebted; there was no way he could avoid bringing the fellow. "I had planned for a select few," Jiro sniffed, after sending his reply. "I've put Kato off on other occasions, but I guess the man's bent on worming his way in through the side door. And Shige's weak. First there was that French loom, and now Kato's given him a fat uniforms contract, so he can't say no." Jiro drained his *miso* broth. "Uniforms. How much further can you get from brocade? His father would be so ashamed." He talked to me as if I weren't there, and yet he made it impossibly rude to leave the room. "Why should I have to pay for him to sell out to that *high-collar* fool?" he said. "I mean, how could you live with yourself if you really talked like Advisor Kato?" Under all the peevishness and bluster, I saw a childlike anxiety on Jiro's face, as if Shige were not, at base, inconveniencing him but actually leaving him behind. I slowly became aware that he was keeping me in that room with him. I realized how rarely I saw him by himself.

Because Jiro spent so much time on retreat, it did not occur to me that he might miss his family's company, but as I served him breakfast all alone, Yukako and the boys having left before sunrise, he seemed out of his element. His morning offerings to the ancestors seemed a little uncertain, and I wondered what it meant to him to make them without his children, his link to the Shin bloodline. I wondered if it put him in mind of his first year as an adopted son. He was a grown man facing the ancestors in the queer timid shoes of a new wife. I remembered the way the Pipe Lady (and she was not alone in this) would dismiss her grandsons' wives to their faces: *A womb's a borrowed thing*, she'd say. *We can just as well get others where you came from.* I wondered, had Jiro ever felt that abject? "Usually I see you with your students or guests, or your sons," I observed, and stopped myself, ready to scuttle away.

But Jiro gave me a rare open look and nodded. "Or I'm with my brother, or my *sempai*," he reflected. The word for those ahead of one in rank could have referred to the monks at Sesshu-ji temple, or it could just as easily have meant his older drinking companions.

"Today I'm like your Rie," he said, looking at me. His eyes were soft lamps and there was a catch in his voice. *Who is Rie?* I wondered, acutely aware of his gaze.

I stood uneasily with my tray to clear away yesterday's ancestral offering of rice and tea, and Jiro plucked at my sleeve with his long calligrapher's fingers. "I didn't really think of you as a foreigner until that day you read the play with the boys," he said quietly, not letting go. "You aren't so ugly when I think of you that way."

He pulled my sleeve steadily, harder, yet as if he weren't pulling at all, as if I were the one deciding to sink back to the floor, to give up the tray he took from my hands, to look up as he tilted my chin toward his haunted, lonely face. Still holding my sleeve he circled me with his other arm, fitting the heel of his hand into my sternum, and held me there in place as his brush hand opened the fabric vent under my arm, stole in between my breast and *obi*. I looked back at him as he cupped my breast, this man who had once been the Stickboy. My pity became a swollen, trembling thing, and I closed my eyes, feeling his breath go uneven against my nape. *Yukako wouldn't be jealous*, the thought came to me, and was completed a moment later: *because she thinks so little of him.*

My eyes blinked open, and in a fraction of a second took in the fact that the door to the study was open, the *shoji* to the garden thrown wide. Chio—or anyone—could see us. It would be so easy to lose my place here. My hands closed on the man's wrists. I spent my days lifting iron pots and brimming buckets; Jiro spent his in the tearoom. It was not difficult to take his hands in mine, peel them off my body, push them to his sides, and set them down, *so*. He'd only been seeing what I'd let him do, after all. I stood again and looked back at him on the floor, half kneeling, gazing mournfully up at me. I felt lofty, remote, like Kannon looking down at mortal suffering. I was glad for the tray I took up, because I wanted so much to turn, lay my hand on his forehead, and say something reassuring and stupid. I felt sad for him and, for once in my life, very tall.

And I felt exposed, stirred up and buzzing like a broken hive. I left the tray with Chio and walked, then ran, to Baishian, crawled in through the square door, and shut it tight, shut myself and my thudding heart up in the teahouse. Why would a man who stopped sleeping with his wife when she began looking even a little foreign show any interest in me? We were alone, I supposed. I was there. *I need to be careful*, I thought. My happiness here means nothing to him, and *men like to finish what they start*. Who told me that? *Inko*, I remembered, my hazy night with her returning hot and sharp, as my body, though I did not want the man, convulsed with desire. My breasts felt soft and alert and my thighs felt damp. At that moment, there was just one person in the world I wanted. I jammed my hand between my legs and rocked and shook until I could think again. Think, think, mentally locate a knife in the kitchen I could use to defend my place in her bed, however chaste, at any cost.

Leaving Baishian, I took the long way back to the kitchen entrance, which brought me past the front gate. I saw an extravagant *jinrikisha* that struck me as familiar: painted court ladies hurried across its surface in their swirling black hair and dozen-layered robes, intricate as artichokes. Who had a cart like that? The *jinrikisha* boy, sitting in the cloakroom with Chio's cold barley tea, did not look familiar, but when I saw his elegant master, I froze. A flash of color rippled under the man's gauze robe.

I wasn't surprised, then, to see a dagger hanging in the disused sword rack outside Jiro's classroom door. Had he known of the tattooed man and his deadline before today? I thought not, and my guess was confirmed when I topped up the barrel backstage in the classroom *mizuya*. Jiro's face, drained of ardor, was drawn and tight, and he paid no heed when his student set down the teascoop in one motion instead of two. I felt pity again, and a flare of vindictive pleasure: let *him* feel how fragile his place was!

Between my disturbing exchange with Jiro and the reappearance of the man without a fingertip, I had forgotten about the little brocade-wrapped bomb ticking in Muin. But that afternoon I glimpsed Master Teacher raking the garden more meticulously than usual; at twilight, when the moonflowers, or *evening faces*, bloomed, I saw him rigorously plucking them all, saving the most perfect specimen for the tearoom. *Oh*, I remembered. *Tonight's tea!* The Shin family had not given so much attention to its gardens since culling all the irises when the former Emperor's nephew came to visit, when I was a child. What was he planning?

I RECOGNIZED Shige's voice in the gathering when I ferried trays over from the kitchen, and Okura Chugo's too. Advisor Kato's voice needled through the group as well, loud and callow, forcing even the flimsiest of connections between Okura Chugo and his young engineer. "You like *natto*, Mr. Okura? Why, so does our Mr. Tanabe! What's the difference, would you say, between Tokyo and Kyoto *natto*, Mr. Tanabe?"

The young man spoke in a cool and reticent voice and, to his credit, seemed embarrassed by Kato's brashness. "Kyoto's is richer and more subtle," he said diplomatically. "I'm so grateful to be here."

"I wasn't planning on this, but you've inspired me, Advisor Kato," Jiro said, his voice frosty. "You will be pleased to know that the tea-scoop you'll see tonight, New Moon, was named for the teahouse you destroyed to build the Ladies' School. The bamboo was taken from an especially lovely example of ceiling work."

The Advisor was too thick-skinned to feel the dart. "It's all worth it if the girls are learning, right? Perhaps you have a niece or cousin who'd like to join Mr. Shige's girl next spring?"

I heard Jiro shift his weight, surprised. "This is news," he said.

"Well," said Shige.

"True, true. I waived the tuition. We've finally got him on board for the canal; it was the least I could do, eh, Mr. Shige?"

"Is that so?" said Jiro. His voice sounded strangled at this new revelation.

Advisor Kato filled the uncomfortable silence that followed. "But my deepest gratitude goes to your brother. It was my pleasure to award him the contract for digging the canal, considering his level of support."

At this third blow, Jiro's voice was a pained squeak. "Congratulations."

"We should break ground in September," the Advisor said, beaming.

Jiro looked like he would topple when he left the tearoom. He sat on the floor and pounded his numb feet, savagely trying to work the pins and needles out. I wondered if he wished he could abandon the evening entirely. But he'd taken such pains! It was still not clear to me what he had wanted from the *chakai*, let alone if he could still hope to gain it. Whom had he meant to impress? Clearly not Kato or Tanabe.

I was surprised to peek in and see that while I could not make out the scattering of men in back, Shige was the main guest again, with Jiro's older brother Okura beside him. They both came so frequently; why had Jiro gone to all the extra trouble? Along with Chio's elaborately prepared morsels, he'd ordered boxed delicacies from a restaurant, and the *tatami*, already new when we switched from the winter hearth to the summer brazier, had been refaced once again. Its new-grass smell, like the painted fan that hung in the display alcove, like the ice-clear jellied sweets in their green glazed bowls, added to the sense of coolness Jiro worked to evoke in this evening *chakai*.

My questions were answered during the intermission between the meal and tea ceremony halves of the event when Jiro, hands shaking from the cascade of unpleasant news, brought the wrapped tea bowl out from the tearoom alcove and set it down in the *mizuya* beside a fresh pine box. Instead of *Shunrai, Spring Thunder,* the box bore a different name. I made out the large *kanji* on the lid: *Rain Field.* The two together composed the character for *Thunder,* or *Kaminari.* Wasn't that the name Shige had suggested Jiro call his Shunrai bowl at their springtime tea? In poetry—I just barely knew this; the knowledge shimmered in me half formed—the only season *Thunder* evoked on its own was summer. At Shige's bidding, Jiro had turned a spring bowl into a summer one.

While, during the tea meal, I had felt spitefully glad to see things go badly for Jiro, when I saw the box he'd painted, the same pity that had drugged my body that morning welled up in me again. Poor Jiro. Bad enough that he was about to unwrap a tea bowl he wasn't expecting. Worse, it now seemed that he had staged the whole tea gathering as an opportunity to make Shige—or his brother—buy the Shunrai bowl. Or maybe, before he knew they'd been won over by Advisor Kato, had Jiro meant to make a gift of the tea bowl to his friend or brother, to grease the way for asking for an enormous loan? Was this how he'd planned to pay back our debts? I remembered his shrill voice the morning Yukako laid the bill from Chojiro's Heir before him: *You'll see there's no need to meddle.* I bit my lip. Thanks to me and Yukako, when Jiro unwrapped his beloved Rikyu bowl, broken and mended with gold, he would be forced to part with it. *We've made a terrible mistake,* I thought.

As Jiro reached to untie the knot on the brocade bag, I moved without thinking. The Muin tea hut, like most Japanese buildings, stood a foot or so off the ground, to protect it from insects and rot. Unheard beneath the sound of Shige and the others strolling out to the waiting arbor, I took out my last tray for the kitchen, flattened myself on the pebbled walk, and slid under the teahouse.

I saw nothing. I felt damp earth and ooze. I heard deep silence overhead. And then I heard a burst of footsteps leading to the main house. A burst of footsteps back. Urgent, angry whispering. Someone walking twenty paces toward the storage tower, first passionate, then stunned, then sleepwalking. Then the walker stopped, seemed to come to a decision, turned, and firmly walked back to Muin.

IN THE TEA WORLD there is a phrase, *ichigo ichie.* One moment, one meeting. Every moment is what it is. Even though tea people watch each other constantly for slips in form, and gossip shamelessly about one another's technique, in the end, in the deepest sense, there are no mistakes. This is what the Mountain meant to teach in giving his students the precious antique with the crack, the flaw, certain to break with use.

For years I blamed myself for my mother's death, that I could have stayed home and saved her. That I could have done something, and had failed. But it was no more cause for blame, I understood, flat under the house that night, than to be the one for whom Rikyu's bowl finally gave up its bowl-ness and became clay again. She died, and I was not there. There are no mistakes. *Ichigo ichie.* Actors know this, plunging ahead as they drop a line here, a cue there. Jiro knew this, mending the bowl with gold, and he knew it again as he summoned the great calm required to slide the low square door to the tearoom open, giving the sign for his guests, whether he liked them or not, to return to Muin.

I COULD FEEL the night coolness seeping from the earth into my chest where I lay on the ground. My eyes adjusted to the dark and made do with the light of a candle in a small stone lantern, low to the ground by the square guest door. The candlelight shone yellow on the paving stones, and the wooden sandals of the four guests stood in the light like miniature bridges. And then an unexpected fifth pair of feet became visible. In the dark tearoom, I had made out only Shige and Okura, and I had heard only the voices of two others, Kato and Tanabe. I hadn't known there were five guests. And what was wrong with those feet? Something curious, confusing: I saw hands, fingers, strings. A man was taking off a pair of foreign shoes! Those must be Advisor Kato's, I thought. Bad enough to barge in and crow about his canal, but wouldn't he know what a purist Jiro was? The kind of man who let his wife run around in foreign dress because he still hadn't gotten over the shock of her teeth and eyebrows. The last man on Migawa Street to wear his hair in a queue. A man who wanted the Japanese to be *Japanese*.

A man who wants foreigners to be foreign, I thought, remembering what he said before he touched me. I shuddered and made myself take deep silent breaths, listening to the *temae* overhead. I heard the guests shift softly, seeing the utensils Jiro brought in. I heard the splash of water on water and realized Jiro was performing a special *temae* for high summer, in which the host brings out a tea bowl full of water, a linen cloth suspended inside like a white lotus. When the host wrings out the linen cloth, the sound of splashing water conveys a further sense of coolness to the guests. I imagined the sheen of water on the lamplit gold veins of the tea bowl.

I knew I'd be heard if I crawled out from under the house, so I waited, listening to the sounds of water and bamboo, to the guests sliding their bodies across the floor just overhead. My breath caught as Shige asked the ritually prescribed questions about the tea bowl.

"This spring," Jiro said, "You did me the honor of expressing interest in a new black Raku bowl called Shunrai, made by the present heir to Rikyu's first Raku master, Chojiro. To that end I gathered this company here." I heard a strained note in Jiro's voice at these words, underscoring the presence of uninvited guests.

"I wanted to repay your interest with something extraordinary," Jiro extemporized. "When you said I should call the Shunrai bowl Kaminari instead, I had to hold my tongue, because there is already a tea bowl by that name. As muffled and weak as spring thunder is to summer's, so is Shunrai to the tea bowl you hold. Kaminari was made for Rikyu himself, by Chojiro." He sounded as assured as if he'd meant to use the gold-mended bowl all along.

As the guests exclaimed in surprise and pleasure, I heard the engineer Tanabe's soft voice repeating Jiro's elegantly improvised tale. No, not quite repeating. What was I hearing? I heard Japanese, but it made no sense. And then it did: a Japanese voice, using Japanese syllables, was translating Jiro's words into another language. There was a foreigner here! I listened and listened, but the language wasn't French or English. And then a voice repeated the translator, asking something in a harsh, sour tongue. It was the Dutchman from the Expo.

I almost cracked my head against the floor beam above me, I was so surprised. Was Jiro so appalled by Kato's presence—and his brother's and friend's defections—that the further insult of a barbarian guest went unnoticed? He must be one of the canal people, I thought. Tanabe had been too polite, it seemed, to translate the earlier posturing among the men. I was impressed that Jiro allowed only a tiny strain in his voice when he said, *I gathered this company.*

At the end of the *chakai*, after Jiro had carried all the utensils out of the tearoom and reentered to bow his guests good-bye, I heard the Dutchman's voice, and the uncomfortable syllables of Tanabe hushing him. The Dutchman repeated his short question, and Tanabe, laying his hands on the floor for a deep bow just over my head, asked Jiro something in the most elaborate, humble Japanese imaginable, as if to emphasize the foreigner's rudeness by compensating for it. He was asking if Jiro would be so kind to consider, at some later date, entertaining an intermediary to discuss the possibility of engaging in negotiations, at his convenience, relating to a matter of mutual interest.

"Ah, is that so?" asked Jiro. I knew the only thing he wanted less in the world than to sell that tea bowl to a barbarian was for his brother

and Shige to see him do so. I knew, too, that the tattooed man's deadline preyed on him, and that he had not yet paid for Shunrai. The
thing that would save face, of course, would be for Jiro to show no
encouragement to the Dutchman in front of Shige and his brother,
but to not discourage him, either.

Is that so? would have marked the end of the night if the Dutchman
had not at that moment spoken for himself in broken Japanese,
aggrieved, as if he'd been forced to repeat himself. *"How much for the
bowl?"*

The crude words rang loud. I could feel Shige and Tanabe's embarrassment, and I could feel Jiro's hatred boring a hot dark crater
through the floor. The Imperial Advisor tried to smooth over the
affronted silence: "We're so sorry. It's not even clear whether this is a
matter for discussion at any point . . ."

Then Jiro spoke. Very slowly and clearly he named a sum, an
impossible sum, a sum that traded insult for insult. A sum that made
clear to all that he never wanted to entertain a foreigner in his tearoom
again. Above me, the floor popped and creaked with the shifting
weight of the guests, as if subtly, seated, they were closing ranks with
Jiro against the barbarian.

And then I heard the Dutch voice again, blunt as the sun on a sheet
of tin. *"Hai."*

The room was very quiet.

And then I heard Jiro's voice proving that there are no mistakes in tea,
proving himself worthy, in that moment, in that sacrifice, to be called the
Mountain's heir. *"Hai,"* he agreed. I knew the others would respect him
for keeping his word.

The foreigner then made another request to Tanabe, who refused to
repeat it with a rapidity that surprised me. Undaunted, the Dutchman
repeated himself in Japanese: *"Mo onna."* As if he were ordering another
drink! *I want a woman too.* Or maybe, *I want the woman too.* My jaw
dropped. The disgusting creature, he thought Yukako was for sale.

"My guest has no idea how offensive he's being," said Kato. "I'm so sorry. There's no reason we need to spend another moment on this tonight."

"None, surely," Jiro said, with such mocking dryness that his brother and Shige laughed. No doubt if they were married to Yukako they'd want to be rid of her too. In better spirits, they filed out of the tearoom, the Dutchman mercifully silent at last, tying on his leather shoes.

I lay under the house for a long time as Jiro cleaned the tearoom, wiping down the floor with deft, angry strokes. I was still clenching the cotton thongs of my sandals with my toes, afraid they'd make a sound if I let go. My feet were cramping up. Something crawled across my leg. I squirmed. I heard Jiro leave the tearoom, heard him dismissing his student helpers, heard him clatter off with a lantern in search of the Shunrai tea bowl. I crept out from under the house, shivering in the summer night, and made my way up to Yukako's room, sandals in hand, looking both ways for Jiro first. A thin film of dirt and ooze covered my *kimono*, and I quickly changed into a bathhouse robe. When I heard a familiar clop of shoes outside the kitchen entrance, I ran down to tell Yukako what had happened, but it was a messenger instead.

The young man was dressed in Advisor Kato's colors. "This was written on behalf of my master's foreign guest," he said, showing me a letter as I poured his tea. "He wanted to make sure your Master Teacher saw this tonight. Is he in?"

I heard footsteps down the hall as Jiro searched for the Shunrai bowl. "He's a little busy," I said, staring at the paper dumbly. I made out some numbers and the character for *tomorrow*. I saw the *kanji* for *woman*, too, but I was distracted by a familiar slip of coarse paper tucked into the folded bottom edge of the letter, by a familiar fat square seal.

"What's this?" said Jiro behind me, lantern in hand. He took the paper from the messenger and read, lifting out the label I'd made for Yukako's *setto*. Yukako's *kanji* were torn off, leaving only my English and the red stamped seal, which Jiro held close to his lamp. He took a cold look at me and nodded curtly at the messenger. "That won't be a problem," he said crisply. "Tell him to bring the money at noon."

My heart beat in my throat. *Don't act guilty*, I thought, paralyzed. *Just do what you usually do. What do I usually do?* When the boy left, I self-consciously bent down to take his teacup to the basin, and Jiro seized me by the hair.

Even after years, each new visit from the hairdressers hurt my scalp afresh, with the pulling and the wax, and the slightest new pressure made me wince away. "What is this?" Jiro said, shoving the label in my face. I said nothing.

I was stronger, but I was at a bad angle: I reached for his arm and stumbled as he pulled harder, then fell against the hard handle of the kitchen knife tucked uselessly into my *obi*. My scalp burned. "*Raku. Shin.* What is this?" he demanded. I said nothing, but gasped, staggering toward him to relieve the pain. I heard my knife skid across the floor.

"There's a man who saw the demonstration of tea sets for sale at the Exposition yesterday," Jiro recounted icily. "He'd like to acquire the servant girl in my household who wrote this," he continued, brandishing the label, "provided she's a virgin and good-tempered." Another burst of pain ripped my head as he pulled me up to face him. "Look at your face. You're covered in dirt," he said, his mouth curling. "I'll break you in myself; the pig won't know the difference." He twisted my hair as he pulled it, and I could feel some of the hairs tearing out of my scalp in a wave of rippling pops. I clawed at his wrists as he dragged me toward the water barrel. "Wash, you animal," he said, pushing my face in.

If only I could crawl back and get my knife, I thought, before I tried to breathe and sucked in water. *Oh God oh God*, I panicked, my head burning. I choked a bubbling scream into the water and he hauled out my head. "What makes you think she wouldn't buy Shunrai back, you *bastard*?" I shouted the last word in French, inchoate. "It's better than you deserve."

I wish I could have told myself this as a child in my uncle's lap: if a man is menacing you, ask him something. I don't know why it works. "What are you talking about?" Jiro demanded, confusion loosening his grip on my hair just long enough for me to elbow him in the groin and run, quick, out the kitchen door in my bare feet, into the lamplit courtyard outside, where Yukako was just walking home.

I was panting with rage and terror. I tried to speak and couldn't. I just kept opening and closing my mouth, facing her, as Jiro walked out behind me, his dagger in hand. "Get out of the way, Miss Urako," he said quietly, looking at Yukako, livid. The dagger shone, a foot long, curved and single-edged like Akio's bright swords long ago. I thought of my kitchen knife left behind on the floor and gave an inappropriate, hysterical yip of laughter. What had I been planning to do, *pare* him?

Tall in her gauze robe, Yukako fixed her husband and the dagger with the same look she used on her sons when they misbehaved. She gave me a quick glance, both protective and dismissive at once. Without breaking her husband's gaze, she quietly set down a wooden box. I heard the metallic rasp of coins in her sleeve.

Jiro did too. "I want to know what you did," he said, his voice hard with rage. "But first I want to see how much you made on Shunrai. Turn out your sleeves."

"Right now?" Yukako looked at him, amused, and pulled a small bag out of one sleeve and a few coins out of the other. On the bench outside the cloakroom door, under the hanging lantern, Yukako poured out her coins and Jiro sat to count them. I stood in the doorway, a little behind Yukako, the blood loud in my head. "You think I sold your Shunrai bowl to some stranger?" she asked.

"Shut up." At the interruption, Jiro started counting again from the beginning.

Yukako watched him. "I didn't sell it. I pawned it back to Raku for a hundred student tea bowls. Today I sold fifty."

"Shut up!" Jiro snarled, brandishing his knife. He blinked at his stacks of coins and began counting a third time, setting down his knife in order to touch the money with both hands. As effortless and hypnotic as her father making tea, Yukako glided toward him and took the knife. She put it away inside, returned, and said nothing, arms folded.

At length, Jiro finished. He stood facing Yukako, his fists at his sides. "So this is all you got? You took Shunrai for this? I sacrificed the Rikyu bowl for *this*? You cheap whore, you butcher-fucker," he chanted, groping for a word low enough. "You *worm*," he said, and cuffed her across the face.

He *hit* her. I stepped up on the bench and leapt down, tackling Jiro from above, all the advantage mine. I pinned him on the ground and forced his arm behind his back like an Irish bullyboy. "Get your dog off me," Jiro told his wife, gasping.

Standing, Yukako looked down at Jiro where he lay. "I sold the fifty tea bowls," she said, continuing her explanation as if nothing had happened. "And I collected my fee from the Expo. You had some debts in Pontocho that needed settling," she said, referring to the tattooed man. "So I went straight from the Expo and dealt with them. And then, because the last thing in the world I would want would be to upset my lord, I went to Raku and bought Shunrai back again for you." Yukako held up her box by its carrying scarf. "What you just counted is the money I have left over. Urako, you can stop. You're embarrassing him," she concluded.

I eased off and Jiro sat up quietly, cross-legged on the ground. Yukako set the box in his lap with both hands. His expression vacant, Jiro untied the knotted fabric; his long fingers traced his own calligraphy.

Both Jiro's and Yukako's heads jerked up at the woodwind sound of music, and they looked at each other, united for a baffled moment. Jiro began trembling as he parted the silk wraps inside the box and lifted out the night-black Shunrai tea bowl. He stared at it with unfocused eyes. "What do I do with this now?" he murmured.

A small procession appeared: the two boys, carefully leading two cartmen. Holding a lantern, Tai paid the cartmen while Kenji played his long bamboo flute. Jiro's mouth formed a small numbed *O* as the cartmen unloaded fifty Raku student tea bowls, each in its own twine sack.

I looked at Jiro and addressed him, as if in his shock he could hear me. I pointed to the bowl in his lap. "Maybe the foreigner will trade that for the Rikyu bowl you sold him," I said. "Don't try trading me, because I'm not for sale."

Suddenly, Jiro stood, leaving Shunrai in its box on the ground. He seized the bamboo flute out of Kenji's hands, lifted it overhead like a cudgel, and brought it down hard on one of the student bowls.

A Raku bowl smashes with a dull, hollow crunch, anticlimactic, like a man kicked in the chest. The boys watched with open mouths while their father smashed and crushed until the flute broke in his hands, until it was a pointed bamboo stump and tears streamed down his face. Panting, he said something to Yukako. What was it? He was, he'd said, like Rie, like Lear without the rainstorm, betrayed by family and friends, his face naked with desolation. He stared at Yukako. She had smeared shit in his robes as a boy and he had borne it in secret, so that he could become a man like her father. No: so he could live in the dream of being such a man, his own personal *floating world*, one in which it was enough to love tea. Jiro stared at Yukako and said it again, his voice wet with despair, the comic truth of a tragic night. *This is not what I married you for.*

EARLY THE NEXT MORNING, Jiro left for One Pine teahouse, retiring permanently at the age of thirty-three, to take holy orders at Sesshu-ji temple.

. . .

WITHIN HOURS of his departure, Jiro had sent word to his wife that Tai was old enough to head the household on his own. Hearing this, Yukako packed her husband's things up in a fleet of handcarts and sent Kenji with them to his father's retreat to say, if Jiro preferred to stay, that she would gladly fund the renovation of One Pine. Kenji came back that evening with news of Jiro's assent. That very night, as the boys sat in their bath, I helped Yukako carry down their bedding, their few clothes and books and treasures, and install them in their father's garden study. Grave and secretive, the boys weren't children anymore: that night no one came padding back upstairs to share his mother's bed.

I DON'T THINK anyone slept the night Jiro snapped. The boys sat up all hours whispering. Yukako stalked off alone, no doubt to Baishian. Jiro left for his nightly debauch and dragged himself in at dawn, staying only long enough to fumble around for a few things in his room and lurch back to his waiting *jinrikisha.* I know this because I lay awake until the sky went from black to white, my scalp burning, wracked with pity, disgust, fear, and shame. I couldn't stop worrying over the same three facts. I had let him touch me. It was only luck that Yukako had come home in time. The Dutchman was bringing the money at noon. I felt scalded and very alone. The mosquito netting, invisible in the dark, became a cobweb cloud in the gray morning, when I heard Jiro's *jinrikisha* come and go.

The boys feigned sleep when I stirred. I found Yukako downstairs in the family shrine, sitting before an artist's ink drawing of her father, hands folded. A fresh stick of incense burned before the picture, the smoke lifting like milkweed. "I guess you heard him go too," I said.

"*Un,*" she grunted.

"I'm so sorry this happened—"

"There's really nothing to say." Her voice was hard to read, neither angry nor sad but opaque, worn, like glass blunted by the ocean. She was quiet for a long time, and then she decided something. "I guess if he doesn't come back this morning, I'll teach his class for him," she said aloud.

"*Hai*," I said. "Would you like some tea?"

"Very much." Her voice was cold but her hands tightened gratefully around the cup. I told her, ashamed, about the Dutchman, and she laughed. "I'll take care of that." Jiro had taken both black tea bowls, old and new, so when the Dutchman came, Yukako took half his money in exchange for another bowl said to be from Rikyu's time, packing him off with a recommendation on where one might purchase a young girl, as I was sure to give him a nasty disease.

THAT NIGHT, after the boys went to bed in their new room, I lay alone in Yukako's chamber, spent. When she came upstairs, I saw she'd taken every comb, pin, string, and horsehair pad out of her hair, which hung, newly washed, in long wet ribbons. "I think that was my last," she said, bidding farewell to the married woman's hairstyle.

I remembered Inko's story about her mother warding off her husband with a widow's *obako* after two of their children died. I missed her so much. Yukako sat at the mirror, experimenting with a deep-eaves bun like a foreign lady's. "Won't Miss Miki be surprised when she comes tomorrow?" I said. As I sat in bed watching Yukako, I imagined the hairdresser's daughter bringing news from her cousin, by some miracle living in Tokyo again. *She'd have word for me from Inko, a gift.* Exhaustion made it easy for me to daydream, resting my chin on my knees.

I touched my own hair. I'd been hiding my ruptured coiffure under a servant's tented kerchief all day, occasionally pushing loosened bits of horsehair and string into the kitchen fire, my stomach knotting at Jiro's remembered hands. *What would happen when he returned?* I'd worried all morning, and then his message came. He wasn't coming back. Why not wash my hair too, start again? That night I folded my arm around Yukako's chest and slept like a stone, safe.

23

1885

T<small>HE FIRST FORMAL TEA</small> invitation Tai extended as the new head
of the household was, at Yukako's behest, to Imperial Advisor
Kato: Tai was to host and she would assist. With the canal under way,
the Meiji court had asked Kato to focus on Kyoto's public schools, a
problem to which he'd applied himself sporadically since his arrival. It
was autumn, mackerel season, and the venerable tea bowl Yukako chose
was a rare flecked steely blue, like a mackerel's body, inked with a black
lattice *ami*, or fishing net. It was a nod both to the season and to Kato's
choice of plaid *ami* shawls for the Christian Ladies' School.

Though he'd come in *kimono* before, in deference to Jiro's sensibilities,
today Kato wore a three-piece suit and stovepipe hat, which he hung on
the sword rack outside the tearoom. He also took off his squeaky new
Western shoes.

Every detail in Baishian, while in harmony with the early autumn
season, was also clearly chosen to honor Advisor Kato, from the flower
arrangement evocative of his *samurai* father's bamboo-leaf crest (a single
early chrysanthemum in a vase freshly cut from a section of green
bamboo, a few green leaves still attached) to the dish of sweets, jellied

persimmon in lychee syrup, recalling his mother's family's trade as fruit wholesalers.

"Though conditions were not always propitious in the past," Advisor Kato's southern voice burred, delicately referring to the many times Jiro had put him off, "I'm grateful to be here today."

"I know everyone's aware of my husband's tragedy," Yukako said, by way of apology. "His wits were not always with him."

WHEN MY TRAY-RUNNING duties were over, I sat backstage in the Baishian *mizuya*, proudly watching Tai's first *chakai*. The new Master Teacher looked so at ease as he brushed the brazier with its bundle of feathers. Though I privately continued to call him Tai, he had just received his first adult name, Rensai, in Tokyo, when he went to present tea at court: he wore the new name with elegant modesty. His *temae* was clear and understated, his responses to Kato's ritual questions learned but unpretentious, if a bit short. Yukako had to step in and explain why Tai—but really she—had chosen the net-patterned tea bowl, though I understood later that she'd planned it that way. "My son was impressed by your simple yet effective choice of uniform for the schoolgirls," she explained. "What gave you the idea?"

Koito had told us long ago that there is nothing a man likes more than being invited to talk about even the slightest of his accomplishments. Though Advisor Kato, like any good *samurai*, made an effort to sound humble at first, the advice stood Yukako in good stead. "When I worked with the army boys, the most important thing in the beginning was to get the world to see them—and them to see themselves—as one modern unit in the service of the Emperor, not as farmers', merchants', or craftsmen's sons from this town or that," he said. "That's what I insisted on for the canal team, laborers and engineers alike, and that's what I wanted for the Ladies' School. Something that would level them all and mark them as part of the modern world, where daughters aren't just kept at home in boxes. However, men's Western dress is standard issue, more or less," he explained. "But women's Western dress has to be made to measure, and that's too costly for most families. So I chose something affordable that would still convey newness and command respect." His voice took a wistful turn. "And it would be awfully jarring to see all those lovely young girls in narrow little stovepipe sleeves, don't you think?" Yukako's mouth twisted almost imperceptibly at this slight to the clothing she wore as a teacher, and then she joined Kato in a low chuckle.

The most impressive thing about Tai's *temae* was that when Advisor Kato and Yukako began speaking at length, he did nothing to draw attention to himself, though his feet were no doubt numb and on fire. He moved to ease them so naturally that neither guest looked up, and yet they both unconsciously followed his lead.

Yukako listened attentively to her guest and then, thoughtful and hesitant, she spoke. "When my father was alive," she said, instantly causing Advisor Kato to lean forward in sympathy, "he dreamed of Tea becoming a similar kind of leveler, a uniform."

"Imagine," said Advisor Kato.

"When he wrote to the Meiji court, he said the aim of tea was that people face one another as equals. Just as you said, he wanted a way for merchant and *samurai*, commoner and artisan, Kyoto native and Satsuma man," she said, nodding here to Advisor Kato, "to set those differences aside and meet each other in the teahouse as equals, as fellow men"—inspired, she snatched at Kato's rhetoric—"under the Emperor, citizens of a new Japan." I had never heard Yukako speak this way before.

"Some tea people do not think this way," said Kato.

"My husband was not well," Yukako agreed. She paused, then continued. "I know part of your work is to determine what today's young people ought to know." Having dropped the hint she quickly backed away from it. "I so much admire the steps you've taken. How many schools did you say you'd already set up?"

"In Kyoto, five for boys and one for girls so far, not counting the Christian schools. It takes seconds to declare education compulsory," he said, referring to the Emperor's proclamation in early Meiji. "But it takes years to build schools. So we're starting with the sons of the wealthiest fathers, since they stand to gain most by Western training. But give me ten years . . ."

Yukako sat quietly, and then, as if the words had just occurred to him, Kato spoke. "A uniform. A leveler." Yukako made a sound of bland encouragement.

"The old men are complaining about the Women's Higher School in Tokyo—they say it produces girls fit only to be teachers and foreigners' wives. These girls can speak French or dance a waltz at the Belling Stag with the Prime Minister, but they've never made rice or recited from the *Hyakunin Isshu*. I'm opening two new girls' schools in the spring and I've been wondering how to respond to these criticisms. But today . . ." he trailed off, speaking more to himself than Yukako. "What's more, I've earned so much rancor from the priests for closing down the temple schools. They think a *secular* school is by definition a *Christian* school." He paused. "Don't they always say, *Tea and Zen have the same taste?*" I almost laughed at Jiro's self-justifying phrase, uttered whenever he left for Sesshu-ji, spoken in Advisor Kato's thick accent.

"I've always been a man of action," Kato declared. "In our fathers' time we'd wait and hint and go through intercessors, but these are new days. I'll simply ask you, Master Teacher"—here he bowed deeply to Yukako's son—"do you think you and your students might be willing to consider teaching The Way of Tea in the girls' schools we're building?"

Tai's eyes widened. He was a thirteen-year-old boy, after all. I could see him restrain himself from turning to his mother for counsel in front of this man. For a moment he said nothing.

"On the city payroll, of course," Kato added. I saw Yukako look pensive in order to rein back a smile.

"I'd have to think about that," said Tai.

"There are old men who ask, 'Why should we educate them at all?' You don't need to read to give your father-in-law a grandson or obey your mother-in-law in the kitchen. But in the West a girl isn't just a borrowed womb. She's a good wife and a wise mother; she educates her sons and advises her husband. Fifteen years ago, the court sent five girls to grow up in America, to come back and teach Japanese women how to be good wives and wise mothers themselves. The girls came back three years ago; I'm eager to see what comes of the experiment."

I leaned closer: as something of an experiment myself, I wondered too. Kato continued, "My countryman Saigo Takamori used to say we shouldn't toss out the best of the old in favor of the new, and here I agree with him. A wise mother can use tea to teach her sons the Five Constant Virtues; I can't think of a better way to learn them. And a good wife? You know how happy I would be, as a Christian, to see tea in the home instead of in the floating world. Why, every son and husband in Japan would benefit from women learning tea."

I could see that Yukako, while pleased, was a little surprised by the direction Advisor Kato's enthusiasm had taken. "I wonder if boys wouldn't profit by the study of *Ocha* as well," she said mildly. It seemed excessive to point out that her family had been training young lords in the Way of Tea for hundreds of years.

"And where better to learn it than in the home? As your father said so well, tea teaches wisdom, honesty, loyalty to the Emperor. Imagine, all the advantages of a centralized curriculum, transmitted at a child's most impressionable years, in the home! Look at your own results!" he said, with a nod to Tai.

"I know his *temae* is nothing to speak of, but my son *did* learn from his father and grandfather," Yukako gently corrected him. She seemed puzzled and a little huffy. Why was the man harping on these girls' schools when it was clear they were an afterthought?

Advisor Kato's voice turned brisk and assured. "Point taken. You see, the boys' days are scheduled to within an inch of their lives already, at least for the next few years. Engineering, mathematics, science. It's not up to me anymore. I have more latitude with the girls, since these schools are just forming now. I hope, Master Teacher," he said, bowing to Tai, "you'll consider my request. Perhaps we could start in the girls' schools next spring and see what happens? In six years the Ministry of Education will come from Tokyo to see how we've done, and after that, it'll be a good time to try and get *Ocha* in there for the boys."

Uneasy at Kato's presumptuous vigor, and because he had grown up, after all, steeped in his father's distaste for the man, Tai bristled a little at the Satsuma fellow's brash, easy voice. "I'll be glad to consider your request," he said, a bit stiffly.

Advisor Kato's mouth tightened at this display of juvenile hauteur. Yukako gave her son a hooded look.

"I look forward to your response," Kato said, and changed the subject. "As a Christian," he began, "I do have my qualms about the mixed dancing at the Belling Stag Hall, but one place Prime Minister Ito and I are in total agreement is on the subject of *glass*."

"I've heard rumors to that effect," noted Yukako, glad the awkward moment had passed.

The Christian Ladies' School had glass windows, as did the other Western buildings going up in Kyoto, but Advisor Kato was the first Japanese person that any of us at the servants' bathhouse had known to install *garasu* in his own home. Jiro had seen dozens of glass windows in Tokyo and had described them with a shudder, while Yukako and Tai had marveled about them to Kenji when they returned.

"In the new capital we visited an official who had a Western parlor for entertaining foreign diplomats in front and a regular home for his family in back. So he had glass in the parlor and *shoji* paper in the other rooms," she said, the Japanized English words hard on her tongue: *garasu, paaraa*. "Is this your plan?"

"Oh, no. I've found a crew of Japanese *gureijezu*," he said. *Gu-rei-je-zu?* Glaziers! "They install glass in our own doors and windows, right where the paper goes. It's expensive and it takes time, but the money goes right back into Japan, and look at the results!" *Look at the results:* I mouthed Kato's pet phrase to myself, mocking.

"I'm encouraging everyone I can to consider this step, especially anyone personally benefiting from the Emperor's largesse," he said, making us only too aware of our small imperial stipend and his large one. "What better way to show one's commitment to a Civilized and Enlightened Japan than by bringing that Light straight into one's own home? Why, imagine how beautiful this tearoom would be!"

Yukako looked back and forth at the walls and windows of Baishian, the bright milky light softening her son's face. "How interesting," she said coolly. "You'll have to give me the name of your glazier."

EVER SINCE THE BOYS had left the upstairs room, Yukako let me massage oil into her cracked feet at night. She'd brought a bristly foreign brush back from Tokyo, and I would work it through her thick hair: she had not known how much she would enjoy having her hair brushed until she began wearing it foreign-style. I noticed, early in the exercise of my new duties, a dime-sized patch of scalp at the very top of her head, exposed from years at the hairdresser's hands. She had covered it with a knob of false hair before Jiro left, and now her soft deep-eaves bun concealed it. But I could see it at night, as well as the thick strands of white here and there, which I was instructed to pluck. I marveled at these secrets, perhaps even more than I did at the miracle of her lush black mane, silky after years oiled stiff, mine in a way it had never been before, to work and weigh in my hands. Every night I plaited it into a loose braid to keep it from knots, while Yukako drank her *soba-cha*, a hot tea made from roasted buckwheat. I was happier than I'd been in years.

The boys were grown and she was mine to cosset and long for. Not long after Tai and Kenji began sleeping downstairs, I'd once dared to reach for her in the dark, not just to hold her but to grip my wanting body tight to hers. She'd stiffened, turned abruptly, and, without a word, pushed me away.

That night after Tai's first *chakai,* as I brushed Yukako's hair, she fidgeted with the rim of her teacup and frowned. She still had that puzzled, distasteful look. "Girls' schools," she murmured now and then, surprised. I brushed her hair far longer than necessary, until her face softened and she sighed as if she were sinking into a hot bath. "He's an odd man," she said, falling asleep.

If Tai had felt resistant to Advisor Kato's idea, a look at the family ledger was all it took for him to see the wisdom of his mother's position. When the Satsuma man's formal request came, Tai, with Yukako's input, sent word that he'd be glad to supply instructors to teach Shin *Ocha* in the girls' schools next spring, provided that the parents or schools were prepared to purchase—from us, of course—enough utensils for each student. When Kato's assent came, Tai was glad enough to let his mother take on the project, overwhelmed as he was, at thirteen, with the round of tea offerings and classes already expected of him.

Not long after Advisor Kato's visit, Matsu's health began its last decline. When Chio's husband could no longer use the toilet on his own, she and Kuga met with Bozu, the gardener with the shaved head. Matsu's son Nao should have taken his father's place as head gardener, but we hadn't heard from the boy in Chio's photograph—beyond his best wishes for a healthy and prosperous new year—since the year his daughter Aki came to us. Instead, Bozu and his grandson Toru, sweet and daft at fourteen, had taken over Matsu's work during his illness. In

Chio and Matsu's hut off from the kitchen, the adults decided to marry Toru to Aki and declare Toru adopted as Nao's son. The girl, however, was still under ten, so the marriage was postponed until she began to menstruate.

I was many years Toru's senior, but when I was between the ages of fourteen and twenty-four, the slow, pockmarked boy named for Queen Victoria had been among the harelips, hunchbacks, and deaf-mutes the bathhouse girls had talked of as potential husbands for me. Nothing had ever come of such talk, and now that I was nearly thirty, it was unseemly to speak in such a way about a woman of my advanced years. The bathhouse was full of children who called me *Aunt*, and Chio had quietly taken up the girlish sleeves of all my *kimono*: I wore the name and dress that would see me for decades hence.

MATSU DIED in late September. He had been so strong; it was a mercy that he was spared knowledge of his frailty at the end. He had accepted our care with the placidity of an infant, and experienced pain and discomfort with an infant's storm-and-sunshine lack of memory. The anger and tenderness of Chio and Kuga's grief was spent by the time the man died, and I understood: the sight of Matsu's waxy husk asleep in the kitchen drew no tears the way that feeding him had, or the sight of his hands when he first became feebleminded, cupping those imaginary snowballs.

Matsu's theory of why I couldn't speak Japanese at all when I came to the Shin house and spoke fluently twenty years later had been that the fire burned the language out of me, that I had not been *learning* Japanese at Cloud House but *remembering* it. In the summer, when he made shaved ices for the children (his grandson Zoji, at first, and later Tai, Kenji, Toru, and Aki), Matsu always made sure I received a bowlful, even when I had left childhood long behind, to fight the taste of fire. In this way he would take credit for the Japanese I learned. When

I studied with the boys, he'd chide: *Don't ever say you're too old for shaved ice. Just look how much you forgot.* I wished, at the end, that I could have given him as much comfort. When we began leaving food offerings at his grave, the season for shaved ice had passed, and so I left a perfect sphere of white rice, round as his lumps of molded charcoal, white as a bowl of snow.

Perhaps to make up for Matsu's absence, the day he died, Chio moved Nao's photograph from its place in the kitchen to a shelf in her own little cottage. She, Kuga, Aki, and Toru wore black for forty-nine days, avoiding Shinto shrines, blood, and alcohol. This last prohibition proved especially trying for Kuga, for whom *sake* had cushioned the longest vigils with her father. On the fiftieth day, Yukako, Tai, and even Kenji—though Jiro required him to stay at Sesshu-ji most of the time—made it their business to come to the memorial ceremony at the neighborhood temple. Yukako held Aki's hand while Chio, Kuga, and Toru made their offerings and drew water to wash Matsu's small stone.

As we crossed the small graveyard toward the servants' plots, I had the prickling sensation of being watched. There was a man sitting calmly on a bench near Matsu's grave: he stood as we approached, as if waiting for us. He wore Western leather work boots, servants' leggings, and a straight-sleeved short *kimono* coat, like a *jinrikisha*-runner or a carpenter. He did not, however, seem to be here on an errand: his hands-on-hips stance was too calmly expectant, his clothing too clean. He was in his late thirties or early forties, solid as a bulldog, with a boyish cast to his pronounced and delicate cheekbones. He was taller even than Yukako, with hair almost as long as hers. It was tied back with leather thongs but not oiled, which gave him the look of a hill brigand. When Chio's eyes met his, he bowed low before her. "Mother," he said.

24

1885–1890

CHIO FROZE as she faced the man. I had never seen her so tautly still. For a moment I was a child again, arrested by the dim enshrined photograph of a solemn young boy. And then I saw Chio's arm in the air, saw her strike her son across the face, saw him brace himself and take it.

Chio bowed in greeting, the tears plain on her face. "Take this and help us," she said gruffly, handing him her wooden bucket of water for washing Matsu's stone.

"Thank you," he said.

"That's Nao, isn't it?" I breathed.

Yukako shot me a look: *Who else could it be, baka?* Her face was sharp and hard. Her grip must have clamped too hard on Aki's hand because the little girl jerked away.

Nao performed every gesture for Matsu—from lighting the incense to paying the priest—just as Jiro had performed it for the Mountain, just as the Mountain, in place of his interned brother, had performed it for the Pipe Lady. He filled out the form of the oldest son's grief correctly and with sincerity, and yet I could feel, beside the young people's curiosity and Chio and Kuga's thunderstruck disbelief, Yukako's seething irritation.

"WHERE HAS HE BEEN all this time? Doesn't the man have any proper mourning clothes? Has he never heard of a barber?" Nao's wrapped package sat pointedly ignored on Yukako's low mirror table as she undressed, hanging her *kimono* on its airing rack. Nao had brought small gifts for Chio, Kuga, and Aki, and when he found out he had an adopted son, "He just gave the boy Aki's present. 'Take care of this for your wife.' Did you see how the girl looked at him when she found out he was her father?" I nodded, remembering the naked longing on Aki's face.

"I can't believe he's been here all this time and we never heard," said Yukako. "He's got a lot of nerve, playing the grieving son. Did he feed the man? Did he wipe him in the privy?"

"I guess you're not going to open his present," I said. The white-wrapped package seemed to glow in the lamplight, like a private moon. I remembered the tall man looking down at Yukako, his voice humbly offering the gift, his eyes, for a moment, meeting hers.

"You open it," she harrumphed. I untied the letter bound to the gift, written in careful *kana*. After the usual preliminaries, he said, *The enclosed are for ices, offered in the spirit of the one we mourn, and in honor of your triumph one hot August.*

I remembered Matsu hauling up blocks from the icehouse, shaving them with his scraper. I could picture the white shavings mounded in wooden bowls and drizzled with Chio's brown sugar syrup, thick and sweet. "What triumph?" Yukako murmured, puzzled and vaguely insulted.

I read on. *I also wanted to show you a sample of my master's work, as his current employer once mentioned it might interest you.*

"Tasteless," said Yukako. "What else does he say?"

"Nothing, really: *Your humble servant wishes the best for you and your family, very sincerely yours.*"

"Have you ever heard of such a thick-skinned face?" Yukako fumed.

"Should I open it?"

"Go ahead."

I unrolled the cheap but exquisitely pleated paper to find five small objects wrapped in raw cotton and soft tissue: five translucent glass bowls, chilly white banded with blue. I knew exactly what he meant; ice *would* taste colder in these bowls than it would in wood or lacquer. "They're beautiful," I murmured.

Yukako compressed her lips and nodded. "True."

Could I really have not seen a glass dish in nineteen years? "He's one of Advisor Kato's glaziers, isn't he?"

Yukako held a bowl up to the lamplight. A white splash of magnified light fell on her face. "I suppose so," she said.

I watched her think. And I saw it at the same time: the delicate cheekbones, the hands-on-hips stare. There was a craftsman at the *Eppo* who'd watched us too closely: yes. "I know which August he meant," I said, remembering those sweet ices for the foreign guests.

Yukako gave me a wan smile. "I do too," she said.

NAO VISITED HIS MOTHER OFTEN, always bringing some little gift. I felt his sister Kuga's silent reproach on his visits, but Chio never asked him where he'd been all those years, or why he'd been in Kyoto so long without telling them, let alone without coming home to care for his father. She never asked him to live with them now, but seemed content to know he was boarding with his master glazier and fellow apprentices in the workmen's quarter. How could it be that she had missed him for so long and now never insisted that he live with her, remarry, give her grandsons? She seemed even diffident receiving his offerings, embarrassed when he sent masseurs to work on her shoulders and stiffening hands, self-conscious when he brought fabric for her, Kuga, and Aki to have new *kimono*.

He gave Yukako no more gifts, and addressed her with no more than the humble formulae required by the occasion of his visits. Advisor Kato, however, was quick to brag to Yukako that he'd put her on a prestigious, though long, waiting list for the master glazier's windows. Yukako suppressed her discomfort: it was an honor she couldn't refuse.

A few months later Yukako took all four of Jiro's former students who were older than Tai and brought them with her to the first girls' school. Because the school asked that she train female teachers as well as male ones, Yukako also chose four unmarried young women from among her private students and brought the young men and women to the school on alternating days, training them at the Shins' the rest of the week. (The seven-day week, and the Sunday sabbath, had come to us with Meiji too.) I carried Yukako's tools and kept records, noting that while she was patient and thorough with the little students—who folded and tilted and lifted like an earnest if unathletic ballet corps— Yukako was as severe with her teachers-in-training as she had been with Koito years before, though less venomous. The first time one of her trainees gave a lesson, she would correct him or her—a humiliation—in front of the class of girls, but from then on she would only make corrections in front of the other young teachers, which smarted too, but less.

AMONG THESE NEW teachers-to-be, barely older than her students, was Kato's cherub-faced daughter Mariko. The quickest to abandon her ashes in the brazier half laid, the slowest to remember what went where, she was not Yukako's first choice, but the relationship with Advisor Kato was too important to compromise. I still remember the sound of her voice one day as she walked home from the Shins' with the other young women; I'd just been summoned to help them sweep up a cloud of fallen tea powder. Each girl silently knelt, feather in hand, each brushing the endless green tea onto a sheet of clean white paper. The air was thick with blame. They left, still wordless, but I did hear an inimitable squeal on the path. "It was in the *way*," Mariko burst out, kicking a carefully placed stone.

SCHOOLGIRLS STUDIED TEA for two years: from spring until the opening of the sunken hearth in November, they worked on the simplest tray-style *temae*, while from November until spring, they learned how to make frothy thin tea using the sunken hearth. During the second year they learned thin tea with the warm-weather brazier, and both summer and winter *temae* for the sticky thick tea. After training for two years, Yukako's teachers would work in the new girls' schools as they opened, each school purchasing Yukako's tea utensils and contracting with her for the teachers' services. She paid the teachers well, but she kept back a portion of the money she received as a fee for the use of her family's name and tradition. Often I came home from the bathhouse to find the abacus and account book out on Yukako's low desk, and though I spread the *futon* for her, I also ground ink and brought lamps for her late-night reckoning. She was charmed by the Western use of red and black ink for debts and credits, and I was proud to see the column of red numbers taper as she paid off the work on One Pine.

Just as Yukako had begun charging her teachers to use the Shin name, once the schools required more tea utensils than we could carry, she decided to do the same for her craftsmen. She had me help her stamp a license for each whisk and scoop and linen cloth she ordered, and then she sold them to the craftsmen, who would sell the licensed utensils to the schools at a fixed price. The year she proposed this practice, she sweetened the deal by selling scores of licenses to make equipment she bought herself for the next imperial tea presentation, to mark the fifth year of tea education in the girls' schools: one for each lady at court in Tokyo. She paid a higher price for these utensils than the school ones, as the work involved was finer. Furthermore, to keep the craftsmen happy in future years, she agreed to sell a few extra licenses to each so that they could sell equipment to foreigners or nouveaux riches at any price they liked. This work would be closer in quality to the imperial wares than the school wares, but as the pieces were new and not named by a tea master individually, they would still be affordable in a way tea utensils had never been before. They sold.

"What if the craftsmen try to cheat you?" I asked one evening, marveling at Yukako's ingenuity. She had just finished a day in conversation with Chojiro's Heir, who agreed to her scheme provided that the distinction between his own work and that of his apprentices be clearly maintained at all times. Yukako had put him at ease and walked away with licensing money in her sleeves. We were pausing on the way home by the Canal Street bridge, watching the V's of geese overhead.

Yukako chided, "They've been supplying tea things to our family for generations, and now they're making more money than ever before. They're not going to cheat us." Then she frowned. Since her father's death, she'd always had a bit of a crease between her eyebrows; now it deepened. "I could go to the stores and check, or send people they don't know," she murmured. Then she smiled. "If I found out a craftsman was trying to cheat me, I'd sell licenses to his rival too," she determined. "Let them fight it out themselves." Pleased with herself, she flicked a stone across the shallow water. It skipped three times, falling in with a quiet *splish*.

"Where did you learn to do that?" I asked.

"I watched my sons," Yukako said with a shrug.

"That's not what I meant," I said, retying my carrying scarf.

"I think this big order for Tokyo helps." She looked worried for a moment. "Our gift to the court ladies is going to cost buckets of money," she said. "But I think it'll pay off." She skipped another stone.

That wasn't what I'd meant, either. Where had she learned how to manage the outside world, and not be managed by it? Perhaps I was seeing the other side of the word *shade.* Yukako had no one to shade her: no father, no husband, no mother. And it turned out that she was no shy fern: the sun shone hard on her, and she'd grown straight and tall, a ridgepole pine, a mast.

WHEN YUKAKO RETURNED from Tokyo later that season, she seemed uncertain about the reception of her tea *setto.* The court was in a state of transition, constantly changing leaders after two factors had ended the long reign of Prime Minister Ito, the man whose broad, if naïve, vision had posed the Belling Stag ballroom as a way to inspire Western nations to revise their unequal treaties with Japan. A British ship had recently sunk off the Japanese coast, and all the survivors were British, while all twenty-six Japanese on board had drowned. Because of treaties favoring foreigners, the ship captain was tried under British, not Japanese, law, and acquitted. A few waltzes and ball gowns, it seemed, were not going to persuade the foreigners to treat Japanese like full human beings. What's more, Ito was discovered in a compromising position with another man's wife. After Ito's hasty retirement, Yukako said, the Prime Minister kept changing from one Tokyo trip to the next: it wasn't yet clear what the tone of the new government would be.

This was the uncertainty into which Yukako had set loose her gift of tea utensils. Would they seem Civilized and Enlightened enough? They were mass-produced; would they seem *too* Western? I worked her frozen feet between my hands as she talked: the road home was long, as always, and there was already snow at Hakone Pass. "Do you remember the man from the imperial court my father entertained when we were children? The former Emperor's nephew?"

"Of course." How strange to think of Yukako and myself as *chil-*

dren together; when we were nine and sixteen, she'd seemed so much older.

The August Cousin, she told me, still a close confidant of the Emperor himself, had just been named Minister of Education by the new Prime Minister. "*He's* the one coming to inspect the schools this fall," she explained, anxious. He had expressed neither pleasure nor displeasure at Yukako's gift. "His silence made me so nervous," she said. "As if Father were watching."

She was home, home: I rested my cheek on her little cold foot.

25

1891

JUST BEFORE NEW YEAR'S, Yukako had an answer, if not from the Minister, then from the imperial household: she was asked to bring a tea teacher to live and work at court when she came the following spring. "This is quite something," she said, nodding. There were so many red stamped seals on the letter, I was afraid to touch it.

MEIJI TWENTY-FOUR, though it corresponded with the lucky occasion of Chio's sixtieth year, did not open well for her. On New Year's she choked on a bite of *mochi*, a chewy cake made of pounded rice, and her face turned purple. Aki, just fifteen, screamed and screamed as if gasping her grandmother's air for her. Nao, visiting, gave his mother a precise blow to the belly and dislodged the *mochi*, but Chio was never the same after. Some sturdy part of her had been left absentminded, content to follow Kuga instead of lead. In the bathhouse I saw her lose track of herself and wander, half soaped, toward the soaking tub: Kuga and I leapt up and led her back to finish rinsing first. After the second time it happened, we watched her constantly while pretending not to, and in the kitchen Kuga slowly edged her mother out of work involving fire and knives.

After New Year's, Nao got permission from his master glazier to leave the guild for a month or two and work on a project out of sequence: ours. He was able, in that way, to see Chio every day, and between us all, someone could always look out for her. Yukako, meantime, had decided to train her female teachers as boarders rather than day students: the first glass windows on the Shin compound appeared in the newly constructed women's bathhouse. I barely noticed Nao at first. He slept in the little cottage by the kitchen; he worked on the windows; he looked after his mother and kept to himself. If Yukako still harbored the annoyance she had first shown on his return, the feeling, like the project she had hired him for, was a thing she set off to the side.

I wondered why Yukako had chosen such an insignificant part of the house to lavish her glass money on. And opaque panes! With glass windows she could see the tea gardens from her *futon* all year round, if she wanted to, or glass could make a new world out of the dim kitchen.

Then I understood: For all her innovation with tea utensils and teaching, Yukako didn't want a new world. She was giving glass lip service as a way to please Advisor Kato. With the school inspection coming up, she could not afford to do otherwise.

Advisor Kato, meanwhile, was working hard to maintain *his* connections. He couldn't join Yukako for tea at New Year's because he was entertaining guests from Tokyo, courting funds for a new *stage, su-tei-ji,* of the almost-dug canal. The money was released, it seemed, on certain conditions. By the time Kato's guests had left, the announcement had gone out to all the principals, parents, and teachers that starting with the new school term in April, the girls' compulsory dress would shift. Plaid shawls would no longer be required. Instead, every girl was to wear *hakama* over her clothes, be they *kimono* or Western. I was glad the Pipe Lady was not alive to witness yet another slight to her abolished caste: girls in *hakama,* the trouser-skirts worn by *samurai* men!

The Pipe Lady's granddaughter Sumie lived in Tokyo with her late husband's parents now, but once the Meiji government had released her father and oldest brother, they, like many former Shogun loyalists, had moved their family north to Yezo, to homestead as far from Meiji Tokyo as possible. How galling it would be for Sumie's brothers to see the new girls' uniforms, I thought: those boys had vaunted their *hakama* as much as their swords.

Though no one wore *hakama* anymore (except for sacred virgins at shrines, who wore red ones), *samurai* households everywhere kept them in storage. Since *samurai* and merchant girls were the first admitted to the new schools, *hakama* would, like the plaid shawls, be an inexpensive way to standardize dress, but the choice did mark a clear shift from West to East. The boys, similarly, who had been wearing a riotous mix of Japanese and modern dress under their Western uniform straw hats, were instructed to leave their hats at home.

When Advisor Kato finally did join us for tea, it was Setsubun, in early February, the day that fathers wear horned *oni*-devil masks and chase their children through the house, when children throw toasted beans and chant spells to drive the devils out. Kenji was visiting from Sesshu-ji that day, and though at eighteen and nineteen they were far too old for Setsubun games, the two boys bought a mask for Nao and teased and bullied him away from his work until he gave in and uncomfortably chased Aki down the hall. Shrieking with laughter, she hid behind me, though she was taller, and so he chased me, too, until the young men assaulted him with beans, triumphant. Jiro hadn't joined us for Setsubun in six years, I noted: no wonder the boys seized on Nao. Even Chio remembered to hang the Setsubun talismans against demons on the kitchen doorpost: a sprig of holly and the head of a sardine. In the tearoom, Yukako chose an incense box with a lid shaped like an *oni*-devil mask, then changed her mind because Kato was a Christian.

It was the season when plum blossoms make their fearless show in the ice and sleet, and the plates I was to carry from the kitchen held sardines and winter herbs. Yukako decided to perform a special *temae* designed for the coldest months, in which the tea is served in a tall narrow bowl to hold in the heat. She even found a winter tea bowl in storage named Hakama to use in Kato's honor: narrow at the base and flared at one side, like the leg of a blown trouser-skirt.

Kato arrived in a suit and a great thick coat with a silk muffler that he kept on in the tearoom. He wore Western shoes, as always, but they no longer squeaked at his approach. I was aware that the faddish sound made by strips of extra leather added to one's Western shoes had faded from the streets: even Bozu had stopped squeaking as he worked.

After Kato had eaten and drunk and formally appreciated the utensils, he and Yukako spoke a little. "I hope you'll come see your glazier's work in the new bathhouse," she invited, before addressing him seriously. "I'd like to have the girls I'm training as teachers board with me, even the ones who live in Kyoto, if their parents approve," she said, bowing. "I want them to feel as much like family as possible."

"Is that so?" said Advisor Kato. "Interesting idea."

"Miss Mariko's a very good student," Yukako added. Was she angling for Kato's daughter, of all people, to come live with us?

"She can be disobedient," said Kato, politely deflecting the compliment. "Obedience is a Christian *and* Confucian virtue," he said warmly. "I've often thought of writing a little tract on the parallels. All this East-West nonsense! We're more similar than anyone wants to say."

Yukako pursued him on the subject no more. "Do you feel ready for the Inspection?" she asked. She'd heard that not only had Kato gotten funding for the next *stage* of his canal, he was actually ahead of schedule with the latest wave of schools.

From my perch backstage in the Baishian *mizuya*, I saw the big man beam. "Much to do, much to do, but this year's new schools are built and ready for April. Now I'm fitting up the house for the Minister's visit. I'm planning a new guesthouse by the moon-viewing pond."

"I hope that goes well. May I ask, do you think it could be arranged for me to meet with the Minister in private at some point once he sees the girls' schools? I'd like to speak with him about tea in the boys' schools as well."

Yukako was rarely nervous, but after this bald request, I heard her ramble a little to fill Kato's silence. "We talked about it some years ago, that after the Inspection . . ."

"Ah! So we did. And I'm sure he'll love what you've done. No doubt you'll have plenty of opportunities to see him on this visit," Kato boomed, vague and jolly.

Yukako swallowed visibly. "I look forward to it," she said.

"DID THAT MEAN yes or no?" I asked later, after admitting that I'd stayed to listen.

"He's not going to help us," Yukako said, changing into her bath *kimono*. As I carefully set wands of fresh charcoal into the ash and embers in the brazier, Yukako cursed, her hand caught in a sleeve. Kato hadn't even asked to see the new glass.

A FEW NIGHTS LATER, when Yukako sat late bent over her sums—the figure the imperial household would send her for the new tea teacher's services; the amount she would retain before sending the young teacher the balance—her back suddenly straightened. Her face lit up; a drop of ink fell from her brush and flecked the ledger. "Maybe I don't need Kato, to meet with the Minister. Why, I could ask him myself."

JIRO, known in his retirement as Great Teacher, had reached an accord with his friend Shige, the silk wholesaler I'd once called the Bear. The merchant had also sent some of his factory profits to help restore One

Pine, which no doubt sweetened his good intentions. It was a warm spring when Yukako and Tai left for Tokyo that year, with Tai's most advanced student—Shige's second son—in tow. After two years of Tokyo-Kobe rail service without major upset, Yukako had finally decided to forgo the hard mountain road in favor of one of the new trains: she and Tai came back in days instead of weeks, jubilant. Kenji had stayed to look after the house in his brother's absence, and Yukako and Tai returned to find us all in the sewing room, where Kenji was giving Aki a reading lesson whose texts—the swashbuckling tales of *ninja* and *ronin* that he and Tai had grown up on—made good entertainment for the rest of us.

But not as good as the adventures which Yukako and Tai recounted. "We went so fast!" Tai crowed.

"They've sold Ito's dance hall to a private club, can you imagine?" asked Yukako. "There's no more Belling Stag."

"I never even got to see it," said Kenji, disappointed.

"You'll come with us one day, I promise," Tai gusted. "And in Ginza, where all the houses are brick, you can see Western lights all night long! *Ii-re-ku-to-ri-ku* lights!"

I had seen one of those lights at the Expo—a bulky, delicate, faltering thing, more often off than on—but never imagined a whole street lit by electricity.

"I finally understood what Kato keeps nattering on about with his next *stage* of the canal," said Yukako. "They can use the water to make electricity!"

"In Tokyo they're building a Western hotel the size of a palace!" said Tai. "And a cloud-scraper! A building twelve stories tall, can you imagine it?"

Kenji's eyes went wide. Nao was there, sitting by his mother, keeping an eye on Chio's needle and her cold barley tea. Even he, who took a dim view of Shogun-era pomp and Meiji-era dazzle alike, leaned forward, excited. Then he frowned. "I'm sure they'll find an army of

poor sods to wear their lives out climbing up and down twelve stories
to fetch and carry, and count themselves grateful for the work," he
grumbled to Kuga.

"No, no!" Tai insisted. "They're importing an elevator machine
from America! Have you heard of it?"

I never had. While Tai explained how an *erebeta* worked, Yukako
reflected on how, amidst the bright lights and skyscrapers, Tokyo was
turning away from its initial giddy embrace of the West toward a more
selective mode. "I didn't see a single man with his hair done in the old
way," she marveled. "But outside of the Palace, I didn't see a single
Western dress, either, unless it was on a white woman. And just last
year I'd see a few of them in every crowd."

"What's the old style?" Aki asked shyly.

Yukako and I caught each other glancing over at Chio in her
widow's *obako* coiffure, to see if she'd heard.

"Do you remember when my father lived here?" asked Kenji.

Yukako continued. "They're still playing Western games, like *gorufu*
and *tenisu*, but the old ones are back too. I hadn't played an incense-
guessing game since before you two were born," she told the boys.

Tai had clearly heard this before, because he eased away from her to
tell more of his feats of speed and noise. "You can't imagine it," he
told me, both gloating and awestruck.

I remembered my girlhood, a desert train at night through Suez. "I
can," I said gently.

He moved on to Nao, who'd shown interest in the *erebeta*. "The foreigners measure power in how many *horses* it would take to pull the cart,
so I rode hundreds of horses at the same time!"

"Seems like a way to break up what little self-rule poor people have
in their villages and suck them away to work in cities and factories,"
Nao said bleakly. Tai stared. I did too; I had never heard anyone talk
this way. I wondered again what Nao had done in his years away from
home.

Tai turned to Aki, undaunted, and promised her a train ride some-day. "You haven't lived until you've taken a train!"

"Then some of us may never live," said Kuga, with a tart, anxious glance at Chio, who had just stabbed herself with a needle.

"Why weren't you watching her?" asked Nao softly, below the sound of Yukako's incense story.

"*You* were watching her," Kuga whispered, holding a rag to their mother's finger.

"You were too," Nao hissed.

"*I'd* like to take a train ride," Kenji assured his brother stoutly.

"You will," Tai promised.

THOUGH YUKAKO HAD TALKED freely of all the changes she'd seen in Tokyo, she'd said nothing of her mission there. That night, however, in private, she all but purred as I combed out her hair. "So many people ordered tea sets of their own," she bragged. "Everyone wants to wash the taste of Ito and the Belling Stag out of their mouths, and *Ocha* is just the thing for it. Shige's son will have more students than he can handle, and the court wants more teachers!"

"Congratulations," I said warily. I had missed her, and I hated any hint of her leaving again.

"And the women were all over our Master Teacher. When we gave them each a tea set, we gave them each a memento of that pretty boy from Kyoto, didn't we? 'I wish you could stay and be *my* teacher,'" she simpered. "And everyone asked about tea in the girls' schools: 'So when are girls going to start learning tea in Tokyo too?' It's working! It's working!"

She smiled, ebullient, and added a crowning dollop of good news. "And I spoke to the Minister myself. I invited him to a harvest moon tea during his visit, and he accepted!"

"Just like that?"

"He said, 'What could be more lovely?'"

Yukako had a *daruma*, a doll so fat and round that when we made snowmen they were called snow *daruma*. When you buy them at the temple, they have one eye painted in, and when your wish comes true, you paint the other. Yukako capered through the room, ground a little ink, and dotted in the missing eye to my applause. It was so bold of her, too, to fix a date: the full harvest moon falls just once a year, on the fifteenth day of the Eighth Month of the old calendar, or sometime in September in the new. The timid, safer thing would have been to propose a tea gathering and wait to hear more about her busy guest's plans. She was so beautiful, looking up at her two-eyed *daruma* on the shelf, her head thrown back with pride.

26

1891

WE WERE ONLY SUPPOSED to start with three girls boarding as teachers-in-training: Sumie's youngest, the Bear's youngest, and Io, the daughter of the Hikone merchant Noda, who stood to become wildly rich the moment Advisor Kato's canal opened. After Tai's success at court, however, three well-to-do Tokyo men asked if Yukako would train their daughters, too, including the railroad pioneer Sono, recently named a baron for his service to Japan. Baron Sono, who was amassing a second fortune selling Japanese antiques to Western art museums, sent Tsuko, his large-eyed girl. And Advisor Kato, with much clearing of his throat, came to ask if Miss Mariko could continue her studies with Yukako as a boarding student. He was still pushing for his electric *stage* to go smoothly and needed all the support he could rally.

There was an attic in the sewing house where Yukako's mother, like many highborn ladies, had once raised silkworms as a hobby. Yukako had the room fitted up to use as a dormitory for the girls, and arranged for their meals to be served in the little room off the kitchen where Kuga and Aki had slept until Chio took ill, and where the new live-in sewing-girls, two sisters named Tama and Hisui—Jewel and Jade—now slept. Yukako borrowed back her father's *hakama* from the boys, who had dressed in them as children to stage their *samurai* plays. The sober pin-striped trouser-skirts dated from the Mountain's own boyhood, before he'd been adopted into the Shins, who had served, and often married, *samurai* but were technically of merchant caste and forbidden to wear warriors' dress. The Mountain had owned four pairs of *hakama* in a blend of wool and silk: black, navy, brown, and gray. Yukako chose the black pair, I chose the brown pair, and she saved the other two for students from merchant families. The women's bathhouse was ready, glass and all.

The work was complete just after Yukako and Tai returned from the capital and Kenji left again for his father's retreat at Sesshu-ji temple. The next morning, as Yukako laid breakfast before her son in the garden study that had been her father's and husband's, Nao came in and bowed deeply to both of them.

"My *sensei* asked when I was coming back, but if there's anything else you need here . . ." he said, with downcast eyes. He flicked a quick look at the kitchen. Yukako followed his gaze toward the scent of Kuga's grilled eel, half as good as Chio's had been.

I think Tai had forgotten that the man was only with us to do a job. Nao had lent him a book and a scraping plane. He was going to teach him how to hunt with a gun. Tai pressed his lips together and looked at his mother, alarmed; she looked at him. She had no plans for more glass in the house, but she said, "Actually, my son said there's money for you to do the sewing house too, if they can spare you."

Tai smiled. Nao bowed repeatedly, and left.

THOUGH YUKAKO DIDN'T *say* she felt strange wearing a dead man's clothes, she refused to wear the *hakama* until they'd been washed. No sooner had we finished stitching up the cleaned panels, however, than she came to the sewing house to try the trouser-skirts on. Nao was in

the room, washing every last trace of paper off the sliding door frames,
so Yukako took me up the ladder-staircase to the new attic dormitory, a
quiet expanse of fresh *tatami* that followed the shape of the roof, high-
ceilinged at the center and low at the edges, with narrow horizontal
strips of *shoji* window on all four sides.

Yukako had me take off my wide *obi* and stand in my *kimono*. Given
all the undersashes used to put on a *kimono*, the *obi* was not, strictly
speaking, necessary for tying it closed, though no woman called herself dressed without one. But that's what Yukako was demonstrating,
in that dim, milky, floor-level light, as she twisted out of her sash and
stepped into the *hakama*. She pulled the enormous trousers up and
lashed them tight around her with their long streamers: each leg of the
hakama was so wide, she and I could have stood comfortably in a single
pair. The four ribbons tied up like those of an apron and formed a
wide sash in place of the *obi*. The split of the trousers was slung so low,
below the knee, that I couldn't even see a lump where her *kimono*
bunched up and fell open on either side of it; I just saw a double-
barreled skirtlike bell. When she was dressed, Yukako helped me into
my *hakama* and stepped back.

"You look different," she said approvingly. I did; I could feel it.
While my Western dress, based on a pattern for a little girl, fit like a
sack, when I wore a *kimono* my *obi* bound me from mid-breast to mid-
hip, fitting as poorly as a cigar band around a peanut. *Hakama*, however,
designed for exertion rather than display, tied at the actual waist, not
the waist-inclusive midsection that an *obi* gestured toward. While
Yukako looked lankier than ever in her mannish getup, I felt as if for
the first time I were wearing an outfit meant for my own awkward
womanly body: full at the bust, tight at the waist, full at the hips. I felt
good. "Come show us!" called Aki from below.

"There's a mirror downstairs; do you want to see?" asked Yukako,
as if I were a little girl again. Shy but eager, I led the way down the ladder. "*Ara!*" chorused Kuga and the new sewing-girls, and Aki gave me a

look of frank curiosity, one that Nao echoed surreptitiously but held longer. It was strange that in all my years of wearing shifts based on my mother's design, I had never registered as anything to them but a Japanese servant girl dressed up in Western clothing: Yukako's accessory, sometimes chic, sometimes outré. Now, however, as I stood at the mirror with my new silhouette, the room of servants scrutinized me. Aki asked, "Was your father a foreign man?"

"She lost her parents in a fire," Kuga recited. "She doesn't know."

But I saw Nao flash his sister a look, saw her shrug in agreement: *Could be.*

"She had no look of pollution, and Young Mistress took her in, didn't she?" said Chio, surprising all of us. She spoke rarely now, and often seemed lost in her own mind: I bowed to her in startled gratitude.

Then Yukako reached the foot of the ladder and crossed the room to the mirror herself. She was stunning, a *samurai* daughter to the bone. Aki cheered. Kuga and the sewing-girl sisters gasped. Tai, passing by outside, paused to stare. Surprised and pleased, Yukako raised her arms into a fighting stance. "You need a sword!" Tai cried out, grinning.

Yukako laughed, and Chio echoed with a laugh of her own, low in the throat and gently scolding. "Mr. Shuji!"

Yukako's trouser-skirt swirled as she spun to face Chio. *"What?"* she asked, a little breathless. I didn't know what Chio had said, but I'd never heard her use that tone of voice.

"Who?" asked Aki.

Chio blinked drowsily. "What?" she asked in her everyday voice.

Yukako gave her a hard look. Aki continued to stare at me. She asked her father, "If you were born in Kyoto but your father's a foreigner, are you still a Kyoto native?"

"Don't be rude," Nao snapped. "You can't help who your parents are." Flinching, Aki bent over her sewing again.

I hated Aki feeling hurt on my account; I gave her a sympathetic glance. Nao looked at Yukako. "You look just like your brother," he said. It was the first time he had addressed her, just her, since his gift of glass dishes years before.

Yukako stopped staring at Chio and fixed her confusion and shock on Nao. "Oh," she said awkwardly, and went back up the ladder to change. She turned to give Chio a last questioning glance, but the old woman looked straight ahead, squinting into the bright day.

I remembered Yukako once saying that Hiroshi and Nao had played at dressing up in the Mountain's *hakama* as children. "Did people call your brother Shuji?" I asked upstairs, changing back into my *obi*.

"No! That was one of my *father's* childhood names," Yukako whispered.

"Spooky," I said, nodding.

"Isn't it? Him *and* my brother, in the same piece of clothing?" She folded the *hakama* at arm's length, shuddered.

"I bet this is happening to schoolgirls all over Kyoto this week," it occurred to me.

Yukako turned her surprise in a third direction, toward me, for thinking of something she wouldn't have. "I bet," she agreed.

THAT NIGHT, on the way to the bathhouse, Aki lagged behind to walk with me. "I'm sorry I asked that about your father," she said. "It was rude."

"It's all right." I shrugged.

"It's just . . ." she said apologetically. "I wonder. About my mother."

Ah, that was it. "I only know what I told you, Miss Aki."

"Well, no one else will tell me *anything*," she said loyally.

CHIO DIED A WEEK LATER, the day before classes began and the great canal waters opened. She'd gone to take a nap in the little hut off the kitchen, and when Kuga went to check on her an hour later, she wasn't breathing. We all ran in from the sewing room: she was gone. She was quickly cremated, her ashes buried with Matsu's in the servants' quarter of the temple yard, everything tidied away before the students arrived, the boys dressed like bats, the girls like long-gone warriors. When I try to remember her last days, I see a swirl of sober *hakama* and falling petals, the water suddenly flowing high past Migawa and Canal Streets. I mourned her most the first week of school on a boat outing we took with the new students, on water that had just arrived all the way from Lake Biwa. Where Kato's canal flowed widest, on the east side of the city, its banks were lined on both sides with newly planted cherry trees, pink as candy. She'd never see this, I thought. She'd seemed so old when I first met her, but I was thirty-five now, the same age she'd been then. I thought of her in the dim shelter of a room she rarely saw in daylight, laid out on her narrow *futon* beneath the sepia photograph of her son. There were fewer and fewer women who had grown up in the old ways, who had never stopped blackening their teeth, who disregarded, without affectation, the Western calendar. And there had only ever been one Chio. When we found her, Kuga drew a cotton robe over her shrunken body, her little claw feet, so that we could see only her face, both hard and soft, like weathered stone.

ONE OF THE FIRST THINGS Chio had taught me was the importance of gifts, of maintaining social harmony. When I joined the Shin house as a servant, another little girl had already been put forward for my place, and Chio had forced me, my first night in the bathhouse, to bribe her and her mother with gifts of candy to sweeten the injustice. I had not understood the dire importance of this gesture: they were my sweets, I'd thought. Chio had given them to me; why should I part with them? And so Chio had roughly scrubbed at my selfish face, and Little Hazu had made faces at me from behind her mother Fujie's sleeve.

And so it came to pass that Little Hazu, though four or five years my junior, grew up to be one of my greatest tormentors in the bath-house, especially at puberty, as the vaporous lack of language that first marked my difference solidified into grown flesh. I had no accent, with time, but I had no husband, either, and no shame: hadn't Hazu, hadn't everyone, seen me in that queer Western dress?

My one saving grace, as Chio took pains to explain to the other women, was that I wasn't being freakish on purpose. *Okusama* might be strange, but she had saved the household from poverty with no help from that merchant princeling, and if Western dress was what she chose for me, then that's what I would wear; if *Okusama* said I wasn't to marry, then unmarried I'd remain.

But with Chio gone, Kuga would not go out of her way on my account. And Hazu in her tiny clogs, with their fresh-from-the-shop-twice-a-month yellow thongs, was a *jinrikisha* man's wife now, with four children of her own. The week I began following Yukako to the schools in *hakama* trousers, I was singled out for notice by Hazu's youngest, whose shrill whine and itchy barbs won him for me the name Mosquito Boy. When I dropped my scrubbing-bag at the bath one night, he pointed his chin at me. *"Pamari-sensei!"* he cried.

Pamari? I had been snubbed and mocked in the bathhouse all my life, but no one had ever said I looked like that dumpy little missionary woman with the lapdog!

Hazu gasped and scolded her son indulgently. "That's not nice," she singsonged, taking a good look at me. *"Pamari-sensei*, huh?" she giggled. I looked away and adjusted the cloth tented over my hair. The streets were full of student girls in *hakama* now, but no one said *they* looked like foreigners. The last time I had seen so many *hakama* go by was in the Emperor's first procession to Edo, back when it was still called Edo. Western clothing, and the girls who'd worn it, had garnered all kinds of scoffers, but this season, though everyone stared at the girls in men's clothing, no one said a mocking word. It was as if wearing the clothes now forbidden to their fathers had conferred upon the girls a certain gravity, a certain sincerity of purpose. Why did *hakama* make them look earnest and me look silly? Now that they could compare me to real live foreigners instead of red-haired wood-block demons, did I seem less Japanese? Frances Parmalee's sagging, jowly face sprang to mind unbidden: I'd once seen her mincing up the street in her buttoned boots and ruffled bonnet, basket tucked under her arm. A doggy sneeze scissored its way out of the basket, and Miss *Pamari* opened the lid and cooed at the ancient panting creature inside. She looked, as did many missionary ladies, like an old woman dressed as a doll: pale blue ribbons on her bonnet, her bustle, the handle of her basket, the hem of her skirt. Her dress swelled at the hips and bustle and again at the bodice, nipped in at the waist—just like me in *hakama*, I realized, blushing in the oil-lit dimness. We were small round women who did not look Japanese. I ducked under the water for a long moment, mortified. When I surfaced, I saw Mosquito Boy hugger-mugger with a friend. "Don't drown, *Pamari-sensei!*" the boys called.

On the way home, Kuga walked fast, never turning to see if I was behind her.

27

1891

AFTER CHIO'S DEATH, Nao began working in a frenzy, rising as early as Kuga, who had inherited her mother's sleepy eyes along with her kitchen. The glassy clink of charcoal on charcoal in the stove, followed by the wooden clonk of Jewel and Jade taking down the shutters, the distant *whump* of students folding up their cotton mattresses— all these were joined by the sounds of Nao scraping and planing and chiseling as he cut and fitted panes of glass.

Since her children's move downstairs, Yukako had become fiercely protective of her morning sleep: while I lay awake for long minutes, listening for the stove and lacquer sounds that would mean it was time to bring *Okusama* her breakfast, Yukako dreamed on until I set down her tray and touched her shoulder. But something in the tinkling, scraping, squeaking work below made Yukako stiffen each morning; I could feel her heart beat faster and her body tense.

One such morning I was floating in a half-dream. Someone was plucking out a *shamisen* tune, *Auprès de ma blonde, il fait beau, fait beau, fait beau*. Half-awake, my bones liquid with longing, I clung to Yukako as she stirred in bed, to keep the music from evaporating. "Listen to that racket," said Yukako's voice, and I both knew, waking, that she was speaking in the room where we lay and wondered, dreaming, if she meant my mother's tune. I felt her shake off my limp arm, and I woke fully: to Nao working a glass edge with a metal file, to Yukako sitting up in bed, peeved.

She dressed in a gust of irritation, put up her hair, and padded downstairs. I threw on my bathhouse robe and crept behind, blinking and yawning. In the dewy gray light, I saw that Nao had already taken down the wooden shutters that covered the sliding doors to the sewing house. *The dew will damage the paper,* I caught myself thinking—but there was no paper anymore, only glass and holes where glass would go. I rounded the house and saw Yukako, tall and formal in her *kimono,* Nao scruffy in his leggings and thick apron. She beckoned him away from the sewing house for a moment and spoke to him in a low voice.

"Did my son say you could begin work this early?"

"He never said anything either way, Madam."

His downcast eyes and level voice incensed her all the more. "Are you aware that there are students sleeping directly above you? You're disturbing them."

"No one has said anything to me before, Madam," Nao said, but not before noting, with one unedited glance, that *she,* and not a student overhead, was the one who'd risen to confront him.

"You never used to do this; I don't see what the problem is."

Nao met her eyes with a raw, flat, open-faced look.

"I'm sorry about your mother," Yukako said, shamed.

"I'd just like to finish up here and get back to the other glaziers," he mumbled. He didn't say *the other glaziers;* he said *uchi:* my master, my guild. The word *uchi* usually meant *my family* or *my home.*

I saw Yukako take a half-step closer to him. "This place isn't home at all?"

Nao looked everywhere but at Yukako and shrugged, head down. "No."

In her elegant clogs, with her hair piled high, Yukako stood as tall as Nao in his straw sandals. She remained where she was, a little closer than was quite appropriate. "You were quick to go last time, too, right after Older Brother—"

"He was the only thing keeping me here," Nao said. *Oh,* I realized. Just as Chio had been the only thing keeping him here this time.

"Older Brother died, Lord Ii's son went to Edo, and you left," said Yukako, her eyes shining with old hurt.

Nao's nostrils flared. He gave Yukako a long, sullen look. "What do you want?" he said fiercely. I could see the blood beating in his forehead.

"I think you should put glass in my room too," she said, half daring, half cajoling. Then, as if remembering her place, she angrily folded her arms across her chest.

"That's what you want? Fine," he snapped. They faced each other, breathing hard.

Yukako turned on her heel to go. "And don't start work until you're served breakfast," she said.

AN HOUR LATER, when I helped Kuga lay out the breakfast trays, one girl was missing: Advisor Kato's daughter Mariko. "Is something wrong?" asked Yukako when she walked by.

"She's sick," said Tsuko, Baron Sono's girl, touching her abdomen and looking forlorn.

Yukako gave a quick, sympathetic nod: what woman didn't know about menstrual cramps? But then Io Noda choked back a laugh. "What?" menaced Yukako.

"Too much *sake!*" Io said, and the other girls giggled, but nervously, quietly, watching Yukako.

"Well, her stomach hurts too," said Tsuko, with an apologetic bow.

. . .

THAT AFTERNOON, when I followed Yukako to one of the schools, she talked about the incident with the girls at breakfast as if the exchange with Nao had never taken place. "Drunk at seventeen? Do you think her father knows? I wonder if Kuga's selling her *sake*; I know the woman likes her cup. But it was decent of Tsuko to cover up for Kato's girl. She framed it so she wasn't *quite* lying, eh? I don't know what Miss Noda thought she'd gain by tattling." Her voice was reflective and convivial, but her eyes shone again with loss, as they had when she spoke with Nao. "It's clear they all need more supervision," she concluded.

That evening, while the girls were at their dinner, Yukako told me to move her ledger into Tai's study. Then she had me crowd a bulky folding screen up the narrow, ladderlike stairs of the sewing house, followed by her *futon* and coverlets, her mirror and chests of *kimono*. As I huffed up and down the stairs, I thought about Nao's word, *uchi*, and how lucky I was to have this one. This was mine, the woodgrain of the stairs through my worn brown split-toed socks, this very gesture of tying a carrying cloth snug around Yukako's lacquer sundries box. *These are her things*, I thought, pulling the knot tight. *These are her things and I belong here with them.*

At the top of the stairs in the girls' dormitory attic, Yukako partitioned off the far corner of the room with her screen and spread her *futon* on the floor. "Not bad," she nodded to herself, looking around.

"Do you want anything else from the other room? Or should I get my *futon* now?" I asked, still a little winded.

"Why?" she blinked, pulling her lacquer box toward her by its striped cotton carrying scarf.

"Why what?" I echoed.

With one finger Yukako tugged open the cloth knot. "Why are you getting your *futon*?" she repeated, surprised. "If you sleep here, you won't hear when breakfast is ready."

I heard her very slowly, as if underwater. I formed a reply. "Then where am I to sleep?"

"With the others, silly," she said, waving her hand in the general direction of the kitchen while their names came to her. "Jewel, Jade."

"But what if you need something?" I asked, stunned.

"It's time I started sending one of *them* for it," she said, with a decisive nod toward the stack of student bedding. "I want to see what these girls are made of."

In the dimming light, I looked down at Yukako's long hands on the lacquer lid. I'd been wrong. *Uchi* meant one thing to me, I realized: the thing I had just lost.

BEFORE WALKING to the bathhouse, I dragged my *futon* down to the three-mat room by the kitchen where Jewel and Jade slept. I could hear Kuga and Aki serving Nao his dinner in the little house off the kitchen, just as Chio had served Matsu when I was young. I felt numb and remote as I spread out my *futon* by Jewel's and Jade's.

It was only in the bath, after I had unwound my tight *obi* and scrubbed away the dirt of the day, after I eased into the warm arms of the water, that I felt anything at all.

My breath came in little hiccups as I tried not to cry. Why had she left me? She didn't really care about *supervising* her students, did she? I knew Nao had drawn her away, but had I pushed her? If I hadn't reached for her, would she still have left? I remembered my dream that morning, of my mother's voice when I was very young, remembered reaching for Yukako's warm body in the dark. I wept.

WITH MY EYES CLOSED in the water, I became aware of a familiar, loathsome voice: Hazu had arrived with her clutch of children. I could hear her two older sons on the men's side of the room, her daughter and youngest son, Mosquito Boy, nearby.

Though she was talking to her aging mother Fujie at that moment, I felt Hazu's eyes on me as I sniffled, and I composed myself. "Tell Miss Momo about the Sneezing Girl, do you remember?" Hazu goaded her mother.

"It was the most selfish thing I've ever seen. Not long before the girl went off to get married in Osaka, she came to the bathhouse one night with a terrible cold and sneezed right into the water. *Fum! Fum!* Like a crack of thunder! And the slime that came out of her nose?"

"Ew!" cried Hazu's daughter, rapt. Hazu's friends gathered around her in the water, listening, casting occasional glances at me as I tried to control my face.

"Was it green?" asked Hazu's son, the Mosquito Boy.

"Green and brown, and yellow! As big as a dragonfly! We had to drain the whole tub and scrub it out, fill it with clean water and heat it all over again," Fujie concluded.

"Mother said it took *forever* before anybody could soak again," Hazu added. "Can you imagine?"

Hazu's friends leaned toward her as she shrilled with laughter, and their children followed suit. I felt them all looking at me. I sniffled again, bowed good evening, and slid up out of the tub to leave. "Do you smell butter?" one of the women giggled.

In their corner of the tub, Kuga, Jewel, and Jade looked uneasily from the laughing women to me, not wanting to take a side. I left, dried, and walked home quickly, in order to spare them the embarrassment of my company. I kept my lamp low so no one could see my face on the path, and I cried in peace until the others came home. I heard Nao's low voice asking Kuga something outside and I felt a dull flash of hope. *He won't always be here,* I promised myself. *He wants to leave as much as I want him to. And won't Yukako tire of playing mother to seven girls?*

It occurred to me that though I had heard longing in her reproach that morning, Yukako might not actually know she desired Nao: she might experience her desire for him as irritation. She hated the sound of his glass and files, she said, but hadn't she moved her bed that much closer to his worksite? Or maybe, with the small part of her that was aware of her own desire, she had moved because she feared it, because—far more than those students needed *supervision*—she herself needed a chaperone: a whole roomful of girls. Why wasn't I enough? In my *futon*, I ground my teeth and wrapped my arms tight around me. When the other sewing-girls came in, I pretended to sleep.

28

1891

I HAD NOT SEEN IT, but everyone wanted Nao to stay. Tai and the gardener's grandson, Toru, though they had nothing to say to each other, could not stop talking around the man—Toru, his soon-to-be adopted son, acting more like a daughter-in-law, scurrying to and fro with the tobacco tray and teacups. He was the first out with a broom when Nao finished work on the sewing house, and the first up the staircase by the kitchen with a dropcloth when Nao shifted to Yukako's vacated upstairs room.

Whenever he could steal away from his classes and duties, Tai scaled the kitchen stairs, too, and hung about as the tall man worked. He spoke to Nao in a manner I had never heard him use before, a gruff, offhand, masterful voice belied by the thirsty specificity of its questions: How do they control the temperature when they make glass? How do trains switch from one gauge of track to another? How much water has to fall through a turbine to generate electricity? When I passed outside, I'd see him slouching in the window frame, smoking a Western pipe—something he would have never done in his mother's room had she still been there.

Even Kenji, when he wasn't sequestered in the classroom with Aki, patiently correcting her as she read aloud, pausing to offer or elicit commentary on a passage here or there, would emerge to watch Nao from below, standing outside, shyly hypnotized. The radiant festival-child beauty of his boyhood was melting—no doubt from all that time at Sesshu-ji temple with his father—into something more hesitant and tortoiselike. I watched as he fingered the skin- thin peels of wood that drizzled down from the carpenter's plane. "Have you smelled them, Aki-*bo*?" I heard him ask once, as if she were a much younger child.

Of course she had. Aki and Kuga doted on Nao, albeit with a certain injured remove, saying little, as if laying up a store of indifference in readiness for his departure, and yet every pot of seasoned rice, every *kimono* seam, every stroke of the rag across the *tatami* where he slept seemed like an act of worship. The new sewing-girls, however, felt no such ambivalence, and readily whispered about him into the night. "He likes you."

"No, he likes *you*!"

"He has that wife."

"Who?"

"Miss Aki's mother."

"No! He threw her out!"

"No, she's still in Asaka, waiting for him."

"I heard she died."

"I heard he has a mistress, a rich married lady who sees him in the afternoons."

"You made that up!"

"What? *You* lie all the time."

"But he likes you, I can tell."

"No, he likes *you*!"

I would try to fall asleep before they could come around to their giggly refrain a third and fourth time; I lay at their feet with a channel between my *futon* and theirs.

Yukako's students, however, were the most blatant gossips of all, and wellborn as they were, their prattle was more varied: it might be about Mariko Kato and Io Noda getting drunk on Kuga's liquor by the fireproof tower. It might be about how the Prime Minister had chosen Lord Ii—grandfather of the shy, aloof girl Sumie had sent us—to write a poem for the gate to Kato's electric plant, in an effort to build bridges between conservatives and *bunmei kaika* men. Or it might be about Mariko tying a string across Nao's path up the stairs, so that she could help him up when he tripped.

Today, Mariko was whispering in the sewing room with Io: the Emperor had licensed Tsuko Sono's father to open a Japanese art museum in Tokyo. All the fine ladies had hoped to see Tsuko's brother married to their daughters, but the boy had married a considerably older *geisha* on his own. "She's *Sensei's* favorite, have you noticed?"

It was true: Yukako often took Tsuko on errands that had, until just months before, been ours. I found myself listening intently to the girls for Yukako's news, the kind of nightly chitchat I had let wash over me before: the Minister of Education—the Emperor's August Cousin—had a new wife he planned to bring to Kyoto when he came that fall, a former *geisha* who spoke French. In honor of this event, Yukako had commissioned a *patisserie* in Kobe to develop a French sweet that would taste good with frothy green *matcha.*

I wondered if I would be dug up from obscurity to speak French to this woman—but surely not. I remembered Yukako displaying the flower-cutting scissors, not the flowers, during cherry-blossom season, and I could imagine her voice: *To use French food flatters his wife's accomplishments; to speak French would test them. Which do you think will leave him with a better feeling?* I tried to answer her in French in my mind and I caught myself reaching for a word in English. The districts of my brain had been redrawn, so that instead of French and not-French, as I heard the speaking world as a young child, I knew Japanese and not-Japanese.

Though it was excellent form on Yukako's part to include the Minister's new wife with this nod toward France, I wondered how she felt about it. Had so many years gone by that inviting a former *geisha* to tea would no longer stir up unpleasant memories? *The* Geisha *Who Speaks French,* I mused. I wondered what had happened to The *Geisha* Who Did Shin *Temae,* and to her servant girl. I wondered if Inko was still married to the sweetshop boy, if she had children now, if she'd ever gotten the gift I sent all those years before. Suddenly I heard Io tease Mariko. "I bet you're glad your husband's staying on longer, hm?"

"My husband, who?"

"We all know that was no ordinary piece of string! That tripwire was the red cord of destiny!"

"Oh, *him,*" said Mariko, rolling her eyes in the direction of Nao's upstairs worksite.

"Don't play dumb!"

"What?"

"You probably told your father to press *Sensei* about the windows, eh, Miss Kato? Admit it!"

"What?" Mariko snapped.

"You really don't know?"

"Do we have to play this game all day?"

"Sensei asked Mister Red Thread to put glass windows in Baishian for the Minister's visit!"

"Is that all?" sneered Mariko, but as Io gloated over being the one to know first, I saw a tiny smile lilt across Miss Kato's face.

Oh, I hated him, Mister Quiet and Skillful, Mister Cheekbones! Why had he agreed to stay longer? The only thing that had been holding my despair at bay was my sense that he'd soon go. I was glad to be sitting behind Mariko and Io, not in their line of sight, as angry tears blurred the blind seam before me. If he would only leave! Yukako would realize she missed me. I'd have my place back.

I closed my eyes. Since losing my nights and errands with Yukako, I circled from sewing house to bathhouse to *futon,* seeing other rooms only to clean them. Without daily excursions, I was spending more time wiping *tatami* with the other housemaids, our backs bent full, our *obi* knots in the air. We had come out of the early-summer rainy season at last, and this one, sore and soggy, had been my longest ever.

I caressed the small of my back a moment and took a break, ostensibly to fetch tea for the others, but I made a longer walk of it than I needed to. Aki had wandered off from the sewing house too; I saw her by the front gate in the last light of the day, with even less to justify her lollygagging than I: she just stood in the servants' gateway, watching the Starkweather girls walk home in their *hakama*. She was fifteen, skinny as a sweetpick, with a head and eyes that looked too big for her little body. She was eating less and less, I realized, noting how her head rested on the doorframe as if its weight were too much for her. Though her eyes were open, it seemed as if she had flown off from her body and were walking, invisibly, home with the Starkweather girls, her books buckled together with a leather strap. *Linger away while you can, Miss Aki,* I thought grimly. *Any second now you'll get your period and have to marry Toru.* I thought of Hazu at the bathhouse, boasting how she'd lost a tooth for each child she'd given birth to. I was unhappy, I realized, but I was lucky. I'd made my own luck before, and I could do it again.

29

1891

WE LIVED NEAR A TEMPLE, to which I had accompanied Yukako on many visits over the years. Beside it stood a shrine. The temple barred its heavy gates before sunset every day, but the shrine kept its lamps burning all night: the *torii* wicket had no gate to close. The shrine walls enclosed three kinds of venerated objects. First, holy things of the natural world: great rocks or trees with sacred straw ropes around them, festooned with rope tassels and white paper zigzags. Second, objects of Shinto devotion such as mirrors or jewels, protected by stone guardians, like foxes or boars. Third—though they'd been chased off in the first year of Meiji, they'd quickly returned—Buddhist deities that had been adapted to Shinto needs, like a statue of Benten revered as a face of the Shinto goddess of agriculture, or one of Kannon honored as the Shinto goddess of childbirth. There was often a star attraction on Shinto grounds, enshrined in the largest building—at ours, a pair of wise warriors—but so many other sacred beings and pavilions were clustered together on shrine grounds that the main god seemed more like a bright star at a dinner party than a monarch surrounded by his court. Japan would have accepted Christianity without batting an eyelash if it could have just tucked another altar—this one with a cross, guarded by stone angels—into the democratic, capacious fold of sacred earth behind the *torii* gate.

Personally, I think the Buddhist gods returned so soon to the Shinto shrines in case someone needed, as I did when I heard Nao was staying longer, to say a prayer when the temples were closed. Before dinner, I rifled through the drawer in my wooden pillow and tucked the coin I found into my sleeve. I left early for my bath that night, the cicadas whirring in the summer dusk.

I passed through the *torii*. A lamp sat just beside the stone shrine basin, into which a trickle of water spilled down a bamboo pipe. I rinsed my left hand, my right hand, my mouth. A great willow stood between me and the moon-lights of the shrine that housed the Shinto goddess with Kannon's face. The lamp on the ground lit a few leaves green-gold; overhead, the tree was a black cutout against the starry night. I parted the raspy curtaining willow branches with both arms and walked down a lantern-lined stone path.

Between the blowing lamps, deep within a series of smaller and smaller gates and curtains, the goddess was a shimmer of gold. The Japanese called her the avatar of compassion; for me she was the patron of choices, of other possible lives. I said, *Make something happen.* I said, *Make him leave.*

At the bathhouse, as every night, I took off my sandals in the outermost room and left them in their cubby on the women's side. Looking at the honeycomb of shoe compartments lining the walls, each a perfect cube, it was easy to see how crowded the bath would be and who was inside. A certain pair of sandals with fresh new yellow thongs never failed to tighten my shoulders: Hazu was already here tonight.

I went, as always, to the corner of the changing room that had been

Chio's, where we each kept a box with a comb and bran bags, a scrubbing cloth hung to dry on each box handle. Tonight my towel was, strangely, folded and tucked inside. I looked up: had I taken someone else's box by accident? No, that was my cloth, the crane crest of the Shin servants clear enough. Had someone at the bathhouse laundered, dried, and folded them all? No, Jewel's and Jade's cloths were hanging just as they'd left them.

"Miss Urako, excuse me."

I looked up at Hazu. A few of her friends stood nearby, watching us with folded arms.

"Could I talk with you for a minute?"

"Why so formal?" I asked mildly, my stomach knotting.

"Look, my children have been giving you trouble, and I want to apologize."

"Your children are charming," I lied. "They're no trouble at all."

"Could we step outside for a moment?" asked Hazu. She took my box by its handle and walked us both to the shoe-lined outermost room.

"What is it you'd like to tell me, Little Hazu?" I asked, oozing condescension, I hoped, instead of fear.

"Well, you've had to put up with a lot of disrespect and insinuation. And that's not right. So I'm just going to speak directly here. You're not Japanese."

"Is that so?" I said calmly, stalling.

"Maybe no one knew any better when we were all young, but I've seen foreigners and I've seen you. I don't care if some Kobe sailor's sheep whore gave birth to you, the fact is, you are a foreigner and this is a Japanese bathhouse. Do you understand?" she asked, her voice remaining forthright and friendly.

I wish I could have deflected her by pointing out that foreigners had not arrived in Kobe until long after my birth, but I was too rattled to think of this. "I don't see that there's ever been a problem," I said, and borrowing Yukako's mettle I added, "Except the one you're giving me.

And furthermore"—my throat began to constrict here—"I don't think you know a thing about my mother."

"I'm sorry if I said this in a way that confused you before," said Hazu pityingly. "I really am. I should have known better than to expect a foreigner to understand, and that's why I'm trying to be clear tonight. I don't care how your *Okusama* does things and I don't care how o-Chio did things. There's clean and there's dirty, and we Japanese come to the bathhouse to get clean."

I was blushing and I could see black at the corners of my eyes. "I do too," I insisted quietly.

"Look. If you ever—*ever*—get into the bath here again—" she began. I wondered what the end of her threat would be. Was she threatening to break my kneecaps if I dirtied her water? "—we will have to drain the water, scrub down the basin, and start over. Do you understand how much trouble that would cause for everyone?"

I was so stunned I laughed, one coughlike bleat. "That's not what I thought you were going to say."

"I don't think I need to say anything else," she said, handing me my bathhouse box. "Good night." She opened the door behind her and I saw the other women in the changing room had crowded round to listen, including her mother, hawk-eyed and sinewy, and her daughter, a girl as pretty and vain as she herself had once been.

I looked past Hazu to her mother standing in the doorway. The woman looked me in the eye and added a stinging farewell. The meaning of the word for good-bye, *if that is as it must be*—which suggests passive resignation and regret, suggests that we are helpless before the forces pulling us apart—cut tartly against her daughter's decisive actions. *"Sayonara,"* she said.

Cowed, I turned to the wall to collect my sandals. They were gone. On the shining, just-cleaned floor of my wooden compartment sat a small dish of salt. "They were dirty," Hazu's daughter said. The other women nodded approvingly. "So we burned them."

"I hope this will help you remember," said Hazu. She took a step back into the bathhouse and the door to the changing room slid shut.

On my way home, shoeless, shaking, I walked past a loose knot of Shin servants on their way to the bath and bowed to them curtly. Nao saw my face and gave me a questioning look; I all but bared my teeth at him.

I passed the shrine gate. "Well, I prayed for something to happen," I said. A bitter sound, almost laughter, burst out of me.

I HAD NOT SEEN AKI with the others on the path, but when I went to Yukako in the garden office she shared with her son, I saw the girl in attendance and guessed that *Okusama* had kept her home to fetch tea and grind ink. Why not her students? I wondered in the doorway.

"Miss Ura," called Yukako, her voice relaxed and merry. When I entered I saw she was not alone. Her student Tsuko Sono sat with her at the low table under the mosquito netting, looking fresh and earnest in her indigo robe and red-and-white-striped *obi*. "Come in, try this," *Okusama* welcomed.

As I lifted the netting to let myself in, I saw a pot of tea at the table, two little cups, and a tray with the strangest-looking *sembei* crackers I'd ever seen. "Taste this and tell me what you think," Yukako said, as if I'd never been sent to sleep downstairs.

I looked from her to Tsuko, her sober face alight like a child allowed to stay up late with the grown-ups, and understood why Aki, and not the other students, had been called to sit in attendance: the other girls would be jealous.

Controlling my own envy, I took a bite of one of the round puffs on the tray. "It's sweet!" I said, surprised.

"That one's my favorite," said Tsuko, nodding. *"Yuzu."*

The crisp citron-flavored disk melted away quickly in my mouth, with a soft charcoally squeak, like—irritatingly enough—Nao's glass.

"It's delicious," I said dully. It was also oddly, primordially, familiar, and this made me even more angry.

"We'll have them in *yuzu*, black sesame and chestnut. I think they'll go over well with the Minister and his wife," Yukako said, and I recalled The *Geisha* Who Spoke French. "They're called *macarons*."

The labored French accent she used made me recognize the taste from childhood: meringue! I flushed a deep and complicated red, and felt, amid my anger and jealousy, proud that I had defended my mother in the bathhouse. "*Okusama*, may I please speak with you in private sometime?" I asked.

Tsuko looked startled. "No doubt the others are wondering where I am," she said, with downcast eyes. "Please forgive my rudeness for leaving."

"I'm sure it's all right," said Yukako, but the young woman quickly bowed and left. Preoccupied, Yukako nibbled at a *macaron*. "I don't plan to have the Minister's wife in the tearoom, of course, but these ought to make a good impression while she waits." Her tone of voice was frosty, and I could tell time had not mellowed her to the prospect of hosting a *geisha*—even a former *geisha*—at the Shin house.

"So, Miss Ura," Yukako said, with a glance toward the doorway Tsuko had exited. "What do you need?" She seemed disappointed the girl was gone.

"*Okusama*, I have to make a special request." The formal words felt thick in my mouth. "May I please bathe here at night?" I told her, as matter-of-factly as I could, what had happened, steeling my voice whenever it began to wobble. "And may I have another pair of shoes?" I finished. *Take me back*, I didn't say. *Didn't we once drink three cups together?*

Yukako nodded, her face soft with compassion. "Of course. That's awful," she said. "There's no dealing with a crowd like that, if they're all against you. Of course you should bathe here."

"When I first came here, I think Miss Hazu's mother wanted her to work for your family, but you and o-Chio took me."

"I remember her." Yukako nodded wryly.

"I think they've hated me ever since."

"Oh, you mean if you hadn't come along, we would have taken in that woman's Little Hazu instead?" She laughed. "I remember o-Chio complaining about how hard she pushed. *Eta.*"

My eyes bulged. I had never heard a woman, let alone Yukako, say the word for the outcast aloud. The *eta*, reclassified by Meiji law as New Commoners, were the families who handled dead animals as butchers and leather workers, anathema in a Buddhist country. They were so deeply outcast that, though I had spent almost all my life in Kyoto, I had only the haziest idea where in the city they might live. I remembered Chio, the few times we'd had pork delivered, splashing the street in front of the house with water after the non-*eta* middleman came by. "He deals with a rough crowd," she'd grunted when I asked.

They were so despised that, though teenage boys were quick to call one another *baka*, I had never heard of anyone calling even a sworn enemy an *eta*. This made me think Yukako wasn't speaking figuratively. "What do you mean?" I asked.

"That woman always insisted a little too much to the contrary," said Yukako, and it was the third time I realized that she'd avoided calling Hazu's mother by her name, Fujie, or Painted Wisteria. "But we really can't know about her family. Her father's mother was married to a carpenter named Toshio. A very pious woman, four sons. But when she died, it was discovered that she'd had a secret lover the whole time. A butcher. Can you imagine? So did Toshio father those sons? Nobody knows, but listen: except for Hazu's grandfather, the sons all went off on pilgrimage"—under the old laws, no commoner could leave his hometown, except on religious pilgrimage—"and never came home."

Yukako gave me a meaningful look. "You see? O-Chio never could stand her: *I have my grandfather Toshio's eyes,*" she mocked. "*Little Hazu has my grandfather Toshio's chin.* Of course we weren't going to take that woman's child." She shook her head, and I winced when she chuckled. "Really, we kept putting the woman off, but it became awkward. You came along just in time."

Yukako poured me some tea, and I hurried to return the favor. "Poor cuckolded Grandfather Toshio," she concluded with a sigh. "And poor o-Fujie, really," she reflected, in an expansive moment. "So you can see why those two would be heading up the mob to get the foreigner out, to cover up their own bad blood."

It was hard to hear her talk this way. "Did you ever think I might be an *eta* when you found me?"

"Don't be ridiculous. I mean, the thing about them is that they look just like Japanese." They were, in fact, Japanese: they weren't shunned until Buddhism came to Japan. "But they weren't allowed to marry out until Meiji, so they really all look like each other. And you look nothing like them. So."

I looked over at Aki daydreaming in the doorway, tray in hand. Ashamed, I quietly repeated what Hazu had said about the foreigner's whore.

Yukako lowered her voice to match mine. "When I found you, you looked so much like a little foreign thing, a little stray cat from the spirit world. I never thought you were Japanese, though with time and training you seemed more and more like a human being. I know it must have been hard for you. I know the other servants must have thought you were half water-child," she said, meaning a miscarriage, "or maybe half sheep." My eyes widened again, to hear her use the slang word for women willing to sleep with foreigners: I'd never heard her say *sheep*, either.

"Even daughters-kept-in-boxes have ears," she said, with a self-mocking smile. "But whatever the others thought, they couldn't have thought you were an *eta*," she consoled, "because no one would issue an *eta* a license for prostitution. Even if there *were* those who consorted with foreign sailors who didn't know any better, no *eta* would have been allowed to travel far enough to leave a child in Miyako. No *eta* would have been able to afford those foreign clothes. You see? No one could have thought that about you."

I felt so soft with gratitude for all the attention at last, and yet Yukako's words were small red bites under my skin. It upset me to hear her working so hard to make this clear. "Thank you," I mumbled, uncomfortable.

"*Sa*," she said pensively. "I don't think it's appropriate for you to bathe with the students, so why don't you bathe with me?"

"Excuse me?"

"I wouldn't want to deal with what their parents would say."

"What *would* their parents say?" I pressed, still itchy from what she'd said.

"Well, I don't know," hemmed Yukako, hearing the accusation in my voice. "But very possibly they'd feel the way the others at the bath-house do."

"Is this why you don't take me on errands anymore?" I asked, scratching for blood.

"Is *that* what you're upset about?" Yukako asked. "Ura-*bo*, what's gotten into you?" She cupped my face as if I were a child again, and I looked away, embarrassed, not wanting Aki to see, or see how much it meant to me. Fortunately, the girl in the doorway looked half-asleep, her tray dipping in her drooped arms. "Don't you see, I've been doing the most difficult work a mother can do?"

"Sorry?" What was she talking about?

"What do you think I've been doing, spending all this time with these frothy young things? I've been choosing wives for my sons."

What? Those boys? In all my moping, the thought had never crossed my mind. "Really?"

"Of course!" Yukako laughed out loud. "Any daughter-in-law of mine will just have to put up with an unexpected bathmate. She'll have no choice," she assured me. I felt a little hurt to hear her say *put up with*, and a little left behind as her demeanor changed. She stretched, her long trunk expanding with confidence. The soft windy flute of our nights together in her dark room had fallen away, replaced by drummers, bright and proud. "Why, tomorrow I'll have this letter carried to Great Teacher," she said, meaning Jiro. I wondered if Yukako used his title as often as she did in order to get around saying *my husband*, a phrase that really meant *my master*. "Once I get his approval, I'll have go-betweens request Sightings."

"Wives?" I blinked.

"Well, Sono's a dream come true, no? Good family. Excellently positioned in Tokyo. Supports the arts, and lavishly. Great Teacher never cottoned to the idea of the railroad, but I'm sure he'd like having access to the man's collection." It took me a moment to realize that Yukako was evaluating Tsuko Sono's father as a potential in-law. "Sono really jumped at the chance to send his daughter here, so it isn't crazy to hope he'll accept. Besides, his son just married that *geiko*. Even Sumie was angling for that boy for her youngest, but everyone's disappointed now. We look very good indeed." How strange, that Sumie's baby—the one the *geisha* house had once offered to buy—should grow up to be passed over for a *geisha*.

"As for the girl, she's smart but accommodating. Gracious, hardworking, wants to be liked. Nice clean *temae*, learns quickly. She's so eager to start working in the girls' schools, it's touching. And she's pretty enough that Master Teacher won't be mad at me," Yukako added with a knowing smile. As she paused, thinking, she drummed her fingers on the rim of her teacup and I refilled it. "I know, I know, on the other hand some will say I'm burning my bridges, not taking Kato's girl," she mused, pouring tea for me in return. "I mean, that's the obvious alliance. But she could do the family a lot of damage as the Master Teacher's wife. And while Kato can help us in Kyoto, we need roots in Tokyo too." She nodded in the direction Tsuko had left.

"So, what I did was make sure a little breath of gossip made its way to Kato about Miss Mariko's drinking, so he'll know what I've had to cope with here and be grateful I'm taking her at all. It'll be fine if she marries Kenji instead."

I had only a moment to marvel at Yukako's confidence—was Jiro so dependent on her money that he'd take Kato for an in-law?—before a tray clattered to the floor. Aki seemed to shake herself awake and bowed deeply, embarrassed. "Go take your bath, Miss Aki," soothed Yukako. "And get some sleep. I have Miss Ura here; no need to stay up on my account."

I sat up with Yukako as she wrote to Jiro, then followed her to the family bathhouse. In all our years together, I had never seen her wash herself. In place of my bran bag she had a cake of Western soap from Kobe, and used a set of seven washing towels that varied in width and texture for the different expanses of her skin. Quickly and thoroughly, she attended to each limb just once, flicked a few dippers of cold water across it, and moved on. I was still scrubbing when she sank into the hot bath, her face loosening with pleasure.

Her nakedness rendered her unfamiliar to me. When I joined her, I realized I had never seen the way her hair wisped up in the steam, the way her small breasts lifted in the water. The things she'd said still grated at me. Suddenly my foreignness made me something for a daughter-in-law to *put up with*. Wasn't I more important to her than some daughter-in-law she wasn't even related to yet? I fished a crumb of *macaron* out of my cheek and tasted meringue. It seemed extraordinary to me that I had ever tasted this before, that I had ever lived anywhere but here. Was I even really a foreigner? Did I ever eat meringues with strawberries, some long-ago June? I saw a pair of hands and an eggbeater, my mother's small sallow fingers against the glossy white peaks. I could not see her face.

The hot water did its slow work. Yukako's body glowed in the dark bath like the moon-lamps of the shrine. Her beauty and her kindness confused me. She was right next to me, and yet she seemed to be slipping away, the Yukako I thought I knew. I had not seen it so starkly before, that if I had been born *eta*, I would not have been permitted to share this bath with her. I felt as if I were balancing a teacup on the back of my hand, sitting gingerly beside this woman. "Thank you," I said quietly.

"*Iie,*" she said, smiling. *Think nothing of it.*

30

1891

SINCE OKUSAMA'S MOVE to the dormitory, my morning tasks had shifted accordingly. Stealing between the two rows of sleeping girls, I now brought Yukako her breakfast in the sewing house, where she slept upstairs behind her screen. After a first cup of tea, Yukako would rise, dress for the day, and eat while I opened the shutters. While I folded Yukako's screen and *futon* and wiped down her side of the floor, the girls would wake and groan, stack their bedding, wipe their *tatami*, and dress silently under *Sensei*'s watchful eye. Then they'd file down to breakfast, Yukako following behind a minute or so later while I brought her dishes to Kuga.

The morning after I prayed at the shrine, Aki followed me to the sewing house. "You're up early," I said.

"You didn't hear him, either?" Aki drowsily brandished a packet for Yukako. "That messenger woke me up," she groused. "I hope nothing bad happened."

After I woke *Okusama* with her first tea, Aki gave her the little package, stamped with a familiar seal. "I'm sorry, the man said to give you this in person as soon as possible," she said.

Yukako rubbed her eyes and looked at the seal. "Great Teacher," she murmured. We all looked at one another, alarmed. Why was Jiro sending a message so early? "Kenji!" Yukako fretted aloud, all but ripping the paper. Inside was a small bag of coins and a letter; as she read, Yukako's worry faded into annoyed amusement. "He needs his *jar of water from Upper Kamo Shrine, properly transported,* as soon as possible." He'd included a sketch of where to find the jar in the fireproof tower, and money for the *jinrikisha.*

She sighed with exasperation. "He must have some surprise guest he needs to impress. Well, this *can* wait until after I've eaten, and then we'll go to the tower together. Miss Aki, we'll need a young maid to handle the sacred water; why don't you bring it? And you can take my letter to Great Teacher as well. We'll get these boys married faster than I thought."

Aki chirped assent and let Yukako tuck the money into her sleeve. A younger girl, I realized, would have gone giddy over the *jinrikisha* ride, would have preened a little over having been chosen to carry the sacred water. Aki's mien, however, was not that of a child facing a special outing but of an adult pausing over a small, pleasant task, like choosing flowers in a shop. She bowed crisply to go, a grown woman facing the day.

Yukako nodded and took a last rueful look at the letter, her expression more indulgent of Jiro than it had ever been when they lived together. "He always had such lovely handwriting."

WITH THE END of the long rains of June had come the heat of true summer, and a shift in the everyday household drink from hot green tea in iron pots to barley tea in ceramic jugs, kept cold in the kitchen well. All that day I ferried cold tea to Nao as he began work in Baishian. Yukako was clearly anxious about the visit from Tokyo: she had set him to work in the teahouse before he'd even finished glassing the upstairs room. All day, as I set each cold full flask down in place of the one that Nao had emptied, I tried not to hate him. All day he steamed the paper off the doors in patient sheets, working tenderly at the excess glue with a soft damp cloth: I tried not to like him, either.

Later, as I helped Kuga chop the dinner greens, a runner came from Sesshu-ji, just before Yukako and Tai left for a full moon tea event. I found *Okusama* waiting in the garden study, *shoji* doors thrown open to the long evening light. "Excellent," she said, reading Jiro's letter. "He's not happy, of course, but I knew he'd be no trouble. I've started speaking to the go-betweens; we can have them send out the Sighting requests tonight. And Kenji's coming to visit, no?" She raised her eyebrows and I realized that had she lived a generation before, that sly, emphatic gesture might have been lost on a face with shaved brows. "He probably wants to get another look at Miss Kato for himself. Well, at least she's pretty."

"Have you told Master Teacher about your choice?" I wondered aloud.

"I'm looking forward to the *jinrikisha* ride tonight," she said. A hesitant look came over her, and we both remembered a day in the northern *geisha* quarter, a hard blow to the face. "I think they might even be happy together," she said softly.

Before I could ask another question, Tai loped in, a cloth-wrapped gift box dangling from either hand. "Mother, the cart's here."

When I went back to the kitchen, Kuga set me to snapping the ends off a bowlful of long beans. "Did *Okusama*'s letter say anything about Aki?" she asked. "Is she coming home tonight or tomorrow?"

THE NEXT MORNING, while the students were in their lessons, I was startled by the loud clamor of wooden sandals and grunting porters halting just outside our gate. I set down Nao's cold tea and went to look: four men were setting down a wooden palanquin the likes of which I hadn't seen in years. They were led by a *jinrikisha* from which a woman younger than myself, but much faded, scrambled down and minced toward the front gate. Pudgy in her fawn-dappled *kimono* and rich brocade *obi*, she seemed familiar; who was she? I bowed and looked at her kind round face, her tired pretty mouth, the high wispy pouf of her deep-eaves bun, the cross dangling from her neck: it was Mariko's mother, Lady Kato. "Good morning," I said humbly. "Miss Mariko's in her lesson now; should I get her?"

"I'd like to speak with your *Okusama*," she said. I remembered her as a new bride with the first Western woman's coiffure in town, telling Yukako, in a piping little whisper, that her husband wouldn't let her touch his tea utensils. Her voice had dropped an octave.

"I'm afraid she's teaching right now. But if it's an emergency . . ." I trailed off, which in Kyoto meant *There's no way you can see her now.*

"I think you should go find her," she said. I went.

I SERVED YUKAKO and her guest *sembei* crackers and cold barley tea, almost bludgeoning young Jade when she offered to do it instead, I was so eager to hear what had happened. From her tone of voice, Lady Kato was obviously not just dropping by to thank Yukako for the Sighting request. And what had her bearers brought, or whom?

Lady Kato complimented the *sembei* without eating any, and then said, "*Sensei*, my lord is in Osaka and I am left to deal with this matter on my own."

"I hope the go-between gave you no reason to think this couldn't wait until Advisor Kato came back." Lady Kato was silent. "I hope he takes all the time he needs to consider my request, but if he tells the go-between he's not interested, I fully respect his decision. I only hope the friendship between our families remains as warm as ever." Yukako's voice was cordial, with just a hint of anxiety. Why was this woman here? If they already had another boy in mind, why not simply tell the go-between? And if not, why not wait until Kato came home? And the palanquin?

"I see," said Lady Kato. "There is another matter."

"Yes?"

Mariko's mother spoke, at first as prim and formal as the knot of her brown-and-gold *obi*. "My lord's parents and I received your request yesterday evening and we were very flattered. It was in fact Mariko's first offer, and we were doubly happy that it came from your house. Under ordinary circumstances, when my lord came home, I think I can say with confidence that we would have given it our most serious and warm consideration." She paused. "As of this morning, however, I have reason to believe that the marriage would not be a happy one."

This was what I'd wanted to ask Yukako the night before, when she'd said she thought Tai and Tsuko might be happy together: the back of my neck prickled with foreboding. "What are you saying?" Yukako asked.

Lady Kato's accusation swelled her voice in its banks. "I should have known you had no idea where your child was."

Yukako, though she did not know why, knew she was being attacked. "Kenji's father wants him by his side in his retirement," she said hotly. "Who am I to oppose him?"

"Your son is not by his father's side. This morning he was by the side of a young girl whom he evidently prefers to my daughter."

Aki! I thought, and I could tell the same thought occurred to Yukako. Of course: all those reading lessons! Why hadn't I seen it before? Yukako's face went hard with anger. How boorish, how utterly unnecessary, of her son to allow himself to be discovered at his fun. Had he learned nothing from his father? "Is that so?" she asked, with suppressed emotion.

"Indeed," Lady Kato replied dryly. "Usually one tries to overlook such attachments. But——" Her voice broke here, and she sounded, for a half second, vulnerable and frail.

"Yes?" Yukako said.

"When we found them, the children had tied themselves together and tried to drown themselves in the garden. I believe they were trying to tell us something."

KENJI CAME TO US with a broken leg. Aki remained at the Kato home, unconscious. By the end of the day, her father had packed up his glass and vanished, the Baishian windows left gaping wide. After Yukako went to sleep that night in the sewing house room, I slipped away from the other servants by the kitchen and went to the shrine again. I blamed myself. They said Aki's face was like a broken plum.

BY THE END of the week, a letter came from the go-between for Baron Sono, to say His Lordship was delighted by our offer, and was prepared to send, with Tsuko's bridal goods, both a chest of gold *koban* and a selection of antique tea utensils Jiro was known to admire. Also by the end of the week we learned that Aki was neither unconscious nor at the Katos': she was missing.

WHEN I WAS A CHILD I carried secret gifts of food to an invalid who repaid them with poems. Yukako's betrothed had seemed like such a grown man to me; I remember being impressed by his carving, by the cold curved shimmer of his longsword. As an adult, visiting Kenji in that same annex, it occurred to me that Akio must have been just as bored and sullen as Kenji was now. "I can't talk to her," he complained after lying silent when Yukako came to see him. "Because if I say anything, I'll have to say I'm sorry, and I'm not sorry. I'm only sorry we failed. I'm only sorry I can't just get up and find her. Have you had any news?"

"O-Kuga went to the Katos' to collect her and they said she'd already left. That's all I know."

"They didn't have any ideas? Any guesses? Anything she might have said?"

"I wasn't there. I don't know."

"Obasan." Most young people called me Aunt, but from Yukako's son, the word made me wish she still called me her sister. "Aunt, I think if *you* asked them you'd find out where she went."

"Me?"

"You watch things, you hear things. You'd hear more."

"Do you think they know and they aren't telling? Why would they do that?"

"See what I mean? Just now, o-Kuga would have said 'Yes, Master' or 'Well, Master, I don't know . . .'" I resisted a laugh. "You know what I mean. I'm sure she went and said, 'I'm here for Miss Aki,' and they said, 'She isn't here,' and she said, 'Is that so,' and turned around and walked home."

"Don't be mean."

"You know it's true."

"Her husband divorced her. He sold her son. I don't think she was always like that."

"Just, please. Mother asked me to come apologize with her today when she goes to see Advisor Kato. Can't you go with her and ask them?"

"'Well, Master, I don't know,'" I said, both joking and earnest. I *would* be the obvious choice of attendant, to avoid student gossip. But could I help him? I saw again the utter devastation on Yukako's face when Kenji was brought home. She'd sat on her bathing stool that night with her arms wrapped around her, staring at the floor, a forgotten washcloth drooping from a slack hand. *He won't even look at me,* she'd said.

"Is there anything I could give you?" the young man pleaded. "Is there anything I could do?"

The raw need in his voice called forth another day: Kenji with a Western book satchel, walking up the street toward us from Sesshu-ji. I bowed in welcome and his beautiful festival-boy face shone gold in the late sun. *I have a new book for Aki-bo!* he'd announced.

"You were so in love with her," I said, using the English words, *in rabu.* "It was right in front of us and we never even noticed."

"I didn't, either, at first," he said. In the porous, tender silence that followed, I wondered if he was about to tell me the whole story. He cleared his throat. "Please, would you go talk to them?"

"I'll do it for a reading lesson," I said, surprising myself.

Kenji looked uncomfortable. I could feel him looking at my bulbous body, my dropped-on-the-head-as-a-baby face, my first white strands of hair, discovered just these past few days in the stronger light of Yukako's bath. *"Aki wa . . ."* he said, explaining why he did not desire me. He meant both the girl's name and the autumn season, *aki,* which my age no doubt called to mind.

"That's not what I meant," I said irritably. "I just know it's the best thing you have to give, and so that's what I want."

"I knew you were the right person to ask," he said, impressed.

I saw his hope and anxiety, and felt guilty for helping him. "Do you have any idea how much you hurt your mother?" I said. Kenji turned away. That very morning at her tea she'd asked me, *Has Kenji eaten yet? Should I bring him his breakfast?* She'd caught herself and inhaled. *I'm not going to lose my head over this. I'll visit him once a day, and when he's ready to apologize, he'll talk.*

Kenji mumbled something. "We didn't do it for her."

"What?"

"Jump like that," he said, his back to me. And what he said next dislodged something inside me, like a coracle stuck in sand, some not-yet-shaped thought that lifted up in me unmoored: "We did it for each other."

THE MAN WAS VERY HANDSOME. His hair was parted on the side and cut just above his ears, shiny as a crow's wing. He had a finger's-width moustache, a trim goatee, a strong L-shaped jaw. The woman was fresh and young, slightly cross-eyed. The man wore scrub-brush epaulets of gold braid; a ball gown exposed the woman's lovely shoulders. In their hand-tinted pastel finery, they both looked straight at the camera with the wary, challenging gaze of those who have steeled themselves to be photographed well. "Why do those people look familiar?" I asked Yukako as we waited.

"Don't you recognize Their Majesties?" boomed Kato's voice. I jumped and glanced again. Who else's photograph would he hang in the entrance? Yukako gave me a pained look and began bowing to Advisor Kato, adding my ignorance to the staggering debt she had to account for.

"The house is built and ready for the Minister's visit this fall," Kato announced with savage politeness, reminding Yukako of her relative lack of clout. "Why don't you come take a tour?"

Yukako nervously accepted, and I followed some steps behind, as she had not yet given him the gift I carried.

"I hear my glazier's done nice work in your home," said Advisor Kato, digging the knife in a little more.

We had no idea where Nao was. "Why don't you come to tea in Baishian?" said Yukako, her voice brave. "I'm having him leave all the windows uncovered this season. It's a once-in-a-lifetime chance: the fireflies coming in through the empty lattices."

"It sounds like an opportunity not to be missed," said Kato, in a way that expressed no interest.

I remembered Sumie living in this house long before Kato bought it. Approaching the moon-viewing pond where I'd once fed carp, Kato and Yukako swerved away from it toward the newly built house. "You know, in consideration of who her father was, I had the girl nursed back to health. I offered her a job with my wife's family, the chance to support herself in a Christian environment—surely, no man will marry her now—and this is how she shows her gratitude." At this, Kato clenched his pocket watch.

"I offer my most abject apology for everything that has happened," said Yukako, in a tone that indicated she was prepared to say it many times.

The new guesthouse, generous and graceful, boasted a handsome glass-windowed Western wing and a tiny French garden, symmetrical and opulent. There was a Japanese wing as well, with a round paper window opening onto a little dell of raked gravel and stone.

After they withdrew to speak in private, I went back to the pond, out along the narrow platform to the moon-viewing gazebo. I tried to see past the luscious coolness of the water, past the shimmer of the carps' orange bodies, into the minds of the children who jumped. The platform had been built a good few feet above the pond, to offer a view of the eastern mountains. A long ornamental bamboo fishing rod leaned against the railing. I looked behind me to see if anyone was watching, then lowered it in: the dark, mysterious water was quite shallow, actually, its unseen floor jagged with rocks. I knew, then, how Aki and Kenji had been so badly injured. *What a thing to discover on the way down,* I thought.

When a servant brought me tea in the cloakroom, I asked if she knew anything about the girl they had found in the pond. There was no way not to ask it rudely: she gave me a hard look and a shrug for my pains. "She left," she said.

. . .

I FOLLOWED the soft flat knot of Yukako's *obi* home. She had dressed penitently: her *kimono* was a pattern of tight gray and white stripes; her *obi* a green so dark it looked black except in sunlight, with a scattering of green-on-green carp that quietly but emphatically announced her shame. Just so, Kuga—in Nao's absence—had gone that week in her very best *kimono* to the gardeners' hut where Toru lived with his grandfather, to kneel with her head almost touching the ground. I know this because she had me and the other sewing-girls follow behind her, each of us holding a vessel of *sake* to offer in apology. "Aw, it's all right," said Aki's betrothed uncomfortably while his grandfather knelt in the doorway, silently accepting Kuga's gifts. "Really, if you don't mind me staying on to do the charcoal, I don't have any complaints. Wasn't meant to be, that's all."

Kuga said neither yes nor no, but kept her head bent low. The job, the only thing of value her family had to bring to a marriage, was supposed to go to Aki's husband. She was loath to compromise Aki's prospects, but on the other hand, how much more was she going to put herself out for her brother's selfish girl? "Maybe there's a widower who won't mind her," I'd heard her mumbling to herself. "Maybe there's a blind man." I knew she hated parting with that much *sake*.

Toru continued to talk nervously as we knelt with our gifts. "I mean, I'd been kind of hoping to maybe get out of charcoal and learn some more about glass, but it seems like you'd have to move around a lot, and my grandfather's not so young. Charcoal's fine. It's good."

With those words, louder than Mariko upsetting her breakfast *miso*, louder than Tai's glum visit to the Baishian worksite, louder than Kuga grimly scrubbing out her cottage, louder even than Yukako's bright lies, Toru expressed the love they all felt for Nao, and their betrayal at his having left them.

. . .

Yukako paused at the Canal Street bridge and watched the bright water, shallow before Kato's Biwa Canal had begun to flow, deep now. The hydrangeas were in flower, a robust blue squadron. "Well, that's over. He made it as uncomfortable for me as he could without using his claws," said Yukako. "I can't say this hasn't spoiled my prospects with the Minister this fall, but I'm glad he was civil."

"Toru's grandfather was gracious too," I volunteered, telling her about Kuga's apology.

"Poor Toru," said Yukako. "You have to admire Kenji, that business with the sacred water."

"What?"

"A forgery. I'm sure they did it so that as soon as Aki got her first period, she could run away to Sesshu-ji instead of having to marry that boy."

"A forgery?"

"Of course I was fooled. He really has his father's gift with the brush, doesn't he? But I should have known when I saw the *jinrikisha* money. That man never paid for a thing in his life."

"Wait, what do you mean?"

"Remember, the night before Aki gave us the note from that 'messenger' no one else saw? She stayed home from the bath with a bellyache."

"Oh," I said.

She sighed. "If he had just *asked,* I would have happily sent her off to go work someplace near Sesshu-ji. I'm sure Great Teacher would have helped find her something. She could even go now, if the boy still wants her."

And then that beached coracle—that thing that had begun to lift inside me when I spoke with Kenji—began to rise again. *We did it for each other,* he'd told me. "You know, if you apologized to Kenji for not thinking of his happiness, he'd probably talk to you. You could just let them marry."

Yukako's laughter was stunned and bitter. "Kenji's *happiness*! Of course! I could have saved myself the trouble of getting tea in the schools, training teachers, bringing all those *setto* to court. Quick, Matchmaker, tell Toru he'll have to find another job. Kenji can be our new charcoal man, and everyone's *happy*."

"Sorry," I said, hurt. "It's just, what you said about Tai and Tsuko, that they might be happy together . . ."

Calmer, Yukako looked at me contritely. "That was rude of me." She looked down into the canal. "I wasn't thinking of both boys," she reflected, herself a woman who had not married for happiness. "I was thinking of the Shin house."

Leaning on the bridge railing, she watched a leaf dance by on the water. "It's bitter medicine," she concluded. "I'd have to think long and hard before I drank." I felt a poised wariness I remembered from the night she first let me share her bath, as if I were holding my breath, as if I were balancing a cup of tea on the back of my hand.

Yukako clapped to brush the dust off her hands and led on. I clopped along behind her, relieved to have some small thing I could tell Kenji, since our visit to Advisor Kato had yielded nothing. Everyone had their idea of what to do with Aki, if they found her. Yukako's plan to send her to Sesshu-ji, Kuga's blind widower, Kato's Christian home. I stopped.

Yukako kept walking, and I ran to keep up. "Excuse me for not coming in," I said when we reached the Shin gate. "O-Kuga asked me to stop at the market."

"DID THE CHILD tell you she was here?"

My head snapped up. Standing in the front office where a young British secretary had asked me, in halting Japanese, to wait, I'd been gazing absently at two letters on a tall Western table. They were spread wide with paperweights, and in my boredom I'd begun making them out. One was from a carpenter, one from a student's father. Their calligraphies, though wildly different from one another, were clear, even if their statements were vague. The carpenter wrote in *kana* only, while the gentleman had added smaller, explanatory *kana* to show the reading of rarely used *kanji*. I had just worked through the second letter, and was wondering why anyone would leave this sort of thing in plain sight, when an American woman's voice jerked me back to the present: this Western wood office smelling of lemon oil, these English words—*Did the child tell you she was here?* I felt dirty standing inside in my shoes.

"No, I just wondered," I said in my creaky English. She did not look surprised that I spoke her language. "We see your students every day, walking up the street."

"She was certainly quick enough to be one of our students," the American woman said. "My teachers said she read well in Japanese. But we're not running that kind of school; we don't have the funds. We've found that families who are ready to pay for the kind of education we offer are also the ones best suited to launch their girls into environments where that education will make the biggest difference."

My head swam, my neck ached from tilting my head back to see the tall woman's face. So this was Alice Starkweather, with her steel sausage-curls. I could barely keep up with the English she was using. "She came here?"

"In America this would never happen." Miss Starkweather sat down at the desk and left me standing in my servant's indigo *kimono* and wooden sandals. Myself excepted, I had not seen a white woman up close in years. Her nose seemed waxy, powdery, misshapen; her mouth was crinkly with fine lines. I was uncomfortably aware of her blood: the capillaries in her eyes, the blue veins in her hands. "But here in Kyoto," she continued, "there are so few of us, we're learning more about the true meaning of Christianity. I drew her a map and sent her to Mother Margaret."

"Who?"

"Papists! Would you believe it? But the girl wanted to make a life in Christ, so who am I to stop her?"

"Nuns?"

"They're a nursing order. I know they have money for fitting up fallen women for hospital work."

"Excuse me, it's rude, but if it pleases you to draw me a map as well?"

She made me repeat myself, this woman in formidable bodice and glove-tight sleeves. "Your accent is shocking," she laughed.

I blinked at her. Who was *she*, to live in Japan all these years and speak to me in English? "I recommend you fold up your letters," I said coldly, enunciating as carefully as possible. Why, any Japanese person could just walk in and see that the floors were in disrepair and well-known men were pulling their daughters out of school mid-semester.

"Our translator's away, you know; these are waiting for the substitute," she said, as if I'd spoken without insult.

"I see," I said. So she had never learned to read Japanese, nor had she hired a secretary who could. I read each sentence aloud in Japanese, then repeated it in English, very carefully, willing the child I'd been so many years before to rise up, to speak clearly, to talk back to the Irish girls, to tell that nun my mother was more than two arms and a mop. "I'm sure you understand that more tuition will not be forthcoming," I said, proud and angry.

"Why, thank you," she said, impressed. She scrutinized me, this not-so-young woman in pagan rags. *Half a savage,* I could feel her thinking, and then she nodded as if she'd figured me out. "Are you a Eurasian, then?" she asked.

"I'll be going now," I said.

"Excuse me, but our translator, you know——"

What was she going to do next, trot out the foreign sailor and the Kobe whore? I was so angry I could barely hear her. I bowed crisply and turned away. "Pardon my rudeness," I said, by which I meant good-bye.

I had misunderstood. "Whatever the Catholics offer, we can do better," she called out to my back.

I paused, blushing with sudden power, and left.

When I first arrived in Miyako, I had not spent even one night in our new house before it was lost to fire. In its place stood one brick house among many, a place—like the church across the way—I'd never seen, and yet a certain angled light stood my hair on end. I glanced up the street, but I saw a French tailor shop where I expected a red *torii* gate. I heard a startle of bells and saw a clot of old white monks cross the slate church walk in rapt discussion. They looked like bald toads.

I found the convent on the far side of the church block. A Japanese sister asked me to wait by the gate: she had not completely lost the coy, baroque language of the floating world. I remembered the silence of the Pontocho *geisha* quarter after the Emperor left Miyako, and I imagined more than a few of its flowers and willows would have welcomed rescue.

Aki came to the gate holding a pair of butterfly-handled shears, as if she'd been called from gardening and at any moment expected to go back. She wore the rough indigo coat and trousers of a farmwife, with a tea picker's pointed straw hat, but where a farmer might have used just a wisp of mosquito netting to veil his face, a thicker gauze hid hers, like the curtains of a shrine. I felt so deeply ashamed.

"I came because it was you, Aunt." she said.

Because I *had* been an aunt to her, of sorts, the word drove my guilt in deeper. I had prayed for something to happen—anything to make Nao leave—and here it was in front of me, veiled Consequence. "He would have come himself," I said. "His leg is broken; he can't get out of bed."

She did not seem to respond to what I'd said. Instead she asked, "Would you do something for me?" At this I leaned closer, almost touching the barred gate. "I want to stay and train to be a nurse," she said. "If you're a novice, you can stay for three years and then decide if you want to stay for life. In three years I could learn how to do something besides sew and clean. I could go anywhere. You get books, Aunt, and you get to learn the foreign names of body parts and medicines, see?" She tapped different parts of her arm and shoulder while reeling off words that sounded like the Church Latin I'd heard as a child.

Hearing that voice, so very much hers, I felt outrageous hope well up in me. I reached through the gate to the hand that held the shears. "Miss Aki, you're both alive. You could marry him. You could elope."

She took a step back from me, turning away. This wasn't what I'd meant to do. I'd meant to come and listen contritely, to offer any help she wanted, to subtly feel out what Kenji could hope for. "Please! Wait—" I said. As she turned, warily, toward me again, I noticed something. She seemed a shade less painfully thin than she had at home, like the difference between the first and the second day of a crescent moon. A thought struck me: "You've been eating this week, haven't you?" I kept my voice tender and coaxing. "You stopped so you wouldn't get your monthlies?"

"They just started yesterday," she whispered, about to bolt. "Please—"

"Shh," I said. Deliberately changing my tack, I assured her, "Even if you can't stay here, no one's going to marry you off the day you leave." She drew closer as I told her about Toru. "So you could still—" Instead of *marry Kenji*, I said, "—come back if you wanted, right?"

Aki coughed a little laugh and pressed on with her suit. "Listen, they said usually your parents have to pay a dowry if you join a convent, but at this one, they pay for some of the girls themselves. They say they'll let me stay for a little while, and they'll ask their mothers in Rome if I can become a novice. Sister Theresa says I shouldn't, because they need to spend their money on *truly* fallen women, not girls like me. But even *she* said if I had a dowry, they'd let me in right away. They wrote this for me." She reached deep into the sleeve of the *kimono* she was wearing under her gardener's coat and handed me a letter written in English and Japanese. I had spent a lifetime running from nuns, and here was Aki, running *to* them. "Do you think you could ask my father for me? Or maybe *Okusama*?"

I tucked the letter away and stared at the veiled young woman behind the gate, this tea plucker, this beekeeper. I had lived beside her and never known her. "I will if you tell me what happened."

She folded her arms. "What do you want to know?" she said, her voice hard.

I sat down on a bench, no doubt for visiting family, positioned across from another behind the convent gate. "Why don't you come tell me what happened after you got into the *jinrikisha* with the Kamo Shrine water? Was it really sacred water, by the way? Or did Kenji just put any old water in the storeroom tower?" We'd followed the map with ease and found, as instructed, a bentwood jar festooned like a Shinto shrine with paper zigzags and straw rope.

"I have to go," she said.

"I can try to get you the money, or I can tell Kenji where you are, and once he's mended, you know he'll come here every day until they make you leave. It's up to you." Not seeing her face—and my anger at her for nearly killing herself—made me feel bossy. "Why not sit down?"

She sat down. She said nothing for a moment, then began. "I took the *jinrikisha* and I brought the letters, and then he asked me to wait for him at the shrine while he talked to his father. He told Great Teacher he was going to visit home and take another look at Miss Mariko for himself."

Aki paused, then spoke again, her voice deeper. "The shrine was up on a hill, and there was nobody around except for the hawks flying. It was so beautiful up there. Do you remember? We stopped there on the way home from Sesshu-ji a long time ago, when I was a little girl. I remember the wind, the pines, the far-off hills so blue, like another color of sky. I felt—something different. Like except for *him*, nobody in the world knew where I was, and I liked that. I saw two hawks flying in circles; their wings were gold. *That's the two of us*, I thought, *flying above the world.* My heart felt so big inside me. I shouted and I flapped my arms." She giggled a little, a girlish sound dimmed with regret. "And then I saw a hawk flying all alone."

She hesitated and began again on a different tack. "When I was little he once gave me a pair of emperor and empress dolls for Girls' Day, and in my mind I always thought those dolls were us. I never said anything. But then, when I was older, when he first—when we first—well, *he* said he'd thought they were us too."

She turned away as if she had forgotten that I couldn't see her face behind the veil. "But here I was alone in secret," she said, "and there he was lying to his father about Miss Mariko. Suddenly I felt so small. Like once I walked out the *torii* gate, this would be my life from now on, waiting and secrets. I watched that hawk all alone in the air until he came to me."

I was surprised that Aki was so forthright when she continued: "There was a veranda where you could bring a picnic, off past the shrine. He brought food and mosquito netting and we stayed there all night on the hillside. We never spent a whole night together before." Her voice was soft and open, and she said half a line from an old poem: "While we lay there, *in our overlapping clothes,* the moon rose over the trees. We looked at each other. We were both thinking about Mariko Kato, and that moon-viewing pond."

I was awed by the certainty of the voice, just inches from me, that knew what its lover was thinking. "He said he'd rather die in my arms in that pond than visit it as a son-in-law. When I heard that, I felt so big and so small at the same time, and I said, 'Prove it.'" Her voice was forceful and clear.

"You know the rest," she said. "We filled our sleeves with rocks." She reached up and lifted the gauze in front of her face, and I willed myself not to recoil.

Her right cheek was a thick ring of greenish scab, the center of which, including much of her closed eye, looked like raw meat. I shuddered, remembering that shallow, murky water, those sharp stones. "You lost your eye," I whispered.

"Maybe, I don't know. I haven't been able to open it yet, but it's already better."

I made myself continue to look, carefully and tenderly, at what I had been trusted to see. The outside of the scab was crusty and white with repairing skin, and the whole right side of her face was heavily bruised. The left side of her precious face was unbroken but darkly bruised as well, in a pattern like clouds. Or a man's hand.

"What happened?" I breathed, spreading my own hand over my own cheek. "He did that?"

I could barely hear her for a second, as she said yes. Then she spoke louder, pushing me away a little. "When we were tied together in the water. It was an accident," she said, shrugging.

We were both quiet for a moment. "I didn't know how much the body wants to live and breathe," she said, "but it does. His did. More than it wanted to die, or love. Mine too." She lowered the gauze as she said this, so I could not see the expression on her face. "I know in my heart it was an accident," she said in a voice both pitiless and forgiving. "But it was a lesson too."

KENJI WOULD HAVE WANTED me to come straightaway, but my head was full of hawks and shrines and hand-shaped bruises. I told Yukako first.

"How much does she want?" she asked, opening the letter from the nuns. I remembered that morning on the Canal Street bridge, the way I felt like I was holding my breath as I watched her contemplate a marriage between Aki and her son. How still she had stood then, as if pausing at a closed door. How quickly she read now, signaling with a fingertip for more tea. I poured. She looked up. "Done."

Had I ever seen her spend money so fast? I felt, inside my happiness for Aki, a jab of disappointment, enough to knock the held breath clean out of me. Before her tea even cooled, Yukako had counted out coins and summoned a *jinrikisha*. "Her father's not here," she sighed sharply. We'd had no news of him all week. "But I can bring Kuga. We'll have them hold the money in trust for Aki until we can get Nao's approval." Kuga was still untying her *kimono* sleeves from their work strings when the *jinrikisha* pulled them away.

As I finished chopping the eggplants and cucumbers left on the block, I felt my stomach go cold over telling Kenji. I washed the rice, I salted the vegetables, I opened the trapdoor in the kitchen floor and gave the pickle tubs their daily stir. I dried lacquer dishes that were already dry. Just as I decided it was better he hear it from me than his mother, I saw a young man standing in the doorway. *He knows,* I thought, dreading his eager eyes and stumping gait. But it was Tai.

Rough where his brother was smooth, quick where his brother was brooding, Master Teacher burst in, sunny and brash. "I thought it might be you. Those look good," he said, helping himself to a dewy slice of cucumber. "Aunt, I wanted to ask something of you." *You too?* I looked at him in disbelief, which he mistook for encouragement. He took something out of the breast of his *kimono*, a white packet tied in red cord. "About Miss Sono . . ." he said.

"Pardon me," I said, scuttling off to the toilet as if I hadn't heard him. I had enough young lovers to worry about. I was touched, though, thinking about the little white package. His elaborately knotted cord not only alluded to the red thread binding two destinies, it was a play on Tsuko's name: *tsuna* meant *rope*; *tsunagu* was *to tie*; *tsunagari* was a relationship. Lucky boy, to like the girl his mother chose for him. Someone else would help him, I was sure. I slipped outside and went to find Kenji.

"I'M FEELING A LITTLE better today," the boy said, smiling in his *futon*. "Look, I walked around some. I brought this down for you." He nodded at a slender book with starry violet binding-knots.

"Lady Shonagon," I murmured. Jiro had shown it to me once, and the Mountain had lent it to me. I never *had* deciphered it. "Your mother read it as a girl."

"*Un*," he said, opening the volume. Layered into the fold of each page was a loose sheet in Kenji's lovely writing, rendered with great clarity, with explanatory characters beside each of his *kanji*. "I did this for Aki," he said. "It was written in the Heian era, almost nine hundred years ago, so these pages," he said, pointing to the printed book, "are written in the old style. And these," he said, pointing to his own sheets, "I rewrote the way people talk now. All her lists. *Adorable things. Depressing things. Things that gain by being painted*," he recited. I shifted my weight from one foot to the other, wishing I'd brought a flask of tea or something so I could just put it down for him and leave. "We only read about half of it together. But maybe someday . . ." he sighed. "So, did you go with Mother to Advisor Kato's?"

What a long, long day I'd had. "Never mind about the reading lesson," I said. And then I told him.

"Oh," he said. He lay there for a long time, utterly silent. And then he drew both whole and broken legs up toward him as if he were wadding all his hopes into a sack. His voice when he spoke was numb. "Could you get that book out of here?"

· · ·

THE FIRST DAY he could walk outside, Kenji was gone for hours. He'd stopped talking to me, beyond a grunt or two when I brought his tray, as had Tai, once his Sighting went without a hitch, no help from me. That evening, when Kenji came home, I saw his slack face taut with resolve. "This is for you," he said. "One of the nuns gave it to me."

"You found her?" I said. I had avoided telling him where Aki was the day I saw her, and he hadn't asked since.

"How many convents are there in Kyoto?" he asked.

"Oh." I opened the note and moved quickly through its careful *kana*. It said, *You already know I thank you. Please thank Okusama too. And tell him he can wait all day if he wants; I'm not coming out.*

AND HE DID. Except on the day of his brother's wedding, Kenji went to the convent every day and sat by the gate. His father sent for him regularly, but the boy did not go back to Sesshu-ji that summer, and Aki did not leave Mother Margaret's. Yukako, perhaps by way of apology, told the go-between to hold off at least until next spring brought its new class of girls. In Tokyo that season, Kato's friend the Minister of Taxation was killed in his *jinrikisha* by an unknown gunman, sparking all kinds of rumors and grandstanding, but after the upset died down, Mariko was engaged, we heard, to the canal engineer, Mr. Tanabe. At her insistence, and to our surprise, her father declared that she was not to marry until she'd taught tea for two years.

THE NIGHT I found Aki, long after Yukako had returned, eaten, and scrubbed, I found I was too awake to bed down in my corner of the room beside the kitchen. I took a lamp and Kenji's book and stole out to Baishian. Without its paper, the teahouse stood forlorn as a mouthful of missing teeth. I lit a mosquito coil and sat quietly in the two-mat room, looking at the night floating in squares around me. I thought about all the people I had seen that day: Yukako on the bridge, Aki at the gate, Kenji with his crumpled hope. The hand-tinted Emperor, Alice Starkweather, the nuns. Those bald-toad monks chattering in French. *Well, Monsieur. That's the natives for you. When in Rome. When in Rome. When in Rome.* My stomach lurched. I knew that voice. It belonged to a man who had once fed me.

I lay on my back, took deep breaths until the dizziness passed, and sat up again. *"Sa,"* I said to myself. *Brother Joaquin never left Kyoto.* Very well. I blinked back a pair of splayed black boots, a burning house, a glinting gold statue. The next time I saw Aki, would she still be Aki, or would she be shriven and wimpled, Lourdes or Agnes or Pauline?

I fingered Shonagon's book, written close to the year 1000. A lady-in-waiting to the Empress, Sei Shonagon kept a notebook in the hollow compartment of her pillow, and so her jottings are known as *The Pillow Book.* I opened it at random: *One is startled by the sound of raindrops; the wind blows against the shutters.* In the same section, I also saw, *One's elegant Chinese mirror has become a little cloudy.* I was glad Kenji had reminded me that Shonagon was a list-maker because the sentences confused me at first. I moved backward and found the title of the list: *Things that make the heart beat faster.*

I added: *The voice of a monk. A hand-shaped bruise. The word* Eurasian. *One learns the shallowness of water where lovers have failed to drown.*

AND I ADDED, though even as I did, I knew the words belonged, not to me, but to an Urako whose mistress had never disappointed her, one whose heart beat faster with desire, and not, as mine did, with wariness:

One's employer enters the bath, her hair loosely piled with ivory combs. She spreads her long, pale arms across the lip of the steaming tub. Her eyelids droop with relief, her slight breasts rise with her deep intake of breath. When her head eases to one side, a lock of hair no thicker than a writing brush dips suddenly into the water.

31

1891

SHONAGON MIGHT INDEED have written the last term in my list, had she been privileged to see her Empress in the bath. She noted every time she was allowed to grind ink for her sovereign, every gift of paper or silk, every time she was chosen to attend Her Majesty in some other woman's place. I recognized, at a pained remove, my own loyalty in hers.

Shonagon's book came just in time for me that summer, as I faced even less time alone with Yukako. Wanting to avoid the long and failed engagement she had herself experienced with Akio, as well as any chance of Baron Sono changing his mind, Yukako pushed to have the wedding as quickly as possible. Before July was out, Tai and Tsuko were ensconced in the privacy of the room above the kitchen where Yukako and I had slept until that spring. Though Tai and his mother continued to share the garden study as an office, I noted that one book at a time, one brush, his things seemed to climb their way upstairs. Yukako continued to sleep just a folding screen away from the girls in the room above the sewing house, and I could count on seeing her alone only when I brought her breakfast. Now that she was family, Tsuko attended *Okusama* on all her outings, and at night they took their baths together while I soaked nearby.

"How did your and Mr. Kenji's visit go with the Katos today?" Tsuko asked in the water, her voice soft and precise. *What visit?* I looked up. I couldn't believe Kenji had finally agreed to go. Perhaps he had accepted his reprieve from the marriage market as the only contrition Yukako was able to offer.

"You know I wanted to try to smooth things over," Yukako said. "And it's good that Advisor Kato accepted our gifts and Kenji's apology. But now he won't even come to tea," she lamented. "I can understand, first the shame on his daughter, then his friend's murder. Poor man. But at this rate I'll never get a crack at the boys' schools." She paused, worried. "At least I'll have this meeting with the Minister to make my case."

Tsuko wrung the hot washcloth over Yukako's exposed shoulders and the older woman sighed with gratitude. "I wonder if we shouldn't set you and Master Teacher up in Tokyo, near Court," Yukako murmured half to herself. "Would you like that?"

"Whatever you think best," Tsuko said diplomatically. *She misses Tokyo,* I thought.

"Wise girl." Yukako laughed a little roughly and closed her eyes for a moment. Would Yukako go with them to Tokyo? Would I be brought along? Perhaps nothing would come of this plan, but it was galling to learn of it in passing, to overhear instead of being told.

Yukako's voice startled me from my thoughts. "What if I were to buy a *jinrikisha* for the Minister's visit?" she reflected. "So in a way, the *temae* could begin when he left Advisor Kato's house?"

I watched Tsuko think, both sparkling and opaque. On her flat pretty features, her hesitation was distinct and self-contained, like a wisp of red fire in an opal. "In Tokyo I've seen a new kind of *jinrikisha*," she said at last. "It has rubber wheels full of air, like——" Yukako looked perplexed. "Like a belly full of water," Tsuko decided. "Or a frog's throat."

Yukako asked a little about the smooth-riding Tokyo *jinrikisha*, and from Tsuko's answers, it occurred to me that her father might have one of his own. I couldn't help but admire her tact.

"Now, imagine leaving Kato's house in *that*," Yukako murmured, a little competitively. "I shouldn't be like this," she said, stopping herself. "The man's mourning his friend. It *would* be better to have him as an ally . . ." But her voice choked off with anger and she gave in. "But he thinks he's climbed past us, that climber!" she fumed. *Noboru-han,* she called him: Mister-Bumpkin-Visiting-the-Capital.

A rejoinder formed on Tsuko's face; she tidied it away as easily as a girl tucking her hair behind her ears.

"He'll always be a hayseed," Yukako said. "You'll never guess what happened. I walked into his office and there was a stack as tall as a man of those imperial photographs. 'One for every classroom in Kyoto,' he told me. Who would think of such a thing? And then he asked if I'd like one for each of the tearooms! Can you imagine?"

"What did you do?"

"I said he was *so* kind to think of us, especially after everything that had happened, and how honored we were to have the opportunity to join the vanguard of schools using the image of Their Majesties to inspire the next generation, and so forth, but I didn't dare make a move without asking Master Teacher. Of course we'll accept: it would be rude not to. But how ridiculous. It makes me wonder if he ever understood the Way of Tea at all. A photo for every tearoom? How inelegant!"

She used the same word Sei Shonagon had nine hundred years before, describing a hayseed of her own acquaintance. As Tsuko nodded and soothed, more gracefully than I'd ever been able to, I wondered if the Heian court lady had ever written of being upstaged in the eyes of her Empress by some young modern thing. Perhaps it was on a page Shonagon had brushed and burned, a list of *inelegant feelings.*

I read on through the sweltering summer, cooled by Shonagon's spare and lovely prose. *Shaved ice with liana syrup in a silver dish. Duck eggs. Wild pinks. The face of a child drawn on a melon.* Reading Shonagon, the squalid narrowness of my days with needle and wiping-rag expanded into gossamer nights in Baishian. *A clay cup. A rush mat.* I savored those hours, reading alone in the exquisite two-mat house, the lamplight flaring on the basket-woven ceiling, the room as given over to beauty as Shonagon's lines.

I felt most bereft in the mornings, when I cleared away Yukako's breakfast tray, and at night, when I washed myself in silence as she talked with Tsuko, planning every detail of the August Cousin's visit. Since the Minister preferred Western dress, the host would wear Western dress as well, and perform the *temae* the Mountain had created for Western rooms. The stools the Mountain had designed weren't meant for *tatami* floors, but since Yukako wanted to use Baishian—or one of the other tearooms, if the windows weren't ready—she designed stools that could glide freely across *tatami.* "And I've ordered another piece of wood like the floorboard in Baishian," she announced, pointing at a spot on her shoulder.

"Here?" Tsuko kneaded as Yukako talked.

In place of her father's table, Yukako wanted to make use of the central element already in Baishian: the floorboard that divided the host's mat from the guest's. If there were a table in the same place as the floorboard, of the same size and wood, with legs that did not draw attention to themselves, surely it would clutter the tiny room less than a great black lacquer stand off to the side? "Perhaps the stools should be made of the same wood too," she thought aloud. "Oh, I'll need you to serve tea when the cabinetry man comes tomorrow."

"Of course," promised the younger woman, draping a towel over her mother-in-law's shoulders before getting her own. The word for a bride is the same as the word for a daughter-in-law, *yome.* As I watched them, I thought how lucky Yukako was, never to have been a daughter-in-law herself: the girl had to work just as hard to please *Okusama* as she did to please her husband. Still, as they left the bathhouse ahead of me, I knew this: I would rather have been her *yome* than her discarded toy.

AT MY MOST JEALOUS, I felt impatient with Shonagon. The snow mountain she piled up for Her Majesty eased the sticky July heat no more than her Empress's approval eased my loneliness. On such nights, I read quickly and badly, like a brute gobbling up a tea ceremony meal: Shonagon meant to tell the reader *what happened next* no more than a *kaiseki* chef meant to fill the belly. But it was on such a night, skimming past the well-turned lists to see if anything ever came of her love for the Empress, that I found I'd reached the end of Shonagon's book, but not the end of Kenji's.

Pushed tightly into the last fold of *The Pillow Book* was a stack of thin pages in Kenji's clearest hand. Half a generation after Shonagon, he explained, another great writer served in the next Empress's court: Murasaki Shikibu. I knew her as the author of *The Tale of Genji*, beloved by Yukako and Sumie as girls. Like Shonagon, Murasaki also kept a diary of her time at court, and Kenji had rewritten parts of it for Aki as well, her archaic forms and obscure words updated for a contemporary ear. I almost ignored it, as it began with a tediously detailed account of imperial birth rituals, but I read on and discovered a moment when the speaker pulls back the sleeve of a sleeping woman to look at her face. "You look like a princess in a story," she tells her waking friend.

Though the prose was less intoxicating, I felt drawn to this shyer, less arch and worldly voice, this woman less at ease than Shonagon with the court and its gossip, quick love affairs, and lack of privacy. She was not above gossip herself: she envied the witty court of sacred virgins at Kamo Shrine, and lamented the dullness of the Empress's ladies. I laughed out loud to read her characterization of Shonagon as *dreadfully conceited. She thought herself so clever and littered her writings with Chinese characters.*

How interesting to learn that the Empress had chosen Murasaki for
the secret task of teaching her those same Chinese characters. *Very
unladylike!* editorialized Kenji, but he was clearly proud of her: then,
even more than now, he explained, men wrote using *kanji*, the Chinese
ideographs, and women wrote using *kana*, the simpler phonetic characters. Murasaki and Shonagon were unusual in using both systems of
writing. I thought about this book, translated and copied as a gift of
love, and I imagined Murasaki waiting for a secret meeting with her
Empress, a young woman resplendent in twelve-layered robes and
flowing hair, learning as Aki had learned, one brushed *kanji* at a time.

As I read on, I recognized, in Murasaki's drier prose, many of the
moments that had seemed unique to Shonagon. *Her Majesty looked so
radiant this evening that it made one feel like showing her off* . . . and later: *In the
clear light of a small lamp hung inside the curtains, Her Majesty's lovely complexion
was of translucent delicacy* . . . and later still: *Her Majesty has also remarked more
than once that she had thought I was not the sort of person with whom she could ever
relax, but that now I have become closer to her than any of the others.*

In the lamplight, surrounded by Kenji's copied sheets, I looked
from Murasaki's diary back to Shonagon's. With her whole heart,
Shonagon, like Murasaki, loved Her Majesty exactly as she should love
a liege, and Her Majesty, with *her* whole heart, loved Shonagon exactly
as she should love a vassal. Nothing was going to *happen*. I had mistaken
Shonagon's sensual fervor for the thing I heard in Kenji's voice when
that coracle lifted off the sand inside me, when he said why they had
jumped, *for each other*.

THE NEXT DAY, as I sat heavy-eyed in the hot sewing room, my sweaty
fingers thick around the needle, facing one more endless seam, one
more endless afternoon with Jewel and Jade chattering about where
Nao could have gone; facing the robes the students had just soiled, the
robes in the gardens and tearooms they were just then soiling, the robes

they were certain to soil soon; facing all the unsewing and washing and resewing, all the thread and stitches and dirty water that would total the rest of my life—at that moment I spotted Yukako walking outside, her swift, long-bodied gait unchanged in all the years I'd known her. As my chest tightened under my *obi*, all at once I remembered that day in our time of direst want, when in this very room Yukako had preferred to burn her own robe rather than sew it.

My eyes flew wide open. I would do as Murasaki had done, I decided, and as Yukako had herself done. *You can get used to anything*, I'd told her then, gently, because I had not yet discovered the one thing I could not get used to, and her disparaging reply lent me steel now: *Maybe* you *can*, she'd told me.

I left.

32

1891

I BEG YOUR PARDON?"
"Would you be desirous of an English or French tutor?" I said
again in the lemon-polish room, staring at Alice Starkweather, her eye-
whites pink with veins.

"Repeat yourself, child, I don't understand you."

I began to blush in anger and frustration. "Do you remember me?"
I asked.

"Of course I do," she said, nodding at a stack of papers on the
table. The room bristled with wooden legs: the table, the desk, four
wooden chairs, two overstuffed armchairs. Miss Starkweather sat in one
of them, her back as straight, in spite of the cushions, as if she were sitting in the tearoom. "You were an angel with those letters the week our
Noriko left. As you can see, she never did come back." The papers, I
realized, covered not only the table but every chair as well. "It's always
the fathers. Are you here to help?"

I concentrated as I framed my reply, willing my English not to skit-
ter off into Shakespearean murk. "What would you pay?"

She named a figure and I felt myself bowing uncontrollably. "Do you have time today?" she asked.

With five coins in my sleeve, I stopped on my way home, as Yukako had before me, for a few skewers of grilled *dango:* rice cakes slathered in thick, sweet sauce.

AT DINNER, out of habit, I filled my bowl as high as any other night, but I forgot that I had just eaten. Each cake of *mochi* is as filling as six times its volume in rice; for the first time I had trouble finishing a meal at the Shin house. I remembered the way my mother spoke of *les nonnes* when I was a child, and I felt shame that I had walked up the road to those Protestant nuns. But I thought of the freedom Aki had found behind the convent wall, and I thought of my mother's gift, her blessing on my future. *You could be a translator.* The letters Miss Starkweather had not understood, she now did, and I had the full belly to prove it.

We were doing well now, thanks to the money from the schools, and even sewing-girls could eat more if they wanted. I watched Jade lift the lid off the steaming pot of rice and barley and dip in the bamboo paddle for a second helping. When she reached for my bowl, I covered it with my hand. "I'm fine," I said.

I watched the steam climb in the air even after Jade replaced the lid. I ate another slow bite of rice. We all had Yukako to thank for our dinner, her cunning and vigor; the great steaming pot held hours of her life. *This is her rice,* I thought. I was too full to eat another bite: I almost cried. I remembered the way the sewing frame had stood ready as if at any moment I might return and bend over that wretched black student robe again, remembered Yukako receding in the Shin gate, long and straight and tiny as the needle I'd left behind: it felt like the longest road I'd ever traveled, the short walk to Miss Starkweather's school. I used both hands to hide my weeping face. I was too full to eat. My independence tasted like exile.

"Aunt?" said Jade's young voice.

"There was something in my eye," I said.

I WASHED THE DISHES briskly when we finished, dried them with a quick snap of towels. When Kuga was alone, I spoke to her, as Yukako had once spoken to Chio. "O-Kuga, I've found other work in the afternoons. I can still serve and clean, but what would it cost to hire someone to take my place in the sewing house?"

Kuga thought slowly. Kenji would have said it looked like she was chewing. "A friend did ask me yesterday about taking in some sewing," she said. "Her daughter's old enough." She looked at me sideways and slowly named a figure that was patently higher than what Jewel and Jade earned, but still half what Miss Starkweather had offered me. I agreed, wondering how much of the money she planned to drink up herself. "Just bundle up your share here at the door and I'll give it to o-Hazu."

"O-Hazu? From the bathhouse?"

I did not pretend to be happier than I was, but Kuga shrugged. "Do you want me to help you or not? It's not like she's coming inside."

"Oh," I said. Kuga was ready to defer to Yukako's wishes, but if I felt betrayed, it was no concern of hers. "Very well."

AND SO I BEGAN wearing *hakama* again, this time down Migawa Street to the school by the Palace wall. I felt so heavy inside, wearing the clothes I loved for Miss Starkweather instead of Yukako, but sometimes, when I walked in the shade, or when a rare summer breeze whisked at my parasol, I wished Aki could have seen me swishing up the street, like the students she envied, with my modern deep-eaves hairstyle and my billowing trouser-skirts. Usually I took small steps when I walked, so my *kimono* wouldn't flap open and expose me, but with my *hakama*, when my skirts flapped, no one saw. I felt my strides lengthen, my wooden shoes ring out on the street.

Reading and translating Miss Starkweather's letters and newspapers was like learning English all over again. A born teacher, Miss Starkweather was merciless and precise in her corrections, insisting I repeat myself over and over until I had pronounced a word to her satisfaction. *"Required. Required,"* I tried again, eliding *kuwai* into that central syllable, reacquainting my mouth with those sticky double consonants: *kw, rd.* I had never lost the distinction between *r* and *l*, but Miss Starkweather, expecting of me a level of English that would have sorely vexed anyone who hadn't grown up with it, never offered comment or praise. Wherever Noriko the translator was now, I was sure she was happy not to be repeating English words. *"You are required to show this photograph. May I say display?"*

"Yes, it's more appropriate. But not displ*ai*, dear, displ*ei*. Repeat."

"Display." My only English-speaking companions for years had been *Tales from Shakespeare* and *Paris for Travelers*, and I could hear them only in my fickle mind's ear. As July sweated into August, however, I found I remembered more and more, and my accent and usage, seized up from years of solitude, relaxed with exposure to another speaker. My work with the stern and rabbit-eyed Miss Starkweather, though demanding, was like a guided tour of a lost childhood city.

And her work with me was clearly one area among a very few in which she had total control of her environment. Nothing seemed to calm her so much as correcting my English. "You are required to display this photograph in each classroom, or you hazard imprisonment or fine." Had I slipped and used the French word?

Miss Starkweather cast a grim eye on a stack of Their Majesties' portraits. *"Risk,* dear," she said, her voice mechanical and soothing. Another father had recently pulled his daughter out of school, and made so bold as to say why: to improve her marriage prospects. "One day Yoshiko was here, the next she was gone," sighed Miss Stark-weather. "And such a bright girl too."

In a week or two I had read my way through all the mail on the chairs and we had moved on to the table. And then, in the hottest part of August, when bowls of sweet shaved ice puddled instantly into sugar water, as I sat making out a notice from the fire inspector one afternoon, a flurry of lace and ruffles burst into the office announcing Miss Frances Parmalee, red and gasping with news: "Oh, dear, an American has gone and killed some Jap tart in Yokohama. And there was a riot and it's in all the papers."

Miss Starkweather, energized briefly by Miss Parmalee's appear-ance, sank deeper into her chair. "Oh, Fanny, and right before the Obon festival."

"Obon is always a trial here," explained Miss Parmalee, acknowl-edging both my presence and my confusion. We had been introduced but had never spoken. "This is Japan, so the school year runs from April to the beginning of March. But this is a Christian school, so we *can't* take a holiday expressly for Obon. We simply *can't*. But this is Japan, so half the girls just don't show. 'Yes, *Sensei*; no pagan nonsense for me, *Sensei*; see you tomorrow, *Sensei*.' And then they simply don't show. I wish they'd never relaxed that ban." The fires and dances, for-bidden in the early years of Meiji, had quietly returned to Kyoto some nine years before.

Miss Parmalee crumpled into an empty armchair while Miss Stark-weather shook her head gloomily, adding, "And this is the time of year when, if the families mean to marry off our girls, they disappear. And, given the summer so far—"

"And now *this*," moaned Miss Parmalee.

"Another blow struck for international accord. I wonder how many students we'll have left when Obon is over," sighed Miss Starkweather. Her hands, large and red-knuckled, gripped her armrests.

"Don't you think we should just take the whole month of August off?" Miss Parmalee asked me, setting down her ruffled basket. It moved: her venerable dog pushed open the lid with its snout, sniffed the stifling air, and sank back into its cushioned grotto. It was hard to look at this ballooning, tiny-waisted creature without hearing the taunts of the bathhouse children, and yet here was *Pamari-sensei*, in all her absurdity, smiling at me, enjoining me to agree. "American schools take a long summer holiday, after all."

"As if butter wouldn't melt in your mouth," said Miss Stark-weather. "Fanny, don't start with her. Haven't we been through this before? We get these girls for such a short time, we can't squander a month of it every year. Moses was on the mountain for just forty days before his people started worshipping the golden calf."

"And we are not Moses," said Miss Parmalee, finishing Miss Stark-weather's speech.

"And there have never been so many graven idols waiting for those girls as now," said Miss Starkweather somberly, refusing to be derailed. She pointed to the stack of imperial photographs, untouched since their arrival in July. "Look at them. Urako, where were we? I wonder if we need to hang these for the fire inspection."

I did as I was told, but it was difficult, remembering when I came in search of Aki, what Miss Starkweather had said: *We're not running that kind of school.* That girl in Yokohama, what about her?

AT THE SHIN HOUSE, we did take a holiday for Obon. After students and servants alike went home to their native towns and villages, the remaining few of us rattled around in the empty house without them. Those who slept upstairs moved to their verandas to catch a breath of wind: Tai and Tsuko, Yukako in the sewing house attic, two girls from Tokyo who stayed on due to an outbreak of cholera at home. Kenji maintained his nights in the Bent-Tree Annex, his daily vigil at the convent. Kuga remained in the little cottage that had once been Chio's. But everyone else was gone, the room by the kitchen enormous without Jewel and Jade.

I had not been aware of how much their presence muffled the night sounds of the house: when Kuga came in to use the privy at night, she sounded so loud padding past my room, just a sliding paper door away. I remembered, when Nao was with us, how the girls would stop their gossip whenever they heard the outside grille slide open. *Is it him? Is it him?* they'd whisper. *No, it's Miss Aki. No, it's o-Kuga. Are you sure? How can you tell?* When the nocturnal visitor had been to the toilet and left, the girls would collapse in giggles before beginning another round of *He likes you, No, he likes you!* But I'd really had to work to hear anyone pass by, those nights; now, in this hollow-gourd house, the shuffle of Kuga's feet rasped like loud wind in bamboo.

The first night of the Obon holiday, the room felt so empty I couldn't sleep, so I went to Baishian to read, the hot night air moving slowly through the empty window frames. It had been this hot in the city now called Kyoto for hundreds of summers, Shonagon assured me. This time, by my flickering lamp, I read not to tease out her passion for an Empress but to slip into a cooler, petaled world: of snapping banners and twelve-layered robes, of cloudy Chinese mirrors and faces drawn on melons, of women wooed with poems tied to branches, of lovers gliding in at night to trade caresses and vanish with the fresh cold dew. In that room frail as gauze, I felt like a court lady myself, elegant and indolent, prized for my learning and cultivation. *Slow down*, I laughed at myself: translating a notice from the fire inspector requires neither witty repartee nor a vast knowledge of the Chinese classics. All the same, I wafted back to bed more lightly than I'd left.

The next morning I was surprised from sleep by a tap on the door-frame. "Miss Ura!" It was Kuga, with a rarely heard note of sweetness in her voice.

"I didn't hear you making breakfast; I don't know what's wrong with me," I apologized.

"It's not even breakfast time yet," she said. "Look." We'd been summoned to Tai's favorite teahouse, a seven-mat room called Sparrow Hut, for a dawn tea. Kuga gave me a slip of paper from Tai and Tsuko that served as both invitation and assignment: "Young Mistress said I'm third guest, you're fourth." Still bleary as I sat on the waiting-bench, I looked around to realize that everyone left in the house had been invited: Kuga, me, the two girls from Tokyo, and, playing first and second guest respectively, Kenji and Yukako.

I found it charming that on no notice at all, they had decided to hold a tea event for the whole household just as we were, the Tokyo girls still in their sleeping *kimono*, Kuga still wearing her sleeves tied back with work-strings. Yukako, surprised, looked girlishly happy, and even Kenji seemed quietly touched. I was flattered to realize that we were seated, not by rank, but according to how long we had been with the house: family first, servants second, students last. According to this scheme, it was clear Tai was singling his brother out by placing him before his mother. Perhaps by naming Kenji as main guest, he was trying to draw his brother back to the world of the living: I like to think he was announcing his love. And by forcing them to sit side by side, I saw that Tai was trying to add one more thread to the fragile web of peace forming between his mother and his brother. I looked down at my lap, made shy by his goodness.

When we walked down the path to the waiting-bench, a handful of candles lit the way: they guttered out just as the sky went pearly and we entered the tearoom. The paper *shoji* doors had been taken out and replaced with walls made of reeds, allowing air and light to pass through effortlessly. As the night ebbed, the room actually seemed cooler: the contrast between dark reed and bright air increased; the garden visible through the reeds grew more deeply green. Behind us, the moss looked like slatted jade, while in the alcove, also behind us, no flowers hung. Instead, a square window had been slid open completely and hung with mosquito gauze. The window framed a standing stone in the garden whose top formed a rough bowl for water, in which floated one lotus bud. I felt a stab of longing, remembering Inko years before: perhaps this was the morning I'd hear it blossom with a soft clear *pop*.

As our eyes adjusted, Yukako and Kenji murmured together, and then the girls from Tokyo did too. In place of the charcoal brazier and kettle was something I'd never seen before: on a square wooden board, in a deep diamond-shaped iron tray, sat a squat ceramic water jar. I blinked; the tray was full of *ice*.

Tai appeared and set down a bowl of sweets, then began a simple *temae* for thin tea. Then Tsuko appeared in the doorway to play the role of *hanto*: an assistant to the host who ferries bowls of tea to guests and offers explanation. "The night before last it was too hot to sleep," she said, "so we sat up talking about cold things. We had an idea: what would happen if you made *matcha* tea with cold water?" Tai nodded, beaming in such a way that suggested that the idea was in fact Tsuko's.

He looked up and added, "We tried warm water and cool water, and it just tasted terrible, but then we discovered that if the water's cold enough, you could get as much foam as if it were boiling."

"We don't know if you'll like it, so this isn't really a proper event, just thin tea and sweets. We don't want you sitting on your feet all morning. But just among ourselves, you know, it's so hot out . . ." Tsuko trailed off nervously.

"It sounds delicious," said Kenji, rising to the occasion with simplicity and grace.

When had I ever heard a man and a woman conspiring together to give joy to anyone else? I savored the sight of them as much as I savored the sweets: dabs of white bean paste flavored with citron, each wrapped in a translucent case of *kanten*, a seaweed-based gelatin that made them look as if they were suspended in ice. What's more, in the growing heat of morning, the sweets were *cold*, as if they'd been kept all night in a well. They were delightful, and my bowl of *matcha*, frothy and flecked with little splinters of ice, left me refreshed and stirred.

When the *temae* was finished and Tai offered his last bow in the doorway, Yukako, who had been quietly glowing all morning, bowed deeply to her son. "I only wish your grandfather were alive," she said. We all bowed in gratitude and Tai humbly closed the door.

As each guest sat in line to wriggle out of the square doorway, I took a last look back, to see if the lotus had bloomed. I was not expecting to see a man at the alcove window, and my surprise was shared by Yukako as she rounded the teahouse to look at him, at the flat wooden case leaning against his leg the very size and shape of a stack of panes of glass.

"Well," she said, waving the two girls from Tokyo off to change out of their sleeping robes.

Tai, alerted by the sound of us lingering, emerged in surprise, and as Yukako composed her anger, he bowed in genuine pleasure and disappointment. "You didn't have to stand out there watching like that. I wish you had come in and tried some tea."

Nao folded his arms and bowed ruefully at the young man. In his leggings and workman's apron, he seemed leaner and more weary. "Oh, no," he said. "Standing here watching you, I felt like I had really come back to my native village just in time for Obon. I wouldn't trade that feeling for the world."

Tai shrank a little at Nao's tone of voice, devoid of nostalgia. "Well, it's good to see you again," he said.

"I had work to finish," Nao said, bowing.

"Of course he gave his permission about Aki," Yukako told her daughter-in-law as they sat in the bath on the night of Nao's return. "I didn't think he'd mind, especially considering who paid the dowry to the nuns."

"But why did he disappear like that?" said Tsuko. "And just when a girl would need her father most." It was a question designed to invite *Okusama* to vent her evident spleen.

Yukako's reply was surprisingly diffident. "He said the proper thing for a father to do would be to punish Aki and set her back on the right path. But if the right path made her want to die, then maybe it was the wrong path. He didn't want to punish her, so he left." I heard her hesitation and distrust, and at first, it seemed, she was judging him for dressing up his cowardice as fatherly concern. But it was not the voice of a judge I heard. It was the voice of a neglected child who hesitantly, distrustfully, accepts a gift.

I hated him all over again. I hated his pretty cheekbones, his long body, his small sturdy hands. And I wanted to hurt Yukako for the tightness in her voice when she talked about him. For replacing me with Tsuko. For thinking of Kenji's happiness so slowly; for paying the nuns to take Aki so fast. For not being who she'd once been to me; for receding from me even as we sat together in the bath.

After dressing for bed, I paced the windowless three-mat room where the servants slept: in the end, I walked out again to Baishian. My face felt hot and I barely saw the stepping-stones, the moss, the bamboo. In my restless haste, I almost didn't see the light in the teahouse, and when I did, instead of scuttling off to find another place to read, I set down my lantern, stepped out of my shoes, and walked forward.

Yukako faced Nao in the small house. I could see the back of her head, their bodies partitioned into floating squares by the window frames: new split-toed socks and the indigo hem of a gauze robe; rough leggings and squared-off bare feet. A gauze sleeve and a glimpse of thick apron. A woman's coil of black hair and a man's lowered eyes. "It's unacceptable," she was saying.

"Whatever Master Teacher prefers," I heard him reply, his voice bland and amenable. The floor was covered with coarse cloth and glass panes were stacked neatly in the corner. It wasn't what they were saying, it was the fact of them alone at night, breathing together in that room of newly planed wood. When he took a step back, she took a step toward him. When she turned to go, his eyes anticipated her path.

But in the moment before she looked back at him to say good night, he noticed me outside; his eyes met mine; he saw the raw hostility in my face. And smiled.

Blushing, I picked up my lamp and shoes and ran all the way back to the house, my heart thudding as I sat on my *futon* in the servants' room. I heard Yukako clip back to the sewing house; she hadn't spotted me. But he had: I hugged my legs close to me, feeling flayed and skinless, *seen*. At the same time I felt so angry. I remembered that smile when he saw me, smug and greedy. *Yukako would be so upset if I did this,* I thought savagely, and when I heard Nao's footsteps trace the way back from Baishian, I reached for the sliding door. My fingers felt fat and raw; they sweated into the thick paper. When he came closest to the house I loudly slid the door wide, and waited. I heard the footsteps pause, then approach. "Jealous?" said the voice in the dark. He stepped in and slid the door shut.

33

1891

O UR COUPLING WAS BRIEF and matter-of-fact. I rose up away
from myself and looked back, saw the apron and leggings
askew on the straw-pale floor, the dark robe pulled open around the
woman's fleshy thighs, the bodies struggling below me in the lamplight. Slowly I began to feel my body again, a sense of weight and heaving, began to feel the back of my head grind, grind, grind into the
tatami. *So this is what women wait for,* I thought. It was neither better nor
worse than I had imagined.

When he was finished, he began to lick my lips and the inside of
my mouth. "What are you doing?" I said.

"Are you sure you're a foreigner? You've never heard of kissing?"

Of course I remembered kisses from my childhood, butterfly poufs
of lips on skin, but they were nothing like this, all thick tongue and
hard teeth. And who was he to say what foreigners did? "You've lived
abroad?" I asked.

He laughed. "Oh, I learned to kiss near Gojo Bridge," he said,
naming a rough Kyoto red-light district. "But my friends in Yokohama
tell me foreigners do it all the time, even husbands and wives."

I tried it. I reached forward for his upper lip and tongued the inside of it, a single line with a wet brush tip, the character *one*. "Sweet," he said. He cupped my breasts with both hands, as if weighing them. "You *are* a foreigner," he chuckled. "No doubt about it."

Just as I was about to tell him to leave, he began to draw his hand across my skin very lightly and I surprised myself, smiling. It made me feel clean and precious, like lacquer. As if I were the lacquer hearth-frame in the tearoom and his fingers were the bundle of feathers used to brush it clean. What was it called? *"Haboki,"* I whispered. Never had the word seemed so startling, so tender. *"Haboki."* His hand was the wing of a swan.

Then, the way a man who had finished eating might tap his stomach, he tapped my hip gently and repetitively, his hand contentedly flexing and relaxing. I found it annoying. I held his hand. "You know, they rip the feathers out while the bird's alive," he said.

"What?"

"For the *haboki*. So it'll last longer. When I was a kid the old man made us do it."

"You and o-Kuga?" I felt cold again. Why was he telling me this?

"Me and Hiro," he said. Yukako's brother. "We had to shoot the cranes down without killing them, and then I'd hold the bird while Hiro pulled out the feathers. The poor thing screamed like a girl," he said.

He was showing off, a little boy brandishing a toad in a jar. I would not give him the satisfaction of seeing me recoil. I felt glad, then, that when we'd done it I had made no sound at all. "Is that so?"

"Sure looks pretty in the tearoom, doesn't it?" he said harshly.

He was trying to bully me, but into what? "And then Mr. Hiroshi died," I said, trying to gain the upper hand.

"Yes." Nao backed down a little, but it seemed he still had something to prove. "But not before Akio came along and the *haboki* job went to him. Took them twice as long without me." He was sneering, but I heard envy in his voice.

"And then?" I pushed back.

"Hiro died, Akio went to the Shogun's court, and I left before anyone could make me shoot another crane. I stowed away to Fushimi.
Loaded casks for a *sake* brewer who didn't ask any questions. Went to
Edo. Yokohama. Asaka. I wasn't coming back." He tapped my hip
again as he told his story, one tap for each short sentence. I kissed him
to make him stop. "You're a quick study," he said. "Must be in your
blood."

We kissed until I got dizzy and he went inside me again. Again I
watched from the ceiling. Hovering up in the mosquito netting, I
thought I could hear the other sounds of night: the water in the gutter,
the watchman with his clappers, the snoring sleepers. Yukako, I suddenly knew, was wide awake behind her screen, thinking of just one
thing, and when I imagined her, flushed and aching, her long itchy fingers, I flooded down into my body and forced the man harder into me.
I shook, I sweated, I grunted, I rolled aside, panting. I felt triumph. "I
didn't know you felt this way," said Nao, sated and drowsy.

"What way?" I said.

I WALKED TO SCHOOL in my *hakama* the next day, drugged and sparkly,
alert. I remembered how I felt as a girl, after my night with Inko, a private hour in a cloakroom while Yukako taught music, breathing the *neriko*
incense Inko gave me, startled with delight. I felt the same way now, but
more quietly, with less dreaminess and more self-satisfaction, my mouth
and thighs pleasantly sore. The night before, I had felt nothing in bed
with Nao until I could imagine Yukako thwarted. But this morning, now
that my body and my loneliness had remembered their hungers, I wanted
him again so much. *Sweet*, he'd said. He'd liked my breasts. *I didn't know you
felt this way.* He wasn't going to tell me what it meant to him, to torture a
beautiful living thing for his master's pleasure, but at the same time he
had told me: it was enough to make him leave home.

That day, as feared, a number of girls did not come to school. Among the notes of apology I read for Miss Starkweather, one girl's parents sent a gift in a large box: a single melon, lovingly wrapped. "In Sei Shonagon's day they would have drawn a child's face on it," I said. I never chatted gaily like this at work, but for once my life was not so different from Shonagon's world; though my lover had vanished, not on a wave of ineffable sadness at dawn, but instead in a hurry to the bathhouse before closing time—though no pretty page boy had appeared that morning with a poem tied to a stalk of bamboo—I felt like a heroine in a twelve-layered robe: seen, imagined, longed for.

Heathenish. I heard the word, and looked up. "Pardon?"

"It's one of our greatest challenges here. They won't distinguish between the wanton and the pure. They just treasure things because they're old, like those Heian *poetesses*." The way Miss Starkweather pronounced the word, as if it were a disease, made me want to laugh. I felt brazen and worldly all day, acutely conscious of my body as I slid my door open that night.

In bed, I remembered the simple, offhand trust with which Yukako had accepted her breakfast that morning, the way I became invisible to her in the bath that night as she outlined her latest plans for the Baishian stools and table. I savored the lying brightness with which she told Tsuko about going to the teahouse the night before to warn Nao against working too loud or too late. "Tell me if he bothers you and I'll have him stop at once," she said. *Oh yes you will, any hour, day or night,* I thought, with a private smirk.

Alone in my little chamber, suddenly I felt the loss of her so keenly that I almost closed the door to catch my breath and cry a little, but then Nao appeared and I got lost in his body, in kissing his mouth, in his planed-wood smell. I felt softer than I had the night before, and I clung to him when we were through the way I'd clung to Inko as a girl.

He was so beautiful. I covered his face with my hands, feeling its hard and soft shapes. Whose face had I touched last? The boys, when they were small? "What was it like to be a child here?" I asked.

He laughed joylessly. "You know how the students take turns cleaning out the privies?" I nodded. There was so much demand for nightsoil among farmers that the students actually looked forward to the task: they got to keep whatever the *owai* man paid.

"Back in the Shogun's day, do you think any of those little princelings were cleaning toilets?"

I remembered the Mountain's students from my childhood, a softer lot than now, more attentive to their ancestral rank than to their *temae*. I did not remember them cleaning toilets. This had changed, I was dimly aware, after we pulled out of our worst time, when the students began coming again. "So Mr. Matsu must have done it when I was young," I thought aloud.

"No doubt. But that's what I did for ten years, eight to eighteen, every night. And every day I cut the tearoom charcoal. Matsu would beat me if I did it wrong."

"Wrong like how?"

"Cut a piece too thick. Too thin. Too long. Too short. If any bark fell off. If there were any knots in the wood. I got a lash for each bad piece."

"But how could that be your fault? I mean, isn't that how it comes?" When the charcoal man brought his load, it was in the form of trunks and branches, black and silvery, whole trees carbonized in the kiln.

"Sure, but that didn't stop Matsu. He said if the sizes were wrong, the Master's tea fire wouldn't light and it would shame us all in front of the guests. And there's a little truth to that: if you always start a fire with the exact same cuts of charcoal laid the exact same way, you're fairly likely to boil water every time. But you know what? My mother made three meals a day for forty-five years and she never failed at boiling water."

I nodded. I could picture the bin under the backstage floor of each tearoom where the charcoal for ritual use was kept, each piece like all its mates. From overhead they looked like milled Kobe soaps, or candies, perfect identical black-and-silver wheels. I knew Toru and his father cut charcoal, but I hadn't given much thought to what that might mean.

"Until Akio came, when Hiro had a break between lessons, he and Yuka would get saws and help me." *Yuka!* I hadn't heard anyone call her that since Chio's day. "If he cut a bad piece, he'd make me beat *him*." Nao grinned.

"Really?" I asked, surprised.

"Well, not hard. Yuka wouldn't have let me."

"Wait, was she older?"

He shook his head. "No, she was the youngest." He made steps with his hands to show their birth order. "Me, Hiro, Yuka. But she always was"—there was a tiny catch in his voice, something you wouldn't have heard if you hadn't been listening for it—"a little hellcat, and he always was kind of frail."

He drew lazy circles on my back as he spoke. "I still can't believe how much she looks like him in her *hakama*," he mused. I stopped breathing for a moment before he continued, "The charcoal dust made Hiro cough and cough. It got everywhere, and it itched. Sifting the ash was even worse. I'd spit wads of black stuff at the end of the day." He laughed his raw sad laugh. "I don't blame him for stopping, but when Akio came, it was like he'd never helped me." In his words I heard it again, a splinter of the jealousy I bore for Tsuko Sono.

"And now little Toru has to do it," he concluded. "Sweet kid. I really thought if this marriage to Aki didn't work out, he'd find a better lot in life, but he's too stupid to know what a drudge he is. And even if I could spare him, someone else would have to do it."

I wanted to ask about Aki, but his voice had gone light and desultory. "The students could take turns at it," I proposed, matching his tone, "the way they do with the toilets."

"That would be a start," he said. "Then they could caterwaul about it the way they carry on about laying ash. You've heard them."

"Yes." I nodded. After each brazier fire, once Toru sifted the ash, the students took turns shaping the fine dark powder into a prescribed form: the shape of a valley between two mountains. The charcoal fire then sat in this valley. "Doesn't the ash form help the fire draw better?"

"It does. But there are other ways. You could use a sunken hearth, the way they do in the winter. Or you could use an enclosed chamber, like we do with glass. You do the same sort of thing in the kitchen."

"And *we* don't use special sizes of charcoal," I agreed.

"*Un.* So why do you think they lay the ash that way, really?"

I thought of Alice Starkweather complaining earlier that day: *They just treasure things because they're old.* "Because that's how the old masters did it?" I asked.

"Guess again."

He started tapping me again, which made me roll away a little. "No."

"Because they can. They don't have to heat up anyone's bath, or scrub toilets, or dig canals, or sew *kimono*," he said, with a nod to me. "They can sit there and push ash around with their dainty little shovels for an hour and a half until they've made a perfect valley with a satin finish. And then they can burn a tea fire in that ash and do it all over again. They're showing off."

Nao was silent, and when he spoke again, his voice was both soft and harsh. "After Hiro died, they cremated him, and when I had to sift the ash the next time, I almost threw up. *It's just dirt,* I kept telling myself. *It's no one you know.* And then I saw the old man critiquing the students' ash forms and I almost threw up again. It was just dirt, and here I was hauling shit and spitting charcoal so that they could sculpt ash. Ura, these people play with dirt."

"You left," I said quietly. He had always called me Miss Ura before.

"If it weren't for my mother, I would have never come back." True, here he was just in time for Obon, the filial son.

"Though now that I'm here," he added, "I can't tell you how much satisfaction it gives me to piss in the Baishian privy."

I laughed with him, but something had caught my attention. "Why did you say Matsu instead of *my father*?"

"I didn't think you'd understand what I was talking about, Miss Foreigner," he said, half teasing, half cold. He reached for my breasts and flattened them against my torso, flattened me back onto the *futon*.

I felt giddy and enveloped and desired, but I persisted. "But you said *my mother* instead of o-Chio."

"Did I?"

He kissed me; we lavished ourselves on each other's mouths and coupled again, hazy and streaky and sparkling. How strange, to have another human being inside you and still not know him. Afterward, I pressed my cheek into the hollow of his sternum. "Why did you leave?" I asked. "After Aki disappeared?"

"I didn't know what was best for her, so I stepped back," he said. "And I had some responsibilities in Tokyo. It seemed like a good time to go take care of them."

"You always acted like she wasn't even here, and now she's gone," I pushed, surprising myself. "Don't you even miss her a little?"

"I don't miss hearing Akio's name all the time. I don't miss seeing her mother's face." He was hoarding something in his shuttered face, the way a husk hoards its grain of rice.

I kept my voice low and easy. "Who was she?"

"What's it to you?" he snapped.

When I was a child, bored and hungry, I'd take one of the Shins' decorative stems of dried rice and eat it, grain by stiff grain. The trick was to crush the tough husk between my front teeth slowly, just enough to splay open its sharp fibers without harming the rice within. I looked at Nao and carefully applied pressure. "When you wrote that year, you said you lost a friend."

His face was suddenly as open to me as it had been closed before. "Roku. He was like a little brother to me," he said. "Like Hiro before Akio came along. We lived and worked together until he died in a blast. There was a mistake. The roof collapsed and he was still inside."

"The roof? Of the tunnel?" I asked, confused.

"Exactly," he said, but not before a look of alarm shot across his face, as if I'd caught him lying.

I didn't know what to do with that look before it vanished. "I'm so sorry," I said. "When I ran away from the fire when I was young, I heard a child screaming. I still dream about it sometimes. I can only imagine if it was a friend."

"Thank you," he said quietly.

That's when I knew to press on. "And then you met Aki's mother?"

He gave me a long wry look. He exhaled. "Fine, because you're a foreigner, I'll tell you." He pillowed his head on my chest and lay silent for a moment. "Her name was Ruri. I met her in Asaka, while I was doing explosives for the canal. Her family worked clearing away the rubble from the blasts. She was—" He held something back before continuing. "Her family worked as day laborers on farms when there was work, and starved when there wasn't. The farmers needed them and hated them. When they went to get their wages, they weren't allowed into the house, and when they worked, the farmers gave them tea in old cups they'd break when the harvest was over, to make sure their lips wouldn't touch anything Ruri's people had soiled. Her family lived with the other day laborers in a squalid little hamlet out past the farms. Ura, this is what gets me about the tea world: those people were so poor, they had only enough charcoal to heat water for cooking *or* washing. So often as not, they really were as dirty as the farmers said, but it wasn't by choice."

I was surprised by the way Nao talked, with more feeling and less bitterness than he had about himself. "Ruri was seventeen. Her husband beat her every night. When he broke her tooth, I said she could stay with me."

I touched his face as he went on. "It was soon after my friend died; I was so broken up, I didn't mind what the other men on the crew said, I just wanted to save one person's life. I thought I could take her with me to Yokohama. Get her a job as a maid with foreigners, people who wouldn't care what she'd come from. She was so grateful. We talked all night, making plans for her. I was grateful too. It finally took Roku off my mind."

And here he was again tonight, talking late with a woman, I noted indulgently. "The next morning, all the men of her village dragged us out of bed and marched us to her husband's shack with nooses around our necks. Her husband divorced her, and the only way her father would untie me was if I married her. So I let them marry us," he said, with a bitter laugh. "A week later I left her at the lodging house where I was staying and went to Yokohama, found her a job with a good family, and came back to Asaka with the news.

"But she wasn't at the lodging house. She wasn't at her father's house when I looked. I went to her husband's house, and there she was, feeding him the rice I gave her. With a fresh black eye."

"She went back to him," I breathed.

"*'How could you?'* I asked." Nao's face was hollow as the words filled it. "'I was born to this,' she said. 'This is my place.'"

"That's so sad."

Nao looked away, and then at me. "It's not *true.*" He balled his fists for emphasis. "You're not *born* to anything. She didn't *have* to go back to him like that. She didn't *have* to dump her child on my mother, or throw herself in the river. Maybe she thought Aki will have a better life than she had, but *she* could have had a better life. Every time I look at Aki, I want to slap her mother for giving in like that."

A short hot sigh burst out of him, a sound of disgust: "My mother was the same way."

Before I could ask what he meant, he said, "I went along with that farce wedding so everyone could put a good face on her leaving him, but I never wanted to keep her for myself. I went to bed with her that week, but I didn't mean anything by it. But when I came back from Yokohama and saw her feeding that man, I felt as betrayed as if I'd married her in earnest. I went and got my gun and I sat up all night in the tunnel we were blasting. I didn't kill him and I didn't kill her. I just held it. I thought about Hiroshi. About Ruri. About the brother I had lost."

He lay silent. When he looked up at me, his voice was thick and forlorn. "Trying to help just one person could break a man in half," he said. "That was the night I decided I couldn't work on that scale."

"What do you mean?" I asked. "What did you do?"

His eyes shuttered again over his secrets. "Whatever I was able."

"But what about making windows?"

"Well, that's for pay," he said, softening. "And it helps me. I can forget everything when I'm working."

He stroked my clavicles as I lay quietly. "Aki *has* had a better life than her mother, thanks to you," I said. "And look, she tried to run away from a bad lot and she succeeded. She tried to kill herself and failed. She got a black eye and worse, and it's healing up fast," I joked, cajoling.

He nodded, half smiling, but he winced as well, and I realized he'd left after we heard what happened to her face: he hadn't wanted to see.

"And that's without you even helping," I added. He hung his head at the reproach even as he chuckled.

I felt so tender toward him. He sank into my embrace and I felt his heart beating in my palm. When I read Murasaki, I hadn't been able to picture how three nights together could make a marriage, but now I could. I smiled. "You know, if we were Heian lords and ladies and you came a third night, we'd be married. Can you imagine? Just like that."

He went brittle in my arms. He coughed.

"You think that's what I meant? Don't flatter yourself," I jabbed lamely.

"We were never lords and ladies," he said.

His voice held an edge of pity. His face shut me out. He'd said it himself: *I went to bed with her, but I didn't mean anything by it.* I looked down, mortified. Before he could rise to gather up his clothes, I said, "I think you should go now."

THE NEXT NIGHT I saw him and Kuga dancing at the neighborhood Obon fire. I could envision Chio dancing there, too, her strong arms, her unshowy, vigorous movements, as unself-conscious as an animal shaking itself dry. Nao and Kuga shared that, reaching up as if from the center of their bodies, as if their arms were incidental, as after-the-fact as hair. That aside, I reflected, unable to leave the shrine grounds, they looked barely alike. Kuga had once resembled her brother's photograph, but now she simply had a crushed look, one that did not change even as she reached and danced. Nao, meantime, looked hopeful and lupine, his lush hair bobbing with his movements. I stood unable to move, watching him, flooded with embarrassment and desire. I was too proud to leave my door open that night, but sliding it shut took all my will.

AFTER OBON, JEWEL AND JADE returned and crowded back into the three mats by the kitchen with me. Nao finished work on the teahouse and picked up where he'd left off on the newlyweds' upper room, subjected to Yukako's tart scrutiny rather more often than warranted. We avoided each other. I promised myself I'd tell Aki her mother's story one day, but I held it tight to my chest just then, not wanting to say how I'd heard it. The heat of August broke, and I learned I was not pregnant.

34

1891

B AISHIAN WAS RADIANT. The morning of the Minister's visit, the brown and gold wood shone glossy: every surface had been wiped until a white silk cloth could come away white. Fresh *tatami* lay new and green. An ancient scroll hung in the alcove, remounted for the occasion on rich new brocade, one crisp *kanji* on a white field.

The calligraphy Yukako and Tai had chosen bore the simple *kanji* for *kan, barrier* or *gate:* a little figure framed in a great double door. It was a reference to this night, the gate between the waxing and waning moon, and it also hinted at the Shin family's desire to teach tea in the boys' schools as well, to be let in through that gate. Mother and son had decided to use the venerable Hakama tea bowl again, with its narrow base and billow at one side, to allude both topically to the new girls' schools and, more resonantly, to the old dress of *samurai* men, to a time when tea was a part of every *hakama*-wearer's education.

In the center of the room, between the host's mat and the guest's, the floorboard with its darkly blooming wood grain seemed to float between the two *tatami* instead of lying flush with them: Yukako's table was just as elegant as she'd imagined. Two round stools of the same wood sat beneath the table, demure and self-effacing. Though she'd adapted the room for a radically new purpose, Yukako had altered it as subtly as possible, filling it with furniture while leaving it uncluttered.

The windows were just what she'd hoped for. Nao had contrived to cover each window hole with two sliding panels, one behind the other, so that each could be left open or covered in glass, *shoji* paper, or both. As I looked gingerly inside the tearoom that morning, I wished for the Minister's sake that he could come in the daytime too. There was a ghost of autumn coolness in the air those days, enough that the effect of glass focusing the heat of the sun was a pleasant shock to the skin.

For the event, Yukako planned to have all the glass windows covered with *shoji* but one. In the high alcove window, where the moon came flooding in, Nao had incorporated *shoji* and glass into the same panel: a diamond-shaped pane of glass in a milky square paper frame. Into that glass diamond, the harvest moon would float, an orange and majestic balloon. Yukako had timed the tea event—and rehearsed with Tai unobtrusive ways to slow or speed the evening along, depending on the Minister's pace—so that the moon would sail in just after the intermission, during the preparation of thick tea.

I'D CREPT IN that morning to see all the work Yukako and Tai had done the night before, to admire the shelves of the *mizuya* backstage, laid out with their carefully chosen utensils, to revel in Baishian at its cleanest, brightest, and purest, the little square door a lush moss vista, the diamond window poised in wait for the moon. "A teahouse is a net to catch the sky," I murmured.

"Isn't it?" said a woman's voice behind me. Tsuko! "I was too excited to sleep, so I came to admire the teahouse before we all started working," she said.

She didn't have to say it. As Young Mistress, she could have invented any reason in the world that would have asserted her right to be there and tarred me as an impostor. "Me too," I said. I brought Yukako her breakfast feeling humbled: Tsuko really was a tea family's dream come true.

THE DAY HAD DAWNED brightly and the evening promised to be clear and dry, with perhaps even a decorative cloud or two to show the moon in its most poetic aspect. All the food preparation had begun smoothly; the *macarons* arrived early from Kobe, pert and pastel, not a single one broken. The first problem, however, proved to be Tai's rash.

Sudden, spotty, and pustular, the rash cropped up that morning for no apparent reason, frightening all who saw it. "But I feel fine," he insisted, trying not to scratch his face. Standing in attendance as he and his mother spoke, I was careful not to look directly at him.

Yukako bit her lip. "I think it might be visible in moonlight," she murmured, shaking her head.

Kenji paused in the doorway on his way out. Even he had been roused by the occasion, and had promised to come home early from his vigil to bring the Minister from Advisor Kato's in the quiet modern *jinrikisha*. He nodded, straight-faced. "I think it might put the man off his tea."

Tai laughed and Yukako gave him an aggrieved look. "Well?"

"I think you should take his place," said Kenji, meaning that he refused to.

Mother and son had planned to work together as helper and host, Yukako talking and passing things while Tai did *temae*. This way, the Minister would have the honor of tea prepared by the Master Teacher's own hands, while Yukako would be positioned to actually broach the question of the boys' schools.

A poxy Master Teacher, however, might be worse than no Master Teacher at all. They determined that when we all bowed to the Minister outside the gate, Tai would lead us, greeting the Minister from behind a gauze mask and apologizing deeply for his poor health; Yukako would do *temae* and speak as well. It seemed makeshift but dignified enough after we'd all rehearsed it a few times that morning. As it was, tiny Baishian might be better suited to just one host. Tai had never had a problem like this in his life, I mused, bowing at rehearsal in time with all the other servants and students. But if I were nineteen years old and believed my family's entire future depended on how I looked that day, I might develop a rash too. Yukako accepted the new plan with equanimity and went to check on the tearoom flowers.

The second piece of bad news came after Kenji went to fetch the Minister, after we had assembled once more, this time in our new *kimono*. Yukako had chosen a solid color for each of us, as her father had for the Minister's visit so many years before: all together we were dressed in three dozen different shades of blue and green, each embroidered at the nape, shoulders, and sleeves with a crest the size of a large coin, the Shins' crane, sewn with subtle variations depending on the wearer's role in the household. When Kuga had pushed against my back to straighten my *obi*, I could feel the embroidered knots press into my spine like a crane-shaped brand. We looked, lining the street by the gate, like a magnificent willow tree, a shimmering wash of leaves. Nao, I noted, was not present. He had received a *kimono* like the rest of us, even though he was working for the Shins on just a temporary basis; all the same, I could very well imagine him choosing not to take part. Yukako, too, was missing, but I knew she was in Baishian, in Western dress, poised for the Minister's arrival. Tai, facemask and all, was doing a fine job of leading us alone. Tsuko stood with the young women students but no longer looked girlish; she seemed both more serious and more content, smoothing her royal blue robe. I saw her raise a hand toward the zone below her *obi*, and guessed all at once that she might be with child.

We heard a runner's footsteps and leaned toward the sound: Tai looked alarmed. Why was Kenji running? It wasn't the Minister, however, but a messenger wearing Advisor Kato's crest. We stood very still as Tai read the man's elegantly folded letter.

Kato's runner, watching Tai's face intently, seemed disappointed by Master Teacher's even-keeled reply. "It's no trouble at all," Tai said warmly. "Please tell him how much we're looking forward to it."

Only when the runner had bowed deeply and gone did Tai turn to address us. "Due to unexpected circumstances, the Minister will not be able to attend this evening. His wife will join us in his stead." We gasped, and a tiny hissing sound arose as we tried to gossip as quietly as possible. Tai silenced us with remarkable calm. "For my own part," he said, "I'll add that for a Westernized person like the Minister, this is not unusual. In the West, husbands and wives go out in public together side by side, and in England, in fact, they are the same person by law. Therefore, however disappointed you are," he said, fixing his eyes on one or two of his students, "and whatever Madame did for work before she was married"—here he spoke to the whispering girls—"I expect every single one of you to treat the Minister's wife as if she were the Minister himself. Do you understand?"

We barked our *hai*s and bowed as one, but continued to look back and forth at one another, stunned. Tsuko slipped off to let Yukako know of the change in plan, and without a word to anyone, Mariko Kato left us and hurried down the street after the runner. Instead of rushing after her, Tai enjoined the rest of us to keep our places: "Madame will be here any moment."

And she was. A minute later Kenji rounded the corner with the rubber-wheeled *jinrikisha* and we bowed. We made an impressive sight, I know it, a river of reverent silk, a blue-and-green wind. A proper bow is conducted on a count of nine: three to sink, three to rest, three to rise: I could feel us all forcing ourselves to rise as slowly as we'd bowed, not to snap up and stare at whoever stepped out of the carriage. *One two three, one two three.* In one slow, simultaneous whoosh of silk on silk, we rose with all the self-control a life in tea had taught us, and as we rose we looked.

The elegant slim person bowing in return, though she sported the deep-eaves bun of a modern Meiji woman, looked every part the well-heeled traditional wife. She wore a formal black five-crested *kimono* with a pattern that climbed to her waist, her *obi* tied in a modest drum knot. Knowing that she was a former *geisha* made me inspect her dress more closely: the *obi* was a tight grid of muted blue and gold, the *kimono* patterned in feathery pampas grass, which, like the *hagi* planned for the tearoom, was one of the seven flowers of autumn. Wearing a seasonal pattern into the tearoom was a dicey matter: it could complement a tea master's choice of images in a delicious way, or it could run the risk of redundancy. If Madame's *kimono* had been patterned with *hagi*, for example, we would have had to find other flowers at the last minute to avoid repetition; expecting a man in a suit, we'd kept no flowers in reserve. Her choice indicated either extreme sensitivity to the aesthetic of tea—and a willingness to take risks—or total insensitivity to the predicament she might pose her host. I saw this all in the three counts it took to rise from the greeting bow, just before glimpsing the face of a handsome woman in her early forties. *One, two, three.* It was Koito.

I LOOKED AROUND, from Kuga and the sewing-girls to Kenji and the students. I saw curiosity on all sides, but no horror. I was the only one, I realized, who recognized her face. As Tai's most advanced student scurried ahead to lay the tobacco tray on the waiting-bench, I took a page out of Mariko Kato's book and ran, without a word of explanation, down the stone path sprinkled in readiness, through the moss garden, around to the backstage side of Baishian.

The only women I have ever seen kneeling on the floor in a bustle and lace were consumptive opera heroines—and Yukako. Her hands were wrapping a little wet cloth around three chips of sandalwood for the brazier, but her face was looking out the door at me. "What?" she said, brusque and panicked. I really was out of place. The guests should feel, entering the garden, as if they were discovering a secluded glade, an effect easily marred by servants rushing about. I should have been in the kitchen, passing food to the solemn young men from Tai's class who were even now moving into position to bring dishes to the teahouse. "Has he canceled entirely now?"

"No, no, his wife just arrived."

Yukako stood in one motion, gave the *mizuya* a last look, and took up a bucket to add water to the hand-washing stone in the garden: the sound would tell the guest to make ready to come down the path. "But *Okusama* . . ." I said, and time slowed for an instant; I was painfully aware that I now felt more comfortable calling her Honored Wife of the House than I did calling her Older Sister. She looked at me with flashing eyes, a strand of hair lifting out of place. "Before you go see her, listen." I insisted.

FOR A MOMENT YUKAKO stood completely still. "This is like a bad dream," she whispered, blinking very rapidly. "Would you mind repeating yourself?"

I told her again.

Yukako laughed, her voice queer and thin. She held the bucket with both hands, gasping, her corseted torso heaving against its bone case.

"Should I take this?" I offered, reaching for the vessel.

"I need it for the washing-stone," she said numbly. "Just stay out of the garden, stay where you are."

I did, though the *mizuya* for the tiny two-mat room was so small, I was sure I'd be underfoot. Looking for an out-of-the-way spot to slot myself, my eyes fell on Yukako's charcoal: a big wooden bucket for the *mizuya* kettle backstage, a dainty basket for the *temae*, each twig laid

just so. Charcoal! All the large tearooms kept their fuel in a great
sunken storage bin, the wooden access panel built into the backstage floor. Baishian had such a panel, very large for a tearoom this size.
It lay right in front of me, with a thumb-sized hole for a grip, though
I had never seen Yukako move charcoal in or out. Was there a chance?
Yes: it was empty, perhaps never used, a metal-lined well in the floor
some half a mat deep and square. I plonked myself inside and slid the
panel shut.

I blinked in the dark, my eyes adjusting to the slim dart of light
falling through the thumbhole in the *mizuya* floor. Long ago, on Jiro's
last night with the Shins, I had hidden facedown on the ground under
the Muin teahouse: this was an improvement. I could sit tailor-fashion
in my hatch, though not up on my knees without crooking my neck.
My only companion in the bin was a lidded wooden box, dusty and
forgotten, containing some dozen lengths of charcoal cut long ago,
perhaps even in Nao's time: enough for one tea brazier's fire.

As I sat, I became aware of something unusual about the little
space. It was airier than one would expect: between the *mizuya* floor and
the top of the metal box in which I sat, I felt some three inches of open
space, which let in the earthy damp from under the teahouse. How
strange; the whole point of a metal bin was to keep moisture away from
the charcoal. I groped around overhead, however, and found a second
sliding panel that had been left open, an inner liner designed to keep
the fuel airtight. I left it open so I could breathe. I further noticed that
the metal my back was pressed against was smoother than the other
faces of the bin, smooth as lacquer or glaze. I slowly, bulkily, spun my
body around to look; the metal surface seemed to be patterned in some
dim geometric fashion. Perhaps, like the opulent lining of a merchant's
sober jacket, this was—to an absurd degree—a secret display of
wealth, as far from the prying eyes and sumptuary laws of the Shogun
as one could have imagined: a lavish ornamental coal bin. I could
almost hear Nao's bitter laughter.

I experienced all this as Yukako poured water into the cup of the hand-washing stone. The host's next gesture was to open the gate between the inner and outer tea gardens, to give the guest leave to come in. I heard Yukako set down her bucket in the *mizuya*, heard her murmur, "*Now* where is she?" She was talking about me, I realized. Before I could respond, I heard her high-heeled shoes tap gravely on the stones, perhaps a little more gravely than even tea ceremony required. I listened. I heard a pause. In the space between one footstep and the next, I saw Akio's face the night of their Sighting, when a drop of *sake* fell to the floor and a glance leapt between them. I saw Yukako facing Koito that night in the rain. I saw her burning her sleeve. I saw the Mountain raise his hand to strike her. I saw Jiro crushing tea bowls with a bamboo flute. Clearest of all, I saw Yukako at twenty-one, reading calligraphy by her grandfather's two daughters: Koito's mother and her own. And then I heard her foot-steps *tock-tock-tock* their way to the garden. She was at this moment open-ing the gate and meeting Koito's eyes.

WHEN I HEARD YUKAKO return to Baishian and slide open the low square door for her guest, my stomach dropped in alarm: I thought I was experiencing an earthquake, that the walls of the teahouse, of the very bin where I was sequestered, had been rent open. There was no other way to account for the sudden brighter light. But then I realized what I was seeing: a dim version of the tearoom overhead, projected onto a mirror. How ingenious! The glassy smooth surface of the bin, I realized, was not quite at square angles with its neighbors: it was tilted to receive an image from overhead. My vantage, I puzzled out, corresponded with the wide slot of a window high on the teahouse wall: so *this* was the secret room in Baishian that Yukako had once told me about! The Mountain had con-structed a mirrored tube by which a bodyguard could observe host and guest unseen. In a teahouse built for just one host and one imperial guest, I could imagine such precautions making sense.

IT WAS EERIE, however, to see Koito's slim, blurred lineaments in the evening light—clearer when I covered the thumbhole with my hand—and know she could not see me. She entered the tearoom, paused to gaze at the scroll, and took her place. I could see the watery outlines of the two women as they faced each other across the table and bowed, one silhouetted *kimono*, one S-curve corset and bustle. I do not know what they felt, but I can guess.

What followed, as the light dimmed, was a perfectly choreographed ritual meal, executed as if by mannequins. Aside from Koito's polite questions and Yukako's polite answers about the incense box and food, they moved in decorous silence, Yukako's voice inflected with anger, Koito's with apology. I could hear footsteps overhead as the students brought each vessel at correctly timed intervals: the tray with three dishes, the pots of rice, the heated *sake* kettle, the extravagantly lacquered bowl of simmered dainties, the bountiful ceramic trays, the palate-cleansing sip of hot water in its tiny lacquer dish with its tiny lacquer cap, the raw wooden tray with delicacies from the mountains and the sea, one of each meant to fit on that wee lid.

It was the first *temae* I had witnessed since Tai and Tsuko made iced *matcha*. When Yukako brought in the last savory course—as tradition required, the clumped brown cakes of almost-fried rice from the bottom of the cookpot, floating simply in hot water—I could hear Nao scoff. Because the Mountain's holiday meals for the household had only ever included just one course in a *bento* box followed by sweets, I had never witnessed a full tea ceremony meal from inside the tearoom. The memory of Nao's laughter—and something about Yukako in her bosomy flounces, solemnly offering Koito a pot of scorched rice—made me uncomfortable. It was a pantomime, ordained by Rikyu, that told the guest, *You mean so much to me. Though my fare is humble, I give you all I have.* But those of us whose place it was to eat the household's daily burned rice had only tasted the dishes in Koito's meal once or twice in our lives, when there was food left over from hosting tea guests: the velvety morsels of fatty tuna, the rare mushrooms brought from remote mountain towns. What's more, I knew Kuga had made three pots of rice in order to have the best bits of crust to choose from: brown but not black, crunchy but not hard, all the same height and size. As Yukako in the dimming evening, the very image of serenity and self-control, cleared away Koito's dish and laid a three-hundred-year-old vessel of fresh moon-viewing sweets before her guest, I found the word that explained my unease. What she was doing, it was *affected*.

The moment Koito left for the intermission, Yukako's demeanor changed. Her calm, automatonlike grace loosened into outrage as she spoke to Tai in the *mizuya* overhead: "All these plans for Western dress and the woman comes in *kimono*. I want this table out of here and I want the brazier on the floor. She's wearing pampas grass, so I can't use this tea box. None of these others will do. Fill me a good black one instead—Rikyu's if you can find it. Once she's in the tearoom, clear the cushion and the smoking tray off the waiting-bench, splash the path with more water, and clean the privy by the bench."

"The teahouse one too?"

"No need, it's still clean from this morning. She'll use the one by the waiting-bench; she's down there now. Before anything else, I need the scroll down, the flowers up, the second sweet tray ready. Hang those flowers lower than we planned. And have Miss Tsuko bring me a *kimono*." I had never heard her use the blunt verbs of men's speech like this before: her voice had dropped to the Mountain's growl. As Tai and his students, quiet as stagehands, rushed to do her bidding, Yukako slid the windows of the teahouse closed: *shoji* covered each surface except the moon window. Even as the paper windows shut out the wan light of evening and her shape in the mirror became the dimmest flicker of gray on gray, I could see her stance soften for a moment as she slid Nao's cunning paper-and-glass moon-pane into place.

Perhaps Yukako meant to leave my spy-window open, to vent the close air of the brazier fire, or perhaps she was distracted by the footsteps pattering quickly toward her from outside. "Yes?" I heard her say.

I was surprised by a gusty intake of breath and a triumphant screech that could only have belonged to Mariko Kato. "*Sensei*, I found out what happened to the Minister!"

"Did you?" Yukako asked, none too warmly.

"I just ran home and back," Mariko announced, proud of her own daring. She gasped for breath. "Mother told me. He and Father were at a golf game with a big American schools expert. They decided to go out to dinner together, so he sent his wife instead."

"You really went to a lot of trouble for us, Miss Mariko, and I appreciate it," said Yukako, and from her tone I could hear how glad she was not to have Miss Kato for a daughter-in-law. "But now is not a good time for me to hear your news."

"Oh, *Sensei*," said Mariko, responding to the chill in Yukako's voice. "I'm sorry. It was thoughtless. Excuse me." Deflated, but only somewhat, Mariko slipped away. From the pleasure in her voice as she apologized, I think she was planning who to tell next.

FOR A FEW SECONDS Yukako stood above me backstage. "Golf," she whispered to herself, and sighed, a long trembling five-count sigh. A moment later I heard her murmur thanks to Tsuko, who must have brought a change of clothing. "Good color. But there's no time."

YUKAKO RANG A BELL to tell Koito the tearoom was ready for her return, and slid the guest's door back open. A little soft light fell on my mirror. I could hear Yukako refill the washing-stone more clearly than I could see Koito walk in a minute later and sit to look at the flowers; I saw just a long silken line, shadow on shadow, compressing to a kneeling fold. And then, just as she sank down, the mirror went golden. All the color returned to the room at once as the blurry polished metal revealed the green and violet of the cascading *hagi* flowers, the muted blue and saffron of Koito's *obi*, the white of her face gazing at the moon. "It's beautiful," she said as Yukako entered.

Yukako paused: the compliment was all the more sincere for being out of place. In the full yellow moonlight, Koito completed the picture framed by the alcove, framed by all *Okusama's* work as host: moon, *hagi*, luminous woman. "Thank you," she said quietly. She laid the second charcoal and began preparing tea.

"I'm sorry that it's me instead of my husband," Koito said.

Yukako's voice went hard and light. "It can't be helped, can it?"

"I'm sorry you didn't know it was me," Koito persisted. "I just meant to stay in the background this visit, but then he asked me to come at the last minute."

"It can't be helped," Yukako repeated.

"We both did the best we could in hard times," Koito said.

"That's one way of putting it."

"I'm not here to dwell on the past. Think of me as just an envelope, a lucky good news envelope," Koito said, her voice playful and cajoling.

I could hear the whisk rasping as Yukako kneaded the thick tea. "I'm listening," she said, her voice reined in.

"What my husband wanted to tell you was that he's so impressed with what you've done in the schools. The experiment was truly a success; your son is a young man to be proud of. In the Emperor's name, my husband asks Master Teacher to come to Tokyo and make tea part of every girl's education in Japan."

"Is that what he said?" asked Yukako, too overwhelmed to deflect the compliment. Her voice was dense and quiet. I heard in it the proud black-sleeved young nobles of her father's day. I heard in it the trembling sigh that followed the word *golf*. She was silent so long it became awkward. The tines of the tea whisk hissed in the bowl. "I had spoken with Advisor Kato about the chance of bringing up a different matter with His Honor," she said.

Koito tilted her head, and I could imagine her as a *maiko* many years before, a pouty and flirtatious child. "He didn't mention anything else. Nor Advisor Kato. Was it the teacher you left in Tokyo this spring? He's in such demand, it's astonishing. You'll surely be asked for more. Congratulations, *Sensei*." *Sensei*, not *Okusama*? Of course, I thought: that's what they had called each other as young women, studying music and tea.

Yukako noted Koito's choice of address too. "Let's not, as you say, dwell on the past," she said. She bowed to Koito, her head almost touching the floor. "Thank you for this happy news. Please tell His Honor that our family hopes to serve the Emperor to the best of our mean abilities."

A long silence followed. The yellow light began to fade as the moon continued rising. Yukako served thick tea, laid charcoal a third time, brought out a candle and the second course of sweets. *"Macarons, quelle surprise!"* said Koito. Even heavily accented, her French spooked me. Yukako accepted her compliments tersely and whisked the thin tea. "What is the name of this tea bowl?" Koito asked.

"Hakama," Yukako said. To one who knew her, it sounded as if she might cry.

35

1891

"PLEASE, JUST LEAVE ME ALONE," Yukako told Tai, her voice like weathered wood. "I'll have a bath, and then I'll tell you how it went. Tell them all it was a great success and they should take their supper and *sake* now. Have everyone gather after breakfast for my announcement and we'll all clean up together. Please?"

"Mother?"

"It's all good news," she assured him. "Just go."

THE MOON HAD LEFT the window, but Yukako remained in place, the nearby taper illuminating her long hands. They covered her face. They fell to her knees. They fingered her green silk dress. She spread them flat on the *tatami* and I saw her body shake as she cried, heard her breathe in wet little ragged gusts. Her breath went calm again, and she raised her hands to her eyes. I felt ashamed watching her, but I knew she'd hear any sound I made to leave. Suddenly her body tensed. I heard footsteps overhead. "Just go away," she said, looking at the host's door.

"Where is he?" asked a man's voice.

"Oh, it's you," Yukako said tonelessly, as if in a dream. Her voice was empty of fear when she asked, "Is that a gun?"

"Where is he?" It was Nao.

"Put that away," she said. "He never came."

"I only saw the woman leave," he said.

"He sent his wife instead."

"He's at Advisor Kato's?"

"They're having dinner with the American Minister of Education," Yukako said haughtily. "Where have you been all this time?"

"Waiting next door. Clever idea, an ornamental privy." Nao faced her for a long moment. I saw only his blurry underwater outline, but it was enough to make me flushed and queasy. He lowered his arms. "Feeling sad, *Okusama*?"

"What are you doing here?"

"All dressed up and the big man didn't come to your tea party? What a shame."

"Would you please go away?"

"You've suffered so much in this lifetime, *Okusama*."

She was seated, he was standing; her narrow face turned full toward him, her long vulnerable neck tilted up. "Don't mock me," she said quietly. It was an order and it was a plea.

"Don't what?" he said, only half mocking. His face caught a spark of reflected light: he was smiling. He sank beside her. He was a gray shape on the floor; she was a green one.

"Put that thing down," Yukako said. I heard a heavy tap of metal on *tatami* and then the two shapes of them collapsed together, green and gray. I saw flashes of white where her hands reached for him. I heard a scramble of clothing. I heard her scissoring breath. "What are you *doing*?" she whispered.

"You don't even know the first thing, do you?" he said.

"I know enough," she said.

I could hear their serrated breathing, feel the wood-framed house respond to their jerking bodies overhead. The triumph of my sticky August nights curdled into bile. I touched the box of charcoal at my feet: if it came to that, at least I would not have to be sick on myself. I clutched my knees to my chin; I floated up out of my body as I had my first night with Nao, as I had long ago, as a child on my uncle's lap. I funneled up through the thumbhole of the *mizuya*. I stood before those beautiful bodies taking what they wanted at last. I felt like a hungry ghost: greedy, vengeful, and forlorn.

I was so upset by what I saw, I looked away. I made my eyes focus on the shining mirror of my spyhole instead of on the image it reflected. And that's when I saw the scratches, off to the side, six simple *kana* characters, three and three. *Yu-ka-ko. Hi-ro-shi.* They had come down here as children and left their names. I remembered Yukako telling me about the secret room in Baishian when I was a little girl, how she and her brother had promised each other they would never show it to anyone. *Not even Akio. Not even Nao.* I felt superior for a moment then, remembering the smugness in Nao's voice when he said he'd hidden in the privy. Yukako had kept her promise to Hiroshi, never telling me about this place. And Hiroshi had kept his, I realized, never telling Nao.

I could hear them overhead, Nao's fast locomotive grunts and Yukako's blunt sobs. Then he spent himself in a groan: the house rocked in its joints. It was silent, and then I heard her sigh. "No more?"

He laughed. "You've always had everything you wanted," he said tenderly. "It's good for you to go a little hungry."

She drew away from him, remaining seated; I saw the moving white bars of her arms, heard the rustle of her dress. "Are you cleaning yourself off with tea-paper?" Nao asked. I had never heard him giggle before.

"It's to hand," Yukako explained crisply. I heard a weary intake of breath, an angry and regretful exhale. Then she picked something up from the floor and gave it a causal inspection. "Heavy," she remarked. "So, you wanted to kill my guest?"

"That's not a toy, Yuka," Nao said.

"I know," said Yukako. She did not put it down.

"You think I stayed here all these months after Mother died to collect your little commissions? After my daughter's misadventure, I asked for an assignment in Tokyo. I would have stayed there gladly, blending in, but when my brothers heard about the Minister's inspection, they said to go back to Kyoto. This was too good a chance to pass up."

"'Too good a chance'?" Yukako repeated. What was Nao saying? What kind of "assignment"? And why did he need to "blend in"?

"As long as there is an imperial family, nothing will change for the rest of us," he explained.

"Are you part of some kind of revolutionary group?"

"It's a brotherhood," he said tersely.

"That's ridiculous," Yukako said. She sounded fed up, like a teenage girl who has stayed up too late, like she couldn't believe she was having this conversation. There was something almost jaunty about the way she hefted the heavy object, flapping it around from time to time. I could not see Nao's eyes, but his whole face seemed to be watching the gun. "Isn't one revolution enough?" she asked peevishly. "Everything's different now."

"No it's not," Nao snapped. "The rich are wearing different clothes: that about sums it up. The Emperor's kinsman marries a girl from the floating world."

Yukako gasped in irritation. When Nao shared my bed, I'd caught glints of a specific bitterness in his voice whenever he mentioned Akio's name, but now I heard the whole bare knife of it. Perhaps he had never forgiven Yukako's brother for choosing Akio, and with Hiroshi gone, she was the only one he could exact penance from.

"All these years have gone by and you're still bowing to the Minister with your head touching the floor. Does that sound like change to you? Except now he doesn't even bother to come."

Yukako winced visibly. "Everything *has* changed," she repeated more quietly.

"Oh, girls make tea now? Do you think that makes a damn's worth of difference to all the people who wear their bodies to a nub so you can sit here in your pretty little house and"—here he paused, trying to sum up the aim of tea—"feel serene? Carpenters, tea pickers, charcoal men?"

"Tea gives them work," Yukako demurred.

"Tea keeps them exactly where they are. Tea keeps them exactly the way it once kept me."

There was a dull glint of metal in the candlelight. Yukako raised her arms and kept them raised. Nao flinched. "I don't think you stayed in my 'pretty little house' just to be a hero for your 'brothers,' Nao-*han*."

Nao was silent.

"I think you stayed here because you have a gift and a skill. Glass windows don't help anyone any more than tea does, really. I think you got pleasure out of making something beautiful." She indicated the moon window with a tip of the chin.

For the briefest of seconds, Nao's face flicked toward his handiwork and back. He made a reluctant, barely audible sound of assent. *"Un."*

At this, Yukako pressed her advantage. Her voice took on a resonant, voluptuous authority. "And I think you stayed to be near me," she said.

It seemed he hadn't forgiven Yukako for choosing Akio, either: there was a sudden scuffling scramble of limbs and thuds and then I heard something small and heavy fall to the *tatami*. Nao seized the gun and stepped back. "You're wrong there," he said, breathing hard.

"Listen to you," Yukako said defiantly.

"I've had women all over Japan. I've had women here in your house. Foreign whores in Yokohama. Rich wives in Tokyo. I married an *eta* girl in Asaka and I divorced her too."

Yukako gasped.

"She was unfaithful."

Yukako didn't hear him; she was still recoiling. "You *what?*"

"Who do you think Aki's mother was?"

Yukako wrapped her arms around her stomach like she was going to be sick.

"Why do you think she just left the baby here like that? She knew *she'd* be found out herself, but a child?"

I remembered Yukako taking extravagant pains to tell me how I could not possibly be an *eta*. Now she whimpered, a little strangling noise like she was choking.

"You would have paid those nuns off even quicker if you'd known, huh?" I knew that Nao was telling it this way to hurt her, but I had not understood this part of Ruri's story. *Because you're a foreigner, I'll tell you,* he'd said. He must have guessed I wouldn't understand unless he spelled it out. He was right.

I heard Yukako pant to regain composure. "Look, don't soil my brother's memory by being cruel."

Nao paused. *"Un,"* I heard him say again, softly. He paused, and then his voice was harsh again. "Lucky for you he was so sickly, wasn't it? You've made a better Master Teacher than he ever would."

"You're a monster," Yukako whispered.

"I've often wondered what would have happened if I'd taken his place."

What was he talking about? "Stop, just stop. I've had it with you," Yukako said, all in one hissed breath.

"I always wondered why Matsu seemed to hate me. Why he always beat me so hard. And then, after Hiro died, right after the fifty-day memorial tea for the household, Mother made me leave. She saw the way Master Teacher was looking at me and she saw the way Matsu was looking at him. I always did look a little like Hiro, but you'd never notice it outside the tearoom. And then, right after the tea, Mother gives me a sack of rice balls and tells me not to come back. Funny, right? And there you were, the last time I saw you, in your pretty new robe and your shiny new sandals. *Do you like my shoes, Nao-han?* I had no idea where I was going to sleep that night, and that was the last thing you said to me."

"How could I have known?" Yukako protested. "I didn't know o-Chio made you leave."

Nor had I: this wasn't the story he'd told me. "I was going to leave anyway," he mumbled.

Yukako sat very still. Her voice, when she spoke again, was weak and distant. "I don't believe what you're saying."

"You know, your father always gave me the dirtiest jobs. But they were all for tea. Matsu had me scrubbing human shit, but your father only gave me tea work. Ever wonder why?"

Yukako inhaled. "You're dismissed," she said.

"Is that so?"

"And you won't be finishing the upstairs. Do you understand?"

"I didn't think I would," he said cockily. He stood. "Well, thanks, Yuka. I had a nice evening."

"But," said Yukako numbly, "why would you——? If you thought I was your sister?"

Nao shrugged. "You wanted me."

Yukako's face tilted up toward him. She held herself as if she were cold. "Nao-*han*, I loved you. The three of you. I——"

"Now I'm really going," he said, his voice rushed and vulnerable. And he left.

YUKAKO LAY FACEDOWN on the tearoom floor, breathing shallowly. "Nao-*han*. My Kenji——" she whispered. And then she propped herself up on her elbows and vomited. "Oh," she groaned.

I was out of the coal bin in one fluid motion. *"Okusama?"*

After the blurry dim image of the tearoom in the polished metal, everything was so hard and bright and clear. Every ruffle of Yukako's green gown, every foamy bloom of *hagi*, seemed as distinct as a woodblock print.

"Go. Away," Yukako moaned. She sat up, trying to look composed.

"*Shh. Shh*," I said tenderly. "I'm sorry, *Okusama*. I heard everything."

"Oh, what next?" asked Yukako, as if appealing to heaven. It had been a long night indeed.

"Let's clean you up," I said.

I brought in wet cloths and wiped her face, wiped the floor. Yukako sat as limp as a rag doll. "Could you bring me my *kimono* from the *mizuya*?" she asked plaintively.

I found it backstage and carried it in while Yukako, still seated, struggled with her dress, tugging and gasping. "*Shh*," I repeated. I unlaced her bodice and her corset and stroked her exposed back. She shuffled off the architecture of her dress and reached for her *kimono* undergown. I held up the white silk robe and she leaned back, spreading her arms into the sleeves, sinking backward into me. To wrap the left side of the robe over the right was to fold my arms across her chest.

I held her in my arms, in the bowl of my thighs. She sighed, giving over all her weight to me. I felt her breathing with my entire body, long and smooth, the heat of her flesh moving through the cool heavy silk. Then she twitched and her breath caught; she pushed her wrist between her legs and held a fold of her robe there for a little while. She shuddered, jerked, murmured a few thick words, and then lay against me with her eyes closed. She smiled briefly, as if floating. For a moment her body felt light as balsa in my arms.

THEN IT WENT heavy again. She was crying. I loosened her long hair and combed it with my fingers. "*Older Sister*," I whispered for the first time in years, and the last.

"He's right," she whispered. "I've thrown my life away on dust and leaves."

"That's not true. Your family was failing and you made it strong. You took an art that could have died and you made it live, and the world is richer for it. In a small way, you changed the world."

"I *changed the world*," Yukako snorted. "I haven't done a thing. The *world* changed. Now that *woman* can just show up at my house and say I don't even have a chance with the boys' schools—" she spluttered. She was still for a long time.

"You see, I thought I could have it both ways," she explained, nodding toward the moon window. "Baishian with tables and glass. But my father's world is gone," she grimaced. "I should make my sons learn golf."

"Listen," I said, feeling faintly impatient. "Do you remember how much you wanted to learn tea when I first met you? How you watched every lesson and you practiced every day?"

Yukako grunted, wiping her wet eyes.

"Did you want to learn so much because the men were doing it, or because it was beautiful?"

"Because it was beautiful," she sniffled, acknowledging the room around her with a glance.

"And do you remember how you had to sit behind a screen to watch your father teach tea? And you never got a lesson of your own until you were married?"

"*Un.*"

"Because of you, no woman ever has to learn that way again. And that is all by itself a gift to the world. Do you understand?"

Yukako nodded slowly. Her body relaxed completely into mine and she smiled for a moment.

She sat quietly, thinking, the bone globe of her head resting on my shoulder. And then her eyes filled with tears again. "You know what made me so sad, earlier?"

"What?" I knew from her voice she meant when she'd cried after quaking in my arms.

Yukako sighed. "That woman just brought it all back to me. How I'll never see Akio in this life again."

Ah. It had been his name she'd murmured thickly, before falling asleep for a few seconds. "I'm sorry," I said.

The truth was, I didn't feel very sorry. It occurred to me that the thing she and Nao had most in common was a need to waste passion on Akio. Twenty-five years seemed like a long time to mourn a boy who'd told her not to do *temae*, who'd cheated on her in her own house. Who'd abandoned her and Koito to go along with an arranged marriage, and then abandoned his wife and family to go get killed in Satsuma. When Nao left, Yukako didn't literally say *I loved you*. She used the pronoun Japanese people go to great lengths to avoid, unless they are wives addressing their husbands. She looked up at Nao and said *Antahan. You.* And then *You three:* Nao, her brother, and Akio, whom she held in her heart as indelibly as that metal wall held its two scratched names, whom she loved with a tenacity forged in childhood.

As part of me still loved her. She'd just managed to snatch away one of the few moments of unmixed bliss she'd ever given me, and still I held her. I missed it so much, the feeling of being in love with her. I drew my fingers down the black silk expanse of her hair, I traced the long calligraphic line of her back, I caressed her face with the back of my hand, barely touching her. She turned and embraced me: it had not happened since I was a child. I trembled. Her hand lay on my bare skin. I melted inside with longing, and then I kissed her.

I COULD STILL FEEL the soft wet heat of her mouth as she stood on the other side of the room, my chest stinging from the force with which she'd pushed me away. "It was *you*. I can't believe it."

What happened? I stared, dumbfounded, while Yukako dressed briskly, shaking with anger. "He taught you that, didn't he?" she barked. Then I remembered her asking Nao, *What are you doing?*

He must have kissed her, I realized, remembering when he'd first kissed me, how disgusting I had found it. But I had made the pleasure of kissing mine so quickly, so utterly, I'd done it without thinking.

YUKAKO LASHED HERSELF into her *kimono*, bristling. I saw Tsuko had chosen a robe just as formal as Koito's for her mother-in-law: black, five-crested, with an almost waist-high pattern of green maple leaves, a red one here or there anticipating fall. The green shone almost white in the moonlight; when Yukako, dressing with her back to me, spread her *kimono*, it looked as though she were standing behind a wall of glowing leaves. The robe fell six inches below the ankle; she folded up the excess with one swift knife-crease and spun into her *obi* as if throwing off sparks.

She turned to face me again. "Every time I look at you, I'm going to remember this night," she said coolly, as if noting it might rain.

I blinked. Somewhere inside, I found it gratifying to think I might have such an effect on her.

Then she spoke again. "This has been the worst night of my life."

She looked down to tuck a last *obi* cord into place and looked back up at me. "I know you have a job, Miss Urako, so I don't feel bad saying this. You are to leave here tonight, do you understand?"

"Oh," I said.

"In my father's day, the appropriate thing to do in this situation would be to take your own life. But I think that's a bit extreme, don't you?"

I stared at her, appalled. But this was her family, wasn't it? Rikyu, her founding ancestor, had been the tea master and closest confidant of the most important man in Japan, until he displeased his lord and was asked to commit suicide. On the day he died, he invited a few friends for a last tea ceremony, wrote a last poem, and slit his own belly with a shortsword.

My face went hot. I placed my hands in front of me and bowed to hide my eyes as they filled with tears. I blinked, head bent, and as if for the first time I saw my own small hands on the *tatami*, the raw eye of each knuckle looking back at me. *For twenty-five years*, I thought, *these hands have been hers*.

The appropriate thing would be to take your own life. Still bowing, I realized that Yukako had just told me how she cared for me: with her whole heart, like Shonagon's Empress. We were vassal and liege, no less, no more. Like Rikyu, I meant enough to her that she would ask this much of me, that she would dignify what she was asking with a name this grave. For a moment I wished I had Nao's gun to point at my stomach and prove myself worthy of the comparison. *These hands are hers*, I thought fiercely. *This is my place.*

But I heard those words in Nao's voice; they were Aki's mother's words. And I remembered what he'd said after repeating them: *It's not true.*

MY CHEST THROBBED, still, where Yukako had pushed me away. I sat up from my bow. I looked at her and spoke. "I need you to pay for me to go, the way you paid for Aki."

"I beg your pardon?"

Everything in me wanted to shrink back, to say *Nothing, nothing*, to stick a shortsword in my belly and tell her I was hers forever. But I took a deep breath and said, "You gave Aki a dowry for the nuns. I want a dowry."

Yukako shrank back in disgust. I did not move.

When she exhaled, Yukako's sigh was equal parts betrayal and fatigue. "You greedy little foreigner," she breathed. I shut my eyes in pain.

I had depleted my courage, so I just sat there. She did too. I felt so much as the long seconds passed. The heat of my daring cooled off and still I sat there, cold and exhausted and stupefied.

And obstinate.

"This is silly," Yukako said. "The night's been long enough already without this nonsense. There's money in my pillow. Take what you need and go."

I bowed again deeply, and left.

36

1891

A s I passed through the kitchen to collect my things, I saw Kuga alone, deep in her cups, idly stirring the hearth with a pair of metal tongs. It was one of her black nights: I knew the next morning she'd be achy and snappish and not remember much. "Well, I'm going," I announced.

"*Un*," she said, which is what I thought she'd say.

"*Okusama* told me to leave and never come back, so I'm leaving," I repeated.

"*Un*."

I could hear the laughter of the others in nearby rooms. I could hear the last crickets whirring before the cold nights came in earnest. I could feel a wave of grief whelming toward me, as if from far away. Before it flattened me, I asked, "Do you think there's any chance Nao-*han* might be *Okusama*'s brother?"

Kuga moved her metal chopsticks back and forth, sluggishly blotting out her tracings in the ash. She looked like both her parents for a moment: Matsu's hollow temples, Chio's heavy lips. I remembered Chio at the end, calling Yukako by her father's boyhood name. I

remembered her quietly moving Nao's photograph from the kitchen
to her own little hut after her husband died. She would have been so
young when Nao was born. Had the Mountain gone to her drunk on
his own power? Or would he, like his grandson, have been happy to
marry the kitchen maid? I had never wondered: had he even wanted to
be his Master Teacher's heir? Kuga slowly looked at me. "Shut your
mouth," she said, which I took for *Yes*.

I made my way through the hall above the sewing room with a
lantern and found Yukako's lacquered pillow by her screen. She had
begun moving it herself in the mornings, and I was surprised to discover how heavy it was now. A search through its drawer yielded only
poems and ribbons, bits of old *kimono*, Akio's tightly wrapped teascoop, but I could barely lift the wooden pillow-box; I felt the heavy
slosh of metal in its chamber. I poured Yukako's keepsakes into one
of her carrying cloths and tied it neatly for her. Then I took the whole
box. In the dark, with tears starting down my face, I was in no shape
to face some clever secret drawer. *I can't puzzle it out*, I thought. One
poem, however, not by Akio, had caught my eye. *I know who can.*

THE WALK WAS ENDLESS. Tears moved down my face in slow sheets.
My hands went cold and bloodless from my knotted carrying cloths.
Nothing had changed in twenty-five years: the night streets went on
forever and I belonged to no one. I could have been a child again, walking and crying, stunned from the fire. I saw my uncle's boots and the
terrified horses. I heard groaning timbers and the thunderous collapse
of tile. I smelled fire, I smelled fire. I sobbed as I walked: the wet,
inchoate noises I heard were mine.

I remembered Yukako as I first saw her in Baishian, phospho-
rescent, the way she spread her robe across me in the dark. I keened. I
sat down on my burdens between two walls of night-shuttered

houses and dug my sodden face into my hands. The rest of my life would consist of thousands of minutes, and from each she would be gone.

I SAID I KNEW Madame from her *geisha* days, and Advisor Kato's servants let me wait by the door. At length they returned to let me in.

"I wondered whatever happened to you," Koito said warmly after the maid brought tea. "But tonight—it never seemed like the right moment to ask." Kato's new guesthouse was even more lavish on the inside, with gold brocade edging the *tatami* and a fat handsome treetrunk for the alcove post. I noted Nao's workmanship in the graceful round window. It seemed, given her unquestioning hospitality, that Koito assumed I was here to apologize for Yukako's coolness, and was hoping, through me, to make a good impression.

So it was with much awkwardness that I began. "There's a rumor that a man with a gun is looking for your husband," I first said carefully. Nao had ties to both Kato and Yukako, and I did not want to embarrass either one of them.

"Thank you for worrying about us," Koito said. "After this summer, with the Tax Minister, he always travels with a pair of bodyguards, but I'll go send them a quiet word." As she vanished down the hall, I wondered if Nao—or his "brothers"—had had any part in that summer's murder.

KOITO RETURNED with a dish of *sembei* crackers. I told her, ruthlessly keeping my voice from shaking, that for personal reasons I'd had a sudden falling-out with my mistress and that I'd been paid to leave. "She gave me this," I said. "I can't open it."

"Can't open what?" Koito asked, popping open a simple catch. Out slid a tray of *yen* and *sen* coins, enough to cover a small tea gathering or deal with an unexpected tradesman's bill. I'd known Yukako all these years and never seen the latch: embarrassed, I pulled the wooden pillow toward myself to see how to work it.

Koito and I looked at each other. We both heard the rasping metal inside, and indeed, the box seemed no lighter for missing a tray of coins. Koito brought the lamp closer. *"Ara!"* she said, finding a pair of metal pins that had been covered by the coin drawer. She pressed them and the whole top of the pillow-box detached.

The base of the box, we discovered, was a deep tray, filled with *koban*, large oval gold coins from the Shoguns' time. Koito gave me a very long look. I felt hot and itchy. Yukako had not meant me to have this. "I don't know," I said nervously. My chance to ask the thing I most wanted to had come and gone. I gasped for air. "She just gave it to me," I said, which wasn't quite true. "I don't know."

Just at that moment there came a clamor of servants and wooden clappers. I heard Mariko Kato's squally voice. "Excuse me," Koito said. There was a small wooden box on the dressing table, probably of valuables; she took it as she left the room.

Just outside, I heard voices, and someone whistling a ditty from when the boys were young: *"We're not afraid of wearing convict red . . ."* Then the whistling stopped, cut off by a blow to the face. I slid open the window and looked. Seven or eight men were crowded into Kato's dainty front garden; all the house servants held lanterns. I saw Nao standing calmly, surrounded by guardsmen, his lip bloodied. I saw a man carefully wrap a gun in a sheet of paper. I saw Kato bowing repeatedly to a thick-faced man in a swallowtail jacket, who brushed him off with jovial menace. "It's just a little hole," he said, his laughter smug and meaty. "Why don't we take him to the prefectural office tonight and find out what happens to people who shoot *jin-rikisha?*"

Kato looked from Nao to the great man and back, tugging his

tight collar, as the words *glazier* and *gun* moved freely through the small crowd. The Minister's visit had been a feather in his cap; the last thing he wanted was to spoil it with a scandal involving a man he'd hired. "Excellent idea," he said wretchedly, bowing.

"Ah, cheer up," said the Minister, slapping him heartily on the back. The gesture was one Western affectation for which Kato was not prepared; he quailed. "We'll compose moon-viewing poems on the way home, how about it? And you said you had that surprise for me on the Takase Canal; let's have a look."

"Tomorrow," Advisor Kato all but squeaked. "I said it would be ready tomorrow." He bowed again, glum and harried, and then Mariko Kato stepped forward.

"Please, Father. Let me come with you so I can tell them about Baishian," she said.

"Baishian? At Cloud House? Why, I was just there," said Koito's low voice.

"It's gone," said Mariko, bursting into tears that were at least half real. It had always been strange to me that she had stayed on at the Shins' after the disaster with Kenji, but I understood, when I heard her cry that night: she loved the place. "There was a fire."

"Is anyone hurt?" fluttered Lady Kato.

"Just Baishian. The stream was right there, so we could put the fire out fast. But it's *gone*," she lowed.

"What happened?" asked her father.

Mariko sniffled loudly and composed herself. "I think it's pretty clear what happened," she said, turning to the knot of guardsmen. Nao said something; I think it was *No.* I could not read his face as he watched her, but in her voice I heard the steel of a woman scorned.

My last sight of him was the mask of his face as the guardsmen walked him away that night. His straight straight back.

· · ·

"You're crying," said Koito behind me.

I closed the window and turned to her.

She looked down at the untouched gold, and up again at me. "Well, it was you or him. Either you burned the teahouse and took the money, or he burned it. And it's worth this much to your mistress to blame you instead."

"Our falling-out was of a personal nature," I said.

"I see. He's very handsome."

I wiped my eyes and said nothing.

"You can't be seen here, whatever happened. It's too messy. If you stay tonight, you need to leave before sunrise." I hadn't thought about where I'd sleep: I bowed to Koito in gratitude. "Truth be told, I would not recommend you stay in Kyoto," she added. She gave me a long look, tender and discerning. I wanted to ask, then, if I could follow her to Tokyo, but she glanced from my all-too-recognizable foreign face to the box of *koban* and her warning scared the question out of me: "Perhaps not even Japan."

THE NEXT DAY, Koito lent me a Western dress and promised to show me the way to a hotel for foreign tourists. I went to Brother Joaquin that morning and asked him to book me passage to New York. He had once arranged for me to enter Miyako; perhaps he could arrange for me to leave. We stared at each other, the grown woman bowing in her borrowed frock, the aging monk. Like Miss Starkweather, he spoke remarkably bad Japanese: he'd known enough to impress me and my uncle when we arrived, but had never, it seemed, learned more. Uncle Charles, he told me, was presumed dead after the fire, but his body had never been found. I said nothing. I had only ever dreamed him once, I realized, that afternoon before the Expo, long ago. "What a loss of talent," Brother Joaquin sighed, shaking his head. "What a waste. And you, growing up among heathens. If we'd known, we could have found you . . ." he said. "I'm so sorry." Fluent or not, his time here had changed him: we were bowing to each other as he apologized and agreed to help me. I gave him passage money: he knew of a ship leaving Kobe in two days' time; he'd do what he could to get me on it. "It's the least I can do."

I bowed, I smiled. Yes, indeed, it was.

When I saw Miss Starkweather, she blinked at me. "You never told me you could dress properly," she huffed. When I tendered my resignation and asked if she knew of anyone in New York who might need my services, she sputtered; she flustered; she said a sour thing or two about my not giving notice, and then she wrote down a few addresses. I stiffened with surprise when she and Miss Parmalee embraced me and kissed my cheeks, but I softened inside as well.

I paused at a fancy new milk bar, all brass and red velvet, and tried a glass. Was I really going to New York? I could not really believe a place outside Japan existed, and yet here was milk, evidence of my childhood, of a whole milk- drinking world abroad. It had a faint undertaste of chestnuts, the way milk in New York would taste faintly of blueberries when it was about to turn. It made my throat close with the old grief for my mother and the new grief of exile. It gave me a stomachache.

I stopped at a rice-ball stand and bought a few. I ate one right there, and the woman gave me a cup of cold barley tea and a hard look. "Your Japanese is good," she said.

The rust-colored frock Koito had given me was the first grown-up Western dress I'd ever worn, made for a woman with a long torso and a small chest. Even ill-fitting, it gave me a sense of invulnerability as I left the stand. No one had recognized me at the girls' school until I had spoken to them; I saw myself diminish in Miss Starkweather's eyes the moment she realized it was me. And so it was with a certain reckless, evil pleasure that I let myself into a nearby *jinrikisha*-puller's home, took a pair of yellow-thonged sandals out of the shoe box in the cloakroom, and made my way to the bathhouse.

I UNTIED THE BOOTS Koito had given me around the corner, so no one could stop me in the entrance. I stepped out of my shoes, set my money on the absent attendant's stand, took a new bran bag and towel, and had my dress off before any of the three ancient afternoon bathers knew what had happened. I soaped and scrubbed, noting that alongside the portrait of the Emperor hung a whimsically tinted woodblock print in which His Majesty faced a company of young soldiers, the crowd spiny with green rifles, their uniforms lush violet and rose.

"Don't come in here," said one of the old ladies.

"It's not for you."

"*Akahen,*" said the third. *Bad.*

Of course I went in, and of course they got out. I sank into the exquisite steaming water and stared back at them, towels on their heads, their arms akimbo. I soaked as long as I dared, while the old ladies went to find the attendant. She lumbered over to the tub and spat invective at me, pulling the plug.

I felt hot triumph, listening to the water suck away: it was the sound of all the charcoal they were willing to waste on hating me. I looked them each in the eye. Everything was still for a moment and then they started talking together about summoning more people to remove me. I climbed out. "Please give my best to Little Hazu," I said, and tossed her pretty yellow sandals into the tub behind me. They circled in the draining water, dirt swirling in their wake.

Then I hurried into my dress. I'd been more than bold enough. The first empty *jinrikisha* I saw, I hailed.

"Take Migawa Street," I said, still damp, pulling up the awning to hide.

"Your Japanese is so good," the runner said.

· · ·

AND SO I CHOSE TO PASS the Shin house that afternoon, in the glow of my last trip to the bathhouse, my pleasure no less real for being juvenile. My giddy mood crumbled as soon as we approached Cloud House: the little Migawa, high and swollen ever since Kato's canal had opened, was lined with buckets, the street abuzz with people. I gagged; the scent was a knife in the air, ineluctable and acrid. The night before, when I'd remembered the long-ago fire, I was breathing real smoke.

The smell was enough. "Please turn off here," I pointed, sinking deeper under the *jinrikisha* awning, and we pulled away. It would not do to be seen, and there was really nothing to see: Baishian had never been visible from the street. My last glimpse of the Shins was their long low wall in the yellowing afternoon light, broken by the great thatched gate.

When we clattered past the shrine, I saw a group of players rehearsing a piece called *Nonomiya*, about the ghost of a woman who cannot forgive her enemy, and who therefore cannot pass out of this life and be reborn. I saw the actor-ghost at the spirit gate lift a white-socked foot to leave and set it down, unable. In my heart I paused at the nearby Kannon altar. This time I did not ask for anything to happen. I bowed my head twice—forcing myself not to look back and see if Yukako was among the others on Migawa Street—and I made the simplest prayer I had ever heard: *to be happy.*

I WAS FOOLHARDY, going to the bathhouse and the Shins'. Everyone was looking for me, Aki said when I stopped at the convent. She wore a white cloth mask over half her face now, but it gave me such joy to see her good eye and unbruised skin. "I can't believe you're *here*," she whispered anxiously. "Why did you do it? *You*, of all people? The teahouse? The money?"

It was a comfort to know she didn't want to believe it of me. "*Okusama* told me to take what I needed, and I took all of it. I heard the teahouse burned, but that's all I know. Really."

Her narrowed eye widened, and she took a step closer.

"So, I guess you talk to Kenji when he visits now?" I asked.

"He writes to me," she said, looking a little abashed. "Usually he waits around outside all day and I burn the letters. What could they say, really? *A dog just walked by. Your Mother Superior looks cross today, doesn't she? Oh, now I smell you're having lunch.* But today he only came and left a letter, so I worried." She took an embarrassed look back at the convent house. "It's worldly of me, but I read it."

So. Arsonist and thief. I knew where I stood with the Shins. "What did he say about your father?"

"They're holding him for questioning," she said, her voice dropping as she looked down.

"You won't believe me if I say he burned the teahouse, but he *was* there last night. I heard him talking with *Okusama* and he said a few things about your mother. I came to tell you what I heard."

Her gaze had slowly lifted as I spoke; now she looked me full in the eye. She leaned forward and took one of the bars of the gate. I told her what I knew, if not how I'd come to learn it.

Aki's face worked behind her mask when I finished. "*Un,*" she said. "I guessed as much. I even wrote to Kenji like I *knew* it was so, to make him stop coming around, but he said he didn't care. Well, now I know." She stood still for a moment, thinking. "There's still so much I *don't* know," she said. I wished so many good things for her just then, this clear, bright young woman, this new penny shining through mud.

I WAITED FOR KOITO on Third Bridge that evening. The Kamo River was swift and glassy, its rocky spits peopled with egrets. I could see the eastern mountains so clearly in the last pink light: great brooding Hiei, Daimonji with the great *dai* character carved into the bald patch on its flank, tame Maruyama, low and green, decked with temple spires. I had not been past the mountains cupping this city in twenty-five years.

There was so much *I* didn't know, either. What had happened at Baishian after I left? Had Nao come back to burn Baishian for spite? I didn't think so: bedding his master's daughter on the tearoom floor seemed like triumph enough for him. And it wasn't clear to me pre-cisely what had happened when: for Nao to burn the teahouse *and* shoot at the Minister might have required him to be in two different places at once.

Could Yukako have fallen asleep in the teahouse and started a fire from neglect? Teahouses were designed to allow two fires to burn untended, one in the tearoom and one in the *mizuya* backstage. I tried to remember if there had been any earthquake tremors that might have jostled the charcoal or thrown sparks. I was upset then; I can't say for certain, but I remember none.

And Yukako had not seemed likely to fall asleep in the teahouse, or to wander off from a charcoal fire. I winced at my last image of her; it was not what I would have wanted. I tried to remember her in my arms, or even in her robe of leaves, grave and regal as she sent me away. But no, the last time I saw my mistress, she was bent over in Baishian with the knot of her *obi* poking in the air like a housemaid's, wiping down the *tatami* with a cloth. Watching her scrub and swab was like hearing a favorite song on an instrument left slack; it was hard to see all that briskness and purpose flattened into nervous energy. I made a sound or two in the doorway, to show I was leaving. I bowed. She did not look up.

I COULD NOT IMAGINE Baishian aflame, and yet I could think of nothing else. The *tatami* smoking from young green to black to red, the delicate basketwork of the ceiling dropping to the floor in blackened curls. The *shoji* gone in quick puffs, the lattice shining red and sinking gray. And fire does not wait for us to pack up our homes before it takes them: the tea boxes surely burned, with their hundred coats of sanded lacquer. The whisks would burn like feathers. The shelves backstage must have burned, collapsing, all their precious vessels in shards. Even the stems and blooms of *hagi* would have curled, wobbled, and burned, right up to the water still in the vase. And burning slowest of all, the fine wood that framed all my years with Yukako: the satiny moiré of the floorboard, the clean planes of the low square door and the alcove post. The night-black alcove floor, with its white lightning blaze. I heard the rending dull heave of the thatched roof as it crashed, the whinny and groan of timber, the tinkling pop of Nao's windows. I covered my ears.

And then I knew what had happened. I wept on that bridge for Yukako. Not *for* Yukako, as I had all day, because she had sent me away, because she was lost to me. No. For *Yukako*. For what the fire must have meant to her.

I HAD NOT YET asked Koito the thing I most wanted to know. When she came, she had her runner bring us downtown on a street that followed the Takase, a canal fed by the Kamo River a short block away. The stream shimmered in the lantern light; I'd first entered the city by this narrow route, poled on a flat-bottomed boat. Before I could ask, Koito pointed to the street beyond. "Pontocho," she said, "where I first worked."

"Did you meet your husband there?" I inquired politely. "Or in Tokyo?"

"We couldn't have met in Pontocho," Koito chuckled, her voice a rich purr. "We tried, once or twice, but all the Emperor's men went across the river to Gion; Pontocho was for the Shogun's people. I'd never seen him before that big tea at Cloud House, actually, the night I first met your *Okusama*. If I'd known she and Lord Ii's son were engaged, I would never have gone. But you know how things turned out. I'll never forget that angry young girl, the way she tried to tear the robe right off me."

She looked out, lost in thought. I wanted to hear more, so I didn't interrupt with my question. Above each river-light hung a darkened lantern; a high row of them lined the canal. I wondered what they were for. Koito continued, "And then the imperial guards at the end of the block wouldn't let me leave! I just sat in my palanquin, with the bearers smoking and the evening dribbling away. I was supposed to work three parties that night, but I knew it would be so long before I saw the young lord again. Remember how sick he was? I couldn't resist the chance to visit him when I could blend in with the other *geiko* at Cloud House. But there I was, in a torn *kimono*, embarrassed and upset and losing money. And then this handsome young man looked into my box and said, "I don't remember you with the others; who are you?" And it was the Emperor's nephew—my Minister. He made the guards wave me through. It was *love at first sight*," she said in English. "But then the war made everything difficult."

I had never heard Koito like this before, relaxed and chatty and confessional. It was a delight. "I had to make my own way," she said. "The other *geiko* kept getting younger and younger. I learned tea as Rikyu taught it, I learned French, I traded my lead paint for Western white. Anything to make me stand out," she sighed. "And then we met again, by accident, when his wife was dying." She looked at me, her smile both frank and shy. "I'm so lucky," she said. She was.

After a pause, she added, "Mizushi just got married too; remember my little sister? To Baron Sono's son Kazuo."

The boy Sumie wanted for her daughter. I gasped. How small this world was. It occurred to me just then that the Mountain might never have known why his adoptive father had wanted to call a teahouse Baishian,

and that I might know now. "What was your grandmother's name?" I
asked suddenly. "Your mother's mother?"

"Why, it was Baishi," Koito said, a little embarrassed as the name
of the teahouse floated unspoken between us.

"I thought so," I said. The moment passed, and then it felt easy, by
the flickering water, to ask the most important thing.

No sooner had I opened my mouth, however, but there came a
sound I'd never heard before. A tingle of metal on metal, a crackling
whir. The delicate pop of one era in a city's life ending, a new one taking hold.

And then the lake waters that lapped Akio's home in Hikone
coursed down the Biwa Canal and fell through a turbine in East Kyoto;
the force of their falling shocked the strung wires overhead, and the
dark lanterns over the canal were seized with light. It was like a loud
sound, a deafening brilliance, as the electric lights behind me, then
the ones overhead, and then each one before me, came on, on, on,
on, on.

THE JINRIKISHA MAN dropped his poles and covered his face with both
hands. I clung to Koito in terror and she laughed. "This must be Kato's
surprise for my husband! I'd guessed as much. Look! It's like Tokyo!"

Hearing her, the jinrikisha-puller nodded, took a long look down
the shining canal, and dabbed the sweat off his forehead. "Un," he said.
He took up his poles again and drew us down the row of lights. I
stared at the Takase water, the illuminated sheets of it, like a dazzling
road.

KOITO BROUGHT ME to the hotel and sat with me in the bar a few
moments before leaving. I finally asked her what I most longed to
know. Among the few things I had brought from the Shins' were five

black pearls of incense, a small white cup. "What happened to Miss Inko?"

"She really took a shine to you, didn't she? My favorite maid ever. You know she married in Tokyo?"

"A man from a sweet-shop family," I said, a little impatiently.

"He died young, ten years ago, maybe," Koito said. "They had three boys and a girl, all recently married. I saw her not too long ago; she's the same as ever. Loud, funny. You remember."

Inko, a mother! Almost a grandmother! I set down my plum wine. "Is she happy?" I pressed.

"Life hasn't been good to her, to be honest. Her husband dying. All those sons, and her in-laws still make her sleep in the entrance like a new bride. I thought when her boys got married, she'd have a houseful of daughters-in-law to serve her hand and foot, but it sounds like her husband's parents have taken them over for themselves. And they're in their fifties, you know. They're going to live forever."

In case I somehow lost the pillow-box, I was also carrying a few gold coins in the reticule Koito had given me. Each was worth a fortune, she'd said. "Give Miss Inko these, when you see her," I told her. "And ask her to come visit me in New York someday."

Koito's eyes widened. She hailed the barman for a writing brush, and he produced an inkwell and a pen with a metal nib. By the electric light falling in from the street outside, I wrote the only address in New York I'd ever learned. And with painstaking Roman letters, I spelled out a name: Aurelia Corneille.

Epilogue

1891–1929

I TRAVELED A GRUELING three-week route, first by sea to San Francisco, then by train to New York. A red brick wall, a yard of stones, the last green leaves of the sycamores: I had come so far for this, a name and two dates. I took fierce pleasure in pulling up the weeds and rough grass that covered my mother's small marker. In all this world, it was mine. "Claire," I whispered, crying a little as I swabbed out the dirt from the cut grooves of her name. My mother had died when I was young and I knew where her grave was: I was surprised by how much comfort this gave me.

While I was gone, Lafayette Street had been widened, the Brooklyn Bridge hung, Broadway strung with electric lights. The church on Mott Street had burned and been rebuilt. Maggie Phelan had died young, of cholera.

I FIRST LIVED just a few doors down from the very building where I'd been raised, in the nuns' Residence for Women Travelers. More so than my mother could afford to be, I was grateful for their hospitality. I picked up translation work quickly, and at night gathered with my fellow Women Travelers at the nuns' long refectory tables, watching my neighbors to learn again how Western people ate. "I don't like the way she stares," I heard a girl tell her mother. But how did a body bring soup to the mouth without lifting the bowl? English was a rough glass wall each woman raised around her: I could see through it, but not as well as I could before she'd spoken.

THE NEW FACE at dinner one night was a female rake. After tumbling all the young girls who would have her, by the end of the week, she reached me. She talked nonsense, but I followed her to bed and found in my own body a storehouse of delight. I looked in the washstand mirror the next morning and saw that I would have been a reasonably pretty girl had I grown up in New York, a black-and-pale *gamine*. At thirty-five, I was a handsome woman.

"I'll write," the rake promised. She did not, nor had I expected as much. But for a good week after, I smiled each night through the idle conversation of the Women Travelers, the rock crystal walls of their English grinding at me like teeth, gnashing my thoughts into the shape of an English tongue.

WHEN THE OLD BARBER around the corner died the next spring, I bought his house with Yukako's gold: across the street from the brick churchyard wall, the small empty building was home to an apartment and a shop, a cat-haunted patch of weeds in back. I welcomed the silence, though it scared me. I ate when I was hungry: bread, fruit, cheese. Alone in the house, adding coal to the fire or hauling in water from the tap, I felt like I could vanish at any moment.

By September, I had not yet touched the barber's vacant shop. I knew I ought to rent it out, and one Saturday morning after the summer heat broke, I went downstairs to give the place a good cleaning and put up a sign. I had just rolled up the heavy shutters when a hansom cab rounded the corner, led by a flock of nuns.

I understood what had happened before the cabbie began setting the cloth-wrapped boxes on the sidewalk, before the nuns reached me, brandishing the paper with my name and their address. The moment I saw the two figures in the carriage bow to each other in their seat, with just the degree of formality of two cordial strangers taking leave, I knew. My heart leapt in my chest. She must have made an English-speaking friend en route who'd helped her find me.

I stood openmouthed, still gripping the shutter handle, and it was Inko. The same narrow close-set eyes, the same reckless grin.

"You look just like yourself!" she cried. I blinked, hearing Japanese, and I bowed to her in the street. "Well, here I am," she said. "If we get along, I thought I might stay with you, and if we don't, I'll go somewhere else."

Breathless with disbelief, I looked at this woman, her rogue's face like mine, youngish but not young. Stemmy in her Western dress, she was lean with years of work. I saw a grown woman, the decades of her hardship unknown to me, and I saw the brash, glamorous girl I'd known. The shutter handle dug into my palm; I was so happy. She cocked her head as if to take me in one eye at a time, and then her glance was a flash of color skimming over the street trees, the church-yard wall, the barbershop window. When Western-style barbers appeared in Kyoto, they set up candy-striped poles just like the ones in New York. The *toko,* pole, in the Japanese word for barbershop, *pole-shop,* was the same as the *toko* in *tokonoma, post-room,* the display alcove defined by an extra post. Dark and glittering, Inko looked from me to the barber's pole and back, raised an eyebrow. "Say, *Tokoya-han,* can I have a shave?"

Shaky with joy, I nodded to the cabbie. "You can put her things in here." I took her hard small hands. "I'll draw you a bath," I said.

. . .

I LOVED HER ARMS. I loved her calves. I loved her little mouth with its crooked tooth. I loved her spooling dark hair. I loved her hard brown feet and soft scant breasts. I bathed her and we made a feast of each other in the barber's brass bed, sleeping and loving and eating apples spread with honey. As the day ebbed toward evening, a pink light stole over the white walls and I held her pillowed on my chest, drowsy in the warm air. "What are all those boxes downstairs?" I asked.

"Do you know how much all those *koban* were worth?" she asked. "More than enough to go and come back. So," she inhaled, her eyes lighting. "I thought I might open a sweet shop."

INKO UNPACKED her pots and molds and strainers into the shop downstairs and became indispensable to Japanese visitors—winning the trust of a few steady buyers in Chinatown, too—for her finely strained red bean *an*. Because of American immigration laws (which Inko had sidestepped thanks to Koito's husband), there were far more men than women among the twelve thousand Chinese downtown; perhaps Inko offered them a taste of, not home, but something less far. The nationalist wave that washed me out of Kyoto kept swelling after I left: during Japan's brutal war with China, Inko's buyers accepted her gifts and apologies with wan thanks. They continued to place orders for her sweet bean paste, but the invitations to their New Years' banquets dried up, never to be extended again.

Snooping her way into confectioners' kitchens, Inko also taught herself to make chocolate—not so different, in texture, from bean paste, after all—and built a brisk trade in the neighborhood. She has become a resident curiosity, the Japanese candy lady, and with time the local children and their parents have come to add a few Japanese holidays to their own: Girls' Day, March third, has become the Day of

Free Chocolate Dolls; Boys' Day, May fifth, has become the Day of Free Chocolate Fish. Each of her children has visited us, but none have decided to stay. Ten years ago, after a last trip to Japan, Inko began training her successor, a warm-faced young widow whose new husband runs a watch-repair stand. All our Sicilian neighbors are so surprised that poor barren Lucia remarried at all, and a Northern fellow no less, that they haven't seemed to notice that her long-fingered Genoese is no man.

I keep the ledger for Inko's shop, deal with English troubles when she needs me, and translate as I find work. At night, while Inko dreams on bakers' hours, I devour books by lamplight. When I was a girl, the novels ended in marriage and the poems rhymed. The Great War changed people here as much as Meiji changed them in Japan: I am by turns baffled and delighted by the stark new cadences of the young writers. They etch the soft phrases through which I see the world into harder, tighter lines, just as today's columnar, *kimono*-shaped dresses once again blunt the bustled and corseted silhouette that flattered me when I first arrived. When I finish reading, I curl into bed: Inko smells like chocolate, like the lemons she floats in our bath.

IT HAS TAKEN ME almost forty years to put words to the unhappiness of my youth; perhaps I have been granted this much time so that someday I can attempt the greater feat of describing the happiness of my middle age. But what is the form best suited to the minutiae of happiness, to its grandeur? I mean to learn it.

LAST OCTOBER, when I went to the Japanese Embassy for a client, I discovered, among the official brochures and leaflets, a long out-of-date issue of a gazette called *Cloud House Monthly*. My skin prickled into gooseflesh: Tai had begun printing up a leaflet for tea people, which included news of his own family. "Do you have more of these?" I asked the Embassy clerk.

YUKAKO WAS DEAD, I learned, reading at home that night. She had died some twelve years before, in 1916.

My very first response, as with almost every interaction I had with Japanese people, was embarrassment: how rude of me to think she'd never die! How selfish! My second response was surprise: how could she have succumbed to anything so petty, so ordinary, as death? And my third was a cauterized feeling where guilty regret should have been: I would never know if Yukako had forgiven me. For taking the money. For taking Nao to spite her. For wanting her more than she wanted me.

I wrote Tai a numb little letter of condolence and went out to the churchyard. I tried to summon the image of Yukako in the white cremation robe in which she'd once been married, her eyes closed, her long body rigid. I saw nothing. I felt nothing, and felt monstrous for it. My face was wet only from the wind in my eyes. The stars were small and far.

IT ARRIVED THIS MORNING, the wooden crate from Japan, just as I was finishing Virginia Woolf's new book, *Orlando*, my ears abuzz with the aeroplanes her Elizabethan heroine lived so long to witness. Among the *kanji* brushed on all sides of the box, I found my address inked in, serifs and all, exactly as it had been printed on my stationery. Inside the crate lay a letter from Kenji, written on his brother's behalf, conveying Tai's best wishes and Aki's as well. They had married after his mother's death, and Aki had surprised them both at forty with a daughter they called Shinju: Pearl. Yukako's suffering, Kenji said, had been intense but brief, and she had gone about dying with the same attentiveness and vigor with which she'd lived. Among the parcels she'd assembled to distribute to friends and family, she had made up a box for me, which they had accordingly kept in storage all these years. She had said to send it with some pressed-sugar sweets and powdered tea, which he enclosed. *For me.*

I BEGAN OPENING my package inside, but after Kenji's powdered *matcha* and the sweets, when the next thing I discovered was a whisk, it was clear Yukako had decided I should receive tea utensils. It was a soft bright day; the paulownia were in bloom. I did not want to face whatever she'd chosen for me inside.

Paulownia are *kiri* in Japanese; their wood is fine-grained and highly prized by cabinetworkers; they have spade-shaped leaves the size of a man's head and regal tiered blooms in May. The tree in the churchyard formed a green canopy over me as I sat on the grass near my mother's grave. I set out a flask of hot water, Kenji's powdered tea, and the box of pressed-sugar wafers. He had chosen ones shaped like irises at a time when surely the plums would have been blooming, both in nature and in the shops. I was touched that he had anticipated how long it would take the sweets to reach me.

Yukako's bundle, packed in a shallow wooden box using tied cloth in place of a lid, included a few new things: the whisk, never used, the tips of its tines still curled like petals; a pad of tea-papers; a new white linen swab; a red silk tea-cloth. And she had chosen for me the practice utensils she'd used as a girl: I recognized the plain tan teascoop, the small student's fan, the dull-red diamond used for serving sweets, the round tray for the simplest *temae*. And the black lacquer tea box, the underside of whose lid I had neglected to clean so many years ago. I saw no wastewater bowl and wondered why.

The tea bowl was in a plain, unsigned box, well wrapped, of the size brought along on picnics, smaller than a tearoom bowl. I had never seen it before, but I saw, in its billowing walls and smoke-colored surface, an unconscious echo of Hakama, the bowl from the last tea held in Baishian. It must have felt like seeing a lost friend in the face of a child, to pass this tea bowl in a shop somewhere: if it gave me a frisson of recognition, all these years later, what must it have done to Yukako? With a sudden flash, I *knew* she had bought the bowl meaning to smash it, to silence its mocking rhyme, and then thought better of it, tucked the little piece away into storage.

And so she had made me her confidante again, after all these years. I was the one she chose to tell the story of her discomfiting day, her head turning as she passed some potter's stall, the tea bowl leaping like an insect into her field of vision. Passing the stall twice more to find herself irritated afresh each time. Finally buying the bowl so as never to have to pass it again. Walking moodily home.

I cupped the bowl with both hands beneath the *kiri* tree, its leaves loud in the wind. Before filling the tea box with powdered *matcha*, I wiped down all the utensils with tea-papers and splashes of hot water, then laid them out as if setting up for *temae*. I was not surprised that Yukako had chosen not to write to me, but I still swelled with hope as I flattened the sheet of soft paper she'd wadded into the tea box, only to find that she had buried a coin in its depths, wrapped in a sheet of paper of its own. It was just the size of a five-*sen* piece, exactly what I'd used to buy my exotic glass of milk the day after the fire. I fingered its hard edges through the paper and shuddered with guilt and defensive anger. Was she insulting me with a few *sen* after all these years? I heard her voice, then, low and sneering: *Are you sure that's all you need? Don't be shy; here, take this too.*

And then I unwrapped it, black with age, the talisman that had put me, a lifetime ago, under the protection of Saint Claire.

I shook, I cried, in the green light that poured through the *kiri* leaves. She had held me dear for so long. I loved her, my Older Sister, the woman who had taken me under her protection, a foreign girl, a stray. I pressed the medal to my throat and took deep quavering breaths. I took a strand of the rolled-paper cord used to wrap the sweets and tied the medal around my neck.

It felt so good to weep, to feel my frozen grief start to melt, to feel the cold metal like a hole in my throat, the air pulled raw into my lungs. I filled the tea box, shaking, because it was the next thing to do, and then I arranged the tray and sweets. I could do this one thing in her memory.

I set the things I wasn't using behind me: the tea-bowl box, Kenji's crate, the box Yukako had packed the utensils into, still half in its carrying cloth. And then I felt metal fittings through the cotton cloth and paused to look.

It was the base of a wooden pillow. Yukako had packed the tea set into a wooden tray just like the one she'd once filled with gold coins.

I held the medal tight at my throat a long moment. Older Sister, elegant and inventive to the very end. And then I held the box in both hands, inspecting it with care. In this choice I did not discern sarcasm. Together with my medal, it bespoke generosity. It said, *Yes, you took it, and I give it to you again freely.* And it spoke apology: no one knew better than she, after all, that I had been unfairly blamed. On the underside of the box, inked in the tight hand of a keeper of accounts, I saw a dated column of clear brushwork. *Wastewater bowl made for Shin Yukako, with wood salvaged from Baishian.* I knew she'd always felt the teahouse hers. Hers for nights alone, hers to fit with glass. Hers to burn.

As I purified each utensil under that *kiri* dome, I felt her beside me, prodding me here and there with her fan: *like so. Like so.* I felt her as I had when I was small, folding her fingers around mine, her hands now as blasted with age as my own. Together we gripped the handle of the scoop with the silk cloth, together we raised and lowered the whisk, making sure the little thread knot turned full circle. When I dipped it in clear water, the tines of the whisk slowly unfurled in the tossing green light. I gently tapped tea into the bowl, hearing Yukako more with my hands than with my ears. Her voice was like light through an amber glass bottle, reciting her father's mnemonics for each gesture. *Kotsun. Kotsun. Sara sara sara sara.* My body had known hers this intimately, I thought. When I lifted the tea bowl in thanks I held it much longer than necessary.

I had not tasted *matcha* in so long, nor tea sweets. I heard a tiny sound as the liquid saturated the dry sugar wafer on my tongue, a squeal of escaping air, and then the taste flooded me.

Sharp. Sweet. Grass. Green. That bowl of tea was all things in all places. A pivot between the living and the dead. I drank, and she was there. *She told me to go.* I drank again, and she was there. *She sent me away.* I drained the bowl, and she was there, her capacity to hurt me undimmed with time.

I packed the tea things up and left, went home to bed, and wept as if I were spitting out my heart.

AND THEN I WASHED my face, brushed down my dress, and went downstairs again, back into the May morning. Inko said she'd break for lunch and meet me at the park. I walked until I reached Reggio, the new café near Washington Square. I gave the man at the counter our flasks to fill and bought sandwiches, then waited for her on our favorite bench.

I sat with my hot coffee, sugared and foaming with milk, dunking little bites of *biscotto* into my flask-cup as I drank. If Yukako had given me one single-edged gift, it was this: how to love this soft air, this wash of light-flooded leaves, this sun hitting red brick, this one day in all the world.

MY HEAD JERKED UP: I heard Japanese and French. Two young flappers sat with a picnic on the bench next to mine, chatting in their *cloche* hats, switching between languages like darting insects, spreading butter and jam on bread. They were lovely, the French girl with her gray eyes and flushed cheeks, the Japanese girl with her cat chin and minx mouth. She giggled as she displayed a pinkie finger, the knuckle dabbed with apricot jam.

"Oh, you poor girl, just look at you," teased the other, and then, quick as a swallow, she took the girl's hand, caught the little knuckle in her mouth, and swiped it clean with a flick of her tongue. I almost dropped my coffee.

"You'll get us killed, you're so bad!" pouted the Japanese girl fondly.

I watched those two girls beside me, the very fact of them: their overlapping hands, their complicit laughter. I had never forgiven Yukako for not being in love with me. I forgave her.

A WOMAN CIRCLED the fountain selling lilacs. A girl ran to her mother, red ribbons down her back. A flock of boys winged by on bicycles. Two students tossed a book in the blue air. Nets of pigeons reeled overhead. My eyes filled; I heard bells clamor in their tower. A bee landed on my mouth and did not sting me: it sucked sweet coffee from my lower lip. I felt joy.

"HELLO, YOU," said Inko, perching close to me. "What was in the box? This?" she asked, touching the thin rolled-paper cord around my neck. Then she spotted my mother's medal. "The one you lost?" she breathed, taking my hand.

I nodded. "I'll tell you everything," I promised. "But look," I said, glancing at the flappers. I whispered what I'd seen.

"*Ara!*" Inko exclaimed, grinning. Startled at the sound, the Japanese girl dropped her mesh purse at my feet, and I picked it up for her.

"Thank you."

"It's nothing," I said in Japanese, and in French, "Not at all." They gasped audibly in concert and glanced at each other, then at Inko's hand on mine.

"How long are you in New York?" I asked.